COLD SILENCE

TONI ANDERSON

Cold Silence

Cover design by Regina Wamba of ReginaWamba.com

Print ISBN: 9781988812885

Contact email: info@toniandersonauthor.com

For more information on Toni Anderson's books, sign up for her Newsletter or check out her website (www.toniandersonauthor.com)

ALSO BY TONI ANDERSON

COLD JUSTICE SERIES

A Cold Dark Place (Book #1)

Cold Pursuit (Book #2)

Cold Light of Day (Book #3)

Cold Fear (Book #4)

Cold in The Shadows (Book #5)

Cold Hearted (Book #6)

Cold Secrets (Book #7)

Cold Malice (Book #8)

A Cold Dark Promise (Book #9~A Wedding Novella)

Cold Blooded (Book #10)

COLD JUSTICE – THE NEGOTIATORS

Cold & Deadly (Book #1)

Colder Than Sin (Book #2)

Cold Wicked Lies (Book #3)

Cold Cruel Kiss (Book #4)

Cold as Ice (Book #5)

COLD JUSTICE – MOST WANTED

Cold Silence (Book #1)

Cold Deceit (Book #2)

"HER" ROMANTIC SUSPENSE SERIES

Her Sanctuary (Book #1)

Her Last Chance (Book #2)

Her Risk to Take (Novella ~ Book #3)

THE BARKLEY SOUND SERIES

Dangerous Waters (Book #1)

Dark Waters (Book #2)

SINGLE TITLES

The Killing Game

Edge of Survival

Storm Warning

Sea of Suspicion

For Gary.

PROLOGUE

DECEMBER 15

FBI Special Agent Shane Livingstone calmly straddled the metal bench on the outside of the MD530 Little Bird helicopter as the pilot buzzed so close to the ocean Shane swore he could see his own reflection in the surface of the ebony water. One of the FBI's Hostage Rescue Team's K9 members lay on the floor behind him, leaning out of the open door near enough that his drool dripped onto Shane's exposed neck.

At least it was warm, unlike the sea spray that felt like bullets of pure ice piercing his flesh.

Good times.

Adrenaline buzzed his system and he grinned. This method of transportation was a thousand times preferable to that of the last training mission when Gold team had accessed a remote coastal installation using Rigid-hull Inflatable Boats. They'd been dropped into crashing surf that had been nut-cracking cold and rough as the wildest rollercoaster, especially fun when carrying sixty pounds of gear that seemed to weigh ten times as much when wet.

This current infil was positively first-class luxury by comparison. Shane's fellow Gold team Echo assaulters were all revved up and ready to go. These men were more than his colleagues. They were his friends, his brothers. And, unlike last time, this wasn't a training mission.

According to the tactical operation briefing, five white nationalist terrorists, who were vocal online supporters of long-dead cult-leader David Hines, had taken over a courtroom and were threatening to kill everyone inside the courthouse if they and the defendant weren't allowed to walk free.

Never gonna happen.

Three of the attackers had military training, as did the defendant. The other two were self-proclaimed "militia." Wannabes with dicks the size of Shane's little finger and brains to match.

These particular whackos had already shot dead the court reporter and were threatening to shoot another hostage every hour until their demands were met. So, even though the Crisis Negotiation Unit was on scene and negotiators were attempting to talk the bad guys into coming out, everyone inside the FBI knew that Judgment Day was coming.

But probably not in the way the tangos envisioned with their corrupt version of Christian values and morals Satan would get a kick out of.

The signal to "get ready" came through his earpiece. The pilot pulled up the nose of the machine and the terrain beneath Shane switched from inky sea to dense shadowy trees then houses, before morphing into taller buildings in the downtown area that the pilots navigated around with apparent ease.

They were close now. The pilot climbed in altitude before descending rapidly and hovering over what must be the roof of the courthouse. HRT's second helicopter was barely visible in the darkness.

These machines were quiet compared to most but, even so, the FBI were trying to deflect the hostage takers' attention away from what might be happening on the roof. Shane recognized one of the FBI negotiators who was helping disguise HRT's arrival by talking non-stop on the bullhorn. A police cruiser chose that exact moment to turn on the siren and speed away from the courthouse as another distraction.

"Go," came the order over the comms.

Shane unclipped his safety strap and threw down a chem light as heavy ropes were deployed onto the roof.

Thick gloves stopped his flesh from being ripped off his hands as he wrapped his lower legs around the cable and threw himself off the side of the chopper before fast-roping twenty feet to the flat roof. He took up a defensive position with his H&K 416 D10RS carbine while Cowboy, also now on the roof, released the dog from his harness. The pilot held steady in the darkness as the rest of Shane's seven-man team, plus kit, descended with rapid efficiency.

In a matter of seconds, the helicopters were flying away, someone inside gathering up the ropes.

Shane grabbed his breaching ram as the assaulters stacked up at the door. Shane stepped forward to take care of that obstacle after Cowboy checked to make sure the door was, in fact, locked. Shane much preferred explosives or his modified Remington M870 loaded with breaching rounds but today they were using the ram on this door because that's what acting Gold team leader Payne Novak had ordered. The closer they could get before the hostiles knew for sure they were coming, the more chance they had of saving innocent lives.

Shane didn't think knocking a door off its hinges with a breacher was much quieter than blowing one off its hinges with a slap shot but, having served in the Green Berets prior to becoming an FBI agent, Shane knew when to follow orders and when to beg for forgiveness later.

Gold team's other assaulter unit, Charlie, had been dropped on the opposite side of the roof and were preparing to abseil down the outside of the building and enter the courtroom via the windows. HRT snipers had the building surrounded, ready to take out any visible cultists as soon as the signal was given. Shane's

Echo assaulters were to work their way down the building, floor by floor, and neutralize any bad guys who'd fled the courtroom in a last desperate bid to make a stand or attempt a daring escape.

Shane took a deep breath in, held it, then released it. Repeating the process as his eyes scanned for possible danger. Deliberately calming his body, settling the adrenaline that wanted to ramp up his heart rate and influence his physiology. This natural response was why they trained *all* the time. A firefight was less shocking when you walked into one every single day.

Cowboy waited for Charlie unit to get into position to begin their rappel. As soon as Charlie unit reported they were ready, everything changed. Tension snapped through the air like static.

Game time.

They communicated using hand signals. Sound carried and they didn't speak on an op unless they absolutely had to.

As planned, it went completely dark as the City cut the power to the block. HRT immediately activated their night-vision goggles. Cowboy counted down with his fingers and, with a single precision strike, Shane slammed the metal ram into the door beside the deadbolt. The wood around the lock shattered.

He stepped back, swapping his ram for his carbine as he followed his team inside and down the stairwell.

Intel had all the hostage takers in a second-floor courtroom, but things changed fast in a dynamic situation and it wasn't always easy to tell the bad guys from the good guys using thermal imaging or radar. Quickly reaching the fourth floor, the team swept into the main office area with a blast of flash bangs and godawful noise and overwhelming firepower that should make any sane individual shove their empty hands high in the air while simultaneously pissing their pants.

Holiday decorations looked garishly out of place under the circumstances and the inflatable Santa in the corner almost earned himself a double tap when he floated back-and-forth.

Thankfully no one shot it.

The press loved nothing better than to crucify law enforcement and while Shane agreed with some of what was said, it wasn't exactly a walk in the park figuring out good guys from bad in these kinds of conditions.

They didn't find anyone, which suggested the tangos had rounded up everyone in the building earlier. Like all the operators, Shane moved in a smooth, slightly crouched gait. It kept his aim steady while allowing him to cover ground quickly and silently.

Off the main office area was a series of rooms down a long narrow corridor. Shane was at the front now and Echo assaulters swiftly cleared three rooms before finding another locked door. He swapped the carbine for the ram again as the team lined up either side of the barrier. Suddenly, Shane paused, shook his head and pointed to the wall instead. Something didn't feel right and the need for silence had long been replaced by the use of speed and overwhelming force. Doorways and elevators were always the most dangerous places in a building, followed closely by stairwells and corridors. His sixth sense was telling him this doorway was either a storage room no one ever used, or a deathtrap.

He never ignored his instincts and Cowboy respected them, too. They all trusted one another with their lives. They had to. The team reassembled and Shane set the explosive charges on the wall.

Once again Cowboy counted down. They all momentarily closed their eyes to avoid getting blinded by the flash in their night vision goggles as Shane blew the charges. Scotty tossed in a flash bang and the assaulters were through the opening, kicking out jagged sheetrock as they went.

Shane heard a shot before his team returned fire.

"I got one," Scotty said quietly into the comms.

Shane nodded to himself. He'd made the right choice.

"Gold Echo assaulters to TOC," Cowboy spoke calmly. "We have one dead subject."

The team filed out and Shane quickly continued down the corridor. Flash bang powder burned his eyes, but he ignored it.

"Charlie unit has three dead subjects."

That left two tangos unaccounted for, including the defendant.

Echo unit continued to spread out and search the area. There was a second set of stairs leading down to the third floor on the north side of the building.

Shane saw movement but recognized a civilian running for cover. Her hands were empty, and she was sobbing in fear. He let her go and watched her cower into a corner as the K9 unit took up protective stance beside them. Scotty went over and put wrist restraints on the woman and told her to hold position until someone came to rescue her.

They couldn't risk she was in league with the cultists. It might seem harsh to treat terrified people this way, but better than accidentally putting a bullet in someone they mistakenly assumed was a threat. That would be a bad day for everyone.

Shane looked through the small glass window of the fire door. On the other side a marshal lay in a pool of his own blood. Shane checked as much of the area as he could through the glass, but the range was limited.

"Charlie unit heading up the main stairwell to the third floor."

Cowboy checked through the window also and replied to TOC. "Echo unit entering the north stairwell heading down to three. One dead marshal in stairwell and one female civilian secured on the fourth floor."

Shane opened the door and covered the others as they moved into position. When he headed down the stairs to the next switchback, a bullet hit the wall above his head. He didn't pause, didn't flinch. He locked onto the target and kept moving forward to engage. He didn't have a clear shot but with the large windows to the north he didn't need one.

The sound of a high-power bullet traversing glass before lodging in the attacker hiding behind a frightened hostage had them all moving forward toward the danger. The sniper had done his job. The tango wasn't going to hurt anyone else ever again.

Cowboy reported into the TOC. "Tango down in north stairwell. Hostage secure."

They kept moving and held a defensive position as Scotty stopped beside the woman who Shane belatedly recognized was the judge. Luckily, he hadn't already slapped restraints on her.

Cowboy reported, "We have Judge King. Repeat, Judge King is in our possession. Echo unit bringing her out via the north exit."

Cowboy signaled for the group to split up. Shane was with the group who were to get the judge to safety while the others helped Charlie team clear the third floor.

"Roger that." Shane nodded. He led the way while Scotty and Keeme supported the judge between them. Cadell and the dog watched their six.

The earlier noise of bullets and explosions had quieted down, although he could hear HRT and SWAT moving through the building.

A sudden shiver of apprehension rolled down his spine. A reaction to the operation, or something else? He raised his hand to signal the others to stop. Then he edged forward and poked his head quickly over the banister. It was pitch black, but the night vision revealed a flat green world that appeared empty.

Shane wasn't sure what had bothered him. In all likelihood the tangos had gone to ground in one of the offices.

He gave the hand signal to move forward. At the bottom of the next switchback the dog growled and Shane felt the hairs on his neck rise.

He knew what he was going to find before he even saw him. The defendant. Del Renfro. An asshole who'd driven from Idaho to DC with a trunk full of explosives, prepared to carry out an attack on a federal building. He hadn't cared which one.

A flat tire on I-95 and a sharp-eyed traffic cop had ended the man's evil intentions before they'd come to fruition, but not without a bullet hole in the brave law enforcement officer. Now the asshole held a young Black woman in front of him, the marshal's 9mm sidearm pressed to her cheek.

Shane put a bullet in the guy's fat skull, calculating and praying the ricochet off the wall didn't hit the hostage.

Del slid to the floor and the young woman stood there, screaming, her hands covering her face. Shane put another bullet into the man on the ground to make sure he was dead.

He touched the woman's arm so she knew where he was because he doubted she could see anything and must be terrified.

"FBI. You're safe now, miss."

He nudged the bad guy's weapon away from the body and Cadell picked it up.

"Gold Echo unit to TOC. Dead tango on lower north stairwell. We have a second hostage we are bringing out the side door."

He held the young woman by the arm and looked up to scan the area as they approached street level. Everything happened in slo-mo as she stumbled in her high heels, holding onto his left arm with the strength of the Rock on steroids and he knew he was going down, too. He tried to roll so her fall was cushioned by his body as they crashed headfirst down the stairs.

Panicked, she twisted and somehow landed with all her weight on the midpoint between his wrist and his elbow. He heard the double snap at the same time she let out a scream that could shatter glass.

Or maybe that was him.

The others held their position and he didn't tell them his arm was fucked. They'd heard the bones break. They knew. He carefully pushed himself to his feet using his right arm and then pulled the woman upright with the same hand, steadying her.

"You okay?" he asked.

"Yes," she said, a little breathless. "Just sore. Thank you."

"No problem, miss. Follow me outside where the police officers will question you. They will restrain you until they can verify your identity. Don't be scared. It's standard procedure."

Then he let her go and surreptitiously cradled his injured arm, leading the way until he had the door open. Officers rushed forward to grab the rescued hostages.

Scotty paused beside him, wedging the door wider with his boot. "You okay, buddy?"

Shane shifted and gritted his teeth hoping his best friend wouldn't notice through the NVGs the fact that Shane wanted to hurl.

"Sure."

He followed the rest of the guys outside and they headed to the rendezvous point to meet up and debrief. He paused to carefully flip up his NVGs as the power was restored and the world came glaring back to life.

Unfortunately, that meant the others could now see the unnatural angle of his lower left arm as it rested across the top of his carbine.

Gold team leader Payne Novak met him halfway with their medic. They wrapped his arm in a temporary splint and slipped a sling around his neck. All Shane could think about was how much it was going to suck getting out of his favorite flight suit.

When Novak indicated that the ambulance drive toward them, Shane balked. "I can walk."

"And risk severing an artery?" Novak snapped.

Well, maybe not.

"You shouldn't have moved once you realized it was broken." Novak sounded pissed.

Shane was valiantly trying not to vomit all over his friend and boss, so he didn't bother to argue. Suddenly going to the hospital didn't seem such a bad idea.

Shane swallowed and asked quickly, "We lose anyone?"

"No. Nor any hostages. From what we can gather, they killed the marshal who you discovered, plus the unfortunate court reporter before we started our assault." Sobering news which proved the white supremacists had been serious about their intentions. "All six hostiles are dead," Novak told him and Shane felt a crushing weight release off his shoulders.

"In fact," Novak smiled slightly as he indicated Scotty get in the ambulance with Shane. "You're the only HRT casualty today."

Shane groaned, as much from embarrassment as pain. "The woman who came out with us, is she okay? And the judge?"

Novak nodded. "Yep. Both shaken but no obvious injuries. There are easier ways to impress women, you know."

Shane shook his head, knowing he was never going to live this down.

"I'll expect a full report when you get back to Quantico." Novak closed the ambulance doors and thumped the back to tell the EMT to get going.

"Fuck." Typing up FD 302s with his non dominant arm was going to take forever.

"Of all the ways to be brought low—a woman in high heels was not on my bingo card today." Scotty grinned.

"Always expect the unexpected."

The EMTs blasted the lights and sirens, more for fun than necessity in Shane's opinion.

One of the medics started to come through to the back but Shane waved him away with his good hand. "This field cast will do until I get to the emergency room."

The guy nodded, seeming a little intimidated and Shane remembered he was in full battle dress and laden down with weapons and explosives.

They went over a pothole and Shane swore again as pain streaked up his arm and lanced his shoulder.

"You sound worse than Grace when she was in labor with Katie." Scotty gripped Shane's good arm hard though. Shane knew his friend was worried about him.

"Grace is a badass."

"Strongest person I know," Scotty agreed about his wife.

"I have no idea what she sees in you," Shane told the guy, though in reality Shane had never met a more compatible couple. Nor a couple more in love.

"I got lucky. If you weren't such a cry baby and, frankly, so fugging ugly, you might find true love, too."

"No sane woman would put up with our bullshit schedule or workload."

"Are you calling *Grace* insane?" Scotty gave him a mocking glare.

"Well, she did marry you."

Scotty grinned again. "The guys are probably taking bets on exactly what you broke and how many pins it'll take to fix and how long you're gonna be out for. I'm guessing ulna and radius. Three pins but if you hear anything different, I want the skinny."

"I'm not going to need an operation." Shane narrowed his eyes, trying to ignore the increasing pain radiating from his snapped bones. "I don't need to be off the team. I can do my job wearing a cast."

"Sure you can. And you can breathe fire and shoot bullets out of your ass while you're at it. We know this already—unless you have really bad gas..."

Tears streamed from Shane's eyes more from laughter than pain, but some of it was pain and that was humbling for a member of HRT. "I love you, man."

Scotty ruffled his hair like he was a little kid. Shane didn't recall removing his helmet.

"I love you too. But if you ever embarrass me like this again, we're over."

"Next time, *you* take the beautiful young woman in high heels and I'll take the judge, okay?"

Scotty grinned. "Deal, but no one will ever be as beautiful as my Grace."

Sudden claws of envy scraped Shane's insides, but he ignored them. He wasn't ready to settle down. Maybe when he stepped away from HRT if there was anything left of him to give. Not everyone was lucky like Scotty and Grace Monteith. Not everyone got their happily ever after...

1

SEVENTEEN DAYS LATER

A living nightmare was playing out in real time on Yael Brooks's monitor.

Horrifying didn't begin to cover it.

Her fingers raced over the keyboard as she scanned the flow of information streaming onto her second screen. She was searching for the location of the computer currently playing a live feed of a young woman strapped to a stainless-steel gurney in a room with breeze-block walls and a cement floor.

The atmosphere in the Command Center was taut. The Joint Task Force had taken over a corner of the FBI's Houston Field Office. The people assembled consisted of agents from cyber-crimes, FBI headquarters, a large group from the FBI's Critical Incident Response Group including profilers, negotiators, and operators from the Hostage Rescue Team, agents from the local field office and the original detective who'd been hunting this killer since the first known murder in Georgia. It also included a small team of civilians, including herself and some of her colleagues from Cramer, Parker & Gray.

All the loaded weapons in the room made Yael nervous and she had to force herself to keep doing the job she was paid to do, the job that meant she belonged in this room, with these federal agents, chasing this monster.

Terror was visible in every strained line of the captive's face and body.

Yael's mouth became so dry it was difficult to swallow. Anya Baker was a brilliant young chemist who could have gone to school anywhere on a full ride. Instead, she'd chosen to live with her mom and dad and attend Rice University. This past summer Anya had interned with the FBI's Houston office. She'd disappeared three nights ago after visiting a bar with friends.

Anya's parents were worried sick. From what Alex Parker had told Yael, they had every reason to be.

Yael's heart pounded and she knew she needed to dissociate herself from the fact it was a real woman on the screen, one who'd recently woken up, looking absolutely petrified, after being kidnapped by the freaking psychopath who went by the moniker Evi1Geni-us. Yael wiped her sweaty palms on her favorite black jeans. She couldn't think about Anya Baker as a real person. If she did, she wouldn't be able to focus on doing her job. Instead, she mentally shifted to gaming mode where she needed to win at all costs to take this bozo down.

Tim Theriault, a new hire at Cramer, Parker & Gray, pushed awkwardly through the heavy door with a tray of beverages from a local chain.

"Not in here," a scary female Asian American FBI agent name of Ashley Chen told him tersely. "Put it in the break room."

"But other people will take them…" The guy trailed off under Chen's steely gaze.

"Do as Agent Chen says," Alex told him without moving his eyes off his monitor. "Then get back in here and help Laura."

Evi1Geni-us flaunted his dirty work via the dark web. Every three months, Evi1Geni-us kidnapped someone—random or targeted they weren't sure yet—and auctioned off their method of torture and death to the highest bidders.

Choose Your Own Murder Adventure.

Yael's colleague and best friend Laura Bay was tracking the cryptocurrency—or trying to as it was in multiple currencies being routed through more than one crypto exchange.

"I've got something," said Alex Parker.

All heads swung in his direction. Her boss's specialty was cellular communications although he was scary good at almost everything. Yael loved her boss. She also loved his smart, gorgeous wife, and their cute-as-a-button baby daughter.

"In Houston?" Ashley Chen was the most aesthetically perfect person Yael had ever encountered in real life. Chen was also crazy good with computers, which proved the world really wasn't fair.

Yael had once been considered exceptional when working with code and tracking people over the internet. Nowadays, with the new crew she hung out with, she figured she was slightly above average—but the crowd she hung out with now were *exceptional.*

Yael side-eyed the scrolling code on her screen even as she watched Alex nod in response to Chen's question.

"About twenty minutes northwest of here." Alex checked a map.

The intensity in the room cranked up another notch even as a swell of relief crashed over them all. Sweat started to form on Yael's back. She swallowed to loosen her dry throat and turned her attention back to the information zipping down one panel on her screen. The task force hadn't been one hundred percent certain Evi1Geni-us was still stateside, let alone in Houston. Based on past "events" the FBI behavioral analysts figured the auction would likely go down in the vicinity of where the victim had been kidnapped—at a storage location, empty property, or unused warehouse nearby. Unfortunately, in this part of Texas, at this time year, that didn't exactly narrow things down.

They hadn't even been positive Anya Baker had been taken by Evi1Geni-us or that she was the intended victim for today's macabre online auction until the bastard had turned the camera on ten minutes ago. Alex Parker had had a strong enough hunch that they'd all flown down here the moment the monster had posted an auction was imminent approximately an hour after Anya had disappeared.

The task force had spent New Year's Eve setting up this Command Center before crashing at a nearby hotel for a few hours' sleep. Anya's kidnap fitted the killer's MO even though they hadn't figured out exactly how the asshole chose his victims. That was one of the reasons it had taken so long to get even this close to the sicko.

Three heavily armed, black-clad men hunched over their own monitors coordinating with the tactical units. Members of the Hostage Rescue Team were currently loaded into vehicles idling at two separate locations around the city. An Enhanced SWAT team made up a third group on the east side. She heard one of the three HRT guys in the room get on the radio to tell Echo unit to head northwest. They all knew Evi1Geni-us was tricky and he could be spoofing Alex in some way so the tactical units wanted to split up to cover as much ground as possible.

"First voting option is up," Agent Chen said quietly.

Option 1: Removing the bitch's clothes using, A) Knife, B) Scissors, C) Bare hands.

Immediately the votes started pouring in. Out of the corner of her eye Yael watched her boss's mouth tighten.

The vultures who'd tuned in—at a cost of five thousand US dollars a feed, capped at one hundred feeds—got to vote on exactly how things went down from here. Each vote cost another thousand dollars. All attendees had to commit to a minimum of five votes per auction. The more votes someone made the more likely they were to receive an invitation to the next party. It was an exclusive club and demand far exceeded available slots.

What viewers might not appreciate was that anyone who watched a murder without reporting it was facing possible accessory charges. Anyone who paid to watch a murder was looking at definite accessory and possible accomplice charges.

"Scissors," Alex told Chen who was sitting at her console with her mouse hovering over the vote buttons.

The way Alex said it made Yael's stomach churn. He'd been chasing this guy for a long time and she didn't want to imagine what happened to Anya if the watchers voted "knife."

The feed from the crime scene was being shown on a large screen on the wall. Yael kept her eyes away from the images and concentrated instead on the software, which was coded in Python.

One of the Hostage Rescue Team operators sat heavily in the empty chair beside her. "What sort of psycho spends their New Year's Day terrorizing women?" He sported a sling and plaster cast on his left arm and a lethal-looking gun in a thigh holster on his right.

Yael frowned and sent him a quick glance. He met her gaze with the greenest eyes she'd ever seen. He looked pissed.

"Maybe it's not their New Year." She fixed her attention back to the screen, determined to ignore the presence of this very large, armed male sitting so close by.

"Good point." Ashley Chen gifted her a nod. "We need to send that observation to the profilers and see if it fits any other patterns of behavior."

The man on screen—dressed completely in black except for the scary *Scream* mask—moved out of sight and a second camera came online, this one with a bird's eye view of Anya Baker's face. Evi1Geni-us walked over to a table and picked up a pair of tailor's shears. He dramatically snipped them in front of the camera before very carefully starting to cut up the woman's jeans leg from the bottom to the top.

Anya's expression suggested she was screaming but there was no sound. There was never any sound on these videos, which lent the whole thing a surreal quality that was also stomach churning.

Yael tried to breathe slowly in and out, the way she'd been

taught when dealing with stressful situations. *Don't look at the screen.*

According to Alex, Evi1Geni-us had started selling the actual sound recordings as exclusive non-fungible tokens (NFTs) on the dark web. Yael didn't know which was worse—Evi1Geni-us for doing the crime, or the customers buying this shit. Only so many of the attendees could be law enforcement and she knew Alex had spent a lot of time and effort creating several shady personas to be in a position to receive multiple invitations.

"Getting some information off the blockchains. It's a lot easier doing this in real time than trying to figure it out after the fact," said Laura.

After the auctions, Evi1Geni-us transferred the money to hardware wallets that were then disconnected from the internet and put in "cold" storage, which basically made them untraceable until he decided to spend that money. Unfortunately, he could probably cash out in a crypto exchange before they even caught up with the fact he was online.

Identifying the people who were paying to watch however… much simpler.

Yael spotted something in the script, scrolled back up the screen, leaned forward and typed in a few more commands. "I found the proxy server he's using."

"Can you trace it?"

Yael glanced at the HRT guy who was now leaning forward in his chair with a look of fierce concentration on his face. She could smell the piney scent of his skin and a trace of something sweet and metallic that made her recoil when she realized what it was. Gun oil.

He caught her reaction and raised a brow.

Damn. He was handsome as hell and probably knew it.

"It's probably better if you don't speak." Her voice was gruff.

Humor twinkled in his eyes. "You sound like all my ex-girlfriends."

"And your boss." The tall, blond HRT operator who seemed to be giving the orders quipped with a forced grin.

Rather than looking annoyed like most men she knew would, the operator sitting next to her gave her a slow smile, and then pressed his thumb and forefinger together and dragged them across his lips.

It was obvious these men were trying to lighten the grim mood that had settled over everyone in the room, but hard to do that when a woman was being tortured online for paid entertainment and it was Yael's job to find the torturer.

She went back to her data, painfully aware of the man at her side but concentrating on the inflow of information despite the distraction. She didn't like being on anyone's radar. She liked to be unobtrusive and forgettable. And she absolutely hated guns. Ironic, considering she now worked for a security firm.

His black-clad knee briefly brushed hers as he shifted position but he didn't seem to do it on purpose. There was a lot of him and not a lot of space underneath her table. A quick glance at his face showed her he wasn't paying her any attention. His focus was glued to the screen and he looked as if he wanted to crawl inside her monitor and throttle the sick bastard responsible for all of this.

If only it was that simple. Except…if it were, she wouldn't feel so safe, so removed from real-life consequences when she was online—a sentiment this Evi1Geni-us guy probably related to in spades.

Evi1Geni-us relied on his ability to cloak his identity while committing his heinous crimes. Anya was depending on all of them to get past his defenses and expose him—to save her, and then lock up her attacker where he couldn't hurt anyone else ever again.

It didn't take Evi1Geni-us long to strip Anya completely naked. The woman was bleeding from where the shears had occasionally snipped her flesh.

Yael's stomach rolled. She couldn't imagine enduring Anya's fate.

The HRT operator shifted again, clearly uncomfortable with what was happening onscreen.

Join the club.

"What happened to your arm?" she murmured, unable to stop herself even as she kept one eye firmly on the code.

He held it up. "Snapped my ulna and radius helping someone down some stairs. Boss wouldn't pass me for active duty even though I'm as good with my right hand as I am with my left."

"You're the breacher, Livingstone. You can't handle the breacher if you have a broken arm," the HRT team leader replied with practiced patience.

"I could have used the shotgun and no one would have known the difference," he assured her with a quirked brow and cocky grin.

Maybe it was a defense mechanism or maybe that innate confidence was why he was an HRT operator. The banter lightened the mood for all of two seconds before the next poll went up.

Option 2: Hot Candle Wax. A) Eyes, B) Nipples, C) Mouth.

Yael's stomach gave a hard lurch.

"Shit," the man beside her said between clenched teeth.

Alex looked across the desk, clearly reading the appalled expression on her face. "Don't watch."

He'd warned her about what she was getting into and she'd thought she'd been prepared, but how did any sane individual prepare themselves for something this monstrous? It was impossible to prepare for the unimaginably cruel. She should know that by now.

Yael swung her monitor with the live feed away so she couldn't see what Evi1Geni-us was doing to the poor woman—as long as she didn't look up at the big screen on the wall. There was no way she could concentrate if she watched, not even if she tried to pretend it was a game.

"What's taking so long?" the man beside her whispered impatiently.

Long? They were making incredible progress. "He's running a VPN and bouncing off a second proxy server." Her fingers raced over the keyboard.

"I have a tentative geolocation based on triangulated cellular data of an area near this high school earlier today, but there's no cell transmitting right now." Alex pointed to a map he put on another monitor.

Yael didn't let Alex's words distract her because proxy servers could be anywhere in the world and they might tell them a different story. She also knew Alex had developed the ability to fake geolocations—be it cellular or computer. They used it when the people they were guarding truly needed to disappear. That software was a closely guarded secret and accessed by only a few trusted employees. However *nice* her boss was, no one wanted to cross him. But if Alex had managed it, others might too.

She followed the streaming information as closely as she was able. Given the sheer volume, it was impossible for the human brain to keep up, but she'd written a program to assist and the laptop she used to run it on was specially designed to handle massive amounts of data without crashing. She'd built it herself.

"Come on. Come on." Her new friend spoke between gritted teeth.

"You really need to stop talking," Yael muttered.

His mouth tightened but the anguish and frustration in his eyes made her regret her words and her loss of focus. She zeroed in on a small piece of code. "Huh."

"What?" asked Alex, still typing on his laptop.

"He's using a cheap off-the-shelf VPN." She clicked open another screen. "Linked to a credit card in the name of Greg Wallander." She did a quick search. "Card was part of a batch stolen a few days ago."

He might have left a trail. She exchanged a look with her boss.

"Can you find him?" Alex asked grimly.

Evi1Geni-us. Not Greg Wallander. Because the former was currently doing something so heinous to the woman he held in his possession that the man seated beside her had gone pale and looked like he might throw up.

Yael drew in a deep breath and ignored the way the HRT operator's eyes latched onto her so intently.

"I'm trying," she said.

There was something weird about the data but she couldn't figure out exactly what without stopping and going through every line of code and she didn't have time right now.

Excitement surged through her. "I found an IP address." She sent the 32-bit number to a work group chat that allowed all the other analysts at Cramer, Parker & Gray to start doing their own things with the info.

"That tells you his exact location, right?" the HRT guy asked.

"It's a unique identifier that tells us about his online activities and…okay. Found the ISP." She typed it into the chat box and explained. "Internet Service Provider. Which gives us another handle on the approximate geolocation."

"The info matches what I have for location," Alex told her.

Good.

Maybe Evi1Geni-us wasn't as smart as he thought he was.

"We have a ZIP code." Alex reeled it off and the FBI agents started huddling around the map.

Yael opened another window and zeroed in on a map of the ZIP code area. Could they really be this close to catching the guy after all the months and years he'd been leading Alex in circles?

The operator's breath was so close to her cheek now she could feel the minty warmth brushing her skin. She pushed aside her hyperawareness of his proximity.

"Looks like a bunch of warehouses," he said.

"Yeah. And a school over there." She pointed to a building on the right-hand side.

"We are checking for the most likely locations within that area," Agent Chen stated.

"Let's hurry it up." The HRT guy's eyes went back to the live screen even as Chen nodded.

Both of their expressions were bleak.

"What's he doing now?" Yael asked quietly, meaning Evi1-Geni-us.

"You don't wanna know," her new friend said grimly.

"Is she still alive?"

"Unfortunately."

Yael closed her eyes briefly then went back to the earlier code. What was in there that had bothered her? A quick scan told her nothing. She scrolled back to the start of the session even though the feed was still streaming.

"We have a possible address," Ashley Chen shouted over the general din. "A warehouse off Eastman and Grove. It's been empty for two years but the electricity use surged over the last three days."

"Help me find any nearby security cameras," Alex urged her.

"I want to check the code—"

"Grab a couple of surveillance camera feeds first. Then examine the code."

She nodded, zeroing in on a couple of nearby premises that likely had cameras.

"If your gut is telling you to look at the code, you should be looking at the code." The operator leaned forward resting his elbows on his thighs. He'd rolled up the sleeves of his long-sleeved T and she got a peek at corded muscles and sun-bleached hairs on his forearms. It shouldn't give her a little quiver. Not under the circumstances.

"Alex is my boss." She sounded prim, which was a first for her. She glared at him to cover the fact that she was knocked off balance by everything that was going on, including him.

She pulled up a camera from a nearby factory that was obviously closed for the holidays. It pointed to the main entrance of its own building. She tried another. A drive-thru coffeeshop but again, it didn't show the warehouse.

"I bet Alex Parker hired you for your computer skills, not your ability to follow orders," the operator murmured softly.

She glanced at him sharply and he leaned back. His dark green gaze didn't leave hers. "I'm assuming."

Another feed was added to the main screen. This showed footage from a helmet cam of one of the HRT operators in the field. They'd reached the parking lot of the warehouse and were climbing out and immediately arranging themselves around the front door of the building.

Yael's heart slammed against her ribs. Maybe they could save Anya. Maybe she could help catch this bastard. With a quick look at her boss, she went back to the code.

"I don't see any vehicles at the warehouse," the HRT operator stated.

Yael looked to yet another screen and it showed the overhead view of the building, presumably from a drone.

She realized the third HRT operator in the room was flying that drone.

"What's wrong with the code?" Her current shadow prompted her again.

"I don't know." She blinked and checked the time on her computer. "Hey, what time did the auction go live?"

"Twelve oh three," Alex said. "Why?"

"How long has it been running?"

"Twenty-five minutes. He usually spends at least an hour with each victim," Alex replied.

Sweat ran down the side of her face as Yael grimaced. It felt like only a few seconds to her, but to Anya Baker it probably seemed like three lifetimes.

"What's bothering you?" The HRT guy who'd latched onto her pushed again.

A shiver crawled up her spine. Reluctantly she said, "The

timing is off. The running time of the code and the start time don't match. It's all out of whack somehow."

The HRT operators on screen were following a dog now.

"The dog was given Anya's scent," the guy explained. "He's great at finding people."

Which was also her job although she didn't use her nose.

She frowned. "I think the feed is delayed. I don't think it's live," she burst out even though that didn't make sense.

Alex frowned at her. "How do you explain the live voting?"

"Maybe he's rigging the system?" Yael pressed her lips together. She didn't know but something felt off.

They all turned their attention back to the black-clad operators on screen.

Yael glanced at the feed of Evi1Geni-us. Her stomach heaved as she saw what he was doing to Anya with a drill. From the way the woman's body jerked and recoiled from the pain suggested she was conscious and totally aware of everything the bastard was doing to her.

"We've got him now." The man beside her touched her upper arm. "I'm Shane, by the way."

She glanced at him. She didn't need to know his name. She'd hopefully never see him again after today.

She frowned at the data. She could hear the other HRT guys through the microphone, the slight huff of their breath, the muffled movement of their gear, but she couldn't hear the sound of a woman being tortured in the background. Evi1Geni-us's feed was still playing in silence but presumably Anya was actually making a lot of noise. Maybe Evi1Geni-us worried the victim might scream out clues as to his identity or somehow miraculously rip off his mask. Maybe that's what the weird delay was all about. He could run over and stop the filming and edit out the bits that might give away clues to his identity. Like a super dark version of the Oscar bloopers.

But the silence coming through the HRT mic was puzzling unless Evi1Geni-us had somehow soundproofed the room.

The operators lined up three either side of the door. A guy with a breacher stepped forward.

Shane muttered something that sounded suspiciously like "that's my job, motherfucker" under his breath.

"Can they hear her?" Yael blurted out.

"Do they hear anything?" Shane spoke up so his voice carried to his boss.

The team leader looked back at them and shook his head. "All quiet."

Her HRT shadow frowned. "That's weird."

One guy used his fingers to count down. The guy with the breacher started to swing.

"Boss, tell them to wait—" Shane began.

"Alex, I—" Yael said.

An enormous explosion caused the live feed from the HRT operator's helmet to turn the whole screen white and the noise to roar, then fall abruptly silent.

There was a split second of stunned quiet before Shane jumped to his feet and joined his teammates across the room. "What the fuck just happened? Scotty! Cowboy, report!"

Chaos erupted around her as everyone tried to figure out what had gone wrong. Had anyone been hurt? Was Anya alive? Had they caught Evi1Geni-us or was he still on the loose?

Ambulances were already on the way. She could hear the frantic shouting of someone telling "Scotty" to stay with them over the HRT's feed.

The HRT operators were scrambling.

"We need eyes. What the fuck is going on over there? I need a vehicle," Shane shouted. He dragged his right hand over his features, clearly struggling to rein in his emotions.

A local agent ran toward Shane and they rushed out of the room. Tim left, looking as if he were about to throw up.

Alex exchanged a look with Yael. His expression was calmly furious. "Is it the right place, or did we get played?"

She had no idea. The feed on the right-hand side continued to show Evi1Geni-us doing his gruesome worst with a box cutter as if nothing had disturbed him.

"What's the status of the HRT operators?" Alex called out to the tactical team leader.

The man's expression was stony. "We have several casualties. One serious."

Yael's fingers clenched. This was her fault. She'd missed something.

"Can they see inside the room?" Alex's voice was rough. "Is this the right place? Did they arrest this bastard or is he in the wind?"

Yael shot Alex a look. She wanted answers too but the people on the other end were dealing with what sounded like severe injuries.

She watched the images now coming online from several of the operators' helmet cams. One black-clad man was on the ground being treated by another man. It was the guy who'd held the breacher. The guy who'd taken Shane's place because Shane had broken his arm.

It looked bad.

Tears blurred her vision but she blinked them away.

She needed to figure out what the hell had happened.

Someone wearing a camera looked inside the room and sure enough, a gurney sat there complete with the dripping remains of what had surely been Anya Baker. But no UNSUB. No Evi1Geni-us.

"He's not here. There's a laptop here playing a video of him torturing the girl. But the UNSUB is not here. Repeat, UNSUB is not here." The words crackled over the comms.

"Dammit." Alex ground his teeth together. "You were right. The bastard recorded it. He makes everyone think it's live and that they have a say in what happens during the auction but they are being conned. He's already made up his mind what to do and what the polls will say. The 'live' aspect of the auction is nothing but a fake poll."

That was the least of the man's crimes.

Yael fought nausea. Anya Baker had likely been dead before they'd even had the chance to save her. Even so, Yael felt as if her guts had been ripped out. She'd failed.

"He's never boobytrapped the crime scene before," Ashley Chen pointed out sharply.

Yael banded her arms across her stomach and leaned back in her chair. Sweat formed on her skin and she started to shake as if she'd run a marathon. "I think it was different this time," she gritted out. "I think he knew we were coming."

Suddenly the camera light on her laptop turned green and she found herself staring directly at the masked face of the so-called Evi1Geni-us.

Ice flashed in a cold wave over her skin. He'd somehow gotten into her system and taken control of her camera. He wasn't in that room with Anya Baker anymore. He was somewhere else entirely. Somewhere he felt safe.

This bastard, who everyone else could see as her screen was being fed to another large monitor, was staring straight at her. He could see her face.

And she couldn't breathe...

2

"Hello, *Sphinx*." His voice echoed with distortion. "Such a pretty thing—thought you were clever, too, didn't you? Tut tut. You'll never be as clever as me."

Her pulse pounded as if someone had plugged her into the mains socket.

Alex was typing frantically.

"Anya was pretty too—in the beginning. I wonder what you'll sound like when you beg for mercy? Or perhaps you like pain..."

Alex stuck his thumb over her camera as the rush of blood to her ears deafened her.

Pulling herself together, she launched herself onto her keyboard and tried to follow Evi1Geni-us's tracks as he fled back along the system. She hit a brick wall. Then he vanished.

She could find him. She simply needed a little time.

"Turn it off," Chen snapped.

Yael's stomach flipped as she stared at the agent, her fingers still typing commands. "I can track him."

"I said turn it off." Chen's eyes were hard as they assessed her.

Yael's hands hesitated as they hovered over the keyboard. Given the opportunity she *could* find him and the likelihood was he wasn't physically that distant from where they all sat stunned and defeated. Alex watched her with a fierce expression.

This was the best chance they had of finding this monster...

"Now!" Chen started walking toward her.

"Do as Agent Chen says, Yael," Alex said finally. "Let's figure out how he snuck inside your machine before we race after him and risk compromising ourselves if he set another trap."

Yael blew out a shaky breath. Reluctantly she shut down her laptop and removed the battery to make doubly sure the bastard couldn't do any damage if he'd planted some Trojan or worm.

"Let's establish what he saw and whether or not he got into any of the other systems," Chen said.

"He didn't," Alex assured the FBI analyst.

"As much as I trust your skills, Alex." Chen sent him a look that Yael couldn't decipher. "I want you to check and double check and then triple check. He got into your employee's machine and I want to know how and for how long, and *exactly* what he saw and heard."

The implication was Yael wasn't as good as Evi1Geni-us was, and she hated that Agent Chen might be right.

Alex nodded stiffly.

Yael stood, feeling dizzy and defeated. She quickly left the room, heading for the washroom. She lifted the seat and threw up in the toilet, her stomach recoiling from the horror of what she'd witnessed, the finality of death, and the fact she'd failed Anya Baker and Evi1Geni-us had beaten her at her own game. When she came out of the cubicle she paused. Her friend Laura stood there, looking pale and shaken.

"You okay?" Laura asked.

Yael nodded. Walked to the sink where she washed her face and tried not to remember staring into that monster's eyes glistening behind his stupid mask. She had protections on her system. Solid protections. How had he gotten past them? What had she missed?

She grabbed a paper towel. Dried her face. Forced herself to speak. "You?"

"Hell, no." Laura swallowed audibly. "That was messed up. How did he manage to get into your computer?"

Yael's eyes smarted. "He must have set a trap and I fell right into it."

"It wasn't your fault," Laura protested.

"Some of it was."

"Hey, it could have happened to any one of us. We were all so focused on stopping him from hurting that girl…" Laura crossed her arms tightly against her chest, as if warding off the memories of what he'd done.

If only it was that easy.

Laura stared at the floor. "Alex wants us all to help check the systems."

Yael nodded. It would take time and concentration and she already felt wiped. "I need some coffee first."

She turned the faucet back on and washed her hands again, using too much soap and too hot water. No matter how hard she scrubbed she couldn't get the image of blood and gore out of her mind.

"Are you sure you're okay?" Laura came to stand beside her and put a hand on her back.

Yael turned away as she dried her hands. She didn't like to be touched.

"No." She glanced at Laura in the mirror, ignoring her own gaunt features. "I'm pissed and upset, but I'll survive." Unlike poor Anya Baker.

Yael pushed out of the washroom with Laura on her heels. More HRT guys were streaming down the hallway, presumably heading to the crime scene or the hospital to be with their injured colleagues. FBI agents milled around. She went to her workstation and slumped heavily in the chair.

Alex came over and sat on the table, watching her.

"How did he know we were onto him?" she asked, feeling the weight of responsibility hanging around her neck.

"I don't know." Alex shook his head and that scared her more than anything else had today. Alex knew everything. "Let's get your machine to a secure room and then we can start checking the systems here to make sure he doesn't plan to launch any more surprise attacks. You up for that?"

She nodded. "Yeah. We need to catch this guy."

Alex's mouth pinched. "We do. But we also need to make sure your *identity* isn't compromised and that your personal security is sufficient."

She blinked.

Did Alex know the truth? She was sure he did although he'd never mentioned it. The idea that the secrets she so carefully guarded could be exposed by this evil monster…

"Why do I feel like I'm not about to like what you suggest?"

Alex smiled humorlessly. "Because you have good instincts. The HRT operator was correct when he told you to follow them. I shouldn't have ordered you to do something else. Next time I'll trust your instincts too."

"You don't think I messed up?"

Alex's eyes narrowed. "I think we all underestimated him, but what I really want to know is how the hell did he know we were onto him?"

"You think we have a leak?"

"Might not be a person on the task force. Could be a software vulnerability we or the FBI need to patch. But Evi1Geni-us knew we were here in Houston and part of me wonders if he didn't plan to lure us here all along."

Shane didn't register anything from the time he left the Houston Field Office to the time he arrived at the scene of the explosion.

The agent riding shotgun had given him directions and then held on for the drive.

Patrol cars and cops surrounded the warehouse, but Shane jogged right through them, making his way to an ambulance where a prone figure was being loaded into the back.

He spotted Cowboy who had blood running down his face, and Nash who was being treated near the doorway.

Shane caught the ambulance door with shaking hands as the EMT was about to close it. "I'm riding with you."

One look at his face and the paramedic jerked his head to tell him to get inside.

Shane moved to sit near Scotty's head while the medic worked on his friend's injuries. Shane's mouth turned to ash at the sight of mangled flesh of Scotty's hands and arms. But it was the jagged piece of steel embedded in his best friend's chest that had him seriously worried.

"At least I won't have to type up any 302s, huh." Scotty's voice was hoarse and flecks of blood bubbled out of the corner of his mouth.

Shane reached out and gripped Scotty's shoulder so tightly it had to hurt but he couldn't relax his grip or let go.

He cleared his throat. "We're taking bets on how quickly you'll be back on the team."

Scotty's eyes crinkled at the corners and then filled with calm purpose, silently telling Shane humor wouldn't save either of them this time. "We both know I'm not gonna make it."

Pain scraped its way across Shane's exposed heart. "That's bullshit. You're gonna be fine."

The medic flashed him a glance as he desperately tried to insert an IV.

"Tell Grace I love her. And the kids." Tears filled Scotty's eyes and Shane suddenly couldn't see for shit as his own vision blurred.

"Tell her yourself."

Scotty started coughing and Shane froze at the rattle in the sound.

When the guy finally hauled in a wheezing breath he said starkly, "I'm not stupid, Shane. My body's fucked."

A wave of determination crashed over Shane. "Don't you dare give up on me. The medics have got you. We'll be at a trauma center in a couple minutes tops. They'll fix you up. Just hang on, buddy."

Scotty's gaze locked onto his. "Tell Grace I love her. I will always love her. And Jake and Katie and the baby. Watch out for her and help her out with the kids when you can. Tell her…" The grief etched onto his friend's face killed him. "Tell her to move on when she's ready. She deserves to be loved, even if it can't be by me."

Shane couldn't speak. This was not happening.

"And kiss the baby for me." Scotty's gaze was fading away. "And catch this evil motherfucker and roast him alive."

The EKG was going crazy on the monitor.

Shane turned to stare at the anguished-looking EMT. "Do something."

The man grabbed the defibrillator pads and attached them to Scotty's chest.

Shane removed his hands as the electricity jolted through his best friend's body.

Nothing.

The medic braced himself as the ambulance took a sharp turn. "Clear."

The machine shocked Scotty again and Shane held his breath. Nothing.

"Should we try compressions?" Shane asked, more desperate than he'd ever been in his life.

The medic's eyes trailed to the blood soaking the gurney. "He's lost too much blood."

Shane snarled. "I'll do it."

He pressed down on Scotty's chest with his good hand as the

medic used a device to blow air into Scotty's lungs—but his friend's chest didn't inflate. His heart didn't miraculously restart.

As they pulled up outside the hospital, Shane followed Scotty as he was wheeled into a cubicle where more doctors frantically worked on his best friend. Shane knew it was hopeless when they kept shooting him glances filled with abject pity.

But miracles happened...

After another five minutes of frenzied activity, they suddenly stopped working and stepped back. One of the doctors called time of death and Shane stared at them frozen in shock.

As they turned away, he went over to his friend and slipped his good arm under Scotty's shoulders, raising him up as he sobbed against his chest.

Slowly he became aware of others coming into the room. Cowboy, Keeme, Hopper, Nash, Demarco, Hersh. Novak walked in, expression dialed way beyond bleak.

Shane slowly laid his friend back on the table aware he was covered in Scotty's blood. Shane closed his eyes. "I need to get to Grace."

Novak nodded. "We're on the next flight out."

"He's coming too." Shane indicated Scotty with his chin.

Novak hesitated only briefly. "We won't leave him behind."

Shane nodded. He wanted to lash out but these guys were hurting as much as he was. "Did we at least catch the motherfucker?"

Novak shook his head and rage replaced Shane's grief.

"But we will."

Damn right they would. They'd get this guy if it was the last thing Shane ever did.

Shane held Novak's gaze calmly as if his heart hadn't been put through a grinder. He pushed away and headed outside, ignoring the curious stares as people took in his blood-soaked form.

Once outside, he stared up at the blue sky knowing nothing would ever be the same again. His best friend was dead and all because of a stupid broken arm and some twisted piece of shit.

"I'm coming for you, motherfucker. You're going to wish you'd never started this, you murderous asshole." If it took the rest of his life, he would make sure the so-called Evi1Geni-us paid for what he'd done, for the lives he'd destroyed.

Then Shane went back inside and helped Novak and the others get their brother home.

3

He sat in the secret secure room he had refurbished inside his modest home, eating a chocolate bar and drinking a soda. He'd spent an hour playing a video game but his appetite for pretend had faded because it didn't compare to the adrenaline rush he got from causing real harm to real people.

He went over to his PC and booted it up.

He had an outside source of air he could control plus a high-grade filtration system. He had backup power sources and enough dried food and water to keep him alive for months. It was a survival bunker but he wasn't prepping for the apocalypse.

It was more secure than most bank vaults, but he'd be lying if he said he wasn't freaked out when he occasionally closed the door and locked himself inside. It was too reminiscent of another small room he'd once occupied. One where no-one ever heard him scream. Where people had died and others, who should have cared, barely raised an eyebrow.

His teeth fused with remembered rage. He'd paid back some of the players involved. Not all of them. Not yet. Let them figure out he was coming for them and then let them sweat in fear. Let their nightmares be fueled by memories of the wrongs they'd committed.

They'd always said he was too puny to fight back but brute strength only took a person so far. He worked out now, though. No one called him their bitch any longer.

He pulled up an image on his private phone. Smiled at the memory of making a fat man consume his own testicles. Tension fell away from his shoulders in a wave of relief.

Sometimes life felt very, very good.

He yawned and rolled his shoulders. He was tired but he was about to take a long vacation. He'd earned it along with the fifty million in crypto he'd saved for his upcoming retirement. Another reason for owning his own secure vault.

He pulled up the screen capture he'd taken of *Sphinx* who'd been attempting to get into his machine a few days ago. If he hadn't been waiting for her, watching for her, she might have found a weakness to exploit and found him. As it stood, he'd been the one doing the exploiting, not that it had gotten him very far. Yet.

She was really very pretty.

He'd run reverse image searches and facial recognition programs. She hadn't turned up anywhere. It was almost as if she had something to hide too and that intrigued him more than anything had in months.

Setting up the Feds had been a lot of fun and had given him the information he needed—so sad that Special Agent Monteith had died in the line of duty. A smile curled his lips. Maybe he'd go after the widow next...except she was pregnant and he didn't ever touch children. That was the only line he wouldn't cross.

He turned everything off and decided to hit the sack. He had a few loose ends to tie up. And, for that, he needed a weapon.

He wasn't a big fan of guns. Guns made heroes out of idiots. Made people feel like bad-asses whereas the thought of running a knife over flesh made them piss their pants. It was easy to dissociate from the act of murder when you simply pulled a trigger or lit a fuse. Skin on skin killing took a lot more balls and was a lot more satisfying.

Unfortunately, this time, he didn't think he had a lot of choice. He'd have to settle for a bullet.

4

A week after the disastrous operation in Houston, Shane was still trying to get the image of his friend's dead face out of his mind, but every time he closed his eyes, even to blink, he saw Scotty's blood-soaked corpse. Past experience told him the flashbacks would fade eventually, but Shane wasn't so sure about the guilt or the rage that consumed him from the inside out.

Scotty had died doing Shane's job and Shane would give anything in the entire universe to go back in time and change that, even if it meant sacrificing the victim in the courthouse to a fall that could easily have broken her neck. Even if it meant Shane dying in Scotty's place.

His eyes burned, but there was no moisture left for tears.

Yesterday morning, they'd buried David Andrew "Scotty" Monteith. Scotty had belonged to the US Coast Guard before he'd joined the Bureau. Telling Grace that Dave was dead had been the single hardest thing Shane had ever done. Special Forces training and HRT selection were nothing compared to uttering the words that had destroyed her life. To put a cherry on top of a shit sandwich, Grace was six months pregnant with child number three.

Shane had barely been able to look her in the eye at the service yesterday, but damned if she hadn't grabbed him and held him like a baby while he'd broken down and sobbed all over her.

Tears smarted in his eyes again but he blinked them away. So much for being done with crying.

Fucking loser.

Grace was the one who needed comforting and support. He needed to put the sick murdering fucker who'd killed Scotty and Anya Baker into a prison cell or a hole in the ground. He would prefer the latter but as a law enforcement officer, he knew how to follow the rules. Prison would be hell for the shitbag—he'd guarantee it.

He couldn't sleep so instead he was at work at HRT's compound situated in the heart of the US Marine Base in Quantico. He'd already put two hundred rounds into targets that morning, honing his skills so that when he met that motherfucker face-to-face, he'd be ready. Shane worked on his marksmanship every single day. Screw his broken arm.

Gold team had had a call out yesterday afternoon after the funeral, to help serve a fugitive arrest warrant. Everyone in the team had felt good about putting a wanted murderer in jail where he belonged. Scotty would have been pleased. Shane would spend the rest of his life doing things that Scotty would have liked —firstly catching the motherfucker who'd killed him.

Now it was only seven in the morning and Shane sat in the equipment cage he'd shared with Scotty, cleaning his custom-made SIG Sauer P226 Mk 25 and backup Glock 22.

The familiar smell of G96 gun oil rose up around him, but today it failed to raise his spirits. The room was quiet. He was alone, which suited him fine. Everyone would assemble shortly for the daily 0800 team briefing in HRT's main classroom.

He heard footsteps in the corridor and pressed his lips together.

Dammit. Not so alone.

"Livingstone?" Payne Novak called loudly as he walked into the room with three figures trailing behind him.

"Here." Shane stared at Novak, who looked as pale and exhausted as he felt. Instinctively, Shane knew he didn't want to hear whatever the guy had to say.

"I saw your truck in the parking lot."

Shane raised his brow in question.

"Everything okay?" Novak asked.

It was the wrong thing to ask, especially in front of the new recruits.

Shane looked away, swallowing hard.

Novak exhaled sharply. "Look, Shane, I know you're upset—"

"I am way beyond *upset*, boss." Upset was when you lost your keys or were dumped by a woman you liked. This feeling of utter devastation was like acid corroding his bones and making him feel raw and achy. But he couldn't afford to show how badly Scotty's death had affected him. He didn't want to jeopardize his career. He wasn't ready to quit HRT, not by a long shot, nor did he like sitting on the sidelines. He needed to help catch this guy. He gritted his teeth and forced out, "I'm dealing with it."

Novak quietly appraised him. Payne Novak was a man who didn't say a lot and, until about a month or so ago, hadn't tended to smile much either. Not that they'd had much to smile about in the last week. But when Novak spoke people tended to listen, which was why he'd been promoted to temporary leader of Gold team while their actual team leader was on some super-secret mission to who the hell knew where.

"You remember Will Griffin, Hunt Kincaid and Meghan Donnelly." Novak introduced the people at his side. Shane recognized them all from Selection and New Operator Training School —NOTS.

The three HRT teams—Blue, Red, and Gold—were each comprised of two seven-person assaulter units and one eight-man sniper unit, plus support personnel. Each selection cycle, the teams had different requirements that needed to be filled by new operators after people aged out, moved up the ranks or headed into other sections of the FBI. Or because of injuries…or death.

HRT had never lost a man during an active response. Until Scotty.

Like all the operators, Shane had a say in choosing who he wanted on his squad. Griffin and Kincaid had both helped thwart a major biological weapons threat last spring and—showing immense bravery—had saved thousands, if not hundreds of thousands of lives. Meghan Donnelly had proven herself a team player. Otherwise she wouldn't even be here, and she was just so fucking good at everything and never stopped, no matter what they'd thrown at her. The fact a woman had passed Selection and successfully graduated NOTS was an historic moment for HRT, but right now nobody wanted to celebrate.

Frankly, it was about damn time they had a female operator and Shane was proud to have her on his team, but another glance at his boss and Shane suddenly realized why they were *here* this morning.

"Griffin and Kincaid are joining Gold team's Echo assaulters. Donnelly is joining Charlie assaulters." Novak confirmed Shane's suspicion a second later. "As you're here, I'd like you to show them where to put their gear. Griffin is with you."

Shane's throat closed and he looked away, wishing he was able to give these people the heartwarming welcome he'd received three years ago.

"Sure." His voice was like sandpaper in his throat. "No problem."

Shane straightened his spine and met the dark brown eyes of his new partner. He'd voted that Griffin get a spot on Gold team after he finished his six months of training—so had Scotty. But Shane had never imagined the guy would fill Scotty's prematurely empty boots.

Griffin stared back at him impassively and Shane recalled the guy had suffered his own devastating loss last year. Griffin had been at the funeral yesterday, all the new NOTS graduates had been.

"Kincaid is with Nash. Donnelly is with Steel. Cadell is getting his own cage to make more room for Hugo's equipment."

Shane nodded woodenly. Nash, Cowboy and Cadell had suffered minor injuries last week but were already back at work. Hugo—their K9 team member—had thankfully been fine.

"Spell out to these guys the expectations regarding storing and maintaining their own equipment and ammunition. Then I want you to report to my office after the morning briefing. I have a new assignment for you."

Wait. What? Shane took a step forward. "What do you mean, a new assignment?"

Was he being removed from the team? Had Novak decided he was a liability?

Novak released a slow breath and clasped Shane's good arm. "Shane, I know this hasn't been easy for you—"

He jerked away. "Because it should have been *me*." Emotion was a vise around his throat. "You and I and everyone else in HRT knows it." He raised the stupid cast on his arm. "If I hadn't tripped down that stairwell, I wouldn't have broken my arm. Scotty wouldn't be rotting in a casket six feet under."

Novak's eyes narrowed. "You really think your broken arm is what caused Scotty's death?"

"I didn't *cause* his death but there is no one in this world who can argue the only reason Scotty was holding the breacher last week was because I couldn't."

"Oh. That's funny. You told me you could handle the breacher despite your cast. In fact, you told me you could do it better than ever because the cast helped strengthen your arm. That's what you told me." Novak sounded coldly furious.

Shane huffed. "I was bullshitting you and you knew it."

"That's right." Novak took a step forward until he was right in Shane's face, but the look in his eyes wasn't anger. It was complete ruination. "I did know you were bullshitting and I knew why. If it was up to you, *you* would have handled the breacher even with two broken arms. I'm the one who put Scotty in your position. I'm the one who ordered you to stand down. I'm the one who ultimately signed a death warrant for whoever breached that door. Me. Not you."

Shane could see the same guilt he was feeling, reflected in the wreckage of Novak's eyes.

"But it wasn't your fault. It wasn't my fault either. It was that evil son of a bitch's fault. He's the one who needs to take the blame. He's who we need to focus on, not our own useless self-pity."

Shane blew out a massive breath. He couldn't speak. Novak was right but dealing with the emotions he was feeling wasn't that easy.

Novak continued. "Accidents happen. We can spend our days fast-roping out of helicopters and then trip over the curb and break an arm on the way to our car. It's called life and it isn't fucking fair."

Shane nodded even though there was no way anyone could tell him he wasn't responsible in some way for how things had gone down. But he didn't want to lose his place on the team by arguing the point further. Bad enough being sidelined. He needed back on the team if he were to have any hope of being there when the FBI caught this asshole. He needed to see the psycho pay.

"I've got this, boss." He stood straighter and stared Novak in the eyes—because when you sold a lie to a man of this caliber you had better put your heart and soul into it. "I've made an appointment with the psychologist next week and I know I have to work through the grief process, but I promise it won't affect my judgment or my ability to do my job."

Novak waited a beat, then nodded. "Be that as it may, you are off the team until your arm heals."

Anger filled Shane. He spoke through gritted teeth. "You have got to be kidding me."

Novak ignored his protest. "According to the doc, eight weeks minimum from the date of the accident before you can start training again, which means you have some time left to go."

Shane ground his teeth.

"So instead of you sitting here cleaning your weapon five hours a day, I found you a position as liaison with the Bureau task force hunting this motherfucker."

Shane opened his mouth to argue but then his brain caught up. "Wait. What?"

Novak squeezed his shoulder. "Help the new guys settle in. They've worked hard to get here and earned their spots the same way you and I and Scotty did."

Shane blinked as he looked away. Cleared his throat. "With Seth Hopper taking that temporary assignment with Border Patrol Gold assaulters will still be a man down without me."

"Kurt Montana and Jordan Krychek are due back from overseas shortly. Jordan is going to step in until you're back to full strength. Then he'll swap out with you onto the task force. I want you to update both of us daily on any significant advances in the investigation."

Shane licked his suddenly dry lips. This was a chance to know exactly what the FBI was doing to catch this UNSUB. The lack of information had been driving him nuts since they'd left Texas. No one would tell him a damn thing and the task force was keeping everything locked down tight—which was good, except *he* needed to know.

"Does that mean I have to move up to DC for a few weeks?"

Novak shook his head. "They decided to run it out of Quantico."

Shane drew in a deep breath. This was a win-win. It felt almost too good to be true. He'd always been suspicious of that feeling.

"You think you can handle it, or shall I assign someone else?" Novak asked.

"I can handle it." Shane stood straighter and angled his chin. Damn straight he could handle it.

Will Griffin, Hunt Kincaid and Meghan Donnelly edged to one side of the cage as their boss went to exit.

"I'll leave you all to settle in. See you at eight sharp for the team briefing. Shane, you're to report to Building 64 Room 3A at oh-nine hundred Monday." Novak headed to the door and paused. "And, as tempting as it may be to go after this killer on your own, don't. It will be grounds for dismissal from HRT and possibly the Bureau, understood?"

Shane stood to attention and saluted the way he'd been taught back when he'd been an idiot child who'd thought joining the Army sounded like a good idea. "Sir."

Humor curled Novak's mouth. He shook his head. "Any issues. Any of you," he included the new team members in this comment, "come to me. It's been a rough week for all of us. You need to talk, you come find me."

They all nodded in agreement and then Shane and Griffin looked at one another after the boss left. Griffin's mouth pulled to the corner reflecting exactly what Shane was thinking. No way in hell would any of them go crawling to the boss with "issues."

Shane held out his good hand to the each of the newcomers. "Welcome to the best squad in US law enforcement. Don't fuck it up."

Griffin's hand squeezed his. "I don't intend to."

Neither did Shane. Hopefully.

5

"You could come out for a meal with us." A dimple flashed beside Laura's red-lipstick-painted smile as she slid behind an empty table. "Make it a threesome."

Yael slumped beside her friend who bumped her shoulder.

"I'm kidding."

Yael shook her head, a reluctant smile curving her lips. "I'm too tired to socialize and I have an early start tomorrow."

"You're always too *something* to socialize."

"I think the word you are looking for is 'antisocial.'"

"Well, you're not too old to change, Grandma."

Yael stuck out her tongue at her friend. Laura might be right, but tonight wasn't the night to change the habits of a lifetime. She tried to push aside the downbeat feeling that had been plaguing her for the past week, but the events of Houston had formed the background to every waking thought, every breath.

Laura had begged Yael to accompany her tonight because she'd arranged to meet some guy online for a date. Yael had agreed because, after relocating down here from DC, Laura had spent the last two days helping Yael organize her amazing new home as well as Cramer, Parker & Gray's new satellite office. The company had paid a removal firm to schlep the furniture and boxes, but there were always a million things to take care of.

Laura took a sip of her wine. A couple of years ago she'd been blissfully married to the love of her life. Then he'd left her for a woman barely out of her teens and it had done a number on her friend's self-esteem. Yael had checked out the ex and his new wife online and they looked nauseatingly joyful. A constant thorn in Laura's psyche.

"We should go on vacation somewhere together," Laura mused. "The Maldives or Greece."

Yael stared at the table. She'd always wanted to travel but didn't have a passport. "Maybe."

"You could bring your art supplies and sit around looking all moody and artistic. I could order food and drink and interact with the locals." Laura raised a finely plucked brow suggestively.

The thought of visiting some of the places on her bucket list was tempting, very tempting. But it wasn't that simple and now wasn't the time. They had a killer to catch. "I'll think about it. What time is your date coming?"

Laura checked her cell. "He said seven."

Yael checked her watch too. It was five to. "I'll hang out at the bar until you give me the thumbs up signal."

Why someone as attractive and internet savvy as Laura found dates via the internet Yael didn't know. She didn't trust the apps. The guy was probably nothing like his profile picture and she couldn't imagine hooking up with someone based on their online persona. She knew how fake that could be. Then again, so did Laura and most of the rest of the dating universe. Why was Yael one of the last holdouts when it came to internet dating when she didn't exactly go out of her way to meet people in real life either?

Maybe because the last thing she wanted to do was actually get involved with anyone? Definitely maybe. Celibacy was easier if a lot lonelier. She recalled a pair of wintergreen eyes and let out a heavy sigh.

Laura glanced at her. "You don't need to stay, you know. I'll be fine. If I don't click with this guy, I'll probably head back to DC tonight to avoid the morning traffic. I can give you a ride home first."

A roar erupted from a group of young men playing pool in the back corner of the bar. Yael glanced over at them. Some of the guys were eyeing them. Her fingers clenched into fists in her lap. "Don't worry about the ride. If you hit it off send me a text and I'll order a cab or whatever."

"Okay, if you're sure. I'm heading to the restroom now." Laura kissed Yael's cheek and glanced at the guys playing pool with a knowing glint in her eye, but thankfully didn't suggest anything.

"Be careful. You know how many creeps there are in the world." Yael wiped her cheek as she headed over to the bar to order another drink. She grabbed a stool and slipped out of her leather jacket. Sitting here like a spare part was the least she could do for her friend, even if it meant she was at a bar rather than curled up on her new living room sofa, watching the latest episode of *Survivor*.

Her beer arrived and she paid the barkeep.

A man came in and stood beside her.

She watched him out of the corner of her eye and in the mirror. Medium height. Slender build. Dark hair that looked like it might have a tendency to curl. Blue eyes. Gray suit. White shirt. Blue tie. He looked out of place in this bar full of jarheads, although, given the proximity to Quantico, he might be associated with the Bureau.

Laura's date?

He caught her gaze and gave her a nervous smile. "I hope you don't mind me standing here. I'm waiting for my date to show up and worried I'm about to be stood up because if she looks anything like her profile picture, she's way out of my league." He checked his phone and scanned the bar. His face lit up as Laura returned from the restroom. "But there she is."

Yael smiled. "Well, you're a lucky guy. She's gorgeous." Yael took a sip of her beer, determined not to ruin Laura's chances if it turned out she really liked this guy. He wasn't Yael's type but few men were.

The image of that grim-faced, green-eyed HRT operator from last week once again flashed through her mind. She pushed the image away. He'd filtered in and out of her thoughts all week long and she wasn't sure why. However handsome he might be, Shane Livingstone *definitely* wasn't her type. Even less so than this guy. But they'd shared something on a fundamental level. Something that wouldn't be so easy to forget any time soon.

Laura's date gave Yael a shy smile. "Enjoy your evening."

She looked away and Mister Tinder walked over to Laura and held out his hand, laughing and joking. Yael pulled a face at herself in the mirror behind the bar as she watched Laura and her new beau chat away like old friends.

Her stomach growled rudely and she pressed her hand against it. When was the last time she'd eaten? She checked the mirror. Laura and her date were clearly enjoying each other's company.

She caught the barkeep's attention. "Can I get a basket of chicken wings, please?"

The barkeep nodded and sent her order to the cook. She was starving and hadn't gone grocery shopping yet so there was hardly any food in her new place.

Yael tipped back her beer. She should be celebrating. She'd just purchased her first home which felt like a miracle. She should have ordered champagne but this didn't seem like a champagne sort of joint. Plus, drinking champagne alone seemed even more pathetic than drinking beer alone so…

She raised her empty bottle to ask for another.

After the events of last Friday, Alex had requested she bring forward her relocation to the satellite office that Cramer, Parker & Gray had recently established at Quantico so she could more easily continue on this Joint Task Force that was working to capture this sadistic killer.

She'd been looking for a place to buy down here and Alex

suddenly had a friend from the BAU who was selling and had already moved into a bigger property. It had happened so fast Yael couldn't believe she was finally a homeowner. The house was fantastic and had great security, too. Alex had been fastidious about her personal safety ever since her face had been seen by one of the country's most dangerous serial killers. She knew he was worried about what had happened last week. She'd be lying if she said she was cool with it. More than anything, she was angry. At herself, at Evi1Geni-us. At anyone who thought it was okay to hurt other people for pleasure or because they'd had a bad day.

Her thoughts flinched away from the direction they'd taken.

Evi1Geni-us hadn't broadcast her identity to the world, or doxxed her. Yet.

It was another reason why moving and buying a house through a private sale and via the shell company Alex had set up to thwart anyone trying to track her down had seemed like an excellent idea. It didn't stop someone figuring out where she lived by simply following her home. She needed to be vigilant. Alex had offered to give her some lessons in surveillance detection this weekend which she planned to take him up on.

They'd already gone over her online security and had taken some precautions. The vulnerability in her system had been inserted as an executable script when she'd begun tracking the computer streaming the video. They'd assumed Evi1Geni-us was busy torturing Anya Baker when in fact he'd been doing to her what she'd been doing to him.

Hunting.

And he'd had the advantage. He'd somehow known they were operating out of the FBI's Houston Field Office. He'd set a trap and, despite knowing better, she'd fallen straight into it.

She'd since rewritten her programs to detect anything like it in the future and three independent experts, including a certain pissy Special Agent Chen, had gone over every pixel, every byte, every line of code, and every physical component of her machine —and every other machine in that FBI operations room last week to confirm they were clean. Evi1Geni-us hadn't done any real damage to them. Just shaken their confidence and made them look like fools.

Better than what he'd done to HRT… The memory made her mouth flood with saliva. Agent Monteith had been a good man by all accounts. Yael wished for the millionth time she could somehow change the past, but it was futile.

A young man came over and stood a little too close as he ordered another round for himself and his shaven-headed friends who were playing pool.

"No," she said firmly, as he met her gaze and opened his mouth to deliver what was, no doubt, his favorite pickup line.

He shot his friends a despondent look and they all burst out laughing.

"Ma'am." He nodded as he picked up the beers on a tray and walked away.

She felt a thousand years old.

Her food arrived and she was on her second wing when a new group of people walked in. She recognized some of them from the operation last week even though they were wearing casual clothes today. The Hostage Rescue Team. She was at the end of the bar sitting in the shadows but she saw them catalogue everyone in the place before some of them settled into an empty booth while others ranged along the bar on the opposite side of the room.

Her heart pounded and her appetite faded away.

The Marines might be young, good-looking and in great shape, but the HRT guys exuded an air of rock-solid self-assurance and absolute competence that was compelling. Every one of them looked in peak physical condition. Broad shoulders, lean torsos, powerful legs. And it wasn't even their physiques that was the most impressive thing about them. It was the way they held themselves with the utmost confidence—the tilt of their jaw, the intelligence in their calm but constantly vigilant eyes, the set of their mouths.

The barkeep placed her beer on the bar and she glanced over

her shoulder at Laura. Her date had moved so he sat beside her on the bench seat and they were facing one another, Laura all giggling coyness and animated excitement. The two of them looked absorbed in one another and as if they were getting on wonderfully.

Yael grimaced and took another swallow of beer.

Maybe she was the one with the problem. Actually, she was definitely the one with the problem. She picked at the label on her bottle. At least Shane Livingstone wasn't with the HRT group. Even as the thought popped into her head, the door opened again and in he walked with a good-looking African American guy she hadn't seen before. Shane didn't seem to see her and she put her head down, letting her hair hide her features as she concentrated on her food, hoping to fade into the woodwork.

She hadn't expected to encounter the guy ever again and had been relieved by that thought. He'd seen her fail on every front—even the thing she was supposed to be exceptional at.

Her foot tapped nervously against the footrest. She doubted he'd even remember her. He'd lost one of his colleagues that day and she knew that didn't happen to these guys very often. They trained too hard to mess up.

One of the group raised his beer bottle in a toast she couldn't quite hear over the noise of the jukebox. The others joined him in the salute. She recalled suddenly that Alex had gone to the funeral yesterday of the man who'd died.

They were toasting their lost colleague, Dave "Scotty" Monteith.

Yael rubbed her hand over the base of her sternum as the few things she'd eaten and drunk tonight swirled uncomfortably in her stomach. How disrespectful would it look that she was here having a drink and some food as if nothing had happened?

Did they all know how badly she'd messed up? If she'd been faster or simply better at her job, she might have figured out Evi1-Geni-us wasn't where he was pretending to be. Sure, a laptop had been streaming the video feed of the torture while Anya Baker's blood-streaked corpse had slowly cooled and stiffened in real time—and Yael had tracked that VPN-cloaked computer faster than almost anyone else on the planet could have done. But the UNSUB himself had already left the building after uploading the sound-stripped version of the video with the prepared fake polls. The bastard had also set up cameras to film the HRT explosion from two angles—one inside the room, one outside—presumably recording the footage before cutting the connection and, once again, disappearing into the ether. Apparently, he liked to have video evidence of his crimes which would be great if they ever caught him. It was unlikely he'd trust that sort of information to the cloud. More likely he had multiple copies squirreled away somewhere.

She wanted to help track him down along with that evidence.

Then she wanted him incarcerated somewhere he could never hurt anyone else ever again. *Or dead.*

As much as she was generally opposed to violence, she'd make an exception in this case. She was fine with this man ceasing to exist as long as it stopped the killings.

He'd made over a million dollars last week alone and people had even sent him bonuses when he'd played the footage of the explosion, mocking the FBI and their efforts to catch him. She'd expected her face and online alias to also be streamed at the end of the video. What twisted serial killer/black-hat hacker wouldn't be bragging about turning the tables on the people hunting him?

But he'd held that piece of information back for now.

Once he went public, she wasn't sure what might happen. Would someone recognize her and expose her again? She did not want her past and her present to collide. She didn't want to have to disappear again.

Her hand shook as she closed her fingers around the neck of her beer bottle and raised it to her lips.

"Hey."

She jerked in her seat and beer ran down her chin. She

grabbed a napkin and dabbed at the mess running down her neck and spotting her favorite t-shirt.

FBI Special Agent Shane Livingstone rested his plaster cast on the bar as the Marines playing pool eyed him with amusement, obviously expecting him to get shot down the same way they had.

6

"Didn't mean to startle you."

Yael crumpled the napkin in her fist. Dammit. She couldn't believe she'd zoned out like that. He must think she was a total freak.

"You okay?" He had a slight southern drawl she hadn't noticed before but now made sense. He watched her with an expression she couldn't interpret.

"Yeah. Why?" Even as she spoke, she regretted the sharpness of her tone. One of his colleagues had recently died, someone he'd been close to if his anguish last week had been anything to judge by. She softened her voice. "You?"

"Fine." He looked away, maybe reflecting on the same memories, with the same reluctance to have his feelings probed as she did. He held up his finger to the barkeep for a drink. "I heard what happened after I left."

Yael stiffened.

"Is *Sphinx* your real name?"

"No." But it had been her favorite online moniker. "Why?"

He smoothed his good hand over his short, light brown hair. "Because frankly the idea that Evi1Geni-us might know your real name *and* what you look like would be a little concerning."

She blinked. People didn't usually worry about her. She didn't let them.

"You sure you're okay? You look a little pale..."

She glanced at her reflection in the mirror behind the bar. She looked haggard and the circles under her eyes reflected her inability to sleep lately. She'd better break out the concealer next time she decided to leave the house.

"Yeah. Seeing you guys walk in here reminded me about last week." Not that she'd been able to forget for very long.

"I've spent a lot of time thinking about it, too." Shane propped both elbows on the bar. She noticed he wore a smaller cast than he had last week. This one allowed his elbow to bend. His sling hung unused around his neck. The subtle scent of pine tantalized her senses suggesting he'd recently showered. She shifted away a little because she didn't want to be so *aware* of this man.

"And the fact he is out there planning to do it again pisses me the fuck off."

"Me too," she agreed.

He stole one of her chicken wings and she suddenly felt hungry again so she took another, wiping her greasy fingers on a clean napkin before offering him the bowl. "Help yourself."

"Any chance he can find out where you live?" Shane asked between bites.

A shiver danced over her shoulders as she placed the bones in a separate bowl. She dabbed her mouth. The thought of someone that evil focusing on her was terrifying. Hard to imagine she'd get lucky a second time.

"We've taken some precautions and as a matter of fact I just moved so it shouldn't be a problem."

"Coincidence? Or were you that worried? Because I personally think you should be worried and getting off the X is probably the smartest thing to do." Shane's sharp gaze held hers.

Getting off the X?

She turned on her stool to face him. A groan erupted from the Marines playing pool and money seemed to be changing hands.

"Friends of yours?" Shane asked with a side glance.

"Random dudes doing weird random dude shit." She cleared her throat. "I never told you last week how sorry I was. About your friend. I'll never forgive myself for the mistakes I made. For not figuring out sooner that it wasn't live..."

He leaned back against the bar and stretched out his long legs. He was a lot taller than she was.

He stared at the floor for so long she didn't think he was going to acknowledge her words. Finally, he nodded. "Scotty was a good man. The best in fact. His wife Grace is pregnant with their third kid."

A coil of grief curled around her insides. "Christ."

The barman dropped something behind the bar. It smashed on the floor and she jumped an inch off her stool.

Shane didn't flinch. "It's okay. Just a broken glass." He gave the guy a look and then ignored him. "Anyway, why do you have to be sorry? It wasn't your fault."

"I didn't figure it out in time and people died. Somehow, he exploited a vulnerability in my system. So, it was partly my fault and I'll have to deal with that." Her voice came out a little ragged.

Shane was watching her carefully. "He fooled a lot of smart people."

It was her turn to look away.

"Just keep in mind, this is on him." The words were sharp. "We were trying to stop him from brutally murdering someone. He planted that bomb. He used the distraction to weasel his way into your computer. Don't blame yourself."

She pressed her lips together to prevent any more useless words leaving her mouth. He obviously wasn't buying her feelings of guilt. Probably because he had enough of his own to bear.

"Any news on the investigation?" he asked with feigned nonchalance.

Now she realized why he'd sought her out.

"I'm not allowed to discuss the case outside of the task force."

Even though he was HRT and had been with them in Houston, he wasn't assigned to the joint task force.

"Did you figure it out? How he got into your computer?"

Yael tilted her head to one side. Then she put her forefinger and thumb together and drew it across her lips, mimicking the way he had last week.

Heat flickered in his gaze for a moment and then was gone. Or maybe she imagined it or was mistaking humor for lust.

You look pale.

Ha.

She looked like crap. No way would this guy find her attractive—not that she was looking to start anything anyway. She wasn't. Her phone dinged with a text and she checked the screen. Then spun around.

"Your friend and her date left a couple of minutes ago." Shane had obviously recognized Laura from Houston.

"What?" Yael blinked stupidly at their empty seats. Laura and suit guy had gone somewhere else and she'd been so completely absorbed with this man she hadn't even noticed. "She doesn't even know the guy."

Yael opened the message on her phone.

Laura: *Didn't want to interrupt you and the hunky beefcake…*

A row of emojis suggested Yael was going to get very lucky with a whole array of vegetable matter this evening.

Laura: *Owen and I are going to find somewhere quieter to talk and then I'm going to head home to DC. Enjoy!*

Yael gritted her teeth, then realized Shane was reading the messages too. Her gaze swept to his and heat blazed in her cheeks. She decided to ignore the obvious.

"She literally met this guy tonight off of a dating app." She slipped the phone into her jeans back pocket.

"She often hook up with guys off the internet?"

Yael shrugged. She didn't want to come off seeming puritanical or judgmental. Not everyone shared her trust issues nor her emotional hang-ups. "She likes meeting new people and says sex should be more of a workout than an intimate moment."

Shane choked on his beer then wiped his mouth. "Well, I guess if you do it right, it should be both."

The air between them suddenly charged.

Yael broke eye contact and drained the last of her beer. Her cheeks felt singed with heat and she avoided looking at her reflection in the mirror.

"Well, I was here as her wing woman tonight in case the guy turned out to be a total jerk, but I guess she doesn't need me anymore." She placed the empty bottle on the bar. "I may as well head home."

"You live around here?" he asked in surprise. "I guess that's a dumb question since you said you just moved, presumably you are still on the task force, and you're here in this bar. Unless you're only in Quantico for the task force meeting. Or stalking me." He sent her a self-deprecating grin that made her pulse thrum in a way she'd forgotten could be fun.

She ignored her stupid fluttering heart. "As of two days ago I guess I do live around here."

Something flickered in his gaze then was gone. "You never answered the question. Did you move *because* you were worried about a certain someone or was it a happy coincidence?"

Shane Livingstone sure asked a lot of questions.

She forced herself to unclench her jaw. The tension she'd been carrying all week was making her head start to pound again. "Alex Parker put me in charge of the cybercrime unit of our new satellite office down here, so I'd already planned to move."

"Impressive."

"Because I'm female?"

Those green eyes shifted to disappointment. In her. "Because you look so young."

"Oh." She pushed her hair behind her ear, feeling flustered all of a sudden. "Last week's events and working on this joint task force speeded things up a little. Well, a lot, actually."

She could see his neurons firing at a thousand volts a second. Why was he so interested? Was it because of what she might tell him about the case, or something else…?

"Traceable?"

"Pardon me?"

"Your new place. Can he who cannot be named link it to the image of Sphinx he captured online?"

She shuddered. "No. I bought it using an offshore shell company which seems very suspect but is completely legit. He shouldn't be able to find me online but if he really wants to find me, eventually he will. Given enough time, access to certain databases, or the right social engineering skills you can find almost anyone. You only need a starting point."

"Except him apparently," Shane muttered, taking a swig of beer. "For some reason we can't find him."

Was that a criticism? "We'll find him."

But how many more people would die before that happened?

She felt the weight of Shane's stare and picked nervously at the label on her beer bottle. Being alone with this man who'd seen her fail at the one thing she was supposed to be good at was disconcerting.

She needed to get out of here before he managed to eke out information she wasn't supposed to share. She didn't want to get thrown off the team. She needed to prove that Evi1Geni-us wasn't better than she was. It wasn't ego. She *needed* to help track him down, to prove that she was one of the good guys. The FBI had to catch him. The asshole deserved whatever he got from the justice system.

She pulled out her wallet and tossed some cash on the bar to cover her tab. Then she grabbed her leather jacket off the back of her stool. Swung it over her shoulders and down her arms in one smooth motion.

Shane's eyes flicked over her body without changing expression. Most people she could read, but not this guy.

"I better go." She pushed back her stool.

"Come have a drink with us. I'll introduce you to the guys."

She glanced at their forced cheer. "They'd probably rather not meet anyone new tonight."

His lashes swept down and she knew she'd struck a nerve. Then he looked up again. "They always like to meet beautiful, single women—assuming you're single?"

She blinked at him in surprise. Beautiful? *Ha.* Hardly. Was he fishing for information because he was interested in her personally or did he want to sweet talk her into giving him information or did he want to set her up with one of his friends?

For all she knew he could be married with kids. She glanced at his ring finger. No wedding band, but that didn't mean much.

She looked over at the group of men and women all laughing and joking despite their loss. She had to admire their spirit because she knew instinctively that this had hit them hard no matter how bright the smiles or too loud the laughter.

The tug toward them, the idea of getting to know them, and *belonging,* tempted her, but it would be a mistake.

"I am single, funnily enough." She quirked a brow with forced sardonic humor. "Thanks for the offer but I'm going to head home. I'll catch you guys another time." She brushed past him, ignoring the little jolt of awareness that zapped her skin as the back of her hand brushed his.

She headed past the curious Marines who started to give Shane hell. Which was unfair under the circumstances—he hadn't been hitting on her—but she wasn't about to stick around and listen to him explain how they worked together. She nodded to another guy from HRT whom she recognized from last week but avoided catching the gazes of the others. She didn't want to be an object of curiosity. She didn't want them to know the part she'd played in the reason for them being down a team member.

Outside, she paused for a moment to inhale the bitterly cold January air. It was quiet here, the bar tucked down a road near the marina. No residential houses nearby. She was so close to the sea she could smell the tang of brine on the breeze. The temperature made her shiver and huddle deeper into her jacket.

The parking lot was empty of people. Laura's car was gone from the spot where they'd left it earlier. Yael was annoyed with her friend but she sent her a quick text to check she was okay.

It was about two miles to her new place and if it wasn't for the memory of what she'd witnessed last Friday night she'd have started hiking along the dark road already. Instead, she pressed the icon to call a rideshare.

The door of the bar opened and Shane Livingstone strode out. He stopped in surprise. "Something wrong with your car?"

She laughed softly. "Only the fact I don't own one. Laura drove us here. I'm calling a rideshare."

He tipped down his chin and frowned over his straight nose. "Don't even think about it." He held up his key fob with his good hand. "Come on, I'll give you a ride."

She shook her head. "I don't even know you."

"And you know the Uber driver?" he scoffed.

She hesitated. "I get rides all the time."

He snorted. "You gonna Uber to work? You think the USMC guards are gonna let them past the barriers?"

She crossed her arms. "Firstly, I didn't say I was working on base"—though she was—"and, secondly, I didn't say I didn't have transportation. I said I didn't have a car."

"Who the hell doesn't have a car?" Amusement tugged at his lips and she forced herself to look away. Damn, he was attractive. "Look, I'm heading home and I'm happy to give you a ride. Saves me following your driver to make sure you get home safe, and it also makes me look good to the Marines who are about to walk out this door thinking I got lucky with the hottest chick in the place."

"*Hottest chick*?" she sputtered, half indignation, half surprise. "Wait. Was I the only female in there?"

He grinned and shook his head. "You are a hard woman to compliment."

"Maybe you shouldn't lead with *you look pale* and I might believe you."

"I didn't mean you aren't attractive." He sounded genuinely confused.

Damn, this conversation was mortifying. She wasn't fishing for compliments.

He hunched his shoulders as if to fight off the biting chill in the air, not surprising considering he was only wearing a t-shirt and jeans. "Look, Yael." She jolted as he said her name. "After last week I don't like the idea of you being in a vulnerable position when it's avoidable. It would make *me* feel better if you let me give you a ride home. I promise I won't try to suck your face."

Embarrassment burned her cheeks once again. She hadn't meant to suggest for a moment that he would make a pass at her. This was why she preferred computers to people. She had yet to offend a PC with a socially awkward comment.

Releasing a sigh, she found herself walking beside him. The sidelights of a massive black truck flashed as they approached.

He moved to the passenger side and opened the door. There was a step to climb inside. "Need a hand?"

She shot him a look. Did he really think she couldn't get into a truck?

"You have a broken arm," she reminded him.

He held up his broken arm. "This thing?" He tapped on the plaster cast. "Good as new."

She huffed. "Something tells me your doctor ordered you to keep it in the sling."

His lips quirked. "More of a suggestion than an order."

The Marines chose that moment to stumble out of the bar. She caught the eye of the man who'd tried to pick her up earlier. He gave her puppy dog eyes and she shook her head in exasperation.

"I take it you turned him down?" Shane gave the younger guy a quelling stare.

Yael snorted and got in the truck. "He doesn't look old enough to drink alcohol. I prefer to date grown-ups."

Not that she dated much. Ever.

Shane chuckled and then walked around to the driver's side and got in. "That pretty much rules out the Marines."

"What about you?" She wanted to kick herself for asking a personal question but the man kept imposing himself in her life so maybe he deserved it.

"What about me—as in who do I date?" He sent her another look that she couldn't read. "I also like to date grown-ups, but lately I seem to date women who want more from me than I am willing to give." He grimaced, as if he'd revealed too much. "Which makes me sound like a complete asshole, so I probably am."

Yael could see it. Women would be drawn to the good looks and the competent attitude. She wondered if the words were also a subtle warning, like he knew there was this occasional flicker of attraction between them and for her not to assume it would lead anywhere beyond the nearest bedroom.

Her heart fluttered against her ribs.

He started the engine. "I guess I'm married to my job."

She laughed, relieved as the tension eased. "Me, too."

"Most of the time it doesn't bother me, but…" He turned and held her gaze. The heat in his eyes intensified.

She shivered but not from cold. "Occasionally it's lonely as fuck."

She bit her lip. His gaze shifted to her mouth.

And like that the air between them sizzled.

Shane dragged his gaze away from Yael's full lower lip and shoved his truck in gear, reminding himself that wasn't why he was here. He was here because he wanted to gain this woman's trust. However, her words struck him hard because, occasionally, being devoted to his career was lonely as fuck. Most of the time he didn't even notice.

He thought about Grace and her fatherless children and suddenly being married to his job didn't seem so bad. At least if something happened to him, no one outside his immediate family would have their lives shattered.

Thinking about Grace reminded him his best friend had been murdered and his fingers tightened on the wheel. Yael being in the bar tonight felt like fate. The sort of signal from the universe he'd learned never to ignore.

And that was why he was here.

He pulled back on his natural inclination to mock the Marines as he drove past. There was no real malice involved. It was an expected ritual that harkened back to his days in Special Forces. He didn't think Yael would appreciate the banter though. Women like her didn't appreciate being treated like a winner's trophy and he already knew she did not like being the center of attention. She liked to be what she thought was in the shadows, the gray man. But she was too attractive for men not to pay attention. Plus, a guy like him always paid attention to what was lurking in the shadows. Survival 101.

And he couldn't quite shake a growing suspicion that refused to go away. Evi1Geni-us had known they were coming. Had he simply lured them into a trap? Or had someone inside the task-force helped him? Shane's instincts screamed that Yael was hiding something. He didn't know what, but he didn't like it.

Shane was absolutely positive no one on HRT had gone rogue, but how was a guy like him supposed to figure out whether or not one computer geek was in league with another?

By hanging out with one. By gaining Yael's trust.

Which was turning out to be more difficult than he'd anticipated.

Despite the sizzle of attraction, Yael wasn't giving off vibes that suggested she was looking to hook up. In fact, even though random sparks unexpectedly lit up the air between them, she acted like she'd rather be anywhere but here with him.

Was that because she was worried about what he might find

out? Or perhaps she really wasn't interested and his imagination was in overdrive because his libido had suddenly woken up after a long hiatus.

He was serious about his concerns about her catching an Uber home. Who knew who was behind the wheel? If Evi1Geni-us could hack an employee of one of the top cybersecurity firms in the US, who was to say he couldn't hack the apps and be Johnny-on-the spot when it came to picking up someone off the street?

Maybe that's how the asshole captured his victims in the first place.

Shane headed to the T-junction on the main road. "Which way?"

The leather of her jacket creaked as she sank back against the seat. Even that sound had an effect on him, setting his awareness on high alert.

"Take a right," she said reluctantly.

He flicked a glance at her. She was gorgeous, although, somehow, he'd convinced her that he thought otherwise. Usually he was better with women, but not this one apparently.

Not that he was interested in anything besides tracking down Scotty's killer. Not really. He hadn't lied about being married to his work. Although no-strings sex with a willing, attractive woman… Well, sex was rarely off the table.

He rested his injured arm on his thigh. He was doing what the doctor told him most of the time. Resting it, keeping the arm in the sling. But he didn't want to lose all the strength in his left arm, so he was exercising it a little. Enough to maintain some conditioning, without exacerbating the injury—he wasn't an idiot. The bone ached today though, suggesting he *had* overdone it. Not that he'd admit that to anyone without the infliction of torture.

Which reminded him again why he was driving Yael home.

"What's your address?"

After a brief hesitation she told him. He was glad she guarded her privacy even from FBI agents like himself.

She didn't make idle chitchat. She stared out of the window

and he could see her expression reflected in the glass. Pensive and uneasy. His aim to get her to open up and trust him was not getting off to a great start.

"Was your friend originally supposed to be heading back to your place tonight?"

She turned to face him and the scent of her hit him. Something sweet and dark, like leather with a hint of blackberries.

Silence hovered between them. Did she think he was coming on to her after he'd promised not to? Probably. What if she asked him inside? He'd like to think he was shrewd enough to say no but somehow, he doubted it. What better way to get close to someone?

He shied away from that thought.

Finally she blew out a heavy sigh. "She had her things in her car and said she'd head back to DC later tonight."

Laura and the date had obviously hit it off.

"I don't know how she does it." Yael dragged her hair out of the ponytail and then tied it back up again. "I mean she runs background checks but it's so easy to manipulate information online..."

Shane made himself stare at the road rather than her. Hoped his silence would encourage her to talk.

She laughed self-consciously. "It seems scarier using a dating app down here compared to up in DC. I mean if you don't like someone in DC you can walk out the door and catch the Metro home."

"It's just as easy to walk out on a date around here. If you get a bad feeling you should leave, wherever you are. As long as you don't skip out on the bill or are stuck for transportation." He gave her a slow grin.

What was her friend thinking? Laura Bay had been in the Command Center in Houston. She knew that Evi1Geni-us had seen Yael's face. But she also knew Shane was with HRT. Was she playing matchmaker? If so, why? Did Yael have trouble finding dates? He found that hard to believe.

Laura could also be the leak, along with the young guy who'd acted as her shadow in Texas. But Yael was the one who'd missed the fact the feed was delayed until it had effectively been too late. She was the computer expert who Evi1Geni-us had hacked.

By befriending Yael, he would hopefully keep abreast of the cyber aspect of the investigation and, in the meantime, he could help keep an eye on her safety because he was concerned that if she was an innocent, she was in danger. There was really no downside to his plan.

He glanced at her again. The woman had a mass of glossy midnight hair that she kept pulled back in a sensible ponytail and intelligent eyes the color of coffee beans. Except for the tiredness pulling at her mouth and the shadows beneath her eyes, she was a knockout.

The thought of that psychopath targeting her made Shane's fingers curl tighter around the steering wheel.

"Do you use dating apps?" Yael's expression was curious.

He grimaced. "I used them in the past. When I was in the Army. I stopped when I joined Special Forces."

A smile tugged her lips. "I guess it's easy to find a date when you're *Special Forces*."

He flashed her a tight smile. "The rules about Fight Club..."

"No one talks about Fight Club." She spread her fingers wide and rested her palms on her skinny jeans. Her nails were painted a pale blue. She had a tattoo on her inner wrist he was dying to get a better look at. "I gave up on online dating years ago. I get a little obsessive with running background checks and worried I might get caught hacking police databases. Plus, I never met anyone particularly compatible and there are some real creeps out there."

He bristled at the thought of what those creeps might have done to make her so leery. Cleared his throat. "Dating strangers is always a risk." Intimacy was always a risk. "It pays to be careful."

Her eyes hit his. "Yet you persuaded me to get into your truck."

He checked his mirrors and took a left turn away from her home address. Her eyes widened in alarm.

"Firstly, I'm not a stranger. You know that I'm a member of the FBI's Hostage Rescue Team. Secondly, my teammates saw me leave shortly after you did. If you disappeared or wound up—" he cut himself off. "Anyway, you can trust me and you can trust them. We are the good guys."

She turned toward him, back pressed against the door as she asked, "So why aren't we heading straight to my place?"

He was glad she had a good grip on the town's geography even though she'd only recently moved here. He checked his mirrors again and took another left.

"You're making sure no one is following us." She relaxed as the words rushed out and pressed her hand to her chest. "See, this is why I don't date people I don't already know. Or hook up with strangers. People are crazy."

She really didn't trust easily. Which made his mission more difficult, but not impossible. He liked a challenge. "Not all of us."

The sound of her laugh raced unexpectedly down his spine. "*Oh, please.* You guys are crazier than most. You jump out of airplanes and helicopters and go after bad guys when the rest of us run and hide."

"We're US law enforcement's only full-time counterterrorism unit," he said quietly. "We train non-stop so we can do our jobs as safely as possible. We're not reckless crazy. We're prepared crazy." He raised his broken arm in annoyance. "Which is why snapping this when helping someone down a few stairs is so damn annoying."

She flinched slightly. "That fall probably saved your life."

A wave of guilt and grief washed over him.

"It wouldn't have happened to me." He'd have set the blasting caps on the wall or noticed the strange quiet and known something was off. It wasn't Scotty's fault. He'd been filling in for Shane. It was Shane's job.

"As I said. You're all batshit." She turned away again and the sound of rubber over asphalt was the only noise in the cab.

Maybe they were all batshit but the operator mindset was one of invincibility—that bad things wouldn't happen to them. That's why they practiced all the damn time, which made being outwitted by some sadistic computer jockey all the more infuriating.

They neared her place and he took a right instead of a left and then pulled a U-turn and sat at the side of road with the lights killed watching the guard in his cubicle and observing the light traffic on the main road.

They sat in silence. The only sound was that of the engine cooling and the occasional car passing by. The townhouse complex was gated but Shane knew the security wasn't foolproof. He could definitely break in if he wanted.

"Do you carry a firearm?"

Yael hunched into her jacket. "I don't like guns."

He turned in the seat. "Guns are simply tools."

"Yeah." She raised her hand as if to ward off his argument. "So are chainsaws and I don't carry one of those around either."

He watched her. She appeared genuinely agitated by the idea of a firearm. He wanted to get close to her, to get her on side, so arguing about this likely wasn't the wisest course of action. He started the engine and, now that he was satisfied no one was following them, headed to the guard post. Once Yael flashed her ID, they were through.

Minimal security, although it was better than nothing. Sort of.

He drove around the curve in the road and pulled up in her empty driveway. "I could teach you some self-defense moves."

Her head shot up. Her eyes went wide.

"Not tonight." From her startled expression she definitely thought it was a come-on and he felt a little stab of disappointment that the idea freaked her out so much. It was obvious they shared some level of attraction and he wasn't completely hideous and had good southern manners his grandmother had ingrained in him from the day he was born. "I'm off this weekend. I can teach you some basic moves if you want. The weak points on any man."

She raised an unimpressed brow.

"Not only the groin area—the eyes, the throat, the knees."

She pulled her purse up off the floor and hugged it to her chest. "I'm good. My boss offered to train me."

Shane had heard of Alex Parker. Knew he had a good rep. Rumor was he'd once worked covert ops for the CIA.

"Doesn't hurt to practice. Give me your phone."

She drew back with a reluctant laugh. "What?"

He held out his hand. "Go on. Give me your cell."

With a sigh she unlocked the screen and handed it over.

He entered his personal cell number. "Now if you change your mind or have any trouble, you have someone local to call. Someone who isn't your boss." He handed it back. "And you can always delete it."

She slipped the cell into her jeans pocket. "I won't call you."

"Wait," he said sharply.

"What?"

He'd startled her again. He got out of the truck and jogged around the front. Opened her door and offered her his good hand. She frowned and tentatively took his fingers in hers, her expression clearly saying she thought he had a screw loose.

There was that electricity again, that *zap*, that neither of them wanted to acknowledge. She quickly withdrew her hand. She was spooked and he could respect that. He walked her to her front door. Watched her unlock it and disarm the surprisingly sophisticated alarm system.

When everything appeared to be secure, he took a step back and nodded. "Goodnight, Ms. Brooks."

"Goodnight, Mr. Livingstone."

He grinned. She'd done enough research to figure out his last name which had to mean something. He backed away and she watched him with a mix of amused surprise and innate suspicion.

His plan to get her to trust him had hit a roadblock but Shane understood the value of the long game and how to overcome obstacles. He and Yael Brooks were going to become friends despite her natural reluctance. And then, one way or another, she was going to help him catch this motherfucker and put him either behind bars or six feet under—Shane didn't care which.

Yael just didn't know it yet.

7

Although the joint task force hadn't stopped searching for Evi1Geni-us, this was the first time they'd assembled for an in-person team briefing since the killer had handed them their asses ten days ago.

Yael parked her scooter, put down the kickstand and got off. She locked her helmet in the box on the back even though it should be safe enough here. Old habits died hard even on the hallowed grounds of the FBI's National Academy. She pulled out her map and shifted the heavy bag on her shoulder, glancing around to orient herself.

The FBI's facilities were situated inside the massive Marine Corps Base Quantico and she'd had to go through several armed roadblocks to gain access. Every time she'd been stopped and questioned, she'd envisaged Shane Livingstone's eyes crinkling with amusement at her powder blue mode of transportation.

The main FBI Academy was visible to the left so she set off, heading in what she hoped was the correct direction. Rolling grassy areas were surrounded by dense forest. Shouts could be heard in the distance—probably Marines training. Far off, there was the almost constant sound of gunfire.

A shiver rushed over her skin and her teeth chattered in time to the branches of the surrounding trees rustling in the wind. The fact she was walking calmly rather than crouching in fear at the noise was a testament to how far she'd come in the last fifteen years. Although it was humbling to realize that more than half of her life had been overshadowed by one traumatic event.

But here she was, dealing with it.

The powers-that-be at FBI Headquarters in Washington DC had decided after the Texas debacle to centralize the "EGMURD" investigation at Quantico. Everyone directly on the task force had been given five days' notice to relocate. A few consultants who were assisting part-time, like Laura and Tim in their hunt for cryptocurrency and blockchain clues, were allowed to work remotely from recognized secure facilities. Alex needed Laura in DC for other projects but he'd ordered Yael to work exclusively on this case for the time being.

She spotted people heading to work or jogging along various tracks around the base, but she didn't see anyone else on this narrow path that led to Building 64.

Her computer seemed to weigh more than usual and she adjusted the strap to stop it cutting into her shoulder. Obviously, she'd parked in the wrong spot, but she liked walking so it wasn't too big a deal.

Virginia was nothing like where she'd grown up. Colorado for the first fourteen years. Arizona with her beloved grandparents for a couple of years after that until they passed. She was sure stress had contributed to their early deaths. Stress and sorrow. After that she'd moved around a lot from job to job.

She liked living on the East Coast but this winter seemed gloomier than normal, the sky duller, the earth gray and lifeless, the leaves more black than russet even when still clinging to the trees. Maybe it was a residual effect of the horrors she'd witnessed on the first day of the new year, but it dragged at her mood.

The *rat-tat-tat* of automatic gunfire made her step falter. Saliva pooled in her mouth and her heart began to pound. She forced herself to take in a deep breath and hold it. Some of the recent images had triggered other unwelcome memories. She'd given up on therapists years ago but maybe she needed to revisit the idea or at least start actively looking for some joy in her life.

Or maybe she was simply overtired…

She'd spent part of the weekend setting up her home and gathering supplies, stocking up the fridge and freezer so she didn't need to leave the house too often except for work.

The memory of Shane Livingstone hovered in the back of her mind. She'd been so tempted to take up his invitation to call him over the weekend. The fact she'd resisted should feel like a victory but instead felt hollow and depressing. She didn't like that either.

Yesterday, Yael had gone to her boss's house where Alex and Mallory had shown her some basic self-defense moves in their home gym while they all took turns entertaining baby Georgina and their cute Golden Retriever, Rex.

Alex had also offered to teach her to shoot in the small range he'd had built in his basement. She'd declined and he hadn't looked surprised. She was pretty certain that, although they'd never discussed it, he knew her full history. He knew why guns freaked her out so much. He hadn't pressed and she was grateful.

Yael reached Building 64 and stared at the small plaque that told her she was in the right place. The structure was a bland, two-story affair with all the personality of a cardboard box.

She was an hour early for the meeting, but she liked to be set up and prepared before other people turned up. Voices nearby spurred her into motion.

She pushed inside and searched for Room 3. She found it easily enough on the ground floor and heard more voices suggesting others had arrived before her. She opened the door and came to a complete stop.

Shane—Shannon Marcus Livingstone III—originally from Madison, Georgia—because give a hacker a small amount of data and they simply couldn't help themselves—stood near the front of the conference room near a white board covered in various images and pieces of information. He wore green tactical pants and a black t-shirt with boots and was armed. All FBI agents were armed, she reminded herself, but somehow he looked more dangerous than those she'd previously encountered. He held a paper handout, talking to Ashley Chen, his cast, for once, obediently nestled in its sling.

"Yael. Good, you're early. Set up over here." Ashley Chen indicated a desk to her right that had a power strip on the floor beneath it. Yael nodded without speaking and headed reluctantly to where Ashley pointed.

"You two met in Texas, correct? Shane Livingstone, this is Yael Brooks. Yael, this is Shane." The agent introduced them again.

"Yes," Shane told Ashley with a serious expression. "We met."

"Shane is acting as HRT's liaison on the task force until he is medically cleared for full duties."

"I see." Yael gave him a pointed stare.

Ashley turned away to attend to something on her laptop and Shane walked over to where Yael stood.

Had Friday night been a test? To see if she spoke about the case outside the task force? Did he think she was stupid or maybe wasn't taking this seriously? Or worse…did he suspect her of being complicit in some way?

"All settled into your new place?" His tone was clipped and professional. Had she imagined the warmth and humor of Friday night? Had the attraction been an act designed to get her to tell him things she wasn't supposed to, and maybe get her kicked off the task force?

She gave him a curt nod.

"Your friend made it home safely?"

She cleared her throat. "Yes."

To her surprise he came around the table and pulled out the chair beside her. Sat.

Her mood took another nosedive.

"Exactly when did you find out you were on the task force?" she asked out of the side of her mouth while Ashley went about setting up various workstations.

"Friday morning," he admitted.

"And you didn't think to mention it?" She didn't bother to conceal the tartness of her tone.

He crossed his arms and leaned back in his seat. "I didn't think it would make any difference to our conversation."

"Why not?"

"I didn't think you'd believe me for a start. Not without verification."

"I wouldn't have."

"Good. That's why I didn't bother saying anything." He started reading through the handout Ashley had given him and Yael exhaled slowly, unsure what to think.

Alex Parker strolled in with a guy wearing an elegant three-piece suit who swept the room with an icy blue gaze. To her surprise the stranger locked onto her and came over with his hand held out. She scrambled to her feet.

"Lincoln Frazer. How are you enjoying your new place, Ms. Brooks?" His hand was warm, belying his cool expression as he gently squeezed her palm.

It clicked then. "Oh, you're the previous owner. I love it, actually. Thanks for the great deal on the place. I'm now worried there's something wrong with the foundations."

Frazer laughed. "Nothing wrong with the foundations. We found the perfect spot for us and wanted a quick sale. Apologies for any remnant smell of wet dog. My fiancée's mutt likes the river and has a particular fondness for rolling in dead fish."

"Seems fair." Alex smiled.

Yael wasn't quite sure how to respond. "It's great. No wet dog odor."

"ASAC Frazer," Ashley commanded in full-on scary mode. "You're over here." She pointed to one of the workstations.

Frazer sent Yael a wry look and stage whispered, "Ashley thinks I'm an idiot when it comes to computers."

"She's not wrong," Alex muttered.

"I have other skills." Frazer smirked. "Like keeping secrets."

Alex said nothing but sent Shane a direct look that the HRT operator calmly returned. Alex was probably wondering why Shane kept sitting next to her in meetings. Next, he'd be thinking they were friends...or something more. Her cheeks heated again. Alex followed Frazer to the other side of the room and sat beside him.

Shane leaned in so close his breath tickled her ear. "You may not know it, but you just met the Bureau's most legendary profiler."

Yael blinked but she shouldn't be surprised. Alex's wife Mallory worked for the BAU-4 and Yael knew the person she'd bought the house from was Mallory's boss.

"No wonder your alarm system is top of the line," said Shane.

More people started to crowd inside the large room. Detectives, federal agents. Analysts from the Strategic Information and Operations Center attended virtually via a large monitor. Finally, at eight sharp, a blonde woman with shadowed eyes, wearing a charcoal suit and crisp white shirt walked into the room and strode to the front.

Her eyes scanned everyone assembled and she nodded to Ashley. "It looks like everyone is already here. Good. My name is Assistant Special Agent in Charge Carly Sloan and I've been given command of the task force investing the EGMURD case. Let's start with what we do know about this so-called Evi1Geni-us. Ashley, would you mind giving us a breakdown summary?"

"Yes, ma'am." Ashley Chen took over the briefing. "From what we have seen online he—and we believe it is a male suspect from the general build—has been running these 'choose your own adventure' murders on the dark web for approximately two years. Alex Parker from Cramer, Parker & Gray first brought this killer to the FBI's attention a little over a year ago."

Ashley turned on a visual presentation, because of course she did, and up popped the faces of the victims. The images included the official FBI headshot of Dave Monteith, the HRT operative who'd died in Texas.

Shane stiffened beside her. Yael shot him a glance. His jaw flexed as his gaze fixed unwavering on the screen.

"So far we have nine known victims at roughly three-month intervals, ten when including our HRT colleague, Agent Monteith." Ashley's voice grew emotional but she pushed through it. Yael blinked away the sudden blurring of her own vision.

"Nothing connects these victims in terms of gender, age, race, religion or location that we know of yet."

"Except they are all adults and, as far as we know, Evi1Geni-us only operates in the contiguous United States," Lincoln Frazer cut in.

Everyone in the room tensed at his words. The idea of that monster doing these things to a child... Yael's hands started to shake so she slipped them under her denim-clad thighs.

Ashley nodded. "Let's hope that continues."

"A-fucking-men," Shane muttered under his breath.

"We have worked up extensive victim profiles which you can access through the secure portal we created exclusively for this task force. Bear in mind that this guy is sophisticated enough with computers he might try a phishing attack to gain access to this investigation, which is why you'll need fingerprints to access the files as well as assigned passwords. If you lose your password or suspect you have been compromised in any way, call me directly. I'd rather we are proactive about this than reactive. I left my card near the door. It's a lot easier to change the passwords than risk this UNSUB gaining access to our files."

Alex stood and began handing out Ashley's business card to everyone assembled. One of the things Yael really liked about her boss was the fact he might be a rich CEO married to a senator's daughter, but he didn't mind pitching in with even the most mundane of tasks.

"We have forensics from each of the crime scenes but nothing that definitively belongs to the UNSUB as opposed to some other individual who may have been using the areas before Evi1Geni-us decided to set up for his own purposes. Nothing has popped in any of the DNA or fingerprint databases. He wears gloves and we think he even wears disposable booties over his footwear as we haven't found any overlap in possible shoeprints as yet."

Alex cut in. "I've tried to determine how he might find the property to commit his crimes. My best guess is he accesses tax records stating whether or not the building is declared vacant. Presumably he also cases the joint. If it were me, I'd have a backup location in the event my primary venue fell through and I had a kidnap victim in the trunk all ready to go."

"Always good to have a secure location to hold a victim when you kidnap them." Ashley sent him an arch look.

Alex grimaced.

"Then we have the issue of how he is choosing and kidnapping these victims and where he keeps them until he is ready for the show—presumably he uses a vehicle of some kind. Is he randomly grabbing people off the streets?"

Yael nudged Shane with her knee.

He nudged her back. "What?"

"Tell them your idea about rideshare apps."

"Agent Livingstone?"

Shane grunted when Ashley stared at him with a raised brow.

"Is there any chance the victims are calling for a rideshare? This UNSUB is hacking into the program, picking victims up off the street? Once they're in the car, he only needs a gun and child locks on the doors, or even some other threat that stops them from jumping out and screaming for their lives."

"I started checking into Agent Livingstone's idea over the weekend, but I needed more information to lock down exactly where each victim disappeared. If this hacker is as good as he thinks he is, he may have deleted the electronic trail and even removed the app from the victim's phones and deleted their user accounts. It might be difficult to find out anything after all this time, although we could check bank statements for any previous payments made to rideshare companies."

Shane glanced at her in surprise.

"What? It was a good idea."

He carried on staring at her with an expression she couldn't decipher.

"We have most of the victims' bank records. We can look for that activity." Ashley added a note to all the other leads they were following before continuing with her summary. "Unfortunately, payments to him are proving harder to locate after the auction closes. As you all know, he's being paid in anonymous cryptocurrencies in a foreign crypto exchange. We can't subpoena foreign companies."

Yael and Alex exchanged a look. While they generally followed the rules, they occasionally veered into territory that would be thrown out of a court of law. But the dark web was the wild west of the internet and you couldn't hope to patrol it with a gun and a shiny badge. You needed to blend in and bend the rules.

Ashley continued. "Cramer, Parker & Gray are working around the clock to trace the crypto but we suspect Evi1Geni-us takes the money offline and obviously knows how to cover his tracks. We'll get him eventually but it's taking longer than we'd hoped and he might already have cashed out into offshore bank accounts."

"Where are we on tracking the people paying to watch?" Sloan asked.

"This is *much* easier. We have collected various aliases and are connecting these to real people at real IP addresses despite their best efforts to cloak their identities with VPNs," Ashley assured the task force leader. "They will face charges of accessory and in some cases accomplices to murder."

"Good. I want them all prosecuted. Every one of them." ASAC Sloan rested against the desk at the front. "The cyber angles are out of my area of expertise and I know your cybercrime team Agent Chen, and Mr. Parker and his associates, are amongst the very best at what you all do. I am going to assume you know the best way to proceed. But are there any ideas as to how we might figure out who this guy is using old-fashioned criminal investigation techniques?"

"Traffic cams?" Frazer suggested. "See if the same license plate shows up in nearby towns or cities around the times of the kidnapping and murders? Same with cell phone data?"

Sloan pointed her finger at him. "That's a good idea."

"I've been looking at cell data. Nothing yet," Alex stated, looking pissed. "He is probably using burners or swapping out SIM cards. Also, he could be using a rental vehicle."

Ashley wrote down both items. "Traffic cams are still worth pursuing but going through the traffic cam data is something that will take up a lot of time and either manpower or computing power to examine."

"I can get someone in my firm to set up a program to crawl over the data if I can have access to all the law enforcement systems involved," Alex said.

Her boss was pouring a lot of company resources into the hunt for this monster. After Texas, Yael understood why.

Sloan spoke to a woman Yael didn't recognize. "Get me a list of all the agencies involved and request the information or access credentials from each authority. As they all have an unsolved murder in their jurisdiction, I don't see them objecting."

Quiet settled over the room. They'd had all these questions before Texas and nothing had been resolved since. Frustration welled up inside Yael.

"Do we have an offender profile?" Sloan asked Frazer.

Frazer coolly returned her stare. "We're working on it, but aside from young male, twenty to forty-five years old, who has a driver's license and is competent with computers—"

Yael snorted.

Alex smiled grimly. "He's way beyond competent."

Frazer nodded. "I suspect he would have been considered gifted as a child. He was probably approached by one of the tech giants in high school. And he probably worked for a tech firm at some point."

"He might still work for a tech company. It could be why he travels around the country." Ashley Chen looked thoughtful.

Yael grimaced. Which might make him potentially even harder to trace because he might be able to disguise or erase his electronic footprint as he went.

"If he's working for a firm then how likely is he to be permanently based near Houston?" Shane pointed out. "I mean, how many workers are sent on the road over the Gregorian New Year?"

Yael's lips twitched as he qualified the type of New Year. Maybe she'd had a good influence on him after all.

Frazer sent him a look. "This is why the profile is taking time, although my team are working on it. We don't have enough starting information. Is he still actively working in the industry and doing this in his spare time, versus being a full-time killer for entertainment purposes? We know little aside from the fact he enjoys ruthlessly torturing people to death and fleecing others while he does it."

"Is he doing the crimes for the money or because he enjoys it?" Ashley noted the questions in her list.

"If he only wanted cash, he could kidnap the victims and demand a ransom," Shane said.

"Or perform ransom attacks on various critical entities or search for zero-day vulnerabilities and sell them on the black market," Alex added. "K&R might be too risky for him. Maybe he's afraid the victims can identify him."

"I suspect he not only enjoys inflicting pain, but he also likes drawing others into the crime too. As voyeurs and making them complicit without losing control of every aspect of the scenario," said Frazer. "And the fact that he's deceiving them too as he has already tortured the individuals before the punters vote? This guy is probably a narcissist and a psychopath."

Yael looked around. She hated speaking up but it didn't look like anyone else was going to comment. She cleared her throat.

"He might not always conduct murders the way he did in

Texas." She froze as the whole room stared at her. "I mean, he might run it in real time under normal circumstances. But he rigged the place with explosives this time. He's never done that before."

Shane went rigid beside her. "This time he knew we were coming."

"We don't have a leak unless someone is feeding the bad guy information in face-to-face conversations," Alex stated. "Ashley and I checked everyone on the team's electronic communications after Texas and everyone checked out."

Shane shot her a quick look. People in the room appeared shocked they'd been actively investigated. Yael wasn't. Although there were other ways to communicate online—chat rooms, message boards, game consoles, burner phones, or old-fashioned dead drops. She suspected Alex and Ashley Chen would have pursued those avenues as much as possible. Still, it didn't jibe with the type of people who worked for the Bureau in general. Why join the FBI only to get in league with a killer? She hoped anyone like that would have been weeded out during the application process. But there were other civilians like her on the task force. She wondered exactly how deep Ashley Chen had dug into her past.

She exchanged a glance with her boss and he held her gaze, seeming to read her mind. He gave a slight shake of his head that was both disturbing and reassuring. He definitely knew about her past and yet he'd hired her anyway. She swallowed the knot in her throat.

"Do we think he knew specifically that a task force had been formed to investigate his crimes or was he targeting law enforcement in general?" Sloan asked.

"I'm speculating that he somehow knew a special joint task force was commissioned." Frazer leaned forward. "Which is probably why he chose that particular victim. Anya Baker interned for the FBI last summer and was planning to apply for the Bureau after college. She didn't hide the fact either. Wrote and published an online article about her experiences."

"He knew or assumed we were onto him and used this specific victim as bait to lure us into traps both online and in the real world," Shane said bitterly. "How much danger do you think Yael is in now he knows what she looks like?"

Yael squirmed in her seat at once again being the focus of attention. "I have an alarm system."

"You need better security. You ride an *electric scooter* for Christ's sake."

She flashed him a surprised glance. She obviously wasn't the only one who'd been doing a little snooping over the weekend. "Okay, Shannon," she murmured.

"*Ouch.*"

"The security in Yael's new home is excellent—I installed it," Alex stated. "And Yael's more than capable of keeping herself safe online, especially after what happened in Houston."

Yael relaxed a little at her boss's support. It meant a lot to her. But Shane didn't look convinced.

"I agree on the issue of transportation. I was planning on raising the concern after this meeting. We can lend you a company vehicle from the compound," Alex offered.

Yael bit her lip, not feeling as if she had any choice. She hated giving up her autonomy but she'd known she'd probably need to buy some sort of car for winter. A scooter was fantastic in the summer but icy roads were not Myrtle's friend.

Although, it wasn't like she ever went anywhere except work or home. Bumping into Shane in a bar was a one-in-a-million-chance encounter.

"Any possibility the UNSUB could hack into the DMV database and discover Ms. Brooks's real identity using facial recognition?" Ashley asked with concern.

Alex shifted in his seat. "It's an outside scenario we've considered and planned for. We altered Yael's photo in the DMV database enough to make his comparison image useless should he be able to access the system."

Yael's mouth went dry as everyone stared at her. It wasn't strictly legal but officially Alex had done it to test the system against potential future security breaches, which was what the government paid their company to do.

If Cramer, Parker & Gray, Security Consultants could do this, then maybe so could others. The government needed to have a system in place to monitor for this type of manipulation. Not to mention, the CIA would be very interested in their findings and how it might be used to help shield its officers' identities. In the meantime, Yael had a little more peace of mind.

"Any other databases that might have Yael's face?" Sloan asked.

Yael stiffened. She felt Shane's gaze on her profile but refused to look at him.

After a long moment Alex spoke for her. "Yael doesn't have a passport or any criminal convictions, nor is she active on social media with her own identity."

That was true.

"I can't say what private companies might be out there scooping up images and data but it would take EG time and effort to figure out. Easier to sit outside our offices in DC and wait for her to leave work. And, yes, we have safeguards against all those kinds of activities at all our premises."

Yael swallowed. There were pictures of her online but she'd been much younger then. Over the last decade she'd tried hard not to have her face appear in any digital form. She had a few anonymous accounts to monitor the internet but nothing that could lead back to her, or even to her real IP address.

Her Sphinx persona was blown. No going back to that. She'd wiped all trace of that avatar from the web, just in case there were any unconscious clues left behind.

Shane worked a crick out of his neck. He appeared relaxed but Yael could feel the energy pouring off him. Then he said, "I assume you have people from TEDAC looking at the explosive device?" For a split second his southern accent slipped out before the guy reined it back in.

TEDAC was the Terrorist Explosive Device Analytical Center.

"TEDAC scientists immediately traveled to Texas to gather the evidence and took it back to Huntsville to examine." Ashley pulled up a report. "The explosive was C-4. Blasting caps were military issue but we haven't been able to trace them. The device was set to blow as soon as the door opened."

Shane rolled the pen against the empty pad of paper on the table with his right hand. The muscles in his forearm were clearly defined. "I doubt EG learned this stuff off the internet. He either has explosive experience or hired someone to help him. If the latter, that someone is a weak link and we need to find them."

"I agree. TEDAC is working with forensics to collect any additional evidence." Sloan stood. "This UNSUB has left behind a stream of wreckage since he started his murder spree. We seem to be chasing around cleaning up his mess but never getting ahead of him. If he's true to form, we have less than three months to stop him striking again. Let's meet here again at eight on Wednesday morning and every other workday after that. I want to hear measurable progress from everyone at each meeting."

That didn't sound good to Yael. That sounded like Sloan was settling in for the long haul. The longer it took, the more the online trail disappeared. The internet might be forever but it was also ephemeral when someone knew how to erase data.

"What about the stolen credit card that was used to purchase the VPN?" Yael asked.

"Sold on the dark web in a batch of thousands," Ashley said with a downward twist of her lips.

Damn.

Everyone started packing up as Ashley made sure they all had a specific lead to follow up.

Yael turned off her laptop and packed it away. This meeting had been a waste of her time. She hadn't learned anything. She could have been working on the code and seeing if there were any clues in it that might have turned up in other places online. She jumped when Shane's arm brushed hers. As much as she generally didn't like to be touched that wasn't why her body reacted so strongly to Shane. It was some weird hyperawareness that made the hair on her nape tingle.

"Want a ride to Alex Parker's compound to pick up that vehicle?"

"I've got it." A part of her wished she could accept his help but it went against her nature. She couldn't depend on anyone else. She'd learned that the hard way.

Alex came over. "I can drive you over there now."

"What about Myrtle?" she asked.

"Who?" Shane asked, frowning.

"My scooter." Thankfully her boss knew she'd named the Vespa.

Shane held out his hand. "Give me the keys and I'll drop Myrtle off after work."

Yael stared at him. Alex looked between them both and then turned to speak with Ashley who'd approached him with a question.

Yael found herself staring into Shane's deep green eyes that were flecked with white like the surface of a choppy ocean.

"What's the problem?" he asked quietly.

Yael shook off the unsettled feeling he gave her. "Why would you do that for me? We're not friends."

He pulled a face. "Because it's a reasonable thing to do for a colleague? And why aren't we friends? We've had a drink together and shared a meal."

Did chicken wings count as a meal?

He climbed to his feet. "Anyway, it's your choice but it is zero trouble as I drive past your place on my way home. And I know I'll feel better—personally and professionally—if you have transportation that some asshole in a smart car couldn't wipe out with a side swipe." His expression grew somber. "We both saw what this guy does to other human beings. What I'm suggesting might be a worst-case scenario, but it is not a stretch and unlike the rest of us, he knows what you look like."

Her fingers curled into fists. She hated that he was right. She blew out a frustrated sigh and dropped the keys into his palm. "She's up in the main parking lot near the Academy. Don't strain your arm putting her in your truck."

"Yes, Mom."

"I mean it." She slid the rest of her belongings into her computer bag. "Get one of your built friends to help you."

He tossed the keys in the air. "Ha. Sassy. I like sassy."

She rolled her eyes. She was definitely not *sassy*. She headed off after her boss, wishing she wasn't so excited by the prospect of seeing the HRT operator again. And soon.

It was a mistake to get more involved, but then again, they were going to be working together until they caught this bastard or Shane's arm healed. Yael really hoped it was the former. The idea that this freak was out there somewhere, hunting his next victim, probably hunting her, made her queasy.

But she wasn't about to stand still and let this predator catch her. She was the one doing the hunting now. She was done with being a victim.

8

It was dark by the time Shane drove up to Yael's townhouse even though it was only a little after five.

Yael had called down to the guardhouse for security to let him in. The gated community backed onto a forest and a small creek which probably gave the people who lived here a false sense of safety. While most petty thieves would avoid a complex like this and look for easier pickings, this UNSUB was not a simple burglar. He liked playing games and he liked messing with law enforcement.

Shane reversed his truck into Yael's driveway and jumped out, letting down the tailgate as she opened the double garage door from the inside. She wore the same tight jeans from earlier but had lost the hoodie and boots, her feet bare now. A pale blue, long-sleeved henley hugged her figure and made his mouth go dry in a way he hadn't anticipated.

He lifted Myrtle one-handed and Yael was there to help him lower the electric scooter gently to the ground.

"If you're trying to show off your manly strength it won't work on me." She caressed the handlebars like the Vespa was a pet.

Like most of the operators on the Hostage Rescue Team, Shane found anyone throwing down a challenge, no matter how flippantly, hard to resist.

"If you're not impressed by 'manly strength,' what are you impressed by?" he asked, closing the back of the truck.

"People who can go for long periods without speaking." She gave him a fat, fake smile.

"Oh, definitely sassy." He suppressed a grin because he could tell she hated being called that.

She wheeled the oversized bicycle into the garage beside a large black SUV with tinted windows he suspected were probably bullet-resistant. Cramer, Parker & Gray protected some important celebs and politicians. That Alex Parker considered the safety of his employee to be equally as valuable made him go up another notch in Shane's estimation. Not to mention the fact he was dedicating his own time and company resources to tracking down this motherfucker alongside the FBI.

Yael came back out onto the driveway and stood with her arms crossed. Despite her disparaging words about his 'manly strength' he hadn't missed the way she'd checked him out in the meeting earlier. She liked his muscles just fine. She simply didn't want to like him.

He could work with that.

Not to get into her pants, although maybe he was lying to himself about that. He'd found himself thinking about her dark eyes and lush lips on and off all weekend. More importantly, she was interesting, and, *ugh*, smart—and smart was his personal kryptonite. So, he wouldn't say no if she offered more than a working relationship, but what he really wanted was to get closer to her to get answers. Answers about her, about EG, about Scotty's death.

And, aside from a little html, computer code was gibberish to him.

Across the cul de sac a man came outside and dumped a neatly stacked pile of cardboard into the recycling receptacle. The stranger waved at them and Yael waved back.

A *For Sale* sign in the stranger's yard swung in the breeze. Yael didn't have a sign. The perks of a private transaction.

Late twenties, five nine and slightly built with dark hair and thick black glasses, the man walked toward them wearing a goofy grin.

"Hey, I just moved in across the street. Kevin Karvo. I wanted to introduce myself to my new neighbors."

Shane eyed him narrowly as the guy took Yael's hand and shook vigorously.

Yael pulled quickly away and crossed her arms, hunching her shoulders against the chill. She opened her mouth to speak but Shane held out his good hand and interrupted. "Welcome to the neighborhood, Kevin." Shane squeezed the other man's hand firmly before letting go. "Betty loves it here, don't you, honey?"

Yael raised her dark brows and looked at him as if he'd lost his ever-loving mind.

She caught on quickly though. "Yes, Billy. It's a great community. I'm sure you're going to love it here, Kevin. The people are *real* nice."

Shane wrapped his right arm around Yael's shoulders and tugged her to his side. He didn't bother hiding his grin as she fell stiffly against him.

"Nice meeting you. Good luck settling in. Have a great evening now." Then Shane steered Yael toward the garage and locked his truck remotely with the fob. They headed inside as Kevin took the hint and jogged back across the street to his own home.

Shane let go of Yael to walk down the side of the borrowed SUV toward the interior door. He pressed the garage door button so it rumbled shut.

"Mind if I come in and double-check your security system?"

Her arms were still crossed tightly across her chest, her spine and shoulders rigid. "You heard Alex say he set it up, right?"

"I did."

"You know he's one of the best in the world at all that stuff, right?"

Shane glanced over his shoulder. "Security systems become moot if you open your door to an attacker or give out information you shouldn't when you bump into someone on the street."

She exhaled, sounding annoyed. "I wasn't going to tell him anything."

"Sure you weren't. Except your name. And the fact you just moved here too and don't really know anyone either. And the big armed guy standing in your driveway is just some loser from work and won't be here overnight."

"Which he would probably already know if he is Evi1Geni-us and has tracked me down."

"He wouldn't know I'm not staying," he argued and pushed aside the feelings that thought evoked. "But that's not the point. Presumably the UNSUB is not part of your inner circle and you don't want to give him the opportunity to wheedle his way in." He stared down at her and saw the way she shivered in the cold garage. "Don't let the societal need to be polite mean you let your guard down. You can make friends with Kevin after this asshole is caught."

The corner of her lips twitched. "I can't believe I'm being lectured for being too outgoing or nice to strangers. That there is the height of irony."

"You don't like people?" he asked.

"I like some people." She shrugged and moved past him, headed into the house.

He followed her, checking the door and lock which were both high quality. "The attached garage is your weakest spot. Not that difficult to spoof the garage door opener and for the bad guy to wait inside the garage ready to jump you coming in or out of your house."

"Funny." She hiked one delicate eyebrow and he shut down the desire to reach out and smooth his finger along the fine edge.

"Until that monster SUV was parked in the garage, I pretty much had an unobstructed view of every inch."

He grimaced.

"Plus, I have cameras set up on front and back entrances, although…" She trailed off.

"What?"

"Nothing."

"What?" he pushed.

"I am a little worried that he could somehow manipulate the system to either let himself in without tripping the alarm or…"

"Or infiltrate the cameras and spy on you?"

Her lashes swept lower over those dark brown eyes. "Yeah."

"That's good."

"Good?" Her eyes flashed indignantly.

"Sure." Shane walked down the hallway without waiting for an invitation. "Means you won't completely rely on technology at the expense of your instincts. Mind if I grab a glass of water?"

She looked a little nonplussed. "Of course not."

She squeezed past him and he caught her scent again. It must be her shampoo. Some sweet berry that made him want to sink his hands into something that didn't belong to him.

"Any progress on tracking down our killer?" he asked, following her into the bright white kitchen with a six-burner gas range.

"Not really, but I set up a web crawler to search websites for a few specific lines of code he used when he hacked my system. I'm not familiar with them so…"

"How long before you get results?"

She picked up her hoodie off the back of a kitchen stool and shrugged into the soft-looking cotton before grabbing a glass out of the cabinet. The tattoo on the inside of one wrist was a small intricately worked snake. "Difficult to say. I have sparkling water if you want?"

"Sounds good." Whatever took longer to prepare. "Why is it difficult to say?"

She made a bottle of fizzy water and poured him a glass. Put it on the counter rather than risk making contact with him. He didn't know how he knew that except when he went to catch her gaze, she avoided it. He made her nervous but he didn't think it was because she was physically scared of him. It was something else.

Attraction? Or guilt?

He could work with attraction. And he would uncover whatever it was she was hiding. In the meantime, he was happy to keep pumping her for information pertinent to the investigation.

"The sheer volume of websites and pages means it could take hours or days or even weeks to crawl over all the data. On top of that, the code might be something generic that I'm simply not familiar with and yield hundreds if not thousands of hits. In which case I will either sift through the results or ditch the search or refine it."

"Sounds complicated." He took a drink.

She clasped her hands together. "Not really."

"To me it is."

"What you do is complicated. I simply review computer code and assess threats."

He stepped closer. "Don't put yourself down. You search the internet for things that hackers are trying to hide. What you do is important and I think you know it." He reached out and gently freed a strand of her hair that had escaped her ponytail and been trapped in the neck of her hoodie.

He saw the way her eyes dilated when she looked at him. He was pretty sure it was attraction reflected in her dark irises, but he also saw the wariness. He wanted Scotty's killer to pay. He wanted all the retribution he was legally allowed to inflict and maybe a little extra to go with it. To get that he needed to sneak under this woman's guard.

He took another drink of water. Stepped back. "Where are the cameras?"

She blinked in surprise. Good. He wanted her a little off

balance. He needed her to trust him first and foremost, and he had the suspicion that if he made a move now, she'd never let him through the doorway again.

An image of Grace hugging her fatherless children flashed through his mind. It killed the desire that had started to sneak between the cracks of his armor.

Yael pulled out her phone and opened the security app she used. Handed it to him and then walked him across the living room through a sliding door onto the deck. The deck had steps down to ground level with no other entrance out back. She pointed upward to two cameras mounted on either side of the house. Yael was clearly visible on both and there were no blind spots that he could see.

Her teeth chattered from cold as he led the way back inside. He checked the front of the house. There was one camera inside the garage and another mounted on the front door with a view of anyone approaching the house.

"And these are live 24-7?"

She nodded, then took her hair out of the elastic that held it. It fell over her shoulders in a glossy wave.

He wanted to take another step toward her and touch it but knew he'd be crossing a line that would be hard to come back from. He'd already pushed the boundaries enough for one day.

"Monitored?"

"I get a notification whenever anything cuts through one of the beams close to the house. It records constantly and data wipes over itself every seven days. Alex installed a silent alarm that triggers if anyone besides a few named individuals—basically me and him at this point—even attempt to interfere with the system. And a screenshot of whoever is disarming the panel is taken and sent whenever the alarm is disarmed. Obviously, I'll remove Alex as soon as EG is caught but right now, I appreciate the backup."

Shane nodded. The security system could be circumvented but not easily and not without setting off a warning. This was sophisticated stuff.

He opened her contacts app on her cell and pulled up his number and dialed it. His phone rang.

"And now I have your number if I need you for anything." He handed her phone back to her, once again caught off guard by an errant spark that jolted between them. Maybe it was actual static? Or maybe it was because she was off limits? Or actively resisting whatever this thing was between them.

She rolled her eyes. "I can always block or delete you, you know."

"Why would you do that?" He headed for the front door. "Think of me as the backup plan."

He opened the front door and noted Kevin Karvo bringing out more trash across the street. The guy stopped and raised a hand.

Shane nodded in return then turned back to Yael who leaned against the doorframe.

"Yael."

"What is it?" Her brows pinched together.

"Brace yourself."

"For what?"

"I'm going to kiss you so that guy across the street doesn't get any ideas about coming over here to borrow some sugar the moment I drive away." He moved closer, sank his fingers into her hair and gently around her skull. Slowly he pulled her toward him. "Okay?"

Her eyes flicked to the side and she held tense for a fraction of a second before nodding slightly.

"Try not to run away screaming."

A smile touched her mouth, but now her dark eyes were on his lips.

He shifted a little closer, wishing for the millionth time he didn't have a cast on his dominant left arm. He rested his left hand lightly on her hip.

Slowly he lowered his mouth to meet hers, a quick brush of lips. She blinked in response and swallowed. Her lips parted slightly and her gaze stayed on his mouth. He couldn't resist another taste so he lowered his head again. She raised herself up on tiptoe, her breasts brushing his chest and making his IQ drop thirty points. He nipped her bottom lip and then went a little deeper. He almost fell over when her tongue glanced off his bottom lip. Then her hands slid up his chest and around his neck. He pulled her closer, kissing her properly now. Feeling the rush of his body's reaction. Feeling the pent-up desire that heated his skin and made his pulse pound. A quiver ran over his entire frame as he put his left arm around her waist and pressed her against the wall. Pain shot to his elbow and he pulled away, clenching his jaw in irritation. Not at the pain, but at the fact he'd forgotten about his broken arm and that they were in a semi-public space. He'd let his guard down and he was supposed to be helping to protect her.

He let her go, reached out with his good arm to cup her chin. He lowered his lips one last time, telling himself they may as well make it look good. This time, when he pulled away, he didn't have to fake the regret that flooded his whole being.

"Is he still watching?" Yael asked softly.

He glanced to the side and shook his head.

"Good."

"Yeah." He was such a fucking liar.

She swallowed, the delicate line of her throat rippling.

"Keep the doors locked. Call me any time if you're worried or nervous about the slightest thing. Remember." He held her dark gaze. "Your instincts are your best protection. Better than any security system or weapon. Trust them."

She stared at him, seemingly rendered mute. Because of the kiss? It had been pretty incredible. Or was she terrified of him because he'd basically forced himself on her? He took a step back watching her carefully.

He didn't want to freak her out. "And anytime you need a fake boyfriend I am here for you."

That at least made her laugh. "Fake boyfriend, huh? Sounds like all my boyfriends."

He laughed too but he wanted to ask her about that. Why?

Were they online? Imaginary, or not invested, not honest with her?

He couldn't afford to get in any deeper with this woman. Not if they both hoped to get out of this with their reputations and lives intact. But he had questions, lots of questions.

Smart, interesting women—absolute fucking *kryptonite*.

"Lock up behind me. Don't answer the door to anyone. Don't sit out on the deck. Don't go for long lonesome walks in the woods. Not until we catch this guy, okay? And we will catch him." He held her gaze until she nodded, even though she appeared loath to follow orders.

She closed the door on him, still looking a little stunned—because he'd scared her to death? Probably. And that was a good thing. She couldn't afford to take chances. He heard the double locks slide into place.

He glanced over at Kevin's house before heading to his truck. Shane planned to run a background check on the guy before heading home and it wasn't only because he'd recognized that look of male interest in the other man's gaze. It was because he fit the general size and shape of Evi1Geni-us and the timing was suspect as hell.

And if Kevin Karvo was Evi1Geni-us, Shane looked forward to greeting him properly with his SIG Sauer P226 and a pair of stainless-steel handcuffs.

Welcome to the neighborhood, motherfucker.

9

Shane took aim at the target and squeezed off a group of shots with his right hand before moving to the next station and squeezing off a few more. He examined the chamber of his SIG to make sure the gun was empty before checking the targets. He'd shot a set with his dominant broken arm earlier to keep in practice and he was happy with it, despite the ache that seemed to cut through the bone when he pushed it too far.

The day was overcast and chilly. Charlie assaulters were running close quarters battle (CQB) drills in the shooting house. Echo assaulters were waiting their turn in another hour or so. Shane was disappointed that he was missing out on the action, although he planned to observe. See how the new guys integrated with the others.

Gold team snipers had headed over to one of the Marine Corp ranges to sharpen their technique. Marksmanship was a perishable skill and even the best shooters in the world needed constant practice, and that went double for people who trained with live ammunition under dynamic conditions.

He pulled off the ear protection and walked back to a table where he'd laid out his gear.

"Hey, Livingstone! Someone to see you."

Shane glanced over to where Cowboy stood near the compound gate.

Ryan Sullivan was one of his best friends in the entire world but the sight of the guy giving Yael Brooks one of his infamous piratical grins as she stood there looking like a lost schoolgirl nervously clutching her bag to her chest made Shane want to deck the guy.

He drew in a deep breath and placed the weapon on the bench and waved her over. Yael eyed Hugo, the dog, nervously. Cowboy was doing some basic handling work with the Belgian Malinois today in case Ford Cadell—Hugo's usual handler—was ever incapacitated. She headed cautiously down the slope to the range. She was dressed in her usual jeans, boots, graphic t-shirt and old leather jacket.

She wasn't wearing makeup but her lips looked shiny, probably with lip balm to protect from the frosty morning air. He'd tasted those lips…

Shane looked away and took time reloading his weapons, placing the SIG in a thigh holster and the Glock on his hip. Then he swept up the spent bullet casings. Was Yael here because of that kiss? In retrospect it had been a terrible idea, but she had kissed him back.

Was she interested in more?

He looked up. She didn't strike him as the sort of woman to chase a guy, especially not into a compound full of alpha males who ate ammunition and explosives for breakfast.

"Come for that firearms lesson?" he asked when she got near enough to talk to without raising his voice.

As she came closer, he saw her glance anxiously at the weapons. He picked up his carbine, checking the safety before he slung it over his shoulder. Confirming his overall impression that she hated guns her brown eyes went huge and she quickly shook her head. "Not in this lifetime."

She seemed to grow paler. She *really* didn't like guns. Had she gone through some kind of trauma? He wanted to ask but sensed pushing too hard too soon would have her retreating behind those walls she liked to hide behind.

Snipers weren't the only ones who learned the art of patience.

"What can I do for you?" He tried to sound professional and nonchalant rather than intrigued and eager.

"I realized after you left last night that you forgot to give me Myrtle's keys."

Duh.

"I can't believe I forgot to hand those over last night." And it was entirely possible he'd purposely held onto them as an excuse to see her again. Building trust took time and Yael seemed reluctant to warm up to him—not a problem he usually faced.

She raised a skeptical eyebrow that said as clearly as words she didn't believe him.

"Although, that kiss did kind of blow my mind even if it was all for show." He gave her a smile. The deflection worked because her cheeks flooded with pink.

He searched her warm brown eyes for some inkling as to whether or not she had regrets about the kiss but once again her expression was difficult to read.

He gathered up the rest of his belongings. "The keys are inside with my gear. Want a quick tour?"

She looked torn. Very few people were allowed inside this compound but with her working on the task force he didn't see the front office complaining. She might not like weapons but he could tell she was interested in how HRT worked. And even if by some remote chance she was somehow involved in being a leak he wasn't about to show her anything classified or operationally sensitive. He'd keep his eyes on her the whole time.

"Sure."

They headed up the hill past Cowboy who was eyeing Yael with undisguised interest. Shane introduced them, because not doing so would look like he was staking a claim.

"Ryan Sullivan, this is Yael Brooks. She's working on the joint task force with me."

Understanding flickered over Ryan's features but his eyes didn't lose their appreciative glint. Ryan considered himself a connoisseur of women. Shane considered him a bigger dog than the K9 sitting patiently at the other man's feet.

Ryan held out his hand and Yael reluctantly took it even as she cautiously eyed Hugo who was watching them all with his intelligent dark eyes, long pink tongue hanging out the side of his mouth.

"I'm sorry for the loss of your teammate," Yael said to Cowboy solemnly. She withdrew her hand quickly and Shane noticed she wasn't a particularly touchy-feely person.

Ryan's expression immediately turned somber. He nodded firmly. "Appreciate that."

None of them could really talk about it yet. It hurt too damn much.

"Don't mind Hugo." Shane inclined his head toward the dog who was clearly picking up on Yael's nerves. "Friendliest mutt in the FBI, but don't tell the bad guys." Although the dog would bring down the Pope himself should he be given the command.

"Can I pet him?" she asked.

"Sure. He's protective of his pack. He simply needs to know you're part of it." Ryan handed her a dog treat. "Tell him to sit and then give him this. He'll love you forever."

Shane didn't miss the look Ryan shot him when he said those words. Shane rolled his eyes behind Yael's back. The guy was implying that Shane was smitten which was bullshit. Sure, he liked her, but he was trying to get closer to her for intel, not because of her body.

Leaving Ryan behind, Shane led Yael inside the main building which housed support staff, their lockers and equipment cages. Gold team's space was packed to the gills with high-end tech and smelled vaguely like a cross between a football locker room and a mechanics workshop.

Thankfully it was empty with most of the team busy training. He checked his watch. Almost time for the teams to switch out at the shooting house but this was another opportunity to gain this woman's trust and he wasn't sure how many more chances he'd get. He could watch the guys anytime.

"Any trouble after I left last night?" he asked.

"No one came around asking to borrow a cup of sugar if that's what you're worried about." Her dark eyes flashed with unexpected humor.

"You can never be too careful." He smiled.

She dropped her gaze.

Was she shy? He thought that might be part of her story, but not all of it.

He opened his locker and scooped his keys off the top shelf. He removed Yael's keyring from the fob to his truck. "Here you go. Why *Myrtle* by the way?"

She shrugged as she took them from him. "She felt like a Myrtle." She gave him a quizzical glance. "You don't name your vehicles?"

He grinned. "I might name my guns but never my truck."

Her eyes widened. "You name your guns?"

He laughed because she looked as if she thought he'd lost his mind when she was the one who'd named her freaking scooter.

"Nah. Not really. The snipers name their long guns though, but assaulters are not as sentimental as those softies." He closed his locker door and headed to his cage to put the carbine on the rack. He needed to clean all three weapons before he left for the day but considering his useless arm, he figured he had time. He planned to visit the joint task force headquarters later and see if they had any updates.

"This is where you keep all your stuff, huh?" Her eyes widened when she took in the biological weapons suit and the heavy equipment go-bags.

"Yeah. The whole team can be wheels-up in four hours. That includes loading vehicles, helicopters and gear into the transport plane out of Andrews Airbase."

"That's impressive."

He nodded and then frowned as he received a notification on his work cell. It was a code red which meant he had to report immediately to the main classroom for a briefing.

"Damn. Sorry." He looked up and she seemed to realize something was going on. "I have to report in."

"No problem. I have what I came for." She dangled the keys from the chain and slipped it into her tight jeans pocket. His fingers itched to follow their path.

"I'll walk you to the main office and someone will show you out."

"I can find my own way," she protested.

"Rules, I'm afraid."

"Oh, *duh*. Makes sense." She nodded and he let her lead the way down the corridor in the direction they'd come toward the main atrium. Operators were filing through the doorway, some of them sweaty and stinking of gunpowder having finished up in the shooting house.

Yael hugged the side of the hall as the wall of testosterone streamed past them into the classroom. Some of the men glanced at her with obvious interest and Shane tried not to feel territorial. He and Yael *worked* together. He never got involved with people he worked with. Too much room for conflict. Except this was temporary…she wasn't in HRT. She wasn't even in the FBI.

Maybe after this was all over…

He pushed the thoughts aside. Finding the serial killer who'd boobytrapped that crime scene and murdered his best friend was his priority. Not *dating*. He leaned over the desk and asked Maddie Goodwin who was the main receptionist and gatekeeper to the front office if she could find someone to escort Yael to the gate.

"Of course." The woman was usually cheerful but right now she looked pale.

His stomach clenched. Something bad had happened.

"What is it?" he asked her quietly.

She glanced sideways at the bosses who marched out of the

backroom and refused to answer him. Shane felt a shiver of apprehension slice down his spine. It had to be really bad if the top dogs were attending this impromptu team meeting. Operators from Red and Blue teams who were on base also headed inside.

Shit.

"Come this way, Yael, I'll walk you out. Sorry for the chaos." Maddie's smile was forced as she came around the counter, giving Shane a tense expression that said he wasn't going to like what he was about to hear.

"See you tomorrow." Shane called to Yael, but she'd already started to walk away, clearly recognizing something important was going down and that he needed to be in that room right now.

He tried to force her out of his mind. If she *was* in danger, she should be safe enough on base. He hated the push-pull of his thoughts though. The genuine concern that EG might target her, balanced against the insidious disquiet that someone on the task force might be dirty.

It was a stretch to think that that someone might be Yael, but Shane wasn't ready to discount anything when it came to the man who'd murdered his best friend. Not yet.

He shook his head and moved into the classroom. Found a spot on the wall next to Novak.

"What's up?" Shane asked.

"Don't know but it can't be good."

Could be anything from a major terror attack to an impromptu training exercise designed to keep them on the tips of their tactical boots. Could be a prison riot or a nuclear threat or the lead up to the next world war.

Shane inhaled and tried to calm the race of his pulse. Cowboy came and stood on his other side.

"*Yael*, huh?"

"She's on the task force," Shane gritted out.

"Then you won't mind the fact she gave me her number when I passed her in the corridor?"

Shane stared at his friend and whatever was on his face made the other guy grin.

"Kidding, buddy. Just kidding." Cowboy crossed his arms over his chest and settled in against the wall. "I gave her mine..."

Shane wanted to tackle the guy even though he knew Ryan was lying. Probably.

Yael didn't strike Shane as the type to fall for superficial sweet talk or charming smiles. But judging from the number of women Ryan *dated* maybe Shane didn't really know what women liked.

They *worked* together.

She was a means to an end.

And Shane had kissed her and she'd kissed him back. Even if it had been for show.

Shane growled out of the side of his mouth. "Go anywhere near her and I will kill you and toss you into the sea for the fish to feed on."

"Hah. I knew it." Cowboy chortled and elbowed him and Shane shook his head. The guy was one of the best operators on the team but he rarely took anything seriously. Shane knew it was deeply rooted in the fact Ryan was a widower even though he never spoke of his dead wife.

Everyone quieted down when the HRT Director himself walked into the room and took his place at the front.

Daniel Ackers had served on the teams for eight years before heading to DC for a few years at JEH. He'd returned to HRT as the boss two years ago and was a straight shooter who understood their job in a way no outsider ever could.

His mouth was grim. Eyes cast down. He raised his hand to get everyone's attention. "I have some bad news and, considering what happened in Houston recently, I wanted to be the one to break it to you all. You probably know Kurt Montana was due back from a TDY today." He looked up, his usually twinkling brown eyes flat and reddened.

What the fuck...

"Twenty minutes ago, I received word from the State Department that Kurt's flight leaving Harare was involved in a crash. Everyone on board died. There are no known survivors."

It took a second for the information to sink in, to penetrate the instinctive, insistent denial. What followed felt like a lightning strike to the heart.

Montana was a hard man, but he always had your back and would literally take a bullet for his men.

Dead?

It was incomprehensible.

In an accident?

Shane stared hard at Jordan Krychek who'd arrived back at work yesterday. The guy was sheet white. What had they been doing in Africa? Who'd they been working with?

Was this a mechanical error or a terrorist attack? Or some sort of military fuck-up? Questions lined up on Shane's tongue but he knew it was too soon for anyone to have real answers.

"We're obviously going to be searching for more clarity and members of Red team are being deployed to investigate on the ground." Ackers cleared his throat. "But to my immense sadness, I have every reason to believe Kurt Montana died last night. I'm about to go break the news to his family. Agents Novak and Angeletti, I'd like you to accompany me, if you don't mind."

Shane saw Novak draw in a shuddering breath and was grateful the guy had his FBI negotiator girlfriend for emotional support. Charlotte Blood was a sweetheart. Despite his own inner turmoil, Shane made a mental note to text her and warn her. Angeletti looked as if he was gonna hurl. This had hit everyone hard.

Grief and loneliness swelled and settled over Shane as he thought about the lack of emotional support in his own life. Sure, he could call his parents or his sisters, but this would only worry them.

Fuck.

A sudden surge of energy pulsed inside him with nowhere to

go. The world had been turned upside again and was now slamming down on his head.

Cowboy swallowed tightly as a tic worked in his jaw. Then the man pushed away from the wall. "Time to run some drills in the shooting house." He glanced at Shane. "Coming?"

Shane nodded as everyone filed silently out of the room.

He felt hollow inside. To have lost one member of the team was bad enough. To lose two in as many weeks was devastating.

10

Yael yawned so widely it felt as if her jaw was going to dislocate. It was eight a.m. and she was once again trapped in a morning task force briefing at Quantico.

"Last night we zeroed in on a hit on a cryptocurrency payment to a former soldier who was a munitions expert based out of Fort Bragg." ASAC Carly Sloan stood at the front of the room and explained the information that Yael and Alex had spent most of the night ferreting out after Laura had identified activity on currency linked to one of the murders via the Ethereum platform late last night.

Once Yael and Alex uncovered an ID that suggested the guy might be a viable suspect for Evi1Geni-us's explosives expert, Alex had made a few phone calls.

Judging from Alex's absence from the meeting this morning and the fact that half the seats in the room were also empty, the FBI was presumably already en route to execute an arrest warrant.

Yael wasn't the only one who'd noticed how many people were missing. She could sense Shane's seething tension.

"What details do we have?" Shane asked. He appeared stern today, focused, and closed off, not at all the easy-going guy she'd grown used to. She had to wonder if the change in demeanor had anything to do with that urgent meeting that had everyone buzzing yesterday at the HRT compound. Or maybe she'd mistaken attraction for genuine concern about her security. Maybe she was the only one who had been thoroughly disconcerted by that stupid kiss.

"Lloyd Zenko was an infantry soldier who trained with the Explosive Ordinance Disposal unit, but he was kicked out of the program and dishonorably discharged after turning up for duty while drunk sixteen months ago."

"Drinking on the job is not a great quality in a bomb disposal guy," Shane stated bitterly.

Yael yawned again and he shot her a look.

She covered her mouth. Damn. She hadn't gone to bed last night. After she'd left Cramer, Parker & Gray's new Quantico offices at five a.m. she'd decided to shower and then head straight here. She'd arrived even earlier than she had on Monday but Shane had still beaten her in. She'd given him a brief nod and set up in the same spot as last time per Ashley Chen's instructions.

The guy had then once again casually parked himself beside her as soon as she'd settled in. She'd be lying if she said it hadn't given her an unwanted little buzz.

And maybe the seating arrangement was Ashley's doing? The female agent seemed to coordinate everything and everyone. Yael was probably reading too much into things like who sat next to whom. Perhaps Ashley had told him to keep an eye on her. Did the FBI agents suspect her of something? That thought was an unexpected shot to the heart. Or perhaps Shane simply hoped to get her into bed.

She wasn't sure how she felt about the latter, but better than people doubting her integrity. It had been a while since she'd had sex and that kiss had certainly fried her circuits. It had reminded her of all the things she was missing with her self-imposed exile from the world. Loneliness was a given, but she didn't usually notice the lack of physical intimacy quite so acutely. He'd made it obvious he wasn't looking for anything long-term or for any deep emotional connection. But, even so, getting involved with someone she worked with seemed like an unnecessary risk.

She pushed the errant thoughts out of her mind. She needed to listen to Sloan talk about the case, not moon about a hot FBI operator who handled assault rifles with the same ease as she wrote code.

She yawned again and Shane eyed her narrowly this time as if she was deliberately hiding secrets from him.

Technically she was, but she refused to feel guilty about that. It had nothing to do with the case.

She was tired but satisfied. The fact she, Alex, and Laura had discovered this clue from the blockchain data meant maybe Evi1-Geni-us wasn't as savvy as he thought he was. It was a good lead and hopefully would make up for her failure in Houston.

Her mood soured.

It wouldn't bring Dave Monteith or Anya Baker back to life though.

"We've since verified that Zenko's cell was turned off on December 30 and not turned on again until January 2. This suggests to anyone with a working brain he didn't want his movements tracked during that period, which is a huge red flag." Sloan must have confirmed Alex's initial findings. "In the meantime, we are searching for license plate captures or any records of him renting a car and traveling to Houston from North Carolina."

"What's the plan?" Shane asked.

Sloan put her hands on her hips. "HRT have sent a team to assist FBI Charlotte's Violent Criminal Apprehension Squad led by SSA Lucas Randall who some of you obviously know—"

"They've already left?" Shane cut in.

Sloan nodded. "Flew out an hour ago. We were keeping this strictly need to know."

Shane audibly ground his teeth and Yael glanced at him. He caught himself and pulled his lips back into a smile that didn't come close to reaching those viridian eyes.

"They are taking bomb squad technicians with them and the plan is to pick Zenko up when he leaves his apartment."

"Do we have a visual of the suspect?" Shane asked.

Sloan shook her head. "Not yet but we know from radar there is someone asleep in bed inside his apartment. We don't know who yet. We only discovered this information in the early hours of this morning thanks to Alex Parker and Yael." Sloan nodded to her.

She pressed her fingers to her warm cheeks and wished she didn't blush so easily. She wasn't shy. She was simply allergic to being the center of attention.

"You found him?" Shane asked.

"I helped."

"I wish you'd called me. Nice work though." He held her stare for so long her pulse skipped.

She gave him a nod. His gaze fell to her mouth before pulling back to her eyes. Then he looked away as if annoyed with himself. The kiss had apparently unsettled them both.

She didn't like how many times her thoughts had strayed to this man over the last few days. Her finger had hovered over the delete button on his number in her contact list a dozen times, but why delete something she might need during the course of this investigation?

No matter how valid that excuse, she knew she was lying to herself. She wanted to call him. She wanted to spend more time with him even though he really wasn't her type—*because hot guys weren't her type*? She mentally rolled her eyes at herself. She was a complete idiot.

Shane drummed his pen on the table. "What are we supposed to do back here?"

Sloan's eyes narrowed. The task force leader clearly recognized Shane's obvious resentment at being left behind. "Keep searching for this UNSUB and I believe *you* are to report back to HRT with our findings."

"Seems like they know more than I do." He sounded pissed and didn't seem to care if Sloan knew it or not.

Yael glanced at him in surprise.

"I'm not here to babysit your ego, Agent Livingstone." Sloan's expression as well as her tone turned frosty.

"It isn't my *ego* that's bothered by the situation." Shane rubbed the bridge of his nose. "I'd like to contribute in a meaningful way and being kept out of the loop means I'm redundant."

Sloan nodded. "Understood, but there is more than enough leg work to go around. Pitch in however you feel will be most helpful."

"Ma'am." He nodded and somehow it didn't sound facetious. "Any idea how Zenko connected with the UNSUB?"

"Not yet. I'm hoping we can ask him directly later today." Sloan continued. "Techs have set up monitors with live feeds to the HRT and FBI Charlotte agents." She pointed to a door to an adjoining room. "Randall's team are staking out Zenko's apartment and have surveillance in place. We hope to gain access to one of the neighboring apartments shortly. See if we can determine whether or not Zenko is in that bed. One thing to note is his truck is not there, but it could be in the shop or he might have bought a new one. Not sure yet. We'll buzz anyone who wants to watch the arrest should we receive enough advance warning. In the meantime, let's keep after this UNSUB and demonstrate he is more *evil* than *genius*."

The noise of chair legs scraping against the floor filled the room.

Shane stood and went over to Ashley Chen, presumably to ask to be contacted when and if the HRT operators went into action. Yael understood why he'd be anxious about his friends and colleagues after last time.

Yael checked her messages to see if her boss needed anything before she headed home, but he hadn't replied to her last note which meant he was probably catching forty-winks on the flight down to Charlotte. She planned to head back to her house and maybe score a few hours' sleep before going back to her data. So far, she had just under a thousand hits on the code EG had used in his executable file that she was working her way through.

She looked up and realized the room had cleared, everyone going about their business. Shane was nowhere to be seen and she squashed the sense of disappointment that he hadn't bothered to say goodbye.

Another reason not to get involved with anyone at work. The emotional energy put into any relationship was exhausting. All the second guessing, the constant fear of rejection or embarrassment. Better to be alone than always wondering if and when someone was going to walk away. And possibly humiliate you in the process.

She heard Ashley and Sloan talking in the next room. Apparently, Ashley Chen and Lucas Randall had adopted a girl called Becca before the holidays and Sloan was asking after her progress.

Yael was finding that many of the FBI agents knew one another and many considered the Bureau one big family. She'd found working at Cramer, Parker & Gray was similar. The bosses looked after the staff. People genuinely seemed to care for one another. She'd noticed they seemed to employ a lot of people who on first glance might not fit the usual corporate mold, but who were smart and dedicated and honorable. Her colleagues made her want to be a better person, and she suspected many of them had secrets or backgrounds like her own.

Yael was about to close her laptop and head home when a notification popped up on her screen. It was data regarding this guy Zenko.

"What's that?" Shane asked from behind her.

She jumped in her seat. She hadn't heard him come back into the room.

She turned and he was so close she could see flecks of silver in the green of his irises.

He sat. "Sorry. Didn't mean to startle you."

"Do they teach you to creep around like that at the academy?"

He snorted. "No. Special Forces. HRT too. What is that?" He nodded at the screen.

She returned to her messages. "I set up property searches for the Zenko family last night before we figured out he'd rented an apartment in Fayetteville. I included his mother's family and grandparents' names to see what popped."

It wasn't a long list.

She eliminated those that had clearly been sold outside the immediate Zenko family. Shane peered intently at her laptop screen and she forced herself not to react to his closeness.

"Was everything okay yesterday?" She wanted to kick herself for asking. HRT business was highly confidential for obvious reasons.

"No." He clenched the hand of his broken arm into a fist. "We lost another team member." He cleared his throat. "Overseas."

"I am so sorry." She stopped what she was doing and looked at him. "Are you all right?"

His lips pressed together. "Not really but I'll deal with that in my own time and catching this motherfucker will make me feel a whole lot better about a whole lot of things."

The silence crackled between them.

He didn't want comfort. He wanted results. She turned back to the screen because he obviously didn't want to talk about it and she understood that. "Zenko's parents retired to near Jacksonville."

Yael was hyperaware of the brush of his knee against her thigh as he leaned forward.

"Hey, check that out. Maternal grandparents own a cabin on the edge of Shenandoah National Park. Looks like Zenko's mother still owns it." Shane pointed at her screen. "That's only an hour west of here." He checked his watch.

"What are you thinking?"

Green eyes flashed, his expression suggesting he was carefully considering his words. "We could go for a drive and see if anyone is there?"

Yael frowned at her screen. "I thought he was in Fayetteville."

Shane dipped his chin. "He's *probably* in Fayetteville. But if the family have owned that place for a long time, then maybe the neighbors will have a few stories to tell us about little Lloyd. And if he isn't in Fayetteville," he tapped the screen, "that is exactly the sort of place where he'll be holed up."

Yael frowned. She'd love nothing more than to redeem herself by helping to catch this freak. And she didn't think Shane would take her with him if he thought it was actually going to be dangerous.

"Are you going to tell Sloan?"

"Do you want me to?"

"Er. Yeah." Yael pulled up the address on a map. It wasn't far at all. "I don't want to get thrown off this task force."

Shane nodded. "Me neither. I'll go speak to her."

Yael packed up her stuff and when she got to the doorway Shane pointed her way and Sloan nodded and immediately went back talking to Ashley Chen. They seemed to be busy creating a section on the wall dedicated to Lloyd Zenko.

"What did she say?"

"Strictly surveillance only. Told us to pose as tourists going for a hike and not to raise any red flags by asking too many questions." He stared at her feet. "You have hiking boots?"

She liked hiking just fine, but walking alone on quiet trails creeped her out, so she didn't do it. She didn't want to admit her fear to this guy though. She hooked her bag over her head and across her chest. "Do I look like I spend a lot of time hiking in the woods?"

He looked her up and down. "You have two good legs so why not? Those boots are probably okay as long as it isn't too slippery."

There had been a light snowfall overnight that had made her grateful she wasn't riding Myrtle.

"Let's go past your place and pick up a raincoat—you own a raincoat, right?" he asked with a frown.

She couldn't help but smile. "Yes, Agent Livingstone. I own a raincoat."

"I thought we were on first name terms nowadays, Yael?" He lowered his voice to a soft velvety tone and leaned closer. "Considering..."

Gah. He was referring to the kiss. She couldn't believe he'd brought it up even obliquely.

But his smile was hard to resist and Yael started to wonder why she even tried. What harm could it do to be friends with this guy? Even if she slept with him, it was no big deal—probably a good way to get this distracting attraction out of her system. As long as he never found out about her past, she could be whoever she wanted to be—and he'd need to be a lot better at digging into the cyber-verse to figure out her secrets.

Although was changing your name to hide a tragic history really deception? For her it was more about self-preservation.

She shuddered. She'd spent a lifetime moving on and reinventing herself when people she'd trusted eventually found out the truth. But, as she was stuck with this guy, perhaps she should relax her guard a little and simply concentrate on helping catch this killer.

That had to work in her favor, right? One day, she might do enough to atone for the sins of her brother.

Her mind filled with images saturated in blood and her mood soured. She'd never be able to atone for everything. All she could do was try.

11

Shane glanced over to the passenger side of the truck and his conscience felt a rare prick. He hadn't been strictly honest with Yael, nor with the task force leader.

Lying to good people left a bad taste in his mouth, but Shane knew that if he informed ASAC Sloan of his suspicions she'd tell him to wait and see what happened in Fayetteville before sending a team out to the cabin. And if he told Yael he'd lied about getting the task force leader's permission she wouldn't have come. And he wanted her with him.

On one hand, it was an opportunity to bond, and to prove he wasn't going off on his own on some lone wolf mission. He'd make sure she wasn't in any real danger.

On the other, he could keep an eye on Yael. Watch her reactions.

Considering she'd been part of the team to identify Zenko it didn't seem likely that she was in league with EG.

Shane was concerned that Zenko might hear about the FBI raid on his apartment from one of his cronies at Fort Bragg. If the guy was at the cabin, he'd be in the wind before the FBI caught up with him again. Shane not only wanted Zenko to pay for his crimes, he was also pretty sure the guy would roll on this Evil-Geni-us asshole faster than green grass through a goose.

He glanced sideways.

Yael was not exactly chatty Cathy. He was used to Cowboy riding shotgun and, off duty, the guy never shut up. Or Scotty… His gritted his teeth together to fight the punch of emotion that wanted to hit him, over and over again. Each blow felt like a fresh wound.

And now Kurt Montana…

Fuck.

He wasn't sure how he'd gotten through the last twelve hours. Mainly by not thinking about his friends and concentrating instead on this case. Finding Scotty's killer was his entire reason for being right now.

He'd told Sloan that he was going to assist Yael with online searches. The task force leader had looked relieved he was getting out of her way. So he'd misled both women and now he felt like a giant asshole, but at least he was a strategic one.

If they didn't find anything at the cabin then neither Sloan nor Yael would be any the wiser that he'd been a little economical with the truth. If Zenko *was* at the cabin, then HRT could be deployed while Shane and Yael observed from a safe distance. The task force would be so happy with the rapid break in the case that Sloan wouldn't ream him out. This was the theory anyway.

Shane had decided to drive his own vehicle. It looked a lot less government issue than Yael's SUV and although it might not sport bulletproof glass, he was confident in his ability to keep her out of immediate danger. They'd stopped by her house to grab rain gear, then his place to do the same. He'd insisted she come inside because leaving her in the truck seemed like an unnecessary security risk. It had felt weird though and he didn't remember the last time he'd had a woman there. He wasn't big on entertaining. He was on-call almost all the time which tended to ruin any social life except grabbing a beer or watching a game with his FBI or HRT buddies.

He'd quickly changed into black tactical pants, hiking boots and a lightweight fleece and had come into the living room to find her staring at the framed photographs he had of his family hanging on the walls. He hadn't seen any photos at her place but she'd only just moved in.

He'd grabbed his raincoat, which was now in the back seat along with two brand-new walking poles that he'd bought his mother for Christmas but had forgotten to give her.

They worked well as walking aids, which was good as Yael's boots weren't as grippy as he'd like, and could double as weapons. He was carrying his favorite SIG and a few magazines of ammo in his pockets. He had a backup strapped to his ankle and never went anywhere without his tactical knife and another slim blade hidden on his person.

Yael yawned again and he suspected she'd worked most of last night uncovering this lead.

Exactly how much time did she spend at her computer? Though he was hardly one to talk. He'd told her he was married to his job and hadn't lied. After leaving the Green Berets he'd worried he'd never find that same kind of soul-satisfying career in the civilian world. But working for the FBI's Hostage Rescue Team was even better than being in the Army. They not only shot at hostiles, they also arrested them. Shane didn't think there was a better job in the entire universe and he had no intention of jeopardizing his position. However, sitting in a room staring at a computer screen when they had a credible lead on a suspect wasn't something he could deal with either. He was part of the best trained unit of federal law enforcement agents in the US, if not the world, and he wasn't ignoring a potential clue.

Not if it meant Scotty's killers escaping justice.

The landscape whizzed by, growing more and more rural from suburbs to farmland. He kept his speed a little over the limit, not enough to get stopped by traffic cops, but enough to get where they were going as quickly as possible. He didn't want to draw attention by using lights or sirens. He couldn't be certain this

Zenko guy didn't have friends or relatives on the local police force.

Yael was doing research on her laptop. Looking for more background information. She hadn't said a word since they'd left town. She'd withdrawn again and he felt as if he was losing ground without even opening his mouth. He'd sensed a brief thawing in relations earlier but maybe he'd imagined it.

It was harder to fake cheerfulness than usual. Maybe that was the problem. She could sense his inner destruction and wanted no part of his misery.

He cleared his throat. "So, where are you from, originally?"

"All over the place. Colorado mainly, I guess. You?"

He watched her fingers clench in her lap.

She didn't like to talk about herself. She deflected constantly. Nerves or something to hide?

"Georgia, but I suspect you already know that."

She flashed him a guilty look.

"No way would you figure out my full name without checking out the family history."

She rolled her eyes. "I was making sure you weren't descended from plantation owners."

His fingers tightened on the wheel. "Thankfully my ancestors made their money from lumber, not from the soulless enslavement of others. However, destroying the environment isn't exactly something to be proud of either."

"Pretty sure most *old* money was earned from the exploitation of something or someone."

He grunted. "I didn't grow up with a silver spoon in my mouth if that's what you're thinking. My dad's father gambled most of his inheritance away after my grandmother died. He spent the rest on women and booze, much to my mother's disappointment."

She blinked at him in surprise. "That must have been hard for your family."

He shrugged. "Not really. Wasn't my money. And I loved the

old goat." His throat squeezed shut at the reminder of another big loss in his life. His grandfather had loved Shane's grandmother and hadn't been able to cope with her death. Cowboy reminded him of the old man in that regard. "Being named Shannon Marcus Livingstone III is a bit of a mouthful, but I kind of like the fact I have that permanent connection to him, you know?"

Yael frowned. "I guess. How'd you end up being called Shane?"

"My mom wasn't big on the family naming tradition. Didn't want her son to have the same name as her husband." Which he totally understood. "One of my sisters began calling me Shane. And I preferred that to *junior*." He gave a mock shudder. "Shane stuck. You named after anyone?"

"Me?" She folded her arms over her chest then looked out of the window. Her family seemed like a sore point. "My maternal great-grandmother. She was a Polish Jew who came to the States with her parents in 1923."

"Between the wars."

Yael nodded. "She was lucky they left when they did. Congress passed laws in 1924 that made it much more difficult for 'undesirables' to immigrate to the US. Then the Great Depression hit, followed by the rise of the Nazis."

"Fucking Nazis."

"Yeah," she nodded. "Fucking Nazis."

After a few pensive moments of silence she continued, "I met her when I was a little girl—my great grandma. I don't remember much about her, except she gave the sweetest hugs and smelled funny." A sad smile lit her features. "We were never a particularly religious family. My dad was raised Catholic, my mom was fiercely atheist. But we'd light a candle to all those who came before us around the holidays."

"Are your parents still alive?"

She shook her head and crossed her arms as she turned to stare out of the window again.

He wanted to know more but didn't want to push, which went

completely against his inquisitive nature. But from her expression the loss of her parents was fresh enough to still hurt.

Another sliver of guilt slid through him that he wasn't being completely honest with her. However, his interest was genuine and they were working together toward a common goal. It appeared increasingly unlikely she had anything to do with EG given the work she was doing with Alex Parker.

Also, he *liked* her in a way he hadn't liked anyone in a long time.

So he wasn't being completely deceptive in wanting to get to know her better. This was a collaboration between his law enforcement chops and her computer skills, with the focus firmly on the case. Working as an effective team was exactly what HRT trained for. He was adapting and maximizing his skill set while he dealt with the stupid broken arm which currently rested on his thigh.

It was healing. Just not fast enough, dammit.

He wanted to be in the thick of the action again. He wanted to be with his teammates, but he couldn't deny the fact he was enjoying hunting this motherfucker.

He saw a turn off and Yael held on to the grab handle as he took it, barely slowing down. HRT operatives were trained in tactical driving but the roads were a little slick so he understood her apprehension. Silence settled back over the cab once more. It made a change for him to be the more talkative person in a conversation.

"How come you ended up working for Alex Parker?"

She tucked a strand of hair back into the red woolen Bull-dogs knit cap he'd found for her. Wearing his old college colors suited her and affected him more than he wanted to acknowledge.

"I contacted the DoD a little over a year ago and informed them I'd found a vulnerability in one of their systems that they might want to fix. They offered me a cash reward which I refused. Turned out it had been set up as a kind of test by Alex Parker to catch any would-be black-hat hackers looking for zero-day vulnerabilities to sell off to the highest bidder."

"He offered you a job?"

"Yeah. Much to my surprise." She nodded. "Before that I was writing code for a startup company in California. I was about finished there and figured why not? I started working for Cramer, Parker & Gray at their DC office last January." She shrugged. "You pretty much know everything that happened since then."

He laughed. Hardly. There was that deflection again. "That's a big move."

"It was time for a change."

Had she left behind a lover? Family?

Shane bet there were intelligence officers more talkative than Yael Brooks. He wanted to know more about her. Figure out what made her tick. Plus, the last thing he needed right now was some jealous ex turning up. Especially not when Billy had been busy kissing Betty on the front step of her new home.

"Who was it who actually uncovered the Zenko connection?" He changed the subject because drawing her out was obviously a full-time job. Thankfully he excelled at stubborn persistence.

"Laura Bay, you know, my friend from Friday night?"

He nodded.

"She'd flagged some cryptopayment information in regard to Evi1Geni-us. The crypto appeared online again yesterday. Alex and I went through the blockchain information and I set up a web crawler that tracked the payment to a shell corporation in the Caymans. Alex somehow managed to identify Zenko from there. I'm not sure exactly how he did it so quickly. I didn't ask." She shot him a look from under her lashes.

"I'm not about to rat him out." But he understood how easy it was for a case to fall apart because someone hadn't followed lawful procedures. Alex Parker wasn't FBI but he did consult for them so they had to be careful.

They drove down increasingly narrower roads with fewer and fewer houses visible, and an ever-increasing number of trees whose limbs overhung the asphalt and made him feel like he was traveling through a tunnel into another world. Shane followed the directions on his Satnav as he was unfamiliar with the area.

"There's a hiking route on the hill behind Zenko's mother's cabin. I plan to park on the other side of the ridge and hike the trail until we are above Zenko's place. Then we can cut down through the woods and find a position in the trees to observe the cabin. I have some binoculars so we don't have to risk getting too close. If it looks like the place deserves a closer look, I'll go ahead and check it out and rendezvous back with you in the woods."

She stared at him silently. He wished he knew what she was thinking.

"It won't be dangerous. We will both wear ballistic vests under our rain gear just in case."

"Do you really think he might be here?"

The niggle between his shoulder blades had started itching as soon as he'd seen that cabin listed in Zenko's mother's name.

"Honestly?"

She nodded.

"I do. Or he's on a beach sunning himself in Mexico. What he likely isn't doing is sleeping late in some shitty apartment in Fayetteville." Shane tamped down on his anger at the fact this fucker had killed his friend. Emotions clouded his ability to do his job and he wasn't about to screw up.

She rubbed her forearms as if cold and he turned up the heat.

"He might be oblivious to the danger. A lot of people don't realize crypto can be traced. Lloyd Zenko might assume wrongly that we'll never be able to link him to the crime."

Shane took another turn. They were getting close now. "Wouldn't this Evi1Geni-us dude have warned him about that fact?"

"Presumably. Doesn't mean Zenko believed him or listened."

She was right. Criminals weren't always smart and a drunk bomb tech probably wasn't the sharpest blade in the knife block.

Yael turned to him, her eyes suddenly huge. "Do you think HRT are walking into another trap? Are they in danger?"

He shook his head. "Not this time. HRT operators and the bomb squad will clear the place before they move in. If the person inside doesn't come out voluntarily, I suspect the FBI will manufacture a fire alarm or something else to get him out of there. They will be evacuating the units close by regardless."

"Isn't that a risk?" Her brows crinkled over those dark eyes of hers. "What if someone warns him? Or he sees people leaving."

"*Servare vitas.*" He recited the Hostage Rescue Team's motto. "Our primary objective is to *Save Lives.*" He shrugged. Making sure people were safe trumped bursting in on this guy. He'd come out eventually. Should a barricade situation develop, the negotiators could talk to him and maybe do a plea deal that led them to EG who was orchestrating the murders. Sure, it would sting if Zenko—the man who'd probably planted the bomb that killed his best friend—got a lighter sentence, but the guy was going to federal prison regardless. It wouldn't be easy. It wouldn't be fun.

"If he's in that apartment he isn't going anywhere, but I still have my doubts." Shane believed Zenko was here, in this old family cabin.

They arrived at a pull in that had spaces for about six vehicles. His was the only one parked there probably due to the overcast sky, light snow on the ground, and the fact it was the middle of the week.

He reached into the back seat and handed Yael a green Kevlar vest. "Put it under your sweatshirt."

Her mouth tightened in consternation as she took it from him and pulled off her sweatshirt. He forced himself to look away so he didn't ogle her figure. She had curves in all the right places and smelled like his favorite dessert.

He grabbed another vest for himself and slid it easily over his head, tightening the straps with his good arm almost from muscle memory. Then he dragged on a plaid shirt over the cast followed by his green Gortex raincoat. He ditched the sling for this hike.

Instead, he buttoned the shirt to where he could rest his broken forearm comfortably inside against his abdomen whenever his arm started to ache. He checked the weapon in his side holster.

Locked and loaded. Ready to go.

Yael's hair was mussed and he couldn't resist watching as she gathered it up and tied it into some sort of knot at the nape of her neck before pulling the woolen hat back over her head.

Her eyes flashed to his, her expression a frown. She seemed always to be looking for disapproval, or a fight. Why was that?

Her jacket was bright red like the hat he'd lent her, but not a lot he could do about that right now.

"Wait here." He climbed out of the truck and jogged around to the other side. He opened her car door and she looked surprised.

"That's why you told me to wait? In order to open my door?"

"I was raised in Georgia. I appreciate not everyone likes southern manners but I'm more scared of my grandmother's ghost than I am of any pissed-off feminist."

She snorted. "You weren't that polite with ASAC Sloan earlier."

"That was different. The FBI didn't spend millions of dollars training me so that I kept my mouth shut in team meetings—not unless ordered to that is." And that had happened a few times when Kurt Montana had been the team leader.

An enormous wave of grief crashed over him but he shoved it firmly aside.

There wasn't much any of them could do about not surviving a plane crash. Montana would have wanted Shane to do his job, catch Scotty's killer, and raise a few glasses to them both later when the threat was neutralized.

Shane forced the thoughts from his head. Distraction could get him killed.

He held out his good hand and stood back so Yael could climb down from the truck. And even though her fingers were cold he forced himself to let go, to remember this wasn't a date and it wasn't up to him to warm her up. This was work and it might be dangerous so he had to maintain situational awareness at all times.

He dug into the backseat and pulled out the Nordic poles. Adjusted them to her height and handed them over. "Figured these will help on the trail and be useful weapons should you encounter anyone—or want to beat me."

She tested them out and leaned on them, smiling up at him with dark eyes and ruby lips. "It's beautiful around here."

He was surprised by her enthusiasm, especially given the mist clinging to the upper canopy of the trees and the cold edge of frost that had morphed into the wet drip of moisture from the few remaining leaves that clung to the branches. He loved being outside in any weather. He handed Yael binoculars to loop around her neck and suddenly found himself wishing that they could do this for real sometime.

He closed the truck doors quietly, locked it. "Let's go."

He led the way, which went against his ingrained manners but he'd rather be the first to encounter any potential danger as they trudged up the steep narrow path. At the top of the first incline, it widened so they could easily walk side-by-side.

"Makes me wish I had a dog," he admitted.

"Really? I've never had a pet, but I've thought about getting one." A sad expression settled over Yael's features.

"Not even a goldfish?"

She pulled a face and shook her head. "We moved around a lot."

Her expression closed down and Shane let it go.

Baby steps.

The mist hung low on the branches as they climbed higher up the ridge. After about a mile he checked the GPS, which was accurate to within ten meters.

They were only a quarter of a mile from Zenko's mom's cabin now but it was down a steep, heavily wooded incline. The sound of birds singing and squirrels chattering were the only noise that filled the air. The taint of woodsmoke rose on the breeze. Someone nearby had a fire going.

He quelled his excitement. There were at least ten cabins on the other side of this ridge, any one of which was likely to be occupied.

Surely Zenko knew it wouldn't take the FBI long to be onto him? Surely, he'd appreciate the cabin in the woods would be one of the first places the FBI would locate and search?

Yael slipped and he caught her with his right hand before she went down into the mud.

"Easy. The leaves are slippery." He reluctantly let her go.

"Thanks." She shivered and whispered, "Where are we?"

He showed her on the GPS system. She glanced in the direction of the property. Her cheeks wore small flags of color and her lips were a little pale.

"You cold?"

"A little," she admitted, crossing her arms and stamping her feet. "I'll be okay."

The last thing he wanted was Yael succumbing to hypothermia.

"Let's climb a little higher and then cut down through the trees. Here." He slid out of his raincoat and slipped it over her shoulders. "It'll help you blend in a little better." It was better quality than her own raincoat and should keep her warm.

"Won't you get cold?"

"I run hot." He gave her a wide grin and was surprised when she laughed at him.

"I bet you do." She pulled up the sleeves before planting her poles firmly in the ground.

He stared after her in surprise. Was she flirting with him?

They climbed for another hundred feet or so. Then Shane cupped her elbow to get her attention. When she turned to him, he murmured, "Sound travels farther than you might think so let's keep it down when we leave the trail, 'kay?"

She nodded without a word and he led the way down the side of the ridge.

He placed his feet carefully, grateful the leaves were wet rather than crunchy even though that meant they were slicker underfoot. Nothing in the world was louder than dead leaves. Moving through them quietly required skill and a patience he didn't have time to teach Yael. The hillside was steep in places and he held out his good hand to assist her. He would have held her hand the whole way to make sure she didn't fall except he needed to keep his gun hand free.

The poles definitely helped stabilize her in the mud.

On a rocky outcrop that was screened by several large evergreens, he paused to get his bearings. Then he pointed to the right and they eased through the suddenly silent woods.

The hairs on his nape prickled and he stilled, wondering what had set off his survival instincts. Yael paused behind him. She was much better at stealth than he'd anticipated.

He scanned the area looking up for any possible surveillance cameras like the ones they'd encountered in the mountains of Washington State last month when a compound full of survivalists had harbored a suspected killer and HRT had been called in to help resolve the situation. Those guys had installed cameras in the woods around their property, but Shane didn't see or hear anything like that here.

The terrain became rockier and he helped Yael over a couple of larger boulders, enjoying the connection despite the circumstances. It had obviously been a long time since he'd been in the company of a woman if holding hands in the damp woods while trying to do surveillance rang his bells.

They had a partial view of the cabin now even though it was still some distance away. He paused behind a stand of birch trees to observe. Yael put the binoculars to her eyes and adjusted the focus.

"See anything?" he asked quietly.

"Not really," she whispered, her voice low and sultry. "Too many obstructing branches."

"Yeah. We need a better position." Which meant getting closer.

They moved around a large conifer and he thought he heard voices. His foot slipped in the loose soil. Yael grabbed the back of his vest and he turned and gave her a grateful smile before helping her down another step.

A *no trespassing* sign warned him they were approaching the property line. A thick swathe of scrub and bushes blocked visibility and he was forced nearer to the cabin than he'd planned. That was the nature of any op. Adjust as necessary.

A narrow game path ran behind a gnarly old box elder. He went to take another step when something made him glance down. He might not have seen it if it hadn't been for the drop of water about to fall from the wire strung tightly between two tree trunks low to the ground. He froze—grabbing Yael's arm with his uninjured right hand to stop her from moving forward.

"Tripwire," he murmured. "Stand completely still."

12

Tripwire?

A freaking tripwire?

What the…?

Yael's heart thundered in her chest and she found it difficult to inhale especially wearing the constricting flak jacket and several layers of clothes.

Shane gave her a shit-eating grin that reminded her exactly how handsome he was. He looked positively thrilled by this development. He probably trained for this sort of scenario every day.

"Is that an *explosive*?" she asked, gripping the bicep of his bad arm so tightly it was a wonder he didn't wince. He did gather the walking poles out of her hands, probably so she didn't accidentally *blow them up*.

"Not sure. Could be an explosive but much more likely to be some kind of early warning system rigged to prevent anyone sneaking up on him."

"Oh my god. He's here, isn't he?"

Shane's hunch had been dead on. Lloyd Zenko was here and the sicko had boobytrapped his own property.

"I'd say there is a very high likelihood he's here. Yes."

"My heart is pounding," she admitted, letting go of him and putting her hand to her chest. Everything had suddenly become a lot more real.

"That's my fault. Sorry. Don't step anywhere. I want to quickly check the area before we move. I doubt Zenko has many of these else the local wildlife would be setting them off constantly, but the fact he is this worried tells me not only is he here—"

"He's also guilty as hell," she whispered back. "Do you think Evi1Geni-us is here too?"

"I doubt it. EG is too careful to risk getting caught. This Zenko character is a loose end that I doubt EG gave enough thought to. EG wanted to send a message to the FBI," he said, bitterness dripping from every word, "but he forgot he was going to leave more clues as to his identity when he did so." Shane scanned the ground behind them to confirm it was clear, then took her gently by the arm and led her to a rock which he checked to make sure was free of wires and explosives, before propping the walking sticks upright against it.

She released a massive breath as she sat. She wasn't used to this rush of adrenaline. And that's why people like Shane trained non-stop. So this internal freak-out didn't screw with their critical thinking skills. In order to function calmly in extreme circumstances—and still hit a target with a bullet when they needed to.

She'd read somewhere that the accuracy of shooting a moving target was around 4%. Unfortunately, she'd seen what 4% with an automatic rifle could do.

Shane crouched down in front of her and she drew her knees together and leaned forward to hear what he had to say. She didn't plan to screw this up. The thought she might have some part to play in finding this guy who everyone else thought was in North Carolina made her clench her jaw with determination. They hadn't caught him yet, she reminded herself.

"What do we do next?" she whispered.

Shane was so close she could smell his skin over the earthy

scent of mud and rotting leaves. He pulled out his cell. "Damn, no reception."

She checked her cell and scanned the area. "I expect we'd get a signal at the top of the ridge."

Shane stared toward the cabin.

"You don't want to go back in case he escapes," she realized out loud.

"We don't actually know he's in there yet. I don't want to call for backup until I have positive confirmation."

Yael shivered. She'd been enjoying walking in the hills until the hunch they were chasing had become a dangerous reality. Hunting him through the ether of the internet was one thing. It was quite another to stumble over tripwires on the bad guy's rural hideaway on a frigid January afternoon.

"I'm going to move closer and see if his truck is outside. You stay here."

Panic gripped her. "I'm coming with you."

"It'd be safer if you sit tight here," he said patiently.

She shook her head. "Except I won't know if you're okay or not. I will be stuck here not knowing if the next person I see will be you or a bad guy wanting to blow me away." Her words were low and he looked slightly taken aback at her vehemence. But she'd lived that experience and refused to do it again unless there was absolutely no alternative.

"I promised I wouldn't put you in danger," he reminded her.

"I will stay hidden behind a tree or a rock as long as I know what's going on." She bit her lip. "Sloan told you reconnaissance only, remember."

He looked away from her and huffed out a breath. "You promise to do exactly what I tell you?"

She nodded rapidly.

"Then stay here."

Damn. He was annoying. "Except that." At his expression she said quickly, "What if you're injured and I'm sitting on a rock all night like an idiot?"

"I've lost two people I care about recently. I don't want to be responsible for anyone else getting hurt." Emotion shone from his eyes.

"You're not responsible for what happens to me, Shane," she said quietly. "You are not my boss. We are both on the task force and I am perfectly capable of deciding what level of danger I'm comfortable with."

He touched her face, smoothing her hair back under her hat, disarming her fear. "You're already freezing. How about you go back to the truck and sit in the warmth. If I'm not there in an hour you call Sloan and then drive to the nearest police station."

Yael clenched her fingers trying to improve the circulation. The damp frigid cold was seeping into her so much she was starting to shiver. "I can't leave you. I'm your backup. I won't abandon you. I might not be an HRT operator or even an FBI agent, but I can watch from a distance and make sure you're okay."

Shane leaned back on his heels, looking frustrated. "I could handcuff you to a tree."

She gaped at him. "You wouldn't dare."

For a few seconds, he looked tempted and she didn't know how she'd react to that except with a feeling of utter helplessness and shame. She'd never speak to him again.

Whatever he saw in her face finally made him relent.

"Fine. This guy will be armed and we know he's dangerous. If we get to the cabin and I see him outside and figure I can get the drop on him, I will. But I expect you to stay put wherever the hell I tell you to and not to come out even if I am lying bleeding out on the ground. Hide, observe, and then go call for help when safe to do so."

That vision had her reeling. "I don't know if I can promise that."

His expression froze. "Then we both head back to the truck."

Part of her wanted to do that, but she remembered Anya Baker's terrified face and Agent Monteith's mangled flesh. She knew how desperately everyone had been chasing Evi1Geni-us for months now with no real progress. And although this wasn't him, Lloyd Zenko was the closest they'd ever come to finding someone who might be able to identify him.

"I'll do as you ask." Her voice shook. "I will stay hidden when you tell me and then go for help if you need it."

His verdant green gaze held hers for a moment as if assessing her veracity. Finally, he nodded. "Okay. Follow me carefully. Step where I step."

She nodded and picked up the walking sticks in one hand. Terrified but determined. "Let's do it."

Shane pulled her hat off her head and stuffed it into her pocket. Then he zipped up the jacket he'd lent her so none of the scarlet of hers was visible. He pulled up her hood giving her a long searching look she couldn't decipher. Then he took a pole from her and used it to test the ground on the other side of the tripwire, presumably for explosives. Satisfied, they gingerly stepped over the boobytrap. She spotted the next one at the same time he raised his hand, signaling her to stop.

They cleared this one carefully too. Now they were only thirty yards from the back of the cabin. Shane indicated right and she followed him, barely breathing as they headed to the neighboring property which looked unoccupied. Unlike Zenko's mom's cabin, no smoke was coming out of the chimney despite the chill in the air. The next cabin over from that had a white van parked in the driveway but no one was visible. Hopefully the owners didn't call the cops if they spotted her and Shane creeping around the woods.

They worked their way through the bush until they stood behind the immediate neighbor's woodshed. Shane eased open the door and they both stepped inside the cramped space that smelled strongly of dry wood and dead mice.

Shane leaned close to her ear and she could feel his warm breath on her cheek. "I figure he wouldn't set boobytraps on the neighbor's property but don't let your guard down and keep your eyes peeled. I want you to tuck yourself into this corner of the shed keeping yourself behind the bulk of the timber in case any bullets start flying. You can see what's happening through that window."

He pointed to a small single-paned window that was covered in a thick layer of dust and cobwebs.

She hated spiders but she'd promised and knew he was doing his best to accommodate her. "Okay."

He nodded, obviously satisfied she'd do what he said. He removed the binoculars. Aimed them at the cabin.

"See anything?" she asked in a whisper.

The world seemed to have gone eerily quiet but maybe that was her imagination.

He grunted. "Nothing." He handed her the binos and pulled his gun from its holster. Her eyes shot to the weapon. Lord, she hated guns.

"I'm going to make my way across to the other side of the cabin and see if I can get a look at the vehicle under that blue tarp." He cupped her chin gently. "Don't go anywhere."

She nodded, too terrified to move but she wouldn't tell him that.

"If it's Zenko's truck I'll give you the thumbs up sign. If you can get a cell signal, call Sloan."

She nodded, leaning the walking sticks against the wood stack and digging through the layers to find her cell. "Shane."

He raised his brows in question.

"Be careful out there."

He gave her a grin. "Always am."

He slipped out and she watched him through the window as he hugged the side of the house. Then he moved at a cautious jog to the Zenko place, splitting his attention between the windows and the ground, presumably looking for more trip wires. He quickly disappeared around the corner of the building.

At the exact moment Shane disappeared from sight, she spotted a guy walking across the dirt driveway in front of the cabin, having obviously come from the Zenko home. She froze as she watched him cut across the yards. Was that Lloyd Zenko? Had he spotted them? Was he escaping?

It didn't look like his DMV photograph but she couldn't really see his features. He was tall and wore a thick black jacket, brown knit hat and dark sunglasses. Something about the way he moved seemed familiar. He kept his head bowed as he quickly strode away. The stranger disappeared behind this neighbor's house. Then she saw Shane giving her the thumbs up through the window.

Damn.

It was Zenko's truck and she was supposed to call Sloan but Shane obviously hadn't seen the other man leaving...

She tried to get Shane's attention but the glass was too dirty and she couldn't risk making a noise. She stepped out of the woodshed and frantically waved but Shane had disappeared again. He had obviously gone to investigate further.

She pulled out her cell and called Sloan, then hesitated, unsure what to do. The stranger was heading toward the white van. Why would he park there? Was he a neighbor?

Was it Zenko?

The call went to voicemail and she hung up, knowing she had to at least get a photo of the license plate of the white van.

It had started to rain again and the damp seeped further into her bones. She ran across the back yard of the neighbor's house, praying no one was home. Then she crept along the wooden siding until she reached the corner.

She pulled up the camera app on her phone and began filming as the van reversed onto the road before speeding away, around the corner and out of sight.

She had to tell Shane. Zenko could be escaping... Or it might be a friend or a relative visiting and not wanting to park out front for whatever reason. She still didn't know what to do but she couldn't simply hide in the woodshed after this development.

Yael jogged back toward the Zenko cabin when she simultaneously became aware of two things. First, the sight of orange flames visible through the cabin windows, and second, the sound of shattering glass nearby.

Dammit.

She stopped and tried Sloan again. This time the ASAC answered with a brisk, "Yes?"

"We're at Zenko's mother's cabin—"

"You're where?" The task force leader's voice rose in a way that made Yael realize the woman had no clue what she was talking about. Shane had lied to her. And if she outed him, he might lose his job.

Yael swallowed the knot in her throat. Took the fall. "I discovered a property owned by Zenko's mother an hour west of Quantico. I persuaded Agent Livingstone to come with me to check it out." Yael rattled off the address from memory. "I think Zenko was here. I think he drove off a few seconds ago. Now I see flames inside the cabin. Please send the local fire service and cops to this address. But tell them to be careful as there are tripwires around the grounds. I'm going to find Agent Livingstone"—and beat him to death with his own walking poles.

"Ms. Brooks—"

"Sorry, the signal is terrible and I'm worried it's going to drop. Please send help. Oh, Zenko is driving away in a white Ford van. I have video of it but couldn't make out the plate. The area is remote and the cops will probably be able to find him if they set up roadblocks ASAP." Yael hung up knowing she was going to get her ass reamed later.

She stuffed the cell in one of the jacket's pockets, ran towards the cabin. She raced to the front door just as Shane stumbled over the threshold carrying a man over his right shoulder, gun in his left hand. He jumped from the top of the porch all the way to the ground and Yael took a step back.

"Let's get out of here. Gas line was severed. I think it's about to blow."

Shane stuffed the weapon in his holster and grabbed her hand and started running.

Despite carrying another man, Shane was still faster than she was. He led them to the property two down and cut in behind the main structure, laying the injured man in the damp grass. Blood soaked the man's chest. The stench of beer was thick on the stranger's breath, even stronger than the odor of smoke that clung to his clothes.

"Is that Lloyd Zenko?" she asked in surprise.

Shane didn't look up as he started first aid. "Yup. Press down hard on this."

Yael forced herself not to balk as he pressed her hands against a wadded tea towel on the man's chest. The sight of blood made her want to curl into a fetal ball but she forced back the feeling and concentrated instead on doing what was needed.

"Shane, I saw someone leave the house. You must have missed him by a split second. He climbed into the white van and drove away. I took a video."

He glanced at her with narrowed eyes. "Fuck. I saw flames through the kitchen door and found this guy on the couch bleeding out. If we'd been ten minutes earlier, we might have got eyes on the UNSUB. Maybe even have ended this thing." Shane rolled Zenko onto his side to check out the exit wound. He swore, then dragged off his shirt. Pressed it to the guy's injury and rolled him onto his back again.

"I called Sloan. Told her where we are and to send backup."

He looked at her then and guilt was written in the shadows of his eyes and the lines around his lips. He opened his mouth but she spoke over him.

"I told her this was my idea and that I persuaded you to come with me."

He pressed his lips together and shook his head. "Appreciate you having my back, but I'll tell her the truth later."

"And make me look like an idiot and a liar? I don't think so." Yael shelved her fury for now. It wasn't the time. "Do you think the guy in the van was Evi1Geni-us?"

The wounded man groaned and opened eyes that were as

brown as her own. He bared his teeth in obvious pain as he stared at her. "Pretty."

She shuddered in revulsion at the reminder of Evi1Geni-us's words to her in Houston.

"Hey, Lloyd. Wanna tell us who this guy is so he can pay for shooting you?" Shane said roughly.

Zenko's eyes cut back to Shane. He reached up and gripped Shane's vest, dragging him closer. "He's…"

A tremendous *whoosh* ripped through the air and heat flashed through the atmosphere. Shane threw himself at her, wrapping his body over hers, forcing her flat against the injured man as he pressed down, covering her, protecting them both from the burning debris Yael could see in her peripheral vision raining down, crashing onto the nearby road.

After a full ten seconds Shane finally let her sit up.

She was breathing hard and shaking in reaction. They held each other's gaze for another breathless moment. Then she glanced at Zenko but the guy had closed his eyes and his mouth had gone slack. He wasn't breathing. Shane checked for a pulse and swore. He sat back on his heels.

"He's dead?"

Shane nodded.

"Shouldn't we try CPR?" It was ironic how much she wanted to save this man. This killer.

"Pretty sure the bullet hit something vital." He caught her eye. "There was a lot of blood inside the cabin. Too much."

The sound of sirens suddenly seemed to be getting closer. Yael staggered to her feet. "Do you think there are people in these other cabins? Could they be injured?"

Shane took a step away from the dead man at their feet. "I suspect they'd have come outside by now if there had been. I'm going to flag down the emergency services before they rush in. I want the bomb squad going over every inch before anyone goes inside."

Yael looked toward the cabin. A section of one wall had

already collapsed and flames were consuming what remained of the roof.

"I doubt any evidence will survive the fire."

"Probably not, especially once the fire service gets their hoses on it." Shane pulled a cell out of his back pocket. "Hand me an evidence bag out of the inside pocket of my jacket, will you?"

Yael did so and watched him slip the phone into the plastic and then back into a pocket in his pants. "Is that Zenko's?"

"Yeah. I found it on the table beside the couch."

A flicker of excitement went through her as surely the cell would contain evidence or clues...but it was difficult to ignore the fact this man had died and she was covered in his blood, or that Shane had been in extreme danger, and it was likely the man calling himself Evi1Geni-us had been so close she could have called out to him.

"I told Sloan to put up roadblocks. Think the cops will catch him?"

Shane shrugged. "You never know. Plenty of bad people have been caught following a routine traffic stop. We might get lucky."

But she could tell from his tone he doubted they'd get lucky this time. The sound of sirens got much louder and he strode into the middle of the road as the first fire truck came into view.

She staggered away from Lloyd Zenko's dead body to brace herself against a nearby tree. Her hands were stained with his blood and she was shivering uncontrollably. She closed her eyes and did her best not to pass out.

13

The fire truck speeding past almost made him piss his pants.

That was a hell of a response time for such a rural area…and now he could hear police sirens joining the fray. *Shit.* Sweat coated his brow and ran down his spine despite the winteriness of the day. He turned off the main road and headed deeper into the boonies.

Lloyd Zenko had wanted more money. He'd known the guy was going to be a problem as soon as the news coverage about Houston exploded across every news channel.

Zenko had been a loser and a grifter his whole life and suddenly he thought he'd found the goose that laid the golden egg. He'd guessed Zenko would come up here to hide out. He'd known about the cabin before he'd hired the bombmaker. And the tracker he'd attached to the asshole's beloved truck had confirmed his suspicions.

Zenko had been asleep, drunk on his couch when he'd arrived. The guy had had a pistol laying on the floor beside him which he'd kicked away before shooting good old Lloyd at pointblank range with a silenced weapon.

It had been a thrill getting the drop on a former soldier, even a crappy one like Zenko.

He checked directions on the maps he'd downloaded onto the cell he'd stolen last night and decided it was time to switch plates again. He drove along a quiet backroad until he found a secluded area and pulled over before quickly replacing the license plates. Then he pulled out some large magnetic decals he'd had made and stuck them on both sides of the van.

The vehicle was a rental but the company who'd rented it probably hadn't even figured it out yet. It was one of many daily transactions and he doubted they'd realize until the Feds started knocking on their doors in about thirty-six hours.

He tapped his fingers on the steering wheel. Did he head back now and switch cars? Or wait until dark as originally planned?

His stomach growled. He hadn't eaten since lunchtime yesterday and he was starving. He'd go find food and then spend some time taking in the local scenery. He'd traveled all over the US but never explored Shenandoah National Park.

Sticking to the plan was the wisest choice. He'd considered every scenario. Planned for every possibility. He always did.

He sighed. What was he going to do with himself in retirement?

He hadn't quite decided yet. Maybe he'd buy a yacht and learn to sail. Maybe he'd start an animal rescue. Anything that was the antithesis of Evi1Geni-us. He thought about the dark-haired woman who was starting to appear in his dreams. He was looking forward to discovering everything there was to know about her.

How much would people pay to watch a long, cunning stalk followed by a slow, painful death?

He grinned.

He was pretty sure he was going to find out.

14

Shane held the door of Building 64 for Yael and they headed to the briefing room. Sloan had ordered an emergency meeting of the task force. Most of the agents who'd traveled to Fayetteville weren't back yet. Some were helping to process Zenko's apartment and secure his electronics. Zenko had let a friend stay at his place while he went away for a few days. The friend had suffered a nasty surprise when he'd left for a lunchtime shift at a bar and had been detained in the parking lot by twenty heavily armed federal agents.

Another Evidence Response Team was at Zenko's family cabin, or what little remained of it.

Sloan walked up to him and Yael, who had fallen asleep on the drive back and looked exhausted. An EMT had cleaned her up but there were still bloodstains on her clothes and a shellshocked expression on her face.

"I don't know whether to throw you two off this team or give you both commendations."

Yael had sent the video of the white van to Ashley Chen earlier and the entire state had set up roadblocks and BOLOs. Unfortunately, they still hadn't located the vehicle or found the killer.

"Please don't blame Ms. Brooks. I was the one who dragged us out there."

Sloan looked from one of them to the other. "Yael said it was her idea and you say it was yours." She held up her hand to stop him from arguing. "Whoever it was—it was damn good work and frankly gave us leads we didn't have before. Plus, you both survived so I don't have to deal with that paperwork. But next time you go off without clearing it with me first, you'll be done working this case." Sloan held his gaze. "Understood?"

He nodded. "Ma'am."

"Are you okay, Yael?" Sloan asked suddenly.

"Yeah. Shaken. Frustrated." Large brown eyes shot to Sloan and her jaw tightened. "If we'd arrived a few minutes earlier, we might have caught EG but I slowed Agent Livingstone down—"

"What?" he cut in. He hadn't realized she was blaming herself for that. "No. Zenko slowed us down by laying boobytraps."

"I was the one who refused to be left alone in the woods."

Sloan cut in. "And you're the one who provided footage of the suspect leaving the scene. You did good work, Yael."

The woman in question didn't look convinced.

He held out the plastic bag with Zenko's cell and Ashley Chen came over and grabbed it. The agents planned to clone it and then have it examined for physical evidence.

Yael swayed on her feet.

"I think I should maybe drive Yael home—"

She shook her head. "If there's a meeting, I don't plan to miss it." Despite her fatigue, her eyes sparked with angry fire.

He nodded.

She was still mad at him. Rightfully so. But they'd followed the evidence and found Zenko. He was kicking himself he'd likely been close to the bastard responsible for Scotty's death but the guy had gotten away. And sure, Zenko had set the explosives, but he'd done it on Evi1Geni-us's instruction. Somehow, Shane didn't figure EG would find it so easy to recruit anyone else to help him, not now that Zenko's death was plastered over every news station in the country. It would be one less worry to deal with.

Alex Parker walked in and immediately came over to Yael's side.

"Are you okay?" He shot Shane a look that promised retribution if she wasn't.

"I'm fine. We almost caught him, Alex." She scrubbed her hands down her face. "Maybe if I'd allowed you to give me firearms training the other day, I could have made him stop."

Shane felt a flicker of resentment that she'd consider taking training from her boss but not him. It was dumb. He was being ridiculous.

"As much as I want you to have a way of defending yourself, I do not want you confronting this guy unless you have to. Shooting a person takes more than pointing a gun at a target and pulling the trigger. Not everyone is comfortable taking a life or hurting others." He squeezed her arm in a way that had Shane grinding his teeth. "Plus, you were up all last night and lack of sleep can affect judgment as much as drugs or alcohol. You want to go home and sit this out?"

Shane hadn't realized Yael hadn't gotten *any* sleep last night. His guilt grew that he'd dragged her into possible danger.

Yael shook her head. "I think Sloan wants to grill us both about what happened and I'd rather get it over with."

Alex frowned. "Sloan will wait if you need rest."

Yael smiled at her boss and Shane was once again struck by how fucking pretty she was.

Not the time. Not the place.

"If you want to stay at our place tonight, Mal has a bed made up. Ashley is staying with us too. I don't know if you know that she and Mal used to work together. I can't guarantee it will be quiet with Georgie teething, but we can provide ear plugs and a secure place to sleep."

Yael laughed, finally, and Shane felt the weight that had been crushing his chest ease a little. He'd promised to protect her and she'd ended up tending a dying man and then getting blasted by an explosion.

"There's no reason to suggest I'm in any more danger than I was this morning, right?"

Alex Parker nodded.

She crossed her arms. "I'll be okay."

"You better be." Alex sent him a look that told Shane who he'd hold responsible if she wasn't.

He nodded back. He had no intention of allowing anything bad to happen to Yael. The sooner they caught this asshole the sooner they could all get back to normal.

Emotion hit him unexpectedly. His mouth flooded with saliva and his throat grew tight. Scotty would still be gone. Montana would still be dead. But he could get back to normal.

The gaping holes left by the loss of his friends and colleagues felt all-encompassing. He doubted the wounds would ever completely heal. He wanted to take a moment alone but there was no time.

Sloan checked her watch and called the meeting to order. The next hour basically consisted of him and Yael being grilled about every detail of what had happened.

When Yael finally finished her account, she looked about ready to fall over.

"Zenko called me pretty." Yael shuddered. "That was almost the last thing he said before he died."

Yael still looked freaked out by the events and Shane wished he'd grabbed another HRT operator or another agent rather than dragging a civilian along for this afternoon's ride. He hadn't expected things to go quite so dramatically sideways.

"You did great work today. None of us expected the UNSUB to go after Zenko," Sloan reassured her.

Ashley spoke up. She'd been working quietly in the background throughout the meeting. "I think I know why. We found communications on the cell that Agent Livingstone retrieved from

Zenko's cabin that suggest Lloyd Zenko decided he hadn't charged EG enough to end up on the FBI's Most Wanted list."

"Zenko was blackmailing EG?" Shane asked. Bold.

"Looks like."

"Which means Zenko either knew who EG was or thought he had a way of giving the FBI information that would lead to his arrest," Alex Parker suggested. "We need to track Zenko's movements, online and real, until we figure out how these two intersected. Did they know each other in real life? Or did EG hire Zenko specifically to set a trap for law enforcement in Houston?"

Alex Parker checked his watch and Shane heard Yael's stomach growl loudly.

"Time to get some rest but I want everyone back here in the morning to discuss next moves," Sloan said abruptly. "State police have BOLOs out on the white van. SSA Randall's team is going over every detail of Lloyd Zenko's life in North Carolina and he plans to courier any electronics here overnight."

Chairs were pushed back.

Alex Parker came over to Yael. "Want me to follow you home?"

"I'll do it." Shane stood. "It's on my way and the least I can do after dragging Yael into the field today the way I did."

"Yael?" Alex insisted.

She thrust her laptop into her bag. "I'll be fine."

Both he and Alex Parker stood staring at her and she looked up with dark shadows under her eyes. "I'm just tired, Alex. Honest."

"I've got this," Shane put in. "I'll pick up some takeout on the way and make sure she eats."

Yael yawned. "Whatever gets you two to stop treating me like a kid."

"Call me if you need anything and don't go anywhere except home," warned Alex.

Yael nodded and Alex headed over to Ashley Chen and the two of them left together.

"Got everything?" Shane asked her.

Yael seemed to slump as she gathered up her belongings. Shane lifted the bag from her shoulder without asking and led the way outside. He knew she wouldn't let him get far with her precious laptop.

Outside it had started to rain. A light mist that soaked everything. His slicker was in the back of his truck and covered in bloodstains.

He needed to call Novak and Jordan and fill them in on more details from tonight's meeting but there was nothing that couldn't wait.

He headed over to his truck which was parked beside Yael's borrowed SUV. "You planning on going anywhere between now and seven o'clock tomorrow morning?"

She shook her head.

He opened his passenger door. "Get in."

She pulled a face, then reluctantly climbed inside. He closed the door and walked around to the driver's side.

Neither of them had eaten all day. He started the truck and reversed, looking over his shoulder. "You like Thai food?"

"I'm not sure I can wait that long. I'll stick a pop tart in the toaster when I get home and then crash."

A *pop tart*?

"May as well eat cardboard. It so happens you're in luck. I ordered online during the meeting. I just need to pick it up."

She shot him a look. "Did you order enough for two?"

He laughed. "I always order enough for two."

He drove to the restaurant which, to his mind, made the best Thai food in the state.

He'd made sure he wasn't followed after leaving the base and left Yael in the locked vehicle and parked directly under the lights outside the restaurant door. Strode inside and grabbed the food. He added a couple of beers to the order. When he got back to the truck, Yael's eyes were closed. He climbed in and she woke with a start. He said nothing, simply propped the bag at her feet. The smell made his mouth water.

They didn't speak on the way to her place and tension built.

She waved to the guard and opened the garage door from a remote stashed in her bag. He pulled up beside Myrtle. Jumped out before Yael could do anything and jogged around to her side, held out his hand for the food as she opened the door to climb out.

His broken arm ached and he reluctantly slid the cast into the sling. He hated anything that reminded him of his weakness but he had to admit it had been a hell of a day despite not being on the team. He and Yael had had all the fun whereas Gold team had spent most of the day in transit and then watching an apartment containing nothing more exciting than a sleeping bartender.

And finding Zenko had beat the hell out of sitting around thinking about Scotty or Montana and how members of HRT weren't nearly as invulnerable as they all liked to believe.

He flexed his arm as he followed Yael to her door. Yup. Broken bones weren't holding him back and soon he'd once again be where he belonged. He ignored the small niggle of regret that he wouldn't have any excuse to spend more time with Yael. He'd get over it.

He watched her unlock the door from the garage to the house and punch in the combination for the alarm. She glanced over her shoulder, seeming to realize he'd seen and filed away the information.

She caught his eye but neither of them commented. She didn't appear to mind him knowing which made him feel guilty all over again. She could always change it.

He watched the garage door lower all the way to the ground, then locked the door behind him after he headed inside the house.

He placed her bag on the kitchen island as Yael fished her cell out of her pocket and plugged it into the charger near the fridge.

His mouth went dry. Despite everything, he felt a driving need to take a quick look at that cell phone. Then maybe he could completely relax around Yael the way he wanted to. Give her the respect she deserved.

"You wanna take a quick shower while I put these in the oven to keep warm?" he asked from behind her.

Neither of them had had the chance to properly wash up since the explosion and they both stank of smoke and their clothes were stained with blood. Although he was so hungry he could gnaw on a table leg, the need to be clean was overwhelming even for him. He would bet money she'd jump at the opportunity.

"Great idea." She cleared her throat which was probably sore from the earlier smoke and the fact she hadn't had much to drink all day. He should have looked out for her better than he had. He'd been so focused on finding Zenko he hadn't been functioning at his best.

"There's a shower in the utility off the kitchen if you want to clean up too. Towels are in the cupboard," she told him softly.

He nodded. "Thanks. I'll take you up on that. I'll put these in the oven then grab my go-bag from my truck. I've got this. You go."

He watched her leave and heard her tread on the stairs. His eyes were dragged reluctantly to her phone. Though he knew even the faint suspicion was ridiculous, it was still theoretically possible that Yael could have texted EG the address of the cabin and then told the killer when it was safe to exit without Shane spotting him.

He knew it was madness and hated the fact he was violating her privacy, but the operator in him couldn't *not* check. He picked up her cell and entered the number he'd seen her input several times today. He checked her call history and thumbed through every messenger app he could find. *Nothing.*

A wave of relief crashed over him followed by a feeling of self-disgust that made his skin crawl. There was no indication Yael was feeding information to EG. There never had been. She'd done amazing things to help find the man who'd killed his best friend. With a sudden rush of clarity, Shane knew that Alex Parker would never have brought her permanently onboard if he had any doubts at all as to Yael's integrity.

"Jackass." He was furious with himself all over again for doubting her and for potentially putting an innocent woman in jeopardy. What a prick.

He needed to double down on making her safety his number one priority. EG had seen her face and even Zenko had seemed to recognize her, suggesting the two criminals had discussed her in some way. He didn't like that realization. He didn't like it at all. He rubbed his forehead and heard the shower go on. It spurred him into action.

Yael headed past the spare room and bathroom, and her as-yet-unpacked office that was waiting on the delivery of new furniture, to her bedroom. She dumped her dirty clothes in a disgusting heap that she'd probably throw in the trash tomorrow. Moments later, she stepped under a welcome spray of hot water.

It should feel weirder having a man in her house while she was naked but Shane Livingstone had proven he was one of the good guys when he'd pulled an injured man out of a burning building even though that man had, in all probability, killed his best friend. And later, with Sloan, he'd tried to take responsibility for lying about the details of today's road trip even though he hadn't had to.

Quickly she washed her hair and soaped her skin, then stood with her head pressed against the cold tile as she waited for the conditioner to work. Was Shane Livingstone only here because of the case? Did he feel guilty about lying to her about what he'd told Sloan? For the fact that they'd ended up in a dangerous situation? Or was his interest far more basic?

She didn't know. Worse, she didn't know what she wanted the answer to be.

She needed to remember that getting involved always ended

in disaster. And getting involved with someone she worked with… Bad idea.

But they wouldn't be working together for long. Even if the task force didn't catch the killer, Shane was only HRT liaison until his arm healed. Then he'd be off, breaking down doors and saving the world once again.

She closed her eyes and the vision of Lloyd Zenko's face twisting in pain as he lay dying from a gunshot wound filled her mind.

She blinked the image away and rinsed her hair under the spray. Turned the temperature to cold to wake herself up before climbing out and wrapping a warm towel around her body and another around her hair. She stepped into her bedroom and decided to pull on her brushed-cotton plaid pjs. They were hardly seductive and sent a clear message she wasn't looking for anything romantic. And this way she could fall straight into bed as soon as they'd eaten.

Her cheeks heated at the thought of falling into bed with Shane Livingstone and she immediately pushed the idea away.

Bad idea. Terrible idea. And one that wouldn't quite quit.

Her stomach gurgled and reminded her exactly how long it had been since she'd last eaten. She towel-dried her hair before dragging a brush through the straggly mess on her head and quickly braiding it. Her reflection in the mirror looked about fifteen.

Fourteen had been a good age. Fifteen had been utter *Hell*.

She ignored the direction her thoughts had taken, turned off the light and headed downstairs.

Shane stood barefoot in her kitchen pulling takeout cartons from the oven with his bare fingers.

"I have oven gloves somewhere—"

"Not a problem."

He'd found cutlery, dishes and had placed an open bottle of beer on the counter. He started digging into the food, as if somehow knowing she wouldn't be able to eat unless he did so first.

She jumped in surprise when he handed her the plate he'd filled. Followed by the beer.

"Thanks."

Her dining table was covered in boxes of books she should donate but couldn't bring herself to part with. Eating in the lounge on the couch felt too relaxed and potentially dangerous. She climbed up on the breakfast stool instead. The food was delicious. Spicy but not too hot.

Shane stood on the kitchen side of the island and ate standing up.

Despite her exhaustion she was painfully aware that the two of them were once again alone in her home. It felt different from Monday when he'd checked her security. Different from the time they spent together on the task force. This felt intimate, more like a friendship, or even a date. Maybe it was because of that fake kiss they'd shared which had felt more authentic than anything she'd experienced. Maybe it was because they'd gone through hell together today.

She liked him and thought he liked her. But maybe that was wishful thinking on her part. That scrappy *desire-to-belong* thing still fighting to stay alive after all the years.

She hadn't realized how hungry she was until she finished the whole plate without saying a word. Shane went back for seconds and she had a little more Pad Thai.

She frowned as something struck her. "Why didn't we hear the shot? Was Zenko bleeding out on the couch for twenty minutes?"

Shane looked up, green eyes narrowed and laser focused. Frowned. "EG must have used some sort of suppressor. Either homemade or the real thing. It is still surprising we didn't hear anything. I didn't even think about it."

Yael took a drink of her beer and dabbed her mouth with a napkin.

His eyes ran over her features and she suddenly regretted that she was in her pjs with no makeup and wet hair. She felt exposed. Raw. Vulnerable. Her usual armor was gone.

"You're good at this, you know," he said suddenly.

She huffed out a laugh. "Hardly."

He came around to her side of the counter and she shifted nervously. "I mean it."

He moved closer, reached out for her plate. Her hands trembled as she handed it over and he was gracious enough to pretend not to notice. He put the plates in the dishwasher and she placed the containers with leftovers in the bag on the counter for him to take with him.

"Keep it," he insisted, washing his hands in the sink. Then drying them.

"Are you sure?"

He smiled as he stepped closer. Took her hands in his. She went to withdraw but he grasped her tight for a moment.

"Yael." He held her until she raised her gaze. "I don't know if it's me who makes you nervous or men in general—and I honestly don't know which I'd hate more."

Her eyes went wide.

Usually, men gave up on her when she didn't fall all over them. Shane seemed to be made of Teflon when it came to dealing with brush offs. Not in a creepy way. In a way that made her think he might genuinely respect her and be interested in who she was beneath the surface.

He squeezed her fingers. "You don't need to be nervous around me, Yael. You can trust me. I promise I'm one of the good guys."

She wanted to believe him but she'd been here before. Maybe not with a rugged HRT operator, but with other men over the years. Men she'd thought might be worth the risk of intimacy. She'd been proven wrong every single time. She tugged her hands away.

"You lied to me today to get what you wanted. How can I trust what you say?"

His eyes widened in surprise. He might be one of the good guys but he'd been happy to use her to further his agenda. She'd almost forgotten about that fact because he'd charmed her with care and attention. She couldn't afford to forget things like that. Manipulation mattered. Then again, so did lying about your real identity.

Her mood took a nosedive—exactly why she tended to avoid getting to know people better. It was a reciprocal process.

"I should have told you the truth about what I'd said to Sloan."

"Yes, you should have."

Would she have gone with him if he'd told her the truth? Probably not. She didn't want to risk her job nor her place on the task force. And she'd have missed out on capturing a video of EG and the vehicle he was driving.

Lines formed between his brows. "I knew Sloan would have made me wait until after they raided the Fayetteville apartment and I didn't want to do that. My instincts were telling me Zenko was at the cabin." His thumb brushed her cheek, making her skin tingle. "And I always trust my instincts. But I put you in danger when I promised I wouldn't. That was wrong. Next time I'll treat you as an equal when making choices about the investigation."

"Next time?" She realized she was staring at his mouth the same time he seemed to realize he was staring at hers.

She swallowed tightly.

He cupped her jaw, his fingers sliding into her wet hair. His deep green eyes were dark with interest.

She was trapped between him, the stool, and the island, except, the problem was not that she was trapped, but rather that she had no desire to escape. Her earlier exhaustion vanished. Her reluctance to get personally involved took wings and headed south for winter.

He slowly leaned toward her and she stopped pretending she somehow wanted to get away. She slipped her hands up and around his neck. He smelled of some sort of fresh pine scent and it must be his soap or shampoo, and reminded her of long-ago holidays in happier times.

He kissed her. She'd expected gentle and coaxing like last time, but this was hot and demanding in a way she'd forgotten a kiss could be. He parted her lips and took the kiss deeper as she raised herself up on tiptoe and strained to get closer.

Lust exploded along her veins and vaporized all the reminders of why she should stay away from this man and men in general. Her tongue delved into his mouth. Tasting him.

Shane Livingstone wasn't going to stick around. He'd told her that from the start. He was a freaking elite operator of one of the premier law enforcement organizations in the world. He was living the dream. They were temporarily working together, nothing more. Under normal circumstances they never should have met. He wasn't someone she'd have to deal with on a daily basis. He was someone she should enjoy as a short, beautiful, no-strings fling.

She kissed him deeper and scraped her teeth over his bottom lip. He groaned, his fingers tightening on her waist.

A shiver of awareness rushed over her. It had been a long time since she'd had sex. The last time had been with a guy from the marketing department of her last job. He'd watched her for a year and she'd finally taken him up on his offer of a drink and, unfortunately, mediocre sex when she'd known she was leaving town. He'd left without a word in the middle of the night and she'd felt dirty and used, even though she'd been glad he'd skulked away.

Now she ran her hands over Shane's shoulders and felt the strong muscles in his back tense to iron beneath her fingers.

His cell phone buzzed in his pants pocket and he broke away. Stood back. "Shit. I didn't mean to do that. Damn. I'm sorry."

A wave of consternation rushed over her. She'd been contemplating sex and he was sorry about a kiss.

He checked his cell and grimaced. "Seems I need to check in with my boss and I know you're exhausted." He cupped her cheek again with his warm palm.

She wanted to kiss his thumb but didn't want to appear desperate. She slid away, wide awake now, pinning what she hoped was a cool smile to her lips. "Forget it. It was just a kiss."

She didn't look away from his gaze and watched as his eyes crinkled at the edges with either confusion or amusement.

"Okay then. Get some rest. I'll pick you up at 0630."

She led the way to the door and made her expression bland as she turned to face him. "Thanks for the ride home and the food," she said. "See you in the morning."

He paused for a moment, then settled for a silent nod and a look she couldn't interpret.

He hesitated as he was about to climb into his truck. "Call me if there are any problems. I'm five minutes away in an emergency."

She smiled brightly and watched him leave, both of them making sure the garage door was fully closed before he drove away.

"Argh." The sound reverberated around the empty garage, Myrtle the only witness to her distress. Yael couldn't believe she'd kissed him *again*.

Humiliation crawled all over her brain. No way in hell would she call Shane Livingstone for help. Ever.

She checked the locks, the alarm and the cameras. Everything was clear. She put the food in the fridge, grabbed her cell and laptop case to drag them upstairs.

She began digging into her data even as her eyelids started to slide closed. Eventually, when she couldn't stay awake any longer, she pushed aside the machine and drew the covers higher.

As her mind drifted, she began to relive that incredible kiss.

In retrospect, she was glad Shane had called a halt to things when he had. It would have been a massive mistake to take things further. But she had the feeling it would have been the sort of massive mistake she'd remember gleefully for the rest of her life.

15

Shane wanted to bounce his head off the steering wheel. He'd known that kiss was a mistake before it had started and yet he'd been unable to resist. So much for his mental fortitude. So much for his indomitable spirit and laser focus. He'd wanted to kiss her and she'd looked like she'd wanted to be kissed, so his libido had knocked aside all the other considerations and just gone for it. And then, afterward, he'd *apologized*.

He blew out a large breath. Totally fucked up.

Yael's coolness at the end there when she'd very politely shown him the door hadn't fooled him one bit. Calling her on it would do absolutely nothing except embarrass them both.

Ass. Hole.

He called Novak as he drove toward his apartment. It was a little after ten and he braced himself, knowing his boss would have expected to hear from him much sooner than this.

"You went after this guy Zenko yourself?" Novak wasted no time with pleasantries.

"We discovered a lead that was close enough to check out. As no one gave *me* the head's up regarding the little trip to Fort Bragg, I figured it wouldn't hurt to take a look."

It was a dig. Shane had not appreciated being left out of that intel until after HRT had already deployed.

"We already had too many people on the ground," Novak grumbled. "The FBI agents from Charlotte could have managed without our dog and pony show turning up. Anyway, you had all the fun. What happened at the cabin?"

"I wrote it all in my report—"

Novak exhaled heavily, sounding tired. "Shane, I don't want to read a fucking report. I want you to tell me what happened."

They were all still suffering the aftershocks of losing Montana and Scotty. Nothing would make things better anytime soon. Maybe that was the real reason Shane had kissed Yael earlier. To forget. And because he'd wanted to. A small pleasure in a sea of pain.

"Fine." Shane gave an exaggerated sigh to lighten the atmosphere as he pulled into the parking lot outside his building. "We drove—"

"We?" Novak demanded.

Shane realized exactly where this was going before it started. "Myself and another member of the task force drove—"

"The computer hacker?"

"Coder." Shane winced as he found himself defending her even though he was now convinced she was perfectly legit.

"Are you saying, you and an unarmed civilian headed off to check out a lead on the whereabouts of an explosives expert who was known to be armed, dangerous and who was most likely responsible for killing one of our own?"

"The plan wasn't to confront Zenko. It was to confirm whether or not the suspect was there." Shane stayed in his truck as he patiently explained exactly what had gone down. His boss was pissed, which Shane understood, but Novak would have done the same thing in his boots.

"We all know how plans can go to shit in the real world," Novak said.

Amen to that.

"Anyway, I left Yael in the neighbor's woodshed in case things went south while I went to find out if it was Zenko's truck hidden under a tarp at the side of the cabin. I planned to verify and then watch from the woods until backup arrived. Trouble was when I went around one side of the house, Yael saw someone else leaving via the front door."

"She see his face?"

"Unfortunately not."

"He see her?"

The idea sent another rush of alarm racing through Shane's veins. "She doesn't think so."

"I hope not. She already has a target on her back."

Shane grunted. He didn't like being reminded of that fact.

"Does she have protection?"

"She has a great security system and security guards at the entrance to her gated community." Shane could almost see Novak curling his lip.

"What about a weapon or training?"

"No. She doesn't like guns." *Fuck. Shit.* He couldn't believe he'd left her there alone when he'd seen what this Evi1Geni-us guy was capable of. The asshole had drilled a hole in a woman's temple for money or fun—or both.

"Okay, boss, look, I get it." He was an idiot. "I'm heading back to her place to sleep on her couch." Shane's stomach churned as he put his truck in gear and began retracing the route he'd just traveled. Why had he left? Because he'd been worried he couldn't control himself. *He*—who was supposedly a master of controlling himself and his actions. It was what the Hostage Rescue Team *did.*

Why had he been turned inside out by a mere kiss? Why had he run?

"I could request a protective detail from HRT. We could give the FNGs some useful real-world experience and at the same time keep her safe."

For some reason Shane hated that idea and knew she would too. "She's not big on people or fuss and I honestly don't think she'd cooperate. I'll drive her to and from work tomorrow and if there's a gap in security, I'll talk to her boss about arranging some supplemental measures."

"Shane…"

Crap. Novak was about to give him a lecture on not getting involved with people from work although he was a fine one to talk—

"Be careful. I've already lost two friends this month and I don't want to lose another. And this UNSUB does not mess around."

The words hit him like a blow to the chest. "I hear you." He checked his mirrors and took a few extra turns because rushing was when people made mistakes. The last thing he wanted to do was lead this freak to Yael's door.

He drove back to the guard post and he'd become such a frequent visitor that whoever was inside didn't even make him slow down or lower his window to gain access.

Tomorrow he'd have a word with their superior but tonight he didn't want to waste time or give anyone a reason to turn him away, especially when Yael might not be too happy to see him.

But he didn't even have to wake her. Earlier, he'd "borrowed" a spare set of keys and a garage door opener he'd found in the utility room. He knew the alarm code.

If it hadn't been so cold out, he might have stretched out on the backseat of the truck but it was below freezing and all he had for warmth was a bloody raincoat.

He sent a text to warn her he was there then let himself into her house, turning off the alarm before re-arming all the exits and entrances.

A few seconds later his phone buzzed and he looked down, expecting a text from Yael to tell him to get lost. Instead, it was Alex Parker.

"Trouble?" the text asked.

Shane thumbed in a reply. *"I'm watching her six from the comfort of the couch."*

"Let me know if you think she needs a full-time bodyguard," Alex replied.

He was shocked that Alex Parker trusted his opinion. And unexpectedly pleased.

"Will do." The thought of other people guarding her darkened Shane's mood, even though Yael's safety was paramount, not his fragile male ego.

They were spending most of their time together anyway so it was hardly putting himself out by doubling as a protection detail. It seemed redundant to involve anyone else when he was right here. He doubted Evi1Geni-us would attack her in her own home but who knew what this psycho was capable of.

There was a short pause in communication followed by, *"She's a loner by habit. Go easy on her."*

What did that mean?

Shane sent the guy a thumbs up emoji because it seemed the most appropriate response and he doubted Alex would reveal any deep dark secrets to a guy he barely knew.

The kitchen was dark but Shane could see perfectly well using the lights from the stove and microwave. The stairwell was in deep shadow and he couldn't hear anyone moving around upstairs. He checked the back deck and there were no footprints in the frost.

But how did he know for sure Yael was actually safely asleep upstairs?

The only way was either to call her and wake her—which would be embarrassing if she decided to ignore it and here he was, hanging out in her house… Instead, he used the skills that the American taxpayer had invested millions to hone to creep upstairs without making a single sound. He saw her easily enough in the glow of her alarm clock. Her computer lay beside her on the duvet and she was fast asleep.

He took a moment to watch her when her guard was down. There was a softness to her features, an innocence in the way her braid fell over her shoulder and her lips parted softly in sleep.

It made him both regret walking away from her earlier and give himself a big pat on the back. As much as he wished he was currently mapping her naked body with his tongue, he sensed that much of her wariness of him, of others in general, stemmed from a core lack of faith in her fellow humans. And getting her into the sack for a sweaty round of sex wouldn't build half as much trust as him backing away—as he was doing now, before heading downstairs to stretch out on her couch.

He placed his SIG on the floor beside him and dragged a blanket off the back of the sofa. Now he hoped Evi1Geni-us made a move on this place. He'd take the fucker down without blinking.

Yael Brooks had proven herself more than capable when it came to computers. Shane was convinced she was the key to tracking down this jackass. He could protect her back in the meantime.

And maybe he was lying to himself a little bit about why he wanted to stay close to her. He could admit to himself now, after reassuring himself she was on their side and then sharing another kiss that had seared the very edges of his being, that his interest might not be strictly one hundred percent professional. And, as long as it didn't get in the way of him tracking down this killer, what did it matter? They were both consenting adults. It was their business.

He lay there staring at the play of moonlight over the ceiling. He hoped he hadn't completely blown his chances with her because getting to know Yael Brooks better was becoming an increasingly enticing prospect.

The image of Grace's weeping face filtered into his mind. *This wasn't that.* And he thought about how Scotty would have liked Yael. Liked the fact she was generally unimpressed by all things macho. Slowly Shane drifted off, thinking about his best friend and some of the good times they'd shared.

Yael's cell started buzzing and she woke to the smell of fresh coffee.

She groggily raised her head. That didn't make any sense. Was Laura here? She knew the code. Or maybe her boss? Although she couldn't imagine Alex Parker letting himself in to brew coffee even if he held a spare key.

She fumbled for the cell before it vibrated itself off the nightstand.

"Okay. Now don't freak out," Shane Livingstone's voice came through the phone *and* the floor.

"What the hell?"

"I'm in your house."

She scrubbed her hand over her weary face.

"And I'm about to bring you breakfast in bed so make yourself decent." He rang off and then she heard footsteps on the stairs. She struggled into a sitting position on the bed.

"What are you doing here?" She glanced at the time. *Five thirty* a.m. She groaned. "In the middle of the night?"

He came through the door wearing the same clothes he'd been wearing when he left last night. He also wore a warm smile. "Sorry, I'm an early riser which is useful in my job but not so great for everyone else." He placed the tray on her lap and leaned over to grab another pillow which he propped behind her shoulders.

She caught the scent of him. Warm skin and that stupid pine deodorant that must contain some sort of narcotic because she was drawn to it like a honeybee to nectar.

"I'm not even going to bother asking how you broke in here this morning."

A smile curled his mouth. "That's good because I didn't actually break in this morning." He took one of the two coffee mugs off of the tray and planted himself beside her feet. She felt the mattress give and concentrated on the breakfast he'd prepared to avoid the intimacy of the moment. Buttered toast with a side of scrambled eggs and a small jar of marmalade on the side that Laura had left behind when she'd stayed here last week.

Yael picked up a piece of toast and took a bite of the salty goodness. She met his gaze. "This is good. Thanks."

Funny, but last night she'd hoped never to see him again because she'd felt embarrassed. Less than eight hours later she was grinning at him like an idiot.

She took a sip of coffee. It was black with sugar. She wondered how he'd figured out how she took it and decided not to ask. He was very observant and crazy smart. She started on the scrambled eggs while they were warm and almost moaned when they melted on her tongue. She didn't know the last time she'd been treated to breakfast in bed. Probably not since she'd been a kid.

His green eyes met hers as he blew on his coffee to cool it down. "I spent the night on the couch."

She almost choked on a piece of toast. "You what?"

"After I left here, I got to thinking about *you know who* and the thought of him breaking in here and finding you alone and unarmed…"

He sounded genuinely worried and a shudder ran through her bones.

"I have security."

He gave her a look.

"Which you somehow bypassed."

He grimaced. The light from the hallway revealed a hint of red in his hair and a slight bump on the bridge of his nose. "I may have borrowed a key and garage door opener after I showered last night—which was wrong of me, but…" He shrugged, looking unrepentant and took another sip of coffee. "Anyway, I texted with Alex Parker when I came back here. Your security system didn't let you down, but I did circumvent it."

She put her fork down. Wrapped her hands around the stoneware mug which was one of her favorites. "You were concerned enough to sleep on my couch."

His hand tightened around his own mug but he didn't answer. His actions told her everything. He had a perfectly nice apartment to sleep in and he hadn't tried to talk his way into her bed. The idea he was genuinely worried raised her own fears. She nibbled on the toast. Wiped the crumbs from her lips.

"You know I have a spare room, right?"

It was an unspoken signal that she forgave him for letting himself in, for kissing her and then leaving.

His smile was self-deprecating. "Yeah, well, I didn't want to totally overstep the boundaries. By the time I turned around last night, I figured you were probably fast asleep. I did send you a text to alert you to what was going on but when you didn't answer I made an executive decision to use the couch."

His expression turned serious. "Plus, I didn't want to scare you or for you to lose sleep worrying about an imminent attack or that I'm some asshole trying to get into your pjs."

"Seriously?" She blew at the steam on her coffee. "You already turned me down."

He blinked in surprise and then something flashed in his gaze that had her blushing. She'd basically confessed she would have slept with him last night if he hadn't put the brakes on. But that didn't mean she couldn't change her mind now.

Her cell chimed at the same time as Shane's and they both checked their screens. Sloan wanted them in early. Then Yael's cell rang again, only this time it was her boss.

"Alex?"

"I need you as soon as you can get here at the Sunset Motel in Ruckersville."

"Why?"

"I'll fill you in when you get here. Bring Livingstone." Alex hung up.

Shane was looking at her expectantly.

"Looks like we're going on another field trip."

16

The Sunset Motel looked exactly as Shane expected it to look. Straggly weeds growing through cracks in the pavement. Two rows of small units facing one another each with a narrow wooden walkway out front. The traffic on the highway was close enough to rattle the dusty windows in their frames and the overhead sign flickered with eternal vacancies.

To save time, Shane had driven his truck again so they didn't have to head back to the FBI Academy grounds to pick up Yael's SUV. Alex Parker had cleared the way with Sloan and Shane had even checked in with Novak. Covering the bases and his ass and reminding everyone he knew how to be a team player.

HRT did not like lone wolves.

Yael once again had her laptop open to do research on the way over. She'd been quiet but not in a resentful way. She obviously wasn't a morning person.

"Figure out what we're doing here?"

Yael frowned. "No. I don't see anything online. If it's a crime, they kept it off the police scanners."

Shane pulled up outside the main office next to a black Audi sports car. Alex Parker stepped out of the reception and they exchanged a look he recognized.

Trouble.

Shane killed the engine and climbed out. Yael didn't wait for him to open her door. She got out, wrapping her leather jacket tighter around herself to help fight off the razor edge of the relentless January wind.

Shane came around to the front of the truck. "What's up?"

"I think I figured out where EG spent the night before last, before he killed Zenko." Alex led them inside the cramped reception area. A woman of South Asian descent stood behind the counter with a worried expression on her face. A small fake Christmas tree sat on the counter in a belated reminder of the festive season. A door that led to a living area was open and a young girl sat mesmerized by cartoons, her small hand digging into a plastic bowl of dry cheerios which crunched noisily between her teeth.

"This is Sunita Cadre. Sunita, these are the experts I told you about. Don't worry. Go ahead and charge the credit card I gave you for all your rooms tonight. This person," he indicated Yael, "will be looking at your computer system and making copies of your reservation list and any security footage for the last few days."

Sunita bit her lip. "I don't want any trouble."

"You won't have any," Alex promised.

Shane flashed his gold FBI shield and Sunita's eyes went huge but then she seemed to relax. The woman nodded, processed Alex's payment, then leaned over and turned off the vacancy sign.

"Did you happen to note any men staying here Tuesday night?" Shane asked.

Sunita frowned. "I'm not sure. We have a man booked into unit eleven for a week. He checked in on Tuesday evening but I haven't seen him yet. My shift normally ends at six p.m.," she explained. "I don't generally run the desk at night but our night-watchman called in sick yesterday morning and couldn't work last night, so I had to take over."

"You spoke to him?"

She shook her head. "He texted me."

Shane got one of those feelings in his gut, one that told him things weren't looking good for the nightwatchman.

"Can I get his name and contact info?" Shane asked. "I'd like to talk to him. And any information you have on all your guests from Tuesday would be greatly appreciated. Thanks."

She pulled the contact information for the nightwatchman from her cell and wrote it on a yellow post-it.

Shane took it and read the name. Wayne Stockwell. "Thank you. We may need to interview you further so if you could remain available?"

Her mouth turned down at the corners and she backed away a step. She must know it wasn't good when the FBI turned up on your doorstep.

"I need to check on my kids." As soon as she'd moved into the next room, she closed the door.

Alex lowered his voice. "Cops found a white van this morning that matched the description you gave from yesterday, burned out on a rural road about two miles from here. They called the Bureau immediately. FBI has an Evidence Response Team retrieving the vehicle and taking it back to Quantico for forensic examination."

Shane knew there was more.

"I got a hit on a cell phone number that bounced off a tower near where the van was dumped and then off another tower here in town about an hour later. The phone went dead shortly after that."

"He walked into town from where he dumped the van." Shane slid his cast into his sling because the sooner his arm healed, the sooner he could strangle the EG with his bare hands.

Alex nodded. "Then presumably removed the sim card and battery and tossed the phone."

"You think he might still be here at the motel?" Shane rested his right hand on his SIG as his eyes shot to the window.

Alex cocked his head. "Only if he's a fool, which would please me greatly. But probably not. The thing is, the cell phone belonged to one Wayne Stockwell."

The missing night manager.

Hence the reason they were here.

The shriek of a child laughing came through the door.

A crinkle formed between Yael's brows as she pulled up a photo of this Stockwell character. "He doesn't have the same physique as EG," she stated.

Shane's brows rose as he stole a glance. EG was lanky whereas this guy was probably three hundred pounds.

"You think EG stayed here Tuesday night on his way to take care of Zenko." Shane exchanged a look with Alex and knew they were thinking the same thing. Either Stockwell was an accomplice or he was another potential victim.

"I don't understand why Zenko wasn't more wary of EG? Why meet at his cabin?" Yael whispered fiercely. "Zenko must have known he was being hired to kill someone. After the explosion he knew how EG made his money."

Details about the gruesome murders had been splashed all over the news. Ironically, it was driving up interest and Shane bet the motherfucker ended up raising his prices for the next auction.

There wasn't going to be another auction if he could help it.

"Zenko didn't necessarily tell EG where he was. The texts from Zenko's phone indicated they were supposed to meet in Ruckersville today," Alex said.

"Maybe that's why Zenko was at the cabin rather than his apartment," Shane added. "But EG tracked him down the same way Yael did."

"EG caught Zenko drunk and unawares and shot him." Alex nodded.

"The guy was paranoid enough to set tripwires around his own house." Yael shuddered.

"Not connected to explosives. I spoke to a bomb tech and they found C-4 hidden in the guy's bedroom but the tripwires went to a simple mechanical bell system to alert him someone was creeping around in the woods."

Relief filled Yael's features and softened her expression. "I guess that's something."

The tripwires had freaked her out. Amongst other things.

"I think Lloyd Zenko seriously underestimated EG and overestimated his own capabilities," Alex added. "He thought his little improvised warning system was enough to protect himself and then he let down his guard and had a few beers. I don't think the two men were friends. Why else would EG park his vehicle a few doors down?"

Shane glanced out the window again. "How can you be so sure EG isn't here now?"

"He's been ahead of us at every turn and, although we are getting closer, I doubt we're that lucky." Alex's expression was bland. "But I did call you for backup—just in case."

Shane frowned. He was the backup. "What about Yael's safety?"

"I have no intention of placing Yael in danger." Alex sent him a long look that suggested he hadn't completely forgiven him for yesterday. Then he nodded to the doorway where the manager had disappeared. "While I was waiting for you to get here, I made sure there weren't any bugging devices on the premises and also checked EG wasn't able to somehow jump onto the motel's surveillance system."

Shane glanced at the camera above the desk facing the door.

Yael gave another visible shudder.

"I have people monitoring communications coming to and from this property and also flying a drone overhead that will warn us if anyone tries to escape out the back. But the family who runs this motel has been doing so for seventeen years. They're hardworking people with no obvious computer skills. Even the Wi-Fi is dubious at best."

Yael sat down in the chair behind the desk. "You want me to

run the images through the facial recognition software at the same time as copying it?"

"Please." Alex nodded.

Yael didn't waste any more time. Her fingers began flying over the keyboard and she connected some sort of external drive to the motel's PC and then opened another window on the monitor and downloaded some piece of software from a USB drive.

Watching her work was a turn on.

Shane stopped watching. "You checked the reservations for Tuesday night?"

Alex nodded. "One of them was made with a credit card number stolen with the same batch as the card EG used to buy the off-the-shelf VPN in Houston. Jason Jones. Unit eleven. It's the farthest unit along on the far side."

Shane checked his weapon. "How many of the other rooms are occupied?"

"Four. There's no one in the adjoining unit."

"You don't want to evacuate the others before we knock on the door of unit eleven?"

"I don't think it's necessary." Alex glanced at the parking lot through the window. "But I brought a handheld radar system with me so we can take a look inside the rooms before we go in."

Shane nodded. "Good idea."

"You and I can check all the units. See if anyone is hunkered down somewhere they aren't supposed to be."

Yael had her head bent over her keyboard completely absorbed in her task.

He headed outside and Alex dug the sophisticated handheld radar out of the bag in the trunk of his Audi. They stood hidden by the truck as they surreptitiously examined each unit in turn and compared it to the register. "All looks exactly the way it should." Shane confirmed. "Unit eleven appears to be empty."

"Let's check it out. I have paper booties and gloves in my car so we don't contaminate the scene should it belong to EG," said Alex.

The hairs on Shane's nape rose. Not a good sign.

Alex headed into the office. He came back with a key on a large clear Perspex keychain.

"Shouldn't we check that for DNA?" asked Shane.

"It's Sunita's master key. She said it never leaves her side."

Alex popped his trunk.

Shane pulled ballistics vests out of his backseat and tossed one to Alex. "Put it on."

Alex's brow rose in amusement as Shane helped himself to gloves and boot covers which he stuffed into his back pocket.

"No trouble at Yael's house last night?"

Shane glanced at the man. "No indication anyone came near the place but the security guards in the gatehouse need to up their game."

Alex nodded thoughtfully.

"Do you really think Yael is in danger?" Shane asked, disquiet filling him at the prospect.

"EG likes to play games and believes he's smarter than the rest of us. He saw her face. He'll be doing everything he can to identify her. The more difficult he finds it, the more intrigued he'll be."

"He did access Yael's machine. Maybe he already knows who she is."

"It's possible but I doubt it. Why give himself away if he'd infiltrated her computer without her realizing?"

Shane shrugged.

"I checked her systems and they were all clean. EG knew where we were going to be and what we'd be searching for. He made it so we focused on trying to save Anya Baker rather than treading more cautiously when, in reality, Anya was already dead. He used our humanity against us." Alex squinted at the sun that was strong despite the low temperature and gathering storm clouds.

"Could someone inside the task force be helping him?"

Alex's gaze sharpened and hooked onto his. "Did you suspect Yael? Is that why you attached yourself to her?"

Shane felt his hackles rise and reminded himself they were on the same team. "My best friend was murdered. I suspect everyone."

Alex slipped a bullet magazine into his back pocket. "Yael has no motive and doesn't like violence. She isn't involved and if you hurt her, I will personally make you wish you'd never left Georgia."

"Well, you can try." Shane sent him a tight smile. "And I have no intention of hurting her. I don't think she's involved." *Not anymore.* "I am concerned about this asshole targeting her though."

"Which is why we need to get on with our jobs." Alex closed his trunk. "How do you want to do this?"

Shane scoffed. "You're asking me now?"

"You're the senior FBI agent on scene," Alex countered.

Shane snorted. "Sure."

He could tell from how Alex Parker handled himself that he was more than capable of doing this alone. Presumably he wanted Shane's legitimacy as well as Yael's computer skills.

"Let's keep it simple to avoid any panic or speculation from the other guests," Shane said. "Stroll up there and check through the window see if we can spot any evidence of explosives—which I highly doubt as it's one entrance in and out and EG murdered his explosives expert. Then we'll knock on the door and pretend to be housekeeping. See if there's any movement inside."

"Sounds good."

"EG has no reason to believe we could locate him this fast," Shane pointed out. "He might be holed up here."

"He knows we're looking for him," Alex argued. "He planned his getaway before he went to Zenko's yesterday. I highly doubt he'd backtrack."

Alex Parker seemed to have a keen appreciation for how someone might cover their tracks.

"You know there are a lot of rumors circulating about you and your time at the CIA, right?" Shane said softly as they walked across the tarmac.

"Rumors? Such as?" Alex asked, checking his own weapon. A M1911 pistol. Nothing fancy but it would definitely get the job done.

"About why you were locked up in that Morocco jail. And what happened when you and Agent Rooney tracked down that serial killer in West Virginia."

Alex shot him a quizzical frown. "What about it?"

Shane watched the guy but Alex didn't give away anything in his manner or his words. Shane would swear the guy didn't have a clue about the speculation that he'd done wet work for the government. Except Shane saw how this man operated. Like a professional. Like a man who was confident he could take care of himself no matter who he was facing.

Shane held Alex's clear gray gaze and then nodded. "You know what, it doesn't matter."

Alex's lips twitched. "You were Special Forces, right?"

"Correct."

"I was infantry."

Shane flashed him a look. He hadn't known that.

"Never had much time for the CIA when I was a soldier." Alex's expression turned pensive. "All these years later, I can't say my opinion has changed."

Shane nodded, no closer to finding the answers regarding the mystery that was Alex Parker than he had been before he'd started probing. But something told him Alex deserved to keep any secrets he held and Shane was fine with that. The fact the man placed such trust in Yael reaffirmed Shane's own conclusions. She was innocent. Whatever she was hiding had nothing to do with this case, but he'd still like to know what it was.

They reached the door to unit eleven and both drew their weapons. Shane peered through the window. The handheld radar told them there was still no one inside but it paid to be cautious. Electronics could be tricked.

Shane had a good view of the inside of the door through a gap in the drapes. "It doesn't look as if it is rigged."

Alex pulled on latex gloves and then knocked. "Housekeeping."

Shane watched for movement through the window.

Nothing stirred. He nodded to Alex who slid the master key into the deadbolt and eased the lock open. He turned the handle and pushed the door wide. The stench hit them immediately.

Shane twisted away and swallowed hard. They both silently kitted up before going inside. The bedroom was empty. The scent of bleach was apparent beneath that of decay. He pushed open the bathroom door and forced back a gag.

Alex didn't flinch.

A body of a man was in the bathtub, his head covered in a transparent plastic bag that was taped tight around his neck. The smell of bleach was even stronger here and it looked as if the killer had sprinkled some over the man's torso. Shane hoped the guy had been dead at the time.

"Wayne Stockwell? The night clerk?"

Alex backed up a step. "Looks like."

They headed outside, closing the door before walking over to a nearby patch of grass to steal a few lungfuls of cold clean air.

"That guy was, what, nineteen?" asked Shane.

Alex stared unseeing into the distance. "Took the job to help pay his way through college."

Shane fixed his gaze on the horizon. "EG is killing anyone who can identify him."

Alex nodded curtly. "I need to call Frazer. See if the profilers can come up with something more solid to go on. You call Sloan and inform her we have yet another crime scene." He paused. "You know, if those rumors were true, these are the sorts of monsters I'd have gone after. Psychopaths like Evi1Geni-us."

Shane nodded. He wouldn't have blamed him one bit. The wind rustled the brown grass as a crow cawed loudly from gnarled branches. The charcoal clouds and nearby woods had an ominous feel now that seeped into Shane's flesh and ran down his spine like a trickle of ice. As if this killer had left a residual malevolence behind that marred the landscape and tainted the very air they breathed.

Yael copied the footage first and made sure she kept the files isolated from her own machine until she could take a deep dive into the metadata. She wouldn't put it past EG to plant some worm or virus in the surveillance images to attempt to gain access to her machine again.

It took much less time to copy than she'd anticipated and then she realized why. The timestamp jumped from Tuesday afternoon, all the way until early this morning.

The bastard had somehow wiped any footage that might have exposed his identity and delayed the cameras from restarting until this morning. She wasn't sure if he'd done it remotely or in person but there was no obvious footage of him.

She leaned back against the chair, frustrated. He seemed to think of everything. She ran the remaining video through a facial recognition program the FBI had access to. It took about twenty minutes, but nothing popped except for an ex-con who'd also checked in Tuesday—the guy was beefy around the shoulders and, she was guesstimating, way shorter than EG. She made a note of the man's name and sent it off to Ashley Chen to follow up.

Yael checked for some sort of cloud backup system but, not surprisingly, there wasn't one. This place ran on too thin profit margins to invest heavily in security. Most people would only ever visit once, on a road trip or just passing through, and there wasn't a lot to steal around here.

Yael searched the motel's computer hard drive and the online trash looking for anything EG may have overlooked. She found absolutely nothing.

Had he been here, in this chair? Or had he accessed the system remotely?

A text pinged her phone. Shane. The words made her stomach roil. The nightwatchman was dead in unit eleven.

Another childish squeal from beyond the glass door made her glance in that direction. A shiver raced over her skin. If Sunita had been the one to check EG into the motel on Tuesday night, she probably wouldn't be alive now. Would he have killed the children too?

The inner door opened and Yael jumped in her seat. *Shit.*

A little girl about four appeared, followed by a toddler waddling along either because of his short legs or the sheer volume of clothes his mother had dressed him in.

"Would you mind watching them in the parking lot for a few moments while I grab my coat and purse?" Sunita asked Yael.

"Sure thing." Yael stood and went to the front door. The kids darted outside and both immediately knelt to play with a couple of kittens who'd streaked across from the opposite side of the complex.

She smiled. They were cute kids and kittens. She hated the fact EG had plied his sick brand of cruelty so close to them.

Yael leaned against the side of the building and glanced across the parking lot to where Shane and Alex both stood talking on their phones.

Shane turned, saw her, and started heading in her direction. He moved with a smooth gait that she couldn't really describe except it was fluid, full of confidence and sexy as hell.

Alex moved in a similar way, she realized, and then she recalled he'd been a decorated soldier before he'd become a highly successful security consultant. Maybe it was a military thing. Or an alpha male thing. Still, her boss didn't make her mouth water the way Shane Livingstone did.

She turned back to the children who were still laughing and squealing with joy as the kittens darted around them begging for food.

She looked up again as Alex and Shane reached the truck and casually tossed their flak jackets into the backseat. Shane caught her staring and raised a brow. She sank her chin deeper into her jacket and watched the kids enjoy their uncomplicated lives.

Sunita came outside carrying a large tote bag. "I'm taking the children to my mother's for a few days. She said she'd watch them for me."

She secured the toddler into his car seat and Alex helped clip in the little girl. Then he took Sunita aside and spoke to her quietly.

The woman gripped his t-shirt and bowed her head against his chest.

He'd obviously told her that he'd found her missing night manager.

Emotion grabbed Yael by the throat.

Had the woman been fond of Wayne Stockwell? Or did she understand how close she'd come to death? Judging from the depth of her sobs, probably both.

Yael looked away and once again caught Shane staring at her with an expression she couldn't decipher. "What?"

"Nothing."

Alex wrapped his arm around Sunita for a long moment, until she was strong enough to push away.

Shane got another phone call and he walked a few feet away before squatting down to play with the kittens who meowed loudly at him, begging for food. Yael would search for some as soon as Sunita left.

The woman wiped her eyes and Alex said quietly, "The FBI will probably need to talk to you again in the next couple of hours."

The medical examiner's vehicle—which looked a lot like a hearse—pulled into the parking lot and Sunita's eyes once again filled with tears. She stared at the black vehicle until it pulled to a stop outside unit eleven. Then she climbed inside her car and drove away.

"You think she's gonna come back?" Yael asked.

"It's her motel. She doesn't have much choice." Alex stood beside Yael as the wind pulled at her hair.

"I don't think I'd be back." Yael grimaced and hugged herself. "There's no way EG could be hiding in her apartment, right?"

"Only if he locked himself in the refrigerator." Alex sent her a glance. "I had the same thought so I talked my way inside earlier —and took a good look around."

"You bought out the entire place for the night?"

Alex shrugged. "I can write it off as a business expense. These people are gonna be hit hard by the news of a murder on their premises. Least I could do."

Her boss was a softy even though he'd never admit it. "Where's the kids' father?"

"He works for an oil company and is currently on a rig in the Gulf."

Yael grimaced. That was not her idea of fun. "Could he be our guy?"

Alex shook his head. He'd obviously checked him out already. "Find anything on the surveillance tapes?"

"Not a lot. Someone deleted most of the video."

Alex swore. "Which makes it nearly impossible to try to track him on traffic cams in the surrounding area as we don't know exactly when he was here and presumably the van had false plates."

"Vehicle Identification Number might yield something useful." Shane joined them having finished his call.

"I can't imagine he owned that van in his real name," Yael argued.

"But every clue we uncover gives us the potential to track him down. He only has to make one mistake and we have his identity. Once we have his real name and his face, he won't be able to hide any longer," said Alex.

"I assume EG didn't bring his own cell with him? Or if he did, he never turned it on?" Shane asked.

"Probably used a burner, before stealing Stockwell's phone," Alex agreed.

A couple of guests were standing around outside their units now obviously drawn by the medical examiner's rig.

One family was loading up to leave.

"I'll go interview them and take their details." Shane shot Yael another look and then headed across the parking lot.

Yael sometimes forgot that before he'd joined HRT he must have been a regular street agent.

Alex cleared his throat and Yael turned around, realizing she was staring after Shane like some besotted teen.

"Where's Wayne Stockwell's car?" Yael asked to deflect attention away from herself and the direction of her thoughts. "Assuming he had one?"

Alex glanced at her as if that was something he hadn't considered yet. Held up his finger. "Good thought."

Alex called Ashley Chen with a request for information on Stockwell's car. Then they looked around the parking lot but there was no brown Buick.

"Presumably EG stole it. Maybe he stashed it somewhere after he killed Stockwell and before he headed to Zenko's place. Perhaps he didn't think we'd be onto him so soon. Or maybe he always planned to torch the van and knew he'd need another getaway vehicle that couldn't immediately be linked to him."

Alex scanned the area and both their gazes landed on a big box store about a half-mile away across some waste ground.

"EG didn't kill Wayne just because he saw his face. He also wanted a vehicle and cell phone and he didn't want to risk drawing attention by stealing another car off the street. He saw the night clerk and decided to use him." Alex's eyes glinted like silver in this light. "Or maybe he planned it all along. Maybe he'd stayed here in the past..."

"We need to check the records," Yael murmured. "Sunita and her kids are lucky to be alive."

Alex nodded. She wondered if he was thinking about Mallory and their baby daughter.

"It's like a giant game of chess." Yael crossed her arms across her chest in an effort to conserve heat. She wasn't sure if she was cold because of the weather or the fact they were hunting such a sadistic killer. Both chilled her to the bone.

"Only we're not allowed to see the board," Alex agreed.

Shane turned toward them. The guy was so handsome. Worse, he seemed like a decent person. Straightforward. Genuine. So competent she wanted to sink into whatever was going on between them and let it take them wherever it wanted to go. It wouldn't last. He'd said as much on the drive home from the bar last Friday night, but that was probably just as well.

Alex followed her stare. "He seems like a good guy from all accounts."

She gave her boss the side-eye. "You checked him out?"

"I check out everybody, Yael." The look he gave her told her there was no point pretending he didn't know the truth about her past. It would insult them both to believe otherwise.

Yael shrugged. "He's not looking for a relationship with someone like me."

"Sometimes people surprise us," Alex said.

"Somehow I doubt it." She huffed out a humorless laugh. "It's not like I was caught shoplifting. My brother shot up our high school and killed ten people." Saying it out loud made her want to turn away and hide.

"Not to mention murdering your parents." Alex's voice was compassionate and tears pricked her eyes.

"Yeah, not to mention that," she acknowledged, feeling hollow and fragile.

"You weren't to blame, Yael."

She looked away. "That's not how a lot of people saw it." She'd been charged as an accessory and had stood trial even though she'd had no knowledge of her brother's plans.

"You were exonerated."

"The jury were split. I almost went to prison for the rest of my life and the press vilified me. The families…" She swallowed the lump in her throat. She understood their pain but they'd never understood hers. "Every time I've let anyone close or tried to settle down, someone figures out my past and the harassment begins all over again."

"I won't let that happen." Alex held her gaze, calmly.

"You won't be able to stop it." She pushed away the feelings of failure and self-pity. "What do you want me to do now?"

"I want you to help me catch this bastard. I want to put him in a place where he can never hurt anyone ever again."

"He always seems one step ahead of us…" Her voice sounded small and she felt a surge of fury that this one man was able to affect her this way. As if he had a right to run roughshod over everyone else and use them like pawns. It wasn't the first time she'd felt this way and the resentment burned a hole through her chest. She hadn't hated like this in a long, long time. It felt good.

It was love that destroyed.

"We're catching up with him." Alex's smile was determined. "He's starting to make mistakes."

Yael thought about Wayne Stockwell, Dave Monteith, and Anya Baker. All the others who'd come before them. All the innocents who'd been murdered to feed one man's greed and corruption. "Let's get there faster, Alex. Let's catch this bastard before he hurts anyone else."

17

A few hours later, Shane pulled up outside the task force building near the FBI's National Academy. Lights were on inside. "I need to go over to the HRT compound. I'll be back in an hour. Will you pass that message on to Sloan for me?"

Yael nodded. She'd been quiet on the drive back. Her cheeks were pale, mouth drawn, eyes tired.

He was thankful she hadn't gotten a look at the dead night clerk. That wasn't an image anyone needed in their brains. He shoved the memory aside and concentrated on his target. Evil-Geni-us. The fucker was going down. It was simply a matter of when and where.

Yael put her hand on the door lever and he caught her arm.

"You did good work again today." She looked like she needed something to believe in and he wished he had more to give her.

"Two murders in two days, not to mention what he did in Houston. It's a lot." She tried to smile but it fell away before she left the cab.

He watched her enter the building. He wasn't worried about her safety here, not really. But Evi1Geni-us was audacious and conceited. Shane wouldn't put anything past the guy. EG could attempt to sneak onto the grounds by impersonating a Marine or an FBI agent. It was important never to drop your guard although, as all the FBI agents were armed, he doubted EG would have the balls to confront them head-on on their home turf. If he did, he wouldn't last long.

After a team from the EGMURD joint task force arrived in Ruckersville he, Yael, and Alex Parker had hit the local Walmart. The store hadn't had any security cameras that covered the farthest corners of the parking lot but Yael had spotted an intersection that might, and sure enough, traffic cams had revealed a small shadowy figure emerging from the wooded area to the west then walking across the far edge of the parking lot in the darkness. Crime scene techs had been sent to look for any obvious clues—like discarded cell phones—but it was a long shot.

The figure had been too indistinct to make out any features—but Evi1Geni-us didn't know that. They might be able to leverage this angle and manipulate the guy into making another mistake.

EG had driven away in Wayne Stockwell's stolen Buick and agents were now trying to trace his route. Even though he'd probably switched out the plates it was a lead that, considering the lengths EG had gone to in an effort to cover his tracks, Shane doubted he'd anticipate they'd get to this quickly.

They'd managed to keep news of the latest murder out of the press for now. Guests who'd asked had been told someone had passed in their room. EG had booked the motel for a week, so unless the guy could access FBI reports, he might not know Wayne Stockwell's body had been found yet.

Shane drove to the HRT compound and headed inside wondering where everyone was. Funny, he hadn't even thought about the guys today. He'd forgotten how good it felt to work a case. When he was eventually forced to leave HRT because he could no longer keep up with the younger guys, going back to being a street agent might not be so bad.

He strode inside the building and spotted Jordan Krychek deep in conversation with the top dog, Daniel Ackers. Shane paused. He wanted to ask them if there were any more details about the air crash that had killed Montana, but Ackers paused in the conversation then put his hand on Jordan's arm, drawing him away. Jordan sent Shane a look over his shoulder and did not look happy.

Shane got the message. Whatever they were talking about, Ackers did not want them to be interrupted. Exactly what had Krychek and Montana been up to in Africa? Shane wanted to know but it was classified way above his pay grade. Even so, the HRT operators who'd worked with Kurt deserved to know exactly what happened to make that aircraft fall out of the sky. So far no one had given them any answers.

He jogged up the stairs to his equipment cage. He stored everything away, turned around and bumped into Will Griffin. A sliver of guilt moved through him. "Hey, man. How's it going?"

Griffin gave him a stiff nod. "Good. Spent the day running drills in the shooting house. Any news on the injury?"

Shane raised his arm and glanced down at the sling that hung uselessly around his neck. "It's fine. I'd be back to work tomorrow if it were up to me." Except, he realized, that was a lie. He wanted to catch this motherfucker first.

Griffin scrubbed a hand through his short black hair. "Shane, I wanted to say something. I know how difficult it is to lose someone you're close to in an unexpected and violent manner." He swallowed loudly. "And then to pretend everything is okay."

They both drew in long breaths.

"And I get you don't want me here, trying to replace your buddy—"

"Hey." Shane grabbed Griffin by both arms and gave him a little shake. "Don't *ever* say that."

Griffin looked startled.

"Don't ever say that," Shane gritted the words out between clenched teeth. "*I* want you here. Scotty wanted you here. We both voted for you to be offered a place on Echo team." Emotion clogged Shane's throat. He should have made more time for the guy but this case was consuming him. "You joined us at a bad time but I don't want you to ever think that you aren't one of us or that I don't want you here. I do." Shane sniffed and pretended he wasn't being slammed by emotions he'd been busy trying to avoid. "I also wish things were different and that me and Scotty were giving you and Kincaid hell, you know?" He squeezed Will Griffin's shoulders one last time and let him go.

Griffin was visibly moved by Shane's words—which he should have spoken as soon as Griffin arrived. He'd been busy wallowing in grief. Scotty would have kicked his ass if he'd been here.

"I know you lost your fiancée. I know you and Hunt Kincaid both almost died trying to save her and his girlfriend"—not to mention hundreds of thousands of innocent lives from a weaponized anthrax threat—"that's why we chose you. Not because of how many pull-ups you can do or how many miles you can run." Body strength mattered but not as much as heart. "We wanted you because you're an asset to this team. Because you're a fucking good agent. And because you care about your teammates. We chose you for your grit and integrity and Scotty would have been damn proud to call you partner."

Griffin looked down at the floor, clearly at a loss for words.

"Right now, it's rough, and to be honest I am so fucking desperate to get this motherfucker I can almost taste it." Shane rubbed his good hand over his face.

Griffin's gaze narrowed and he held Shane's stare. "*You're* my partner now. You need any help, anything at all, you call me. Understand?"

Shane felt tears form in the back of his eyes. He nodded. There was a noise and Hunt Kincaid and Aaron Nash walked noisily around the corner having clearly gotten back from the gym.

"Everything okay?" Kincaid asked, squaring his shoulders as his gaze went warily from his friend to Shane.

And Shane knew he needed to remember he wasn't the only one in pain around here.

Griffin gave a slow smile. "Yeah. Everything's good."

"Damn right, it's good." Or it would be. As soon as he found and stopped Evi1Geni-us from performing more of his heinous crimes. Shane checked his watch. "And now I apologize that I need to bail, but I have to report in to task force headquarters."

"They found this wet wipe yet?" Nash asked stripping off his sweaty shirt.

Nash was one of the more serious members of the unit, a good foil to Cowboy's unrelenting humor. He was clever as hell and liked to think outside the box when they ran into problems.

Shane shook his head. "We're getting closer though. Don't forget to watch each other's backs," he warned. Because EG liked to play games.

"Who's watching yours? The brunette with the impressive rack—"

Shane had Nash in a one-handed grip against the metal of the cage. "A little respect for the lady, please."

Nash grinned and Shane knew he'd fallen for the oldest trick in the book. Insult the girl to find out how a guy really felt about her.

Shane dragged the guy closer and kissed his teammate on the cheek. "And mind your own fucking business." Then he shoved Nash away and the three of them were laughing and joking as Shane slipped out of the room. Time to head back to the task force and the woman who was beginning to sneak beneath his guard and make him forget his primary focus.

He told himself not to let it happen. Knew he was lying to himself.

What would Scotty think of Yael?

Shane felt a smile stretch his lips as he strode along the corridor. Scotty would get a kick out of her. Scotty would tell him to go for it.

But Scotty was dead and Shane needed to find his killer. Maybe then he'd pursue this thing with Yael a little. See if they had anything in common besides physical attraction.

Maybe.

It was almost ten p.m. by the time Yael was finally able to leave task force headquarters. It was dark and a low fog clung close to the ground, making everything a million times spookier than usual—or maybe that was the threatening shadow that seemed to hover over everything lately. The sense of danger tainting the world in a way that made her resent the serial killer even more.

She glanced at Shane who looked calm and competent in the driver's seat and a feeling of dèjá vu stole over her. He'd insisted on staying at her place for another night while EG was still at large. They'd dropped by Shane's apartment to pick up fresh clothes and check his mail, then to a pizza joint to grab dinner before heading to her townhouse.

On top of all the other happenings of today, Alex had traced the sale of the sound recording of Anya Baker's murder online. Sold as a non-fungible token for forty thousand US dollars' worth of crypto. The law was a little murky around NFTs and the dark web in general but paying for a recording of a murder to use as a source of entertainment had to be as illegal as well as it was immoral. It was also possible Evi1Geni-us had arranged to buy the item himself via proxy to jack up the overall value of the merchandise which wasn't uncommon in this emerging market. The buyer was under surveillance from local police in England as were his communications. He'd be detained for questioning as soon as the FBI gave the word.

The FBI's sound technicians were working to obtain a copy to examine in minute detail. Yael had a few possible ideas for getting hold of a copy.

They pulled up at her house and she opened the garage door. Shane drove inside. She needed to add some additional information to her other searches. Then it was simply a question of waiting. Exhausted, she dragged herself out of Shane's truck as he held her door. She unlocked the house, turned off the alarm, and tossed her keys on the kitchen island.

"Go shower," said Shane as he locked everything behind them and re-set the alarm.

"Want one?" The words left her mouth like an invitation and her heart stopped in sudden terror.

Shane's eyes darkened but he took a step away, into the kitchen. "I'll grab one later if that's okay."

Despite their shared kisses, he seemed determined to keep everything professional between them which she appreciated. There were obvious reasons for not getting involved. If things became awkward between them and they still had to work together it would suck. And maybe the attraction was all one sided. She glanced at him.

The guy was good-looking and built. Women probably threw themselves at him on a regular basis.

Did he spend a lot of time apologizing for kissing people or was that just her? Under normal circumstances she doubted Shane Livingstone would look at her twice but he'd assigned himself as some sort of personal bodyguard for this case and they were stuck together.

She headed upstairs feeling more despondent than ever and not sure why. She made sure there were towels in the main bathroom and that the spare bed was made up. The guy didn't need to sleep on the couch and get a crick in his neck in order to babysit her.

She stood at her window and noticed Kevin Karvo standing in his front room looking across at her. He raised his hand. She nodded and closed the blind and the drapes.

Laura was supposed to stay over tomorrow but Yael didn't really want her friend here. Was her reluctance tied to the fact she didn't want to lose this unexpected intimacy with Shane? There was no guarantee Shane would even be here tomorrow night. She had no idea what was going to happen from one day to the next, but she did crave a little mental space. She hadn't been alone in way too long.

She stopped on the landing and texted her friend before she

could think better of it. *"I need to cancel you staying here tomorrow night. Sorry."*

Yael grimaced as she watched the three dots appear and disappear several times. Laura was outgoing and gregarious. Yael wasn't. She was a terrible friend.

Finally, *"How come?"* Then… *"Do you have a date?!!"*

Laura was always urging Yael to go on dates. As if going out for a meal or the movies followed by some vigorous sex would mean Yael finally, magically, had a life worth living. Yael hated herself but she lied. It was the only excuse Laura wouldn't try to bulldozer. *"Yes."*

Even though the date would probably be eating take-out while working the case.

"Who with?" asked Laura.

"No one you know." The woman was exhausting.

Laura sent through a thumbs up and more vegetables which Yael understood but really didn't want to think about.

"Talk soon." She ended the chat because she needed to shower and revive her brain and she needed *food*. Even though it was late, she and Shane planned to go over the records of the ex-con who'd stayed at the motel Tuesday night—the same night as EG had murdered poor Wayne Stockwell. It might be a coincidence, but they couldn't ignore the possible connection no matter how tired they were.

She scrubbed herself clean but didn't wash her hair. After she dried off, she put on her pajamas along with a baggy white hoodie. She brushed her out-of-control hair and tied it back in a scrunchy. She didn't apply any makeup or perfume. She didn't want to send Shane any of the wrong signals. They were work colleagues. He was protecting her from a murderous psychopath, not planning the fine art of seduction. She didn't want any more apologies.

She slipped quietly down the stairs and found him watching the late evening news.

"Anything?" She knew he was looking to see if anyone had

linked the dead nightwatchman to Evi1Geni-us yet. The longer they could hold off, the less worried EG would be that they were onto him, and the more likely he would be to relax and stop looking over his shoulder, which might give them time to catch up.

"Nothing."

The news item changed and she immediately recognized footage from a school shooting.

"Turn it off." The words came out harsher than she'd intended.

Shane flicked the off button and didn't seem to notice her tone. But maybe she was kidding herself because he didn't miss much.

She grabbed two beers from the fridge and offered him one. Their fingers connected and she pretended she didn't feel the flare of electricity arc between them.

He turned to look at a pencil drawing she'd hung on the kitchen wall, indicated it with his beer bottle. "You drew this?"

It was of a tiny, solitary wren. Every feather was lovingly detailed. She nodded. She'd signed it with a faint single "Y" that was barely visible in the bottom right-hand corner.

"It's fantastic. You ever think about selling anything?"

She shrugged, uncomfortable now with the subject. "It's just a hobby."

She sat on a bar stool that Lincoln Frazer had left behind and grabbed a slice of pizza and cupped her hand under it to stop it dripping onto her clothes.

"Ohmygod," she chewed. "This is delicious."

Shane nodded and devoured his own slice. They'd both been working flat-out since before dawn but he didn't look tired.

She noticed someone had been working on an unfinished crossword she and Laura had started last weekend. "You finished the puzzle?" She pulled the newspaper towards her. "'Pictures of Yosemite' is 'cels'? What the hell?"

"Yosemite Sam. The cartoon character."

"I can't believe you knew that."

He shrugged. "We spend a lot of time hanging around or in

transit. Nash always has a crossword going and sometimes we turn it into a contest."

"Shocking," she said dryly.

He stood there grinning in his green utility pants and tight black t-shirt and she swore her mouth started to water for something other than food.

Damn.

She made herself concentrate on the pizza and why he was here. Not to get lucky. To *protect* her. He was stuck here. She needed to get a grip.

"What are you thinking about?"

She jumped. "Nothing."

He grabbed a second slice. "You always this quiet?"

A slight smile tugged her lips. "I better be. I live alone, remember."

He took a large gulp of beer and Yael watched the way the strong muscles in his throat worked. He put the bottle behind him on the counter. "Have you always lived alone or…"

She concentrated on catching a string of melted cheese. She hated talking about herself. People always pushed for a little bit more and a little bit more after that until they had everything and she had nothing but a need to run and hide. "I've had roommates in the past but I didn't particularly enjoy the experience. And, yes, I've always been quiet." She grimaced. "Unless I've had too much to drink and then, apparently, I don't shut up."

His eyes shone with amusement. "That would be something to see."

Except she never had too much to drink nowadays. Not since she'd been young and foolish and had given away her secrets to a boy she'd mistakenly thought would keep them. She gave Shane a smile she hoped didn't reveal her bitterness. "No, it isn't. Really."

"According to my sister I started talking early and never shut up. I think that was written in every report card I ever received. But by the time I joined the Army I finally learned the value of keeping my mouth closed. Scotty always says—" He cut himself off, clearly suffering from raw and terrible grief every time he forgot his friend was gone.

It was devasting to watch.

She needed to stop feeling sorry for herself and her own pathetic hurts. People were dying. She slipped off the stool and went to him. Touched his arm.

"I'm so sorry about your friend." She withdrew her hand and snuggled deeper into the hoodie. "I know I said it before, but I mean it. I know finding this killer is personal to you. I know why. I promise I'll do everything I can to track him down."

"I keep forgetting Scotty is dead," Shane admitted. "I find myself about to text him or think of a joke to share." He turned sideways. "Sometimes I want to tell him how much I enjoy working with you and how smart you are." His voice got deeper. "How beautiful you are."

Her mouth opened in surprise and she looked away.

"And how you don't like anyone noticing the latter." He stood in front of her and her nerves fluttered.

He dipped his head and kissed her. She stood there, desperate to kiss him back like she had yesterday, but…

He pulled away, his eyes dark and intense. "What's wrong?"

She went with honesty. "Yesterday, afterwards, you said you shouldn't have kissed me."

His lips tugged into a rueful smile. "I was trying to do the right thing." He brushed her hair that must have once again escaped its constraints, back behind her ear. "Now I can't even remember why this might be the wrong thing to do."

She didn't either. She rose up on tiptoes, her breasts pressed against his chest as she kissed his mouth. She ran her fingers through his hair, grazing her nails over his scalp.

He pulled her against him and she felt edgy and nervous knowing she wanted him in her bed but worried it wouldn't be worth the fallout.

He pushed aside the pizza box, lifted her up onto the kitchen island despite his cast and stood between her legs. His fingers seemed to quiver as they tightened on her hip and shifted her forward. He slowly unzipped the hoodie and it slipped easily off her shoulders.

She kissed him again, not wanting to think about why they were together or what would happen if it all went wrong. It had been a long time since she'd desired intimacy and now she'd tasted him she couldn't stop craving him. He tasted of musk and pine and warm male skin after a cold day in the sun.

Her fingers ran over his back and she nibbled his lower lip which made him groan and pull her against him.

Heat bloomed over her skin making her hands tremble.

His fingers went to the buttons of her pajama top and he started undoing them one at a time until they were all undone. He slowly swept one edge of the material to one side, then the other, his eyes going wide with appreciation at her breasts. Her nipples were tight with arousal. He shifted lower to take one pink tip in his mouth and she moaned.

The sensations he created made her shudder with desire.

She tugged on his t-shirt and helped ease it over his plaster cast before he trailed his lips over her collarbone and up the tender skin of her throat.

She'd never been with anyone this muscular or toned before and knew he must put hours into honing his body into a weapon of sorts. She was grateful he didn't seem to mind her softer curves because her spin classes and yoga couldn't hope to compete.

But she liked her body. Liked her curves. She loved the feel of his hands gripping her hips possessively, the sensation of his mouth on her skin, and the heat in his eyes as he discovered her.

His tongue circled her nipple until she was squirming and he let go of her hip to touch her body as if all he wanted to do was arouse her until she burned. Then he pushed her gently back and she rested on her elbows, watching him.

His fingers hooked onto her pajama bottoms. "Lift."

"Say please." Her voice didn't wobble for which she was glad.

"Please." He grinned and slowly dragged the soft cotton down her legs. Next thing she knew she was wearing nothing except a thong.

Thankfully the drapes were closed and the lights were dimmed because Yael was not nor had any desire to be an exhibitionist and the idea of stopping this terrified her. She was reserved and slow to trust but somehow, she trusted this guy. Enough to have sex with him anyway. She couldn't imagine him wanting to stick around once the case was over. This might be her one chance to physically enjoy this man.

His gaze was so intense she bit her lip. He kissed her stomach. Then the tattoo of a raven on her hip and the other one of a snake on the inside of her wrist. "I like these."

Of course, he did.

He traced his tongue lower, over her hip bone and she tensed knowing where he was going and wanting him there but being nervous too. She thought about her vibrator upstairs. It had plenty of plus points but had never gone down on her on the kitchen counter—which happened to be a fantasy she'd believed would remain mysterious and unfulfilled.

He draped her legs over his shoulders and dipped his tongue along the side of her barely there panties.

She shot up.

He laughed. "Relax. I want to make you feel good."

What she was feeling wasn't *good.* It was a mix of clawing desire and desperate want. It left *good* in the dust, along with dry white wine and potato chips. This felt like diamonds and fairy dust. Like castles and dreamscapes. It felt *incredible.*

His short hair gleamed and the stubble of his jaw scraped her skin in a way that made her toes curl. Her eyes closed and her mouth opened on a soft gasp. He licked and kissed until she lay prone against the cold marble feeling nothing except the slow drag of his tongue over her most sensitive flesh, wanting nothing except for it to last forever even as she wanted more of him. All of him.

His fingers sank inside her and the need built higher and

higher, sensation coiling like a spring. She wrapped one leg around his neck knowing she was speeding toward climax faster than she'd ever gotten there before.

He ignored her not so subtle urging and took his time.

"Shane." She didn't beg. She didn't remember ever wanting this desperately in the past. Sex was usually fast fumbles in the dark with people she planned to never see again. Right now, she wanted this man inside her more than she'd ever wanted anything in her entire adult life.

His tongue pressed flat against her clit and her world exploded into a million pieces of light that shattered and sparkled. A shudder of pleasure ripped through her as she cried out.

He lay his rough cheek against her stomach as she slowly spun back to earth.

She squeezed him with her legs and stroked his short hair. "Shane."

"Just give me a moment. I'm trying to be a gentleman about this. You've had a tough day and not a lot of sleep recently. I'm looking for the strength to walk away without doing something you might regret tomorrow."

Her heart gave a little flutter. A warning shot across the bow. This man had lost so much and right now he needed her as much as she needed him.

"I don't plan to regret anything," she said gruffly. "Not after the last few weeks. Life's too short."

He tensed at her words and she thought he was going to pull away again.

18

People didn't live forever and wasting opportunities like this topped the stupid list. Yael's words reminded him he'd lost two people he cared about in the last two weeks.

And, if he was honest with himself, he'd never been as desperate to get inside someone as he was to get inside Yael right now. Making her come had made him dizzy with lust. She'd turned him on with her mix of insecurity and wanton enjoyment. Despite everything, she'd trusted him to make her feel good. To get her to that place they both wanted to go.

A lot of the women he'd dated lately treated sex like a series of expected choreographed moves that they'd read in a magazine or seen in a TV show. More than one had asked him to handcuff her to the bedposts, which he could deal with as long as they had their own fluffy cuffs and didn't expect to use his.

Nothing seemed choreographed or planned with this woman. She'd obviously assumed that coming downstairs in her plaid pajamas would be some kind of turn off, but apparently, he had some sort of previously unknown LL Bean fetish.

They worked together but they were not coworkers.

A relationship wasn't against any rules.

Soon he'd be going back to the team and he'd probably lose

the opportunity to be with this woman—and he didn't like that thought.

She intrigued him.

And if he was being a little disingenuous about why he'd attached himself to her in the first place? His concerns had proven unfounded and he knew they were on the same page about catching this killer. And he certainly wasn't faking his attraction for her. He was so hard even his head hurt. And she knew he wasn't interested in anything long term.

She took the matter out of his hands by sliding off the counter and wrapping her pajama top tight around herself. Disappointment flashed through him for a moment, before she grabbed his good hand and tugged him to follow her up the stairs to her bedroom. He went willingly.

Her bed had a purple satin duvet and mauve sheets. There was a large cream armchair in one corner with a reading lamp and an ereader on a small side table. She went over to the drapes to close a narrow gap in the material.

He followed her across the room and when she turned around, he stopped her, pressed her up against the covered glass and kissed her deeply.

She obviously had no idea what she did to him with her little tattoos and the totally unexpected red fucking thong. She was like his favorite Christmas gift and he wanted to unwrap her over and over again.

She sank her fingers into his hair and he hoisted her higher until her legs were around his hips.

"Your arm," she protested.

"Is fine." He turned them toward the bed and came down on top of her. The room was dark except for the light from the hallway which was more than enough to see the heat in her gaze. He pulled back and removed his SIG and Glock from their holsters and placed them on the nightstand.

She struggled to sit up and opened the drawer. He placed both weapons out of sight and she relaxed back onto the covers again.

He tossed his wallet on the table, grateful he always carried condoms for survival purposes and also because sometimes men were weak when it came to the opportunity to get naked and lucky. As she'd said, occasionally his job was lonely as fuck.

It had been a long time for him.

He'd been caught up with work and avoiding anything that smelled even vaguely like commitment.

But, really, no one lived forever and Grace's tears were proof of that.

Emotion clogged his throat and he didn't want to think about his dead friend. He wanted to think about nothing except burying himself inside this woman with her beautiful brown eyes full of shadows and secrets.

Yael's gaze followed the movement of his hands as he slowly unbuckled his belt and stripped off his boots and pants.

The appreciation in her gaze almost made him blush, but he was more interested in her body. She had the most mouth-watering curves that he wanted to spend all night exploring.

He sank down onto the bed and felt the mattress give. He kissed her mouth and she released a sigh. Then he moved lower, careful not to catch her with the rough edge of the cast on his left arm.

His broken bones ached a little. Enough to remind him he probably needed to take a little more care of his injury, but not for the next hour or so.

She reached out and ran her hands over his chest and shoulders. "You must work out every day."

"Pretty much. It's part of the job."

Her skin was pale but her cheeks were flushed and her eyes were wide as she took him in. The fact she liked his body almost made the brutal workouts worth it. Not so much the gym—but the assault courses and close quarters combat and climbing and general dangling on a rope from a helicopter wearing fifty pounds of gear. That was the incentive to maintain his upper body strength. It was also the main reason Novak had pulled him off the team.

The team was the last thing on his mind right now.

Yael's fingers left a trail of arousal in their wake until every inch of him was on fire. She wrapped her hand around him and sweat burst from his pores.

He caught her wrist. "Wait."

Her brows rose in surprise.

"I want to make you feel good," he said.

"I already feel good." She laughed and the low sound sent a ripple of something that felt a lot like tenderness through him.

He moved so he lay alongside her. "Again."

"Again?" She sounded dubious.

He kissed her mouth. "Again."

He reached up and released her hair. Spread the black mass over the pillow. He nuzzled her neck. "You always smell incredible."

He felt her smile. Why that made him feel good he didn't know. She was wary of men and he figured some of her experiences hadn't been great. He wanted to replace those memories with something good. Keep up HRT's reputation for excellence.

She stroked her hands over his shoulders and pecs. He made his way down her body tasting every inch and finally removing that last tiny scrap of clothing. Her legs were long and her toenails were painted a soft pink that he'd never have predicted.

He tasted her breasts again, unable to resist.

Her fingers dug into his scalp impatiently. "Do you have a condom?"

He couldn't wait either. He winced as he moved up the bed to grab one out of his wallet.

Yael caught his look of pain and her expression sobered. "Are you okay?"

Leaning on his good arm he found the condom, tore it open with his teeth and she helped him quickly put it on. He was better than okay. He was sublime.

He moved between her legs and she guided him to her. She wrapped one knee around his thigh and he pushed inside.

She gasped and his heart hammered as they held each other's gaze for a wondrous hot moment.

He moved, then pushed against her again, and again. She clung to him so tightly and they fit together so perfectly he couldn't think straight. It was exquisite torture as he moved faster and faster and she matched him, her fingers digging sharply into the channel of his spine and then lower as she grabbed his ass which would have made him smile if he hadn't been so focused on her.

They strained against one another, over and over until finally she arched up off the bed and closed her eyes as she cried out.

But his own control slipped and he thrust home one more time as his climax rocketed through his entire body searing his brain in a white haze of pleasure.

When he could breathe again, he realized he'd collapsed on her and she probably couldn't breathe. He shifted his weight and her arms tightened briefly before letting go.

He climbed out of bed and went to the bathroom, getting rid of the condom.

When he came back Yael was curled up under the covers watching him with big eyes.

"Want me to sleep in the other room?" he asked softly.

She shook her head.

That was all the permission he needed.

He flicked off the hall light and climbed into bed. Lay on his back because of his stupid cast and pulled her against him. She was warm. Her cheek rested on his chest, her leg hooked over his thigh. Her skin was soft as velvet and blew his mind.

That had been spectacular sex. He wondered if she'd enjoyed it as much as he had or if he'd added to her list of disappointments.

His good arm tightened around her and she snuggled closer, her scent filling his senses. He felt her pulse slow and her breath deepen. He drifted off slowly, wanting round two but knowing they both needed sleep.

Yael slipped from beneath the covers and used the bathroom. That had been the most incredible sex of her life but she had no intention of mentioning that to Shane. She suspected sex was always like that for him. Energetic, sweaty, *intense*—with women, as he'd pointed out in one of their first conversations, always wanting more from him than he was willing to give. She'd known he'd ruin her for anyone else but she hadn't known how deeply being with him would affect her. How desperately she'd want more of him…

Pathetic.

Just as predicted.

She didn't want to wake him so she grabbed her pajama top off the floor and crept downstairs to put away the pizza and set up that internet search for the convicted felon, which she'd meant to do before falling asleep.

It wasn't what she wanted to do. What she wanted to do was have another unforgettable round of sex with Shane Livingstone but she didn't want to come across as too clingy or demanding. She didn't want to assume anything more than them having a one-off sexual escapade, otherwise she risked setting herself up for disappointment.

They still had to work together and she didn't want her emotions trashed.

She glanced at the clock on the stove. Three a.m. She shivered and stuffed the pizza box into her refrigerator. Then she dragged her laptop onto the counter and plugged it in, turning it on and quickly setting up the web crawler searches she'd meant to initiate earlier.

A noise on the stairs had her looking up.

Shane stood in the shadows wearing a pair of boxers and nothing else. "You okay?"

Her mouth went dry at the sight of him. She nodded mutely. He came to stand behind her and the feel of him hard against her backside had her closing her eyes with delicious want.

His hand slipped under her shirt and cupped her breast. "Finished?"

Again, she nodded mutely.

He closed the laptop with his other hand.

She leaned her head back and his teeth sank gently into the sensitive flesh where her neck met her shoulder. His large hand spanned her stomach, then slid lower. She moaned as he sank his fingers inside her.

A shiver ran over her shoulders and down her spine to the tips of her toes. He withdrew slowly. She turned around and found his eyes intent on hers in the ambient kitchen light.

"I woke up because I was hungry."

She blinked in surprise and expected him to step away to grab some food. Instead, he bent and suddenly she was upside down with her butt exposed as she was carried up the stairs. She squeaked.

He laid her carefully on the bed and came down beside her, pushing her hair back as he stared down into her eyes.

"Guess what I was hungry for?" He smiled slowly, that southern drawl making a rare appearance and curling her toes.

Her heart hammered. "Pizza?"

He chuckled and she felt the sensation reverberate through her entire body.

"Nuh huh." He leaned down and kissed her. "You."

19

Shane sipped his coffee and watched Yael as she peered intently at her computer screen. She hadn't looked at him since they'd arrived at task force headquarters at 0700 this morning.

He wasn't sure if she regretted last night or was having second thoughts about him in general. Or if she was trying to keep their private life separate from work, which he was all for, naturally.

He wasn't sure what he was feeling but whatever it was felt intense, like a HALO jump at night, or plunging forty feet off an old freighter into the James River. The sex had been fantastic but the personal connection…that had felt precious and at the same time fragile. It had been a long time since he'd felt so in tune with anyone outside of HRT. However, he didn't spend a lot of time staring at his teammates while they slept, or wishing they'd wake up so he could make love to them one more time before they had to get to work.

Suddenly Yael looked up and frowned when she caught him staring at her. "I think I've found something."

He strode over along with Alex Parker and Ashley Chen. He leaned over Yael's shoulder and noticed the look Alex shot him.

Did Yael's boss know what they'd done last night?

Shane clenched his jaw. He knew he shouldn't dwell on how incredible last night had been, or whether or not it had been a good idea. Regardless, it was their business and no one else's.

Yael pointed to a second larger screen that someone, probably Ashley, had set up on the desk.

"A few days ago, I set up a web crawler search to look for some of the script that Evi1Geni-us used to hack my feed."

"What did you find?" Alex asked.

Yael dragged her fingers through her hair and Shane remembered how she'd done the same to him last night before pulling him close... And maybe it *had* been a bad idea to sleep together because now his focus was split when he needed to concentrate on why he was really here. To find Scotty's killer.

"At first, there were too many hits. So I went through some of the data we captured during his previous webcasts on the dark web and I also," she cleared her throat, "spent a bit of time this morning examining the sound recording EG sold as an NFT. The buyer loaded it to a private chat room he shared with a bunch of his friends. I sent a copy to the FBI techs. Anyway, these losers appear to be a group of incels who think Anya got what she deserved. I want them to suffer every bit as much as she did." Yael's lip curled in fury.

Atta girl.

The idea grown men would get a thrill out of listening to the soundtrack of Anya Baker's murder repulsed him.

He was now convinced that Yael was the kind of person who'd pursue these suspects to the end of the cyberworld while he and the rest of HRT were happy to follow through in the physical realm. But he didn't like the fact that she'd exposed herself to that kind of toxic masculinity or that she could be in physical danger if they found out what she was doing.

"I isolated a little more code and re-ran the searches." She showed them a list that looked freaking long to Shane.

"It was first developed by a tech company in Silicon Valley five years ago as part of their firmware."

"I'm not sure how this helps," Ashley said uncertainly.

Alex watched quietly as Yael explained further. His faith in his employee was obvious.

"I tracked down all the companies that now use the code in their set up. Turns out it's for corporate security and alarm systems. Expensive top-end gear and software, with a lot of clients."

Shane crossed his arms.

"I crosschecked the dates and locations of the Evi1Geni-us abductions with when a company installed this security system."

"Smart." Shane praised.

Alex smiled.

"I didn't get a match."

Except from the way Yael grinned he suspected she'd found something.

"However, when I ah, *delved* into when client companies requested maintenance or some sort of onsite upgrade of the security system, I found a positive correlation between one individual's activity, including in Houston where a telecommunications giant insisted on doing an upgrade over the holiday period when their main headquarters was essentially closed." She pressed a key and pulled up what looked like an HR file and a driver's license for one Eric Antony Pierce. "This guy."

Shane stared hard at the man in the photograph, cataloguing the details. Good-looking with a narrow face and sharp features. 5′11. Blue eyes. Black hair.

Based in Charlotte, North Carolina.

Was this the motherfucker who'd killed his best friend?

Ashley Chen smiled. "That is good work, Yael." She stood, her fingers gripping the tablet she carried. "I'll tell Sloan. Let's get a team on this guy immediately."

Much to Alex's disgust and Yael's relief, they'd been ordered to sit this one out. They'd headed to Cramer, Parker & Gray's newly finished satellite office at their Quantico compound and hacked into the surveillance feed of a coffeeshop across the street from Eric Pierce's place of work.

It was now four forty-five p.m. According to Pierce's manager he was currently out on a local job and expected back at the office any moment prior to being finished for the day.

FBI agents from the Charlotte Field Office were inside the building, posing as employees and staked out around the complex. The tension was so high Yael felt it choking her despite using her best breathing techniques taken from her online yoga classes to calm herself.

There was always a chance one of Pierce's coworkers would reach out to warn him.

"I wish they'd allowed me to search his house before picking him up." Alex frowned in a rare show of impatience. Baby Georgie was being bounced gently on his knee as she started to fuss. Alex and Mallory employed a part-time nanny, but the young woman had class on Friday afternoons so the couple took turns entertaining their daughter or used the FBI Academy daycare.

Sloan was worried about the potential threat of explosives even though it seemed unlikely in the man's own home. Ashley Chen's fiancé, Lucas Randall, was in charge of this arrest with HRT providing backup as well as surveilling the guy's modest house in case Pierce had ditched work and headed straight home.

HRT were preparing to raid the place as soon as Pierce was arrested and bomb techs declared it safe.

Shane was in Charlotte.

Yael tried not to think about him, nor about last night. Tried harder not to worry about him.

He was acting as an observer and liaising between HRT and the task force, which was his job. Yael hated the fact that she missed him. Hated the fact that she didn't know what would happen between them when this op was over and hated the fact that she wanted anything to happen at all.

"Get a move on already." Laura stood and rolled her shoulders, flicked her blonde hair over one shoulder and checked her watch.

Tim sat beside her. Quiet as always.

"Where is this guy?" Yael grouched. She grabbed a glass of water. Paced as she sipped.

"There." Alex pointed to a figure on the screen who was crossing the road and heading toward the main doors.

Suddenly there was chatter on other feeds which linked to the FBI Charlotte's Violent Criminal Apprehension Squad, the Crisis Negotiation Unit, and the Tactical Operation Center.

Yael gnawed her lip as agents swarmed out of nowhere.

Pierce froze, then reached inside his jacket. He looked as if he was going for a gun and a blast sounded along the airwaves as one of the FBI agents shot the suspect. Innocent people who'd been going about their business paused, looking shocked and startled. One woman on the sidewalk drew up short, gaping in fear.

The suspect dropped to the ground and planted his hands on the sidewalk. His gun skittered across the concrete. Yael heard agents yell at Pierce to lie down on the ground and watched them cuff him even though he was bleeding. She watched them check his face to make sure he was the right guy. And then give the affirmative that they had Eric Pierce in custody.

An ambulance sped into frame and cut off their view.

Almost immediately Pierce was on a gurney with two FBI agents and an EMT climbing into the back with him. The vehicle sped away, presumably to the nearest trauma center.

Yael released a lungful of air. "Wow, that was over fast."

"Reminds me of some of my dates." Laura snorted. "All the buildup and promise of excitement, and over in under twenty seconds flat."

"You need to date better men," Alex stated dryly.

Tim sniggered quietly.

Laura laughed. "Most of the best ones are taken, Alex. We single ladies have to make the best of what we can get."

She looked gleeful though and held her hand up to high five them all. "Good work, guys. You did it. You helped capture him. Now we can all sleep better at night."

Yael slapped her hand. "You helped too. False modesty does not become you."

"I'm not the one who figured out his identity, my love. That was all you." Laura flashed her lashes at Yael and smiled.

The pressure in Yael's chest eased a little. That had been her and it felt good.

Alex called Ashley Chen who was with the Crisis Negotiation Unit. "You're sure it's Pierce? Is he going to make it?" An intent look came over his features. "If he survives, do you plan to keep him down there or bring him back here?" Whatever she told him made his eyes gleam. "Great."

He hung up. "It's definitely Pierce. She has no idea of his injuries or prognosis but I hope he survives. One bullet isn't enough for the likes of him."

Yael crossed her arms. She couldn't agree more and yet she'd never enjoyed the idea of retribution. Probably because sometimes innocents got caught in the crossfire.

"Agents are going to secure electronics from his house before the Evidence Response Team gets in there, to courier them back to Quantico with Shane Livingstone. Tomorrow morning we'll go through them at task force headquarters."

Yael blew out a massive breath. They'd waited all day to watch this arrest. Alex had worked on this case for well over a year. The fact it was over so suddenly felt anticlimactic and weird.

Laura stood and helped herself to a donut that was left over from the morning. Yael needed to figure out how to instigate a healthy food policy here because no one else ever seemed to gain weight from the overload of carbs, but she stacked on five pounds just looking at it.

Laura wiped sugar off her lips and yawned. "I'm going to call my date and cancel. In case anything comes up that requires my amazing skills or talent."

"Don't." Alex checked his own watch. "I'm about to head out and pick up Mal before this little beauty starts hollering for her dinner." He looked at Yael. "I doubt there'll be anything for us to do until tomorrow morning so you may as well get some rest. And Ashley and I can handle Pierce's electronics tomorrow if you guys have plans for the weekend."

Laura rolled her eyes. "None of us would leave the boss to do all the work and you know it."

"I'm not busy," said Tim. He was quiet and shy. Yael had the feeling he had a crush on Laura but figured the other woman was way out of his league.

"I don't mind doing the work myself," Alex insisted.

"And that's why we don't mind helping," Yael told him with a grin.

"I'm down here now and, unless my date decides to whisk me off to Paris for dinner, I'll be at task force headquarters in the morning." Laura checked her nails.

Alex put Georgina on his shoulder. "Last date I had with Mal was before this one was born—unless you count having to attend the senator's black tie Christmas thing." He shuddered.

Laura pointed her finger at him. "Do the Paris thing. You have the company jet."

Alex smiled. "Mal's not into grand gestures."

Laura snorted. "Then maybe she needs to date better men."

"Touché." Alex smiled. "But there isn't a man alive worthy of Mallory Rooney."

Tears pricked Yael's eyes. "Take her on a date where you first met."

He grimaced. "Ironically that would be the FBI's Charlotte Field Office."

"Definitely not there." Laura sat forward. "Where was your first proper date?"

He pulled another face. "DC." Georgina started to cry and Alex snuggled her into his neck and made her giggle by blowing raspberries. Then he stood and maneuvered her nonstop-action arms and legs into her onesie coat and strapped her wiggling form into her car seat.

"There's always the Caribbean," Laura told him sagely. "Or NYC. Dinner and a show?"

"Maybe when I know for sure this is over." He lifted Georgina's car seat easily and gave them all an easy grin.

As soon as he left, Laura raised her brows and released a massive sigh. "Why aren't there more Alex Parkers to go around?"

Yael smiled. The guy was a dream but so was...she snapped out of her reverie. She turned to her friend. "You know, if you do want to stay with me overnight it's okay."

"No way." Laura raised her hands. "I already booked into a nice hotel. I am not getting in the way of your love life. This is the first time you've even thought about going on a date since I met you."

"It's not really a date." Yael shut down the computer. The fact she'd lied about having plans seemed underhanded now. After all, Laura had helped her move and was her closest friend.

Shane and his band of HRT brothers flashed into her mind. When they went their separate ways, he'd still have all his buddies. She mustn't forget to treat her friends with the respect they deserved whatever else was going on in her world. Still, the need for peace and quiet called to her.

"Who is it anyway?" asked Laura archly.

Tim eavesdropped unabashedly while straightening the office chairs.

"No one you know." Yael busied herself by turning off the PC which also killed all the background chatter and cut the cord to the FBI and, inadvertently, her immediate connection to Shane.

Alex liked the computers to be powered off unless one of them was there or running something specific so that they could monitor everything in real time. She cleared her throat. "Actually, it probably won't happen now."

Instead of looking annoyed, Laura grinned. "It's that stud from the bar last week. The HRT operator who was all over you in Houston. I knew it."

"He was not all over me." *Jeez.* Yael couldn't believe the way her friend twisted things.

"Please." Laura kissed her cheek, her lips cool against Yael's hot skin. "Alex said Livingstone would be back in town later tonight. I'm not going to risk spoiling a late-night bootie call because you got cold feet. The company is paying for my hotel so it's no biggie."

Tim stared at them intently. He pulled a self-conscious face when she caught his gaze.

Laura grabbed her purse and pulled out a deep red lipstick using a compact mirror to apply it perfectly. Yael realized how incredibly gorgeous and put together her friend always looked. She was wearing a cream satin shirt over a lacy cream camisole. She unbuttoned another button and swapped out her stud earrings for some dangly ones that sparkled in the overhead lights. Then she gave herself a spritz of perfume from a small bottle in her bag and fluffed her hair.

"How do I look?"

"Like a freaking movie star." Yael looked down at her own long-sleeved *Cure* t-shirt and blue jeans. She wondered what Shane saw in her beside the obvious.

Laura lifted her chin and smiled into her eyes. "So do you, Yael. You are gorgeous and smart and cool as fuck with your shiny hair and pouty lips and cool tats and 'stay the hell away from me' vibe. Now get home and slip into something sexy and text your federal stud muffin to pop by when he gets back later. Make him understand he's one lucky bastard that you even deign to let him in the door."

Yael laughed but the idea made her mouth go dry. What if he wasn't interested in seeing her again? She'd be devastated. "I wouldn't have the nerve."

Laura shook her fist at her. "I see I still have work to do on you. Not to worry. I'm up to the challenge."

She gathered her things. "Come on, Tim. I'll give you a ride to the hotel."

"You have fun tonight." Yael gathered all the cups in the room and stacked them in the dishwasher. When she turned around Laura and Tim were on their way out of the room—Laura threw her a sly smile and a casual wave.

Yael grabbed her jacket off the back of a chair and waved to Jack Reilly.

"Night, Jack." He was the last person in the building, working in one of the glass offices. He waved back and checked his watch in surprise. He ran the personal protection side of the business which was transitioning fully to this site in the next six months.

Yael picked up her cell and checked for messages. Her heart gave a stumble when she saw that she had one from Shane that was a simple thumbs up.

She frowned. Then she realized he'd replied to a message from her that told him to "pop by later."

Mortification hit her in a wave and then annoyance and then embarrassed amusement. She exhaled loudly.

"You good?" Jack was putting on his jacket and turning off all the lights.

"Yeah. You know. Just Laura." Those words were enough and Jack laughed.

"Night." Yael headed outside into the fresh January evening. Maybe she should take a few life lessons from Laura. After all, Yael was pretty sure Shane had said yes to coming over later. And while they might not be dating, she liked his company and she really liked the sex.

Plus, she wanted to know what had happened today. And,

ironically, seeing him helped her to forget the evil and horrors that existed in the world.

Either way, it was too late to admit to him that she hadn't been the one to send that text. Laura might have overstepped but Yael knew she cared about her. She'd figure it all out later but right now she was excited at the prospect of seeing Shane again.

20

Shane sat in a surveillance van with two TacOps agents from the FBI's highly secretive "the Center" as they all pulled on Tyvek suits and surgical gloves. Spanish guitar music played faintly in the background as the agents argued over the merits of the best Argentinian restaurant in DC compared to Buenos Aires.

"You guys were in Argentina?" Shane asked.

They both stopped talking and turned to face him with blank expressions.

Dexter Kim, a big, friendly Asian guy, smiled. "No?"

Shane nodded. He understood. He wasn't allowed to talk about a lot of his missions either. But he recalled there had been a thing in the Argentinian capital over Christmas when the US Ambassador's daughter had been kidnapped.

Shane figured these two guys had been involved and he could only imagine in what clandestine capacity, considering local political figures, Russian oligarchs, and American diplomats had all been suspects in the abduction.

Shane looked out the side window of the van. Eric Pierce had been picked up near his place of work. The fact he'd gone for a gun suggested they had the right guy. Was it the same gun with which he'd shot Lloyd Zenko? Shane hoped so. It would be nice to tie the crimes together in a substantial knot that helped send this guy all the way to death row.

Pierce owned a modest ranch house at the end of a quiet bay that looked ridiculously ordinary for the home of an obscenely wealthy and sadistic serial killer. The neighbors had been warned to stay put.

Agents from the local field office were staging a block away, tasked with knocking on doors and interviewing anyone who might know this guy. An Evidence Recovery Team was kicking their heels waiting for Shane and the TacOps agents to finish the initial walk-through. Shane wanted to examine the guy's place. See if it revealed anything about the person who'd murdered his best friend.

He watched as HRT prepared to move on the bungalow. Shane itched to be part of his assault team but had promised to stay in the van until they'd checked the place for explosives. He knew how tense these operations could be, even the routine arrests. All it took was an automatic weapon in the wrong hands or a bunch of C-4 and a blasting cap on a door and people could get hurt. After Texas, and then losing Montana, Shane didn't intend to be a distraction for the other members of Gold team.

A signal came over the radio. "Clear."

Meaning neither electronic sensors nor canine ones had indicated the presence of explosives. He watched Cadell remove Hugo from the area. Diego was with his handler on Charlie team about to go in with the assaulters even though there didn't appear to be anyone inside.

Gold team got the "go" signal and Shane watched his counterpart on Charlie team set a charge on the front door and everyone crouch in readiness to burst inside the neat little home that still had Christmas lights strung up around the yard.

Shane held his breath as they rushed inside. Watching was worse than taking part. Multiplied by a thousand after Texas.

Before Houston they'd believed their own myth—that they

were unkillable. Now they'd lost two of their own in less than a fortnight and Shane knew it had affected them all.

"All clear," came through his headphones and Agent Kim gave him a nod. They stepped out of the van and headed inside.

The plan was that HRT were to leave as soon as the building was confirmed empty of threats and return to the local field office until they received word they were no longer needed. Then they could fly back to Quantico.

Shane hoped to be on that plane—especially after Yael's text. He'd been worried she'd withdrawn again and wouldn't want to see him once the case was over. Even though it was probably a bad idea in the long run, he wanted to be with her again. Her inviting him over was huge.

His cell buzzed with another text. Pierce was on his way to surgery. Shane hoped the man survived. He wanted him in court. He wanted him in jail and then prison. He wanted him to pay for his crimes.

When and if Pierce was stable, he'd be booked and transported to Virginia. Sloan planned for the task force to start interviewing him as soon as the doctors allowed. So far, the only words he'd uttered had been to demand a lawyer.

Yeah. Innocent men did not draw weapons on federal agents nor demand counsel while bleeding out.

Shane high-fived his teammates as he passed them. They all wore happy grins because they'd finally caught this motherfucker and obtained some measure of justice for Scotty. Not that it would help Grace or their kids, but it beat this guy being on the loose. Shane met Novak in the doorway.

"Nothing obviously hinky," Novak stated.

The two TacOps agents split up. They were searching for all the electronics which Shane would take back with him to Quantico, including any hidden surveillance equipment, along with looking for anywhere this asshole may have stashed his crypto.

"Where are his computers?" asked Shane.

"There's an office at the rear to the west. Doesn't look like he uses it much." Novak looked impatiently at the door. "We're leaving the field office for the airport in ninety minutes unless we hear differently." He headed off with the other operators.

Shane wandered through the house. It was nicely furnished but without any great design statements. Basic middle-class home of a single American male.

Shane found the office where Dexter was already bagging the computer and tech.

Shane took a few photos on his cell and sent one to Yael. The lounge had a worn-out couch and a large-screen TV attached to the wall above the open fireplace. A dusty gaming box sat on the console and even as he spotted it, the other tech guy came over to bag it.

A couple of framed photos sat on the sideboard that Shane took snaps of and forwarded to the task force to investigate. Maybe the guy had lost someone he loved or had some sort of bad experience that had set him on a life of crime. Except the guy was hardly living it up. If Shane had a few million dollars of ill-gotten gains in the bank, he'd at least have a beach house in Barbados or Mexico and not keep working the boring day job.

Not that Shane's job was boring. People would pay good money to get even a glimpse of the sort of excitement he lived every single day.

He was wandering into the kitchen when Yael replied to his photo of the computer. *"There has to be something else. Maybe a laptop?"*

Shane checked the freezer but it contained nothing more exciting than ready meals and ice cream. The fridge had a bunch of salad and cheese. He stepped out to the garage but the place was empty except for a new lawn mower, some paint tins, and some unused-looking sports equipment.

He carefully pried the lid off one of the cans with a screw-driver he found on a shelf. He wore gloves. Found nothing except an inch of old varnish. The other cans were heavy enough to contain paint. He supposed the Bitcoin could be hidden inside in some sort of waterproof container but he wasn't sure that would be the safest place. He left it for the evidence techs who were better at this stuff than he was.

He texted Ashley Chen the image of the office. Wrote back to Yael. *"No sign of a laptop here. Maybe it's at the office or in his car? I'll get Ashley to check."* He fought the urge to call Yael, wanting to hear her voice.

He headed back inside. Dexter had placed the electronics near the door and was proceeding to remove every light switch, electrical socket and forced air grate. The other guy was examining the light fittings and sweeping underneath furniture.

Shane got that feeling again that something wasn't right. "Does this feel like the home of a computer geek?"

Both men paused and looked at one another, and then at him. They shook their heads.

He called Ashley and she picked up immediately. "Did you find anything except that desktop?" she asked sharply.

"No, ma'am."

She swore.

"Did agents find anything at his work desk or in his vehicle?" Shane asked.

"I'll tell them to look again. We haven't found his vehicle yet and he's not saying a word about where it might be but then again, he's been shot. We have people scouring the streets and nearby parking garages."

"Maybe he has a bolt hole? Somewhere he stores all his computer gear?" Shane scratched the back of his neck and looked outside to see the Evidence Response Team preparing to come in.

"Probably. I'll get people to start searching records. Where are you now?"

"About to leave his house and let ERT do their stuff."

The TacOps guys were incredibly efficient and were about finished. They picked up the bags of electronics they'd stacked at the door.

Dexter spoke. "Tell whoever is on the phone there is no

detectable hidden surveillance. We'll give you a ride back to the FO if you want."

Shane nodded. Something didn't feel right but he couldn't pin it down. Maybe he was being paranoid.

"I heard," Ashley told him. "Have them drop by Pierce's place of work first, will you? They might see something the other agents missed. I'll have them hold the aircraft for you."

"I'll ask them." The TacOps agents eyed him as they all headed past the ERTs with nods. "And as much as I would love to be on that flight, don't make the guys wait around for me."

The thing he hated most in the world was the incessant waiting in between the excitement.

"That's not your call," Ashley said quickly. "Blame me if you need a scapegoat, but I want those electronics in Quantico tonight."

She rang off and Shane was left staring at the phone.

"Where to next?" Dexter asked with a wry grin after they'd stowed the evidence securely in the van.

"She wants you to check Pierce's workspace in case the other agents missed anything," Shane said, climbing inside the surveillance vehicle and closing the door.

The bald guy nodded and put the van in gear. Dexter started looking up directions to the office on his cell. The notes of some Latin American song rang loudly through the air in a surreal soundtrack that made Shane ache for the quiet peacefulness of working with Yael, or the boisterous camaraderie of the team. The fact he was more excited about seeing a woman again than working a case was a first. Scotty would have been proud of him.

21

A few hours later, Shane trudged off the transport plane at Andrews Air Force Base. Novak slapped him on the shoulder as the others jumped into vehicles. "Great job getting an ID by the way."

Shane pulled a face. "Wasn't me. Yael Brooks is the person who identified Pierce."

"Tell her from me she did good next time you see her. If Pierce survives and is convicted, that fucker's headed straight to death-row."

In this case, Shane would bring party poppers to the sentencing. "I'll let her know…next time I see her."

Novak gave him a knowing look that Shane refused to acknowledge.

"You coming to the bar later to raise a toast to Scotty and Kurt?"

Shane's throat swelled with sudden emotion. "Don't you have to get home to feed the kittens?" he ground out.

Novak smiled. "Charlotte's home. She promised to pick me up later and maybe join us. Tomorrow, we plan to go visit Grace. Do some chores around her place and give her a break from the kids."

Shane nodded. "I'll drop by on Sunday if there's anything she needs."

He thought about his friends and then he thought about Yael's text. For the first time since he'd joined the FBI, he was torn about which to choose. Maybe she'd wanna come out for a drink too? After all, she was the one who'd led them to Pierce…

"I have to take this evidence to the lab straightaway for the techs to run a bunch of forensics overnight before the computer people can get started analyzing what's on them in the morning." He checked his watch. Twenty-one hundred. "I'll see you at the bar as soon as I am done."

Novak nodded. "See if Yael would like to join us. I, for one, would love to buy her a drink."

Shane huffed out a quiet laugh. He should have known he wasn't fooling anyone. He thought about the misplaced guilt she carried on her shoulders for Dave Monteith's death and how, because of her intelligence and hard work, they'd finally arrested the suspect. Even though he wanted to keep her all to himself it wasn't his call. She'd just moved to the area so she'd probably enjoy getting to know more people.

But how awkward would that be if they stopped seeing one another?

If?

The *if* surprised him.

He didn't remember the last time he'd had a relationship last longer than three weeks. Most tended to end as soon as Gold team actively deployed for their sixty-day operations stint.

He shook his head at himself.

It was early days. He had no idea where the two of them would end up eventually. And he knew he'd have to tread carefully around Yael to have any hope with her at all. She'd obviously been hurt in the past and he didn't want to be the next chump to screw with her.

He felt something for her. He just didn't know what those feelings were or if they'd last. He wasn't sure he even wanted to be in any kind of relationship—Grace's grief and her fatherless children were clear reasons not to get involved.

Shane headed to his truck which he'd left near the hangar earlier. He called Yael but she didn't answer so he left a message saying he was going to be late and asking did she want to join him for a quick drink at the bar with the guys. He headed over to Quantico and followed instructions to drop the evidence at the National Laboratory. One of the scientists was waiting for him when Shane got there. He signed off the evidence transfer and headed off base.

He was tired and didn't really want to go for a beer but they hadn't had the chance to raise a toast to Montana yet. The urge to head straight to Yael's was equally strong. It wasn't only the thought of sex driving him. He wasn't an animal. It was the need to connect with her and tell her what had gone down thanks to her hard work. To thank her in person.

And if thanking turned into naked body worship, he didn't consider that a problem. She'd been responsible for catching this bastard. He would worship her as much as she'd let him.

He checked his phone. She still hadn't called or texted him back. Maybe she was asleep. They certainly hadn't gotten much last night.

Bar or Yael's place?

Shane wasn't even sure which choice he was going to make until he took the turn to the bar almost against his better judgment. He parked and sat there, torn. Even the memory of her soft curves had him feeling restless again and he almost put his truck in gear. But these were his teammates. He didn't really have a choice.

Someone rapped on his window. Cowboy stood there grinning at him.

Shane slid his phone in his pocket, pushed open his door and got out of the truck. He slipped his cast into the sling that hung around his neck because the bone ached and he should rest it.

"Where's Yael?" Cowboy asked with a knowing smile.

Shane shook his head and shoved Ryan aside before pushing into the bar.

The guys were in their usual corner and a few shouts went up when they arrived. He laughed, feeling the warmth of belonging surround him. It felt good to be part of a group like this. A woman with long dark hair that reminded him of Yael's sat next to Hunt Kincaid and was laughing at something Demarco—one of the snipers—said to her. Her arm banded her stomach she was laughing so hard.

What would Yael think of his friends? He checked his phone again. Still nothing.

Charlotte Blood walked in with another negotiator, Dominic Sheridan, and his fiancée. Novak swept Charlotte into his arms and gave her the sort of kiss that could blister paint. Everyone whooped and she blushed. Sheridan put his arms around the woman at his side.

A slow ache of loneliness began to build in Shane's chest.

Cowboy and Will Griffin propped up the bar beside one another. They had a lot in common. Ryan Sullivan had lost his wife eight years ago and had a daughter who was being raised on the family ranch back in Big Sky Country. Shane had met the kid during a visit once. She was cute as hell and loved her dad but the guy was probably right about her being better off on the ranch. She loved it there and the Hostage Rescue Team didn't keep routine hours. It would be impossible for a single parent to juggle working this job.

Novak quieted everyone down then raised his glass. "To Dave Monteith and Kurt Montana. Two of the strongest, smartest, and best HRT operators I ever knew. And the toughest, nicest people I ever had the honor to work with."

"To Scotty and Joe," Nash said their nicknames loudly.

Everyone raised their beer. A bottle was thrust into Shane's hand and he tipped it back and drank long and hard. Another wave of longing hit Shane and it was shaped in the curvy form of Yael Brooks.

His nape prickled and he looked over his shoulder. Yael's friend Laura sat beside her new boyfriend. If Laura's eyes were daggers, he'd be dead. The dude said something to her and they both rose to leave.

Laura came up to Shane on her way out. Went up on tiptoes and whispered into his ear, "You are an ass."

He pulled away in surprise but she was already walking away.

Shit.

He checked his cell when it buzzed in his pocket. There was a message from Yael.

"You're at the bar?"

He released a massive sigh. She obviously hadn't received his message and Laura had ratted him out. But it was only for one drink and this was important.

He texted. *"Raising a toast to Montana and Scotty. I left you a voicemail. Come join us. Same place as before."*

He watched the three dots appear and disappear three times and knew he'd upset her.

Damn, she had no right to be mad with him. They weren't even properly dating. He liked her. Really liked her. But it was early days. They were having fun while he'd been making sure she was protected from a psychopath. If there was a niggle of guilt at the back of his neck because he'd been suspicious of her at first, he was damn well ignoring it.

Finally, the message appeared and he gritted his teeth before he read it.

"Sorry I missed your call. I was in the bathtub. Hope Laura didn't give you hell. Appreciate the offer, but I'm tired and headed to bed. I'm so sorry about your friends. You deserve a few drinks after these last few weeks. Have a good night. See you tomorrow if you're working."

He closed his eyes and released a deep breath. Fuck.

Yael sat cross-legged on the couch in her one pair of silky pajamas feeling a tiny bit hurt and a whole lot foolish. She'd been so excited at the thought of seeing Shane again and now felt idiotic to be so disappointed.

The FBI had just had a major break in their case and she understood why they wanted to celebrate, especially HRT. She should have anticipated it. She could have blamed her embarrassment on Laura but Laura had thought she was helping her out. Her friend had texted her a photo of Shane drinking with his teammates. Yael winced at what Laura had probably said to him when she left.

Her friend had been furious but really, she had no right to be. And Shane had, indeed, left her a voice message while she'd been in the tub, inviting her to join them.

Yael could go to the bar but they were once again remembering their friends and colleagues and she didn't want to intrude on that sort of occasion. Plus, after her hot bath where she'd shaved her legs and moisturized her entire body, she felt so relaxed her limbs were like noodles.

And she was lying to herself.

She stood up and paced. She deserved to celebrate along with everyone else. She didn't have to sit here feeling sorry for herself all the time. Shane had invited her. Maybe it was time…

She froze in the middle of the room and stared at the drawer where she kept the only photograph she had of her family, taken before their whole world went to crap.

She'd already lived through the worst thing that could happen. Nothing could compare to losing her entire family in a single day and then being unjustly vilified for that and so many other tragic losses. Fourteen years old and she still dreamed about it every damn week. She walked over to the drawer and pulled out the silver framed photo and stared hard at the family she'd loved. They were outside and holding hands. Richie was sixteen and smiling, but when she stared at his image she wondered if she couldn't already see the darkness shadowing his eyes.

Fifteen years of hell—of trying to make sense of his actions, his hate, of trying to atone for the unforgivable.

She'd spent years in therapy developing coping strategies but, as the sole survivor, the guilt still ate her up every day. She should have guessed what Richie had planned to do. She should have stopped him. He'd told her to stay home from school that day. She still wasn't sure if that was so he could kill her more easily when he murdered their parents, or so he didn't accidentally shoot her at school.

His girlfriend had dumped him a week before. He'd let alcohol and his idiot friends fuel his rage and then he'd taken their father's assault rifle and killed their parents when they tried to stop him.

For years Yael had tormented herself, wondering if he'd gone upstairs to her room to kill her too. She didn't know. She'd never know.

But his eyes had flashed wide with surprise when he'd spotted her in the school corridor that day. Then he'd shot the boy she'd had a crush on, killed him right in front of her—told her he was doing her a favor—before he'd strode away, shooting kids indiscriminately. And she'd run. She'd run and run and run until she'd gotten home and she'd come to a screaming halt when she'd found a police officer already there. She'd seen the white sheets covering her parents' bodies in the garage and she'd spent the next fifteen years mourning the family she'd lost—even, secretly, the young man who'd morphed from beloved brother into evil incarnate.

She squeezed her hands into fists and forced herself to leave the photo out. Richie didn't deserve to be loved or mourned and she wished she could still hate him the way she had for so many years. That would have been so much easier. But her parents had been good people. She touched her mom's smile and remembered her dad's need to outcompete the neighbors' Christmas light display every year.

But not after that day.

After that day, Yasmine Abbott's world as she'd known it had ceased to exist.

Yael didn't want to disappear again. She'd paid a heavy price for a crime in which she'd been as much a victim as anyone else.

The grieving parents had wanted someone to pay though and she'd been the only one left alive.

Now Yael stared around her nice living room and felt the walls pressing in on her. Was this all she had to look forward to? Was she a prisoner of her own making? She wanted to take a chance at a new start. She wanted to live.

She ran upstairs.

She was done hiding from the past. She wanted to make the most of this new exciting world she was part of now. Make the most of the opportunity Alex Parker had given her. She wanted the chance to get to know Shane better, even though it was bound to end in heartbreak. Maybe it was time for a little risk in her life. Maybe it was time to stop being so afraid of every damn thing.

She dragged on her best underwear and clean jeans and a form-fitting red shirt that she knew looked good with her black hair. She ran back downstairs and was about to pull on a pair of socks and her boots when her alarm started beeping. Someone had entered the cameras' field of view.

Was it Shane? Her heart gave a little flutter.

She stood up to check the monitor when the sound of gunfire shattering the large window off her deck had her ducking down behind the kitchen island, her heart clenching painfully in fear.

Oh my god.

What was happening?

Was this real?

Who was this? Why would anyone attack her?

She knew she had to move. But as bullets flew and glass shattered around her living room, she was too scared to risk it. It felt like that day at the school…

Get off the X.

That was what Shane had said to her once before.

He'd meant move. *Run.*

She lunged for the keys to the SUV and raced out the back door into the garage, ignoring a sharp pain as broken glass sliced into her bare feet. The sound of gunfire tearing up her home never let up.

How long would it take the security firm or police to get here?

Too long.

She sprinted into the garage, slamming the door behind her. Popping the locks, she jumped into the black SUV. The door into her house opened and a man dressed completely in black stood in the entranceway. He was wearing one of those *Scream* masks just like Evi1Geni-us did when he butchered people.

Oh my god.

She was hyperventilating.

He was supposed to be in custody…how could he be here, now?

Yael dropped the keys on the floor and shrieked when the bastard started firing at the windshield.

The SUV shook from the force of the impact but the glass held.

She pressed the button on the garage door opener and scrambled around the footwell searching for the key. Then she realized she didn't need the fob to start the engine. She put her foot on the brake and pressed the start engine button and threw it into reverse. The person kept firing and the glass chipped but didn't shatter. Not yet. She careened out into the street and then put the SUV into drive and accelerated away, swerving madly. She didn't slow near the guard house and burst through the barrier. Her stomach dropped at the guard's shocked expression but he must have heard the gunshots and was already on the phone, hopefully to cops or armed security professionals. She hoped this lunatic wasn't behind her because the guard wouldn't last long in his flimsy structure, although he was armed.

She wanted to call for help but her phone was back in the house. She wasn't sure where to go. Alex's house or the bar?

Was Shane even still there? What if he changed his mind and

went to her place and accidentally confronted this shooter? A pistol was no match for an automatic weapon. She hung on to the wheel like her life depended on it and headed for the bar, not paying attention to the speed limits or the warning beeps the car kept screaming at her to put on her seatbelt.

What if the bad guy followed her to the bar? The idea she might put Shane or his fellow operators in danger didn't sit well but they were always armed and they'd know what to do. She couldn't see anyone following in the rearview mirror and her attacker had been on foot as far as she could tell. Her heart pounded so fast she felt as though she was physically running.

She pulled up directly outside the entrance and ignored the shouts from some guy whose car she almost bumped into, slamming on the brakes just in time.

She staggered out of the SUV, leaving the door wide open and ignoring the pain in her feet as she hobbled toward the building, pushing inside and frantically searching for Shane.

And then there he was, suddenly in front of her, and she grabbed his shirt with both hands and held on tight. He lifted her up and placed her on the counter, pulled away to examine her shredded feet.

"What happened?"

"He ffff-found me." Her teeth chattered and she was shaking so much she couldn't spit out the words.

"Who?" Shane demanded. All the FBI people crowded around in a circle.

Panic squeezed her throat shut. "E-e-evil1Geni-us. I think it was him. He attacked my house with a gun." She gripped him. Concentrated on his dark green eyes because they were steady and calm and she was an absolute wreck. "He might have followed me. You could all be in danger."

22

So close. So fucking close!

Yael Brooks was one lucky bitch. He sloshed through the stream, biting back a curse as the frigid water flooded his shoes. Then he sprinted across a field on the other side, crunching through grass stiff with frost. He placed the rifle in the footwell of the passenger side of the vehicle and covered it with a blanket. He slipped the handgun onto the seat, out of sight but within easy reach.

Adrenaline had his heart hammering and he started the engine of the secondhand Subaru he'd bought in a private sale off some unsuspecting yahoo yesterday.

He drove for a while and pulled over when he was positive he hadn't been followed.

He unzipped his jacket and pulled out the framed photograph of Yael Brooks and her family from when she was a kid. He captured the image with a cell and did a quick reverse image search.

After nothing but frustration when trying to track down this woman's real identity over the last two weeks he was suddenly overwhelmed by the plethora of hits. Not on Yael, who looked a lot younger in the photo, but on her parents, the brother.

His hands shook.

Her brother Richie had killed twelve people in cold blood. He laughed, incredulous. Hell, she'd been tried as an accessory but managed to get off.

Anger burned through him. Why did some people sail through life without any consequences sticking to them while others—including himself—never caught a break?

As a teen he'd hacked into the Defense Intelligence Agency and posted about the vulnerability online trying to earn a little money while giving the feds a heads up that they needed to fix a potential problem. *He'd* ended up in prison being beaten and abused, disowned by his own parents. Didn't matter he'd screamed for help so much he'd lost his voice. Didn't matter how many times he appealed to his lawyer or the warden for help.

No one had heard his screams. No one had paid attention.

He'd been ignored. Hell, his parents had immigrated to the Caribbean but he was hoping for a reunion in the not-too-distant future.

The assaults had only stopped when one of the boys had died, but he hadn't forgotten and he hadn't forgiven.

Should he drive to his house and pick up his hardware wallets? But the FBI still didn't know who he was, let alone where he lived. The information was buried so deep it would take a front loader to uncover. Even if cops did figure out his identity and searched the house, they wouldn't find his secret room. He had at least a million on him and another million tied up and unconscious in the trunk.

Better to find a place to set up his next auction, which he was looking forward to. He had several places he'd previously cased that were suitable. He glanced at the photograph again and another idea formed. He looked at his watch. Time was going to be tight.

He pulled into a drive-thru for some coffee. It was going to be a long journey.

23

Out of his peripheral vision Shane was aware of members of HRT and other FBI agents peeling out to cover different positions inside and outside the bar, but his primary focus was on Yael. On making sure she was okay and prying out the information she was currently too petrified to give.

"Tell me exactly what happened." He squeezed her arms gently. He could tell from her large pupils and ragged breathing that she was terrified and possibly going into shock. He scanned her body to make sure she hadn't been shot but he couldn't see any wounds beyond the cuts on her feet.

Her feet were a mess though, covered in blood and there was a scratch on her cheek, probably from flying glass.

Her teeth rattled. "I'd gotten dressed because I'd decided to come down here and meet you for a drink."

He blinked in surprise. He hadn't expected that. He closed his eyes and tried to bury the fear that had flooded him when he'd seen her run in here.

"I was in the kitchen when I heard the alarm system start doing its warning beep." She gulped air. "And I thought it might be you."

Her eyes flashed to the people crowding around them. He

thought he caught a hint of embarrassment in her expression. Did she think he might be ashamed of her or want to keep their relationship a secret from his friends when her life had been in jeopardy?

"I am so fucking proud of you, Yael." He didn't know if she believed him but she needed to hear it and he wanted to shout it from the rooftops.

She was an incredible woman. He rubbed her arms and took the brandy that the barkeep handed him over her shoulder. Watched as she tipped back the shot and handed him back the glass.

"Someone started firing an automatic weapon through the door to the deck."

Christ. His mouth parched as she told them what had happened. How she'd run out of her home and the fact the SUV windshield had most likely saved her life.

He was so impressed by her. She'd done everything right. And she'd been very, very lucky and could so easily have died. The punch to his gut when he realized exactly how close he'd come to losing her hurt more than the snap of his bones after falling down those stairs last month.

Novak eyed him grimly. Shane knew his boss had called it in already and there would be a team from HRT bearing down on Yael's house as they spoke.

Her hands shook as he handed her another shot of brandy.

She drank it without arguing.

"Did you recognize him?"

She shook her head. "Mask," she croaked.

He rested his hands on her hips but had to force himself to not hold her too tight. She was going to have bruises if he wasn't careful. "I'm getting you out of here to somewhere safe."

Novak slid a key into his palm and said under his breath, "Use my place in case yours has been compromised. I'm barely using it right now and there might even be food and drink in the fridge. First aid kit in the bathroom, although you should probably take her to the ER and get her stitched up."

"Do you want me to come with you?" Charlotte asked.

Shane glanced from her to Yael whose lip trembled and she looked as if she was about to cry. His heart clenched. She'd almost died tonight. He'd thought the danger was over. He'd let down his guard and failed his mission and he'd almost lost her. Son of a fucking bitch.

"I don't want to go to the hospital," Yael said firmly.

"Might be a good idea," he said easily.

She shook her head and her grip on his hand intensified. "I'm not hurt."

He begged to differ.

Noam Levitt, one of the Charlie team assaulters, pushed him aside. He was a trained combat medic and had grabbed the bar's first aid kit from the owner.

"I've got this." He handled her feet gently, cleaned up the blood with antiseptic wipes, pulled out one small piece of glass before closing the two biggest cuts with steri-strips and superglue. Once it had dried, he dabbed antiseptic cream on her foot, then wrapped them both in sterile bandages.

"Nothing too deep," Noam said to Yael. "Keep an eye on them for infection but I don't think you need to go to the ER."

Yael nodded.

"Thanks, man," said Shane.

Alex Parker walked in the door and pushed through the crowd to the bar. "Are you okay?"

Yael nodded but her teeth were still chattering. "How did you know I was here?"

"There's a tracker on the SUV," Alex said.

Made sense.

"When the alarm went off, I checked the cameras. UNSUB left via the backdoor as soon as you drove away. I don't know where his vehicle was parked but HRT better figure that out fast. He can't be far away. Do you have the energy to come back to your house and walk me through events? We can do it tomorrow if you'd rather."

Yael started to shake her head.

Eyewitness statements were more reliable the fresher they were.

"I'll be right there with you, Yael. He's not getting near you again," Shane reassured her. Anger fused his jaw. He should never have left her alone in the first place. "Then we'll go somewhere safe and you can get some sleep."

Her deep brown eyes locked onto his and he felt a surge of protectiveness when she nodded. "Okay. But I can't drive. I don't have my driver's license."

Emotion clogged his throat. That she worried about something so trivial should have made him smile but he couldn't. He wasn't about to let a traffic cop near her.

She let go of him and clutched her throat. Her eyes went even wider. "My wallet, cellphone, and laptop." Her voice rose. "What if he took them? You better tell Ashley to change all the passwords, Alex. ASAP, just in case."

"I will. Let's take a quick walk around your place and you can see if he took anything," Alex told her gently. "He left almost as soon as you did, so I doubt it. I'll deal with everything after that. I'll arrange to get the windows fixed and the place cleaned up." Despite the considerate nature of the words there was a light in the man's eyes that was steely and cold.

Shane had no trouble believing those rumors about Alex Parker now. Shane swept Yael into his arms and waited for Ryan Sullivan to give him the all-clear that it was safe for them to exit.

Shane followed Alex, careful not to knock Yael's feet against anything. Alex stopped for a quick word with Dominic Sheridan and his partner before they all headed outside.

Shane almost stumbled when he saw the damage to the SUV. Holy fuck. It looked like a full magazine had been emptied into it. He exchanged another glance with Alex. If she hadn't been driving that vehicle, she'd be dead. His arms tightened around her and he belatedly remembered his cast but it didn't matter. No way was he letting her go now.

"Sorry about your SUV, Alex," Yael murmured.

Shit.

"Not your fault. He focused on you because of the work you were doing for the company. Anyway, that's why we have insurance."

Shane and Alex shared another look.

"I'll follow you." After a nod to the other man Shane strode to his truck and opened the passenger door, easing Yael carefully inside. Then he climbed in the driver's seat and drew the seat belt around her while she pulled her knees up to her chest.

"I hope you don't mind me coming to find you. I didn't know where else to go," she said quietly.

"I'm so fucking grateful you came to me." She could have gone to Alex Parker but he was glad she hadn't. "That was exactly the smartest choice to make." His throat closed and something suspiciously like moisture filmed over his eyes. He stroked his thumb over her cheek, rubbing away a spot of blood.

She flinched and he drew away.

"I've got you, Yael. He won't hurt you again." Shane had to rein in all the emotions racing through him so he could do the job the way he'd been trained to do it. He followed Alex's black Audi back to the complex and noticed SSA Sheridan and his partner followed behind them, and another truck behind that he was pretty sure belonged to Hunt Kincaid and was full of HRT personnel.

Warmth stole through him that helped calm his mind. These people were more than just a work team. They were a brotherhood—with a new female member. Peoplehood? Or simply *family*.

He'd die for his colleagues and they'd die for him. But none of them wanted to do that. They all wanted to survive and save innocent lives—like this woman beside him.

A bunch of emergency vehicles with cherry lights spinning on top sat outside Yael's townhouse. Crime scene tape was being stretched around the property and his headlights picked up the glint of brass on the ground.

"Did you see a vehicle anywhere? In the street out front?"

She shook her head. She was shivering again. He reached into the back seat and dug around in his go-bag. Found some wool socks and a sweatshirt. "Put these on."

He glanced across the street where a small crowd of neighbors huddled on the sidewalk. The new guy, Kevin Karvo, wasn't anywhere to be seen.

Shane pulled up on the side of the road two houses down on the same side of the street as Yael's. Alex parked in front. Sheridan behind.

FBI agents spilled from the vehicles. Some of the guys jogged around the complex, presumably searching for any tracks in the frosty grass. Others, including Sheridan and his partner, began separating and questioning potential witnesses.

Shane got out and came around and opened Yael's door. Her hands shook as she tried to push him away. "I can walk."

He ignored her and lifted her up, bearing most of her weight with his right arm. "Let me carry you inside. We'll see if whoever is in charge will let you grab some shoes and clothes before we leave."

Alex joined them.

Someone shouted across the street, "Are you okay?"

Yael raised her hand. "Yes. Thanks."

A uniformed officer with a thick waist and granite jaw guarded the scene.

"Special Agent Livingstone." Shane introduced himself and eased Yael to the ground as the patrol cop looked him up and down dubiously. He fished out his creds. The guy's eyes widened in surprise when he realized Shane wasn't kidding. "This here is the homeowner."

"You're unharmed?" the uniform asked in surprise.

Yael nodded and Shane bit down on his desire to argue with

her. Her feet were cut up pretty bad and she was shaken and obviously terrified. He didn't consider that "unharmed."

But at least she wasn't dead.

Reality at how close she'd come to dying tonight hit him all over again.

"Good to see you survived. Did you know the shooter?" the cop asked.

Yael flinched and shook her head.

The man they'd assumed was Evi1Geni-us was currently handcuffed to an ICU bed in Charlotte, North Carolina. Who was this attacker? Or did the FBI have it wrong?

"The FBI will be taking over this case, Officer, but we'd appreciate your help securing the perimeter while we work the scene."

"No problem. Couple of other agents arrived the same time as I did. They already checked inside but the suspect had fled. They went out the back to see if they could track him. Called for a K9 unit. It's a mess in there. Glass everywhere." The uniform went to the trunk of his patrol car and handed them all latex gloves and paper booties. Then he eyed Yael's socked feet. "Want some shoes…? I have some sneakers in the back of the patrol car."

Yael shook her head, her dark hair fanning her shoulders. She pointed into the garage. "Can I grab the shoes I use for yard work?"

On one of the shelves near Myrtle was a pair of rainbow Crocs.

Shane exchanged a glance with the other men who nodded. There was no reason to believe the suspect had rummaged around in the garage. The patrol officer went and fetched the rubber shoes and Shane bent to help Yael place the paper covers over the top of the ensemble. As he squatted down, he spied Kevin Karvo's house, the For Sale sign swinging in the wind, every window dark.

When they were all appropriately clothed, Alex led the way inside and Shane held Yael's hand, trying to infuse support and the feeling of safety into her. Slugs and bullet casings littered the garage floor and her home. They were careful to avoid treading on them, and also on the blood smearing the tile floor near the door.

Shane forced his mind away from so many murder scenes he'd attended as a case agent where bloodstains like these had usually been associated with a corpse.

The idea it could have been Yael, tonight, gutted him.

He should have been here. They'd obviously made a mistake somehow. Either Evi1Geni-us had an accomplice or they'd arrested the wrong guy in Charlotte.

Once inside the kitchen, he could see the shattered windows and bullet-riddled walls. The attacker had gone to town on redecorating the place.

If she'd been anywhere except near the back door, with the car keys within easy reach, she'd have been shot or taken. Shane had no doubt this fucker would want to play some of his sick games with her if he had the chance.

Shane's fingers tightened on hers and she sent him a worried look and he forced himself to relax. He was freaking her out.

Alex moved to the sliding doors where the ragged drapes fluttered in the frigid wind.

Shane spotted Yael's cell on the kitchen counter. She went to grab it but he gently caught her fingers.

"Let the crime scene people check it first."

She looked as if she was going to burst into tears.

Alex came back toward them. "I'll deal with it and, if need be, I'll find you a replacement by morning. Where did you leave your computer?"

"Upstairs."

"Okay, let's see if is still there and then we'll pack you an overnight bag. From the timing on the cameras, I don't think he had time to search your house."

She nodded and they followed Alex up the stairs that Shane was now so familiar with. They were all careful not to touch anything, not even the handrail.

No bullets here. No sign anyone else had been up on the second floor.

Shane glanced at the bed where last night he'd made love to Yael for hours, promising her he'd keep her safe. This fucker had destroyed all that. Made a mockery out of the FBI and their safety precautions. Made a mockery of Shane's words.

"Is this a copycat or is Eric Pierce innocent?" Shane voiced the words he was sure they were all thinking.

Alex pressed his lips together and shrugged. "EG might have had a partner or us arresting Pierce might have pissed someone off." He paused. "Or EG is still out there."

"Why'd Pierce pull a weapon when the agents tried to arrest him?"

Alex shook his head. He didn't know either. He took out his cell and called someone from work and told them to check in on everyone and make sure they were all safe. Then he called Mal, his wife, and spoke to her in a low urgent tone.

Yael went into her bedroom and stared longingly at her laptop which was on a chair near the window, half covered by some silky material. Shane could see she wanted to pick it up but forced herself not to.

She looked over her shoulder. "I'm certain he didn't touch it."

Alex hung up the cell and pinched the bridge of his nose. "I'll take it to the lab for a quick forensics examination and then to the office to run a diagnostics check. We have your prints on file. If they want your DNA, we can supply that tomorrow. I'll have the machine back to you by morning. I promise."

"Thanks." Her voice was small.

Alex walked over and gave her a quick hug. "Mallory says you should come stay at the house." He looked at Shane. "You can both stay if that's what Yael wants. We have the room. No one will get to you there."

Yael sucked in her bottom lip. Shook her head. "I don't want to bring danger to your family. The baby…"

Alex's expression turned icy. "Trust me. No one's getting near my family, Yael. I'm only sorry this bastard seems to have fixated on you."

"It was my own fault he saw my face."

"None of this is your fault. We have all underestimated him time after time. That's not gonna happen again. We're on a war footing with this psychopath and I won't stop searching until we have him for sure."

Yael's bottom lip wobbled and her eyes filled with tears. Then she blinked them away and raised her chin. "I hate this. I hate him."

Shane stepped forward and wrapped an arm around her shoulder. He hated seeing her so upset. "I have a place we can stay. He won't find us there and if he does, he won't live long enough to regret it."

"I can keep you both safe," Alex assured them.

"So can I. I won't let her out of my sight."

"Yael?" Alex asked.

Yael stood straighter and drew in a big breath. "I'll go with Shane. I can't stand the idea of bringing danger to Georgie."

"Okay but call if you change your mind." Alex picked up Yael's laptop and the power cord and took both items downstairs to bag them.

Shane wasted no more time. He went to her drawers and pulled out underwear and then socks and pants and t-shirts. He found sweaters and jeans and stuffed everything into a sports bag he found in the bottom of her wardrobe.

Sloan's voice echoed up the stairs. "Is she okay?"

Yael's eyes shot to his. She was keeping it together but he could see the strain around her eyes and mouth. And she was cold. He dragged a thick gray cardigan off a shelf and wrapped it around her shoulders, pulling her hair out from the collar and ignoring the way the silky tresses brushed against his skin.

Her dark brown eyes were full of fear and uncertainty.

Shane wished he could fix everything for her. Rewind the

clock. Be at her place when this coward attacked. Finish it. Instead, this killer had once again gotten the drop on them.

They made their way carefully back down the stairs and Sloan's gaze shot from Yael to him and the bag he carried.

"Are you okay, Yael?" the task force leader asked.

"Yes." Yael's voice sounded firmer now. Either the brandy had kicked in or the shock was starting to wear off. "I'm not hurt. Just scared and pissed."

"Thank goodness you weren't killed. I don't know how this could have happened." Sloan crossed her arms over her chest. "I thought we'd caught the suspect. I should never have assumed…"

"Don't beat yourself up," Alex said. "We all missed this. We are all equally to blame."

Sloan eyed Yael critically. "Why is he so obsessed with you? Besides the obvious?"

Yael looked startled by the statement.

"Did he take anything?" Sloan asked.

Yael started to shake her head then frowned at the sideboard. "I don't think so," she said slowly.

Shane froze. She was lying. He just didn't know why or about what.

"I want an HRT protection detail arranged—"

"No," Yael stated firmly this time. "I will stay with Agent Livingstone this evening and we can reassess in the morning."

Sloan blinked at her tone but Yael didn't work for her and had clearly recovered her backbone and didn't want to be ordered around.

"I've got this, ASAC Sloan," Shane assured the task force leader. He felt the weight of all eyes on him as he escorted Yael out the front door and back to his truck. He wouldn't let this asshole come anywhere close to Yael. Not tonight. Not tomorrow. Not until they had unequivocally found and detained this UNSUB or put him in the ground.

He was not going to lose anyone else he cared about.

24

Yael paced the area in front of Shane's boss's couch as Shane raided the man's drinks cupboard. She felt stronger now. Shock was rapidly morphing into anger.

"Did anyone find any trace of him yet?" She hated being without her cell phone or any way to communicate. Hated relying on someone else for information.

"I would have heard if they'd picked him up."

"How did he know I was alone?"

"Sit," he ordered. "You're gonna make your feet bleed."

Yael had forgotten about her cuts. Now, with the reminder, her soles suddenly throbbed.

She sat cross-legged on the couch, making sure she hadn't opened the injuries, taking the glass of booze from Shane without even asking what it was. He handed her a pain pill at the same time. She popped it in her mouth and swallowed it down with what tasted like good scotch.

The alcohol burned all the way down her throat and made her eyes bulge with tears.

Shane laughed and sat on the couch beside her. The cushions sank and Yael found herself leaning against him. When he wrapped his uninjured arm around her shoulders, she didn't resist. It felt good being in his embrace again. Almost too good, but she needed the comfort.

He shifted and removed his handgun from its holster and placed it on the coffee table.

She stared at the lethal-looking weapon then glanced at the door. "Are you worried he might follow us here?"

"We have people watching entrances and exits. Plus Novak keeps an assault rifle in a gun safe in his bedroom which I removed and loaded while you were in the bathroom. If that motherfucker comes at us here tonight, he will die."

Yael opened her mouth but didn't know exactly what to say. "I know I hate guns but I hate this guy even more. Thank you for helping me."

Shane put his arm back around her shoulder and she yawned widely. Thanks to the alcohol, she was finally starting to feel sleepy.

"As for why he came at you when you were alone, he probably didn't care if you were alone or not. He probably wouldn't have cared if he'd known you were supposedly being protected by some asshole HRT operator who was stupid enough to believe the threat was over. He had a fully automatic rifle and probably figured that made him invincible. Not true, by the way. I wish I'd been there to demonstrate that fact." His words dripped with guilt.

"It wasn't *your* fault."

He tilted his head to catch her gaze. "Yes. Yes, it was. I'm big enough to shoulder my responsibility in this. I promised you and Alex Parker I'd look after you, and I failed."

"You were in North Carolina for most of the day."

"I was back when he attacked you."

She looked away. Was she only a job to him? She swallowed with difficulty, her throat dry and scratchy.

"Yael." His arm tightened and she looked at him. Those

wintergreen eyes of his stared at her intently. "Are you sure he didn't take anything?"

She blinked rapidly, not expecting the question. She hid her reaction by reaching for her drink and offering it to him. He shook his head and she drained the glass and put it back down on the table. The whiskey still burned but less now she was expecting it —a lot like heartache.

Avoiding his gaze, she snuggled back against him. "Not that I could tell."

His silence felt accusatory and she didn't want to have to deal with the questions that would follow if she told him the truth.

What did it even matter? Everyone in that photograph aside from her was dead. Whoever had stolen the photograph couldn't hurt anyone else in it. Not anymore. They could only hurt her by revealing the truth about her family and telling Shane would accomplish the exact same thing.

She couldn't think about it right now.

It was after midnight. She was exhausted. Her gaze lifted until she reached the honed lines of his face. The stubble on his jaw. Warm skin that still held a touch of a summer tan.

"Shane?" she whispered.

He made a sound that was a cross between a grunt and a sigh.

"Can we go to bed now?"

His face softened. He took her hand in his right and held his handgun in the other. He led her into a darkened bedroom and pulled back the quilt.

Much to Shane's amusement, Novak's FBI negotiator girlfriend Charlotte Blood had dashed back here from the bar to change the sheets and throw a few basic supplies into the fridge. He hadn't missed the strip of condoms she'd put on the bedside table but Shane had no plans to use them tonight. Yael needed to rest.

He placed his SIG on the side table. Then removed the Glock

from the ankle holster. Novak's carbine was within easy reach should someone break down the door. Gold team had set up cameras in the hallways and stairwells, plus had people watching the entrances.

Shane knew Yael was being evasive about what had been taken from her house but he wasn't sure whether or not it was important. Not all lies mattered, but Shane would be lying if he said he wasn't disappointed that Yael still didn't trust him enough to confide in him completely. But he'd also been the guy having a beer when her house was being attacked so maybe he couldn't blame her all that much.

She stripped off her clothes and his eyes almost popped out of his skull when she got down to her underwear even though she was too busy struggling to remove her jeans without pulling off her bandages to notice.

"Sit." He knelt in front of where she sat on the edge of the bed and took her calf in his hand as he eased the material over her socks, one at a time. She smelled so sweet he closed his eyes and swallowed the punch of desire.

"I wore these for you." Her smile was sad as she ran her fingers through his hair.

Unable to stop himself, he pressed his face against the softness of her thigh.

Black lace seemed to have been designed with the sole intention of destroying a man's control. He nuzzled her skin, the warm womanly scent of her wrapping around his senses and snapping him to attention like a flagpole.

He gripped her thighs and pulled her closer to his mouth. He couldn't afford to be consumed by his hunger, didn't want to lose focus. They both needed to rest and they were probably as safe as they could get until this guy was apprehended.

He nuzzled closer and ran his nose over her vulva. She shivered.

He eased his tongue under the material and into the hot core of her and she bowed up off the bed.

"Relax," he whispered.

"That is not very relaxing," she countered.

He pulled away and rolled her gently onto her side. "Stay there. I'll be right back."

He turned off most of the lights in the apartment except for one under-counter light in the kitchen. Then he headed back to the bedroom and climbed into bed, fully clothed. Last thing he needed was to be caught in his skivvies should this UNSUB get past their defenses or should his boss arrive unannounced.

Yael grumbled in protest.

He slipped behind her, spooning her. She snuggled against him, her excellent ass pressed against his doomed-to-disappointment cock. He rested his head on his left arm keeping the cast on the pillow above her head. His other hand slid over her perfect body and cupped her full breasts over the rough scrap of lace. She moaned and squirmed against him. A different sound this time. He rolled her nipple between his thumb and forefinger, feeling the peak grow hard beneath his touch. "You like that?"

She stretched against him and tried to turn over.

"Uh uh. My rules else I sleep on the couch."

She grumbled again but the way she rubbed against him suggested she wasn't too angry with him. Sex was a great stress reliever and if anyone needed help sleeping it would be Yael after what she'd endured today.

His hand returned to her breast, easing the bra cup aside as he nuzzled the soft skin behind her ear and at the same time tormented her nipple.

Then he smoothed his palm over the indent of her waist and over the curve of her hip. He hooked her thigh and wedged his knee gently between her legs and opened her up to his mercy.

His fingers gripped the scrap of lace and he started gliding the rough material gently back and forth through her folds and over her clit until she was gasping. Then he eased two fingers inside her at the same moment he pressed the heel of his hand firmly against her clit. She shuddered and her muscles spasmed as she climaxed fast and hard around his fingers.

He withdrew his hand, pulled the covers more firmly over them both, knowing he was going to burn tonight for more than one reason.

Then he kissed her hair again and she sighed. Thirty seconds later, she was asleep.

25

The task force meeting room was buzzing despite it being the weekend. Yael looked out of the window and wished this was all over. She hated living in fear. She detested this killer besting them yet again. She hated the fact he'd attacked her in her new home and made her run away like a coward.

The room was chock full of agents working hard to catch, and gather enough evidence for the DOJ to convict, this sadistic killer.

Shane wasn't here.

Yael hated the embarrassment that hit every time anyone asked about the HRT operator's whereabouts or mentioned last night or even looked at her for any length of time. She guarded her privacy as much as she valued her integrity, but last night had thrown a spotlight on her actions.

It was like the others knew exactly what the two of them had done in the darkness. How she'd woken in the early hours to feel him still hard against her back. And how she'd destroyed him the way he'd destroyed her.

She'd woken the second time alone. Alone, but a whole lot stronger and more determined that she wouldn't become this asshole's next victim. He'd sent her an unmistakable warning she wasn't likely to forget. She'd received the message, loud and clear. Taking risks wasn't in her MO.

She'd texted with Laura on and off all morning. Her friend was sick in her hotel room with suspected food poisoning. Laura said she felt awful not coming to see her but that the chances of her barfing were high and she didn't want to inflict that on anyone. Yael had promised to drop by later to see how she was doing.

Tim wasn't in yet either, but it was early and the young man tended to be more of a night owl as were many computer geeks.

"Attention, please," Sloan called from the front of the room.

Yael knew Shane would want to hear this. She didn't have her cell but thankfully her laptop was in front of her so she sent a quick message to his work phone. The techs had toiled all night long and there was no evidence EG or whoever had attacked her last night had gone anywhere near her machine.

Techs were almost done checking her cell and then Alex wanted to run some diagnostics of his own. He'd offered her a temporary one but she had declined for now. She wasn't planning on going anywhere.

Alex sat next to a good-looking dark-haired guy and a woman with long brown hair tied back in a high ponytail. The woman wore a sparkling rock on her ring finger. Alex obviously knew them well. Yael remembered seeing them last night. They'd been in the bar and then on her street questioning her neighbors.

The woman caught her eye and sent her a smile which Yael returned. She was striving to appear calm and professional. Everyone must think she was crazed the way she'd run into that bar last night. Like someone out of a horror movie. And then there were her neighbors.

Gah. Her stomach churned.

Maybe she should cut her losses and move already.

She set her teeth. She didn't want to keep running.

"Eric Pierce is awake following surgery but he's refused to talk to law enforcement and his attorney is preventing us from even questioning him yet," Sloan began. "Charlotte PD found his car and it's being transported to the lab here. The bomb squad checked it out and when they opened the trunk, they found several kilos of uncut cocaine."

Yael pulled a face. Presumably the guy was a drug dealer or some sort of mule. He could still be Evi1Geni-us and whoever attacked her last night could be a pissed off ally designed to make the FBI doubt their conclusions. Or Eric Pierce was innocent and being set up.

She frowned. If he was a patsy then Evi1Geni-us had chosen well because the guy apparently had a lot of reasons not to cooperate with law enforcement.

"There was nothing, apparently, to indicate he was a dealer at his house and we are still searching for a secondary residence or property where—"

Shane walked in the door with his boss from HRT, whose bed she'd slept in last night. Her cheeks did what they always did when it came to Shane Livingstone. They heated.

"Sorry I'm late. We had an HRT team briefing to discuss what happened last night so I can report any updates." Shane took the seat next to hers, as always—everyone on the task force had fallen into a smooth working routine. Novak pulled out the chair on his other side and sent her a sympathetic smile.

Something cracked inside Yael's chest.

"As I was saying," ASAC Sloan repeated for them. "Local police found a significant quantity of Class-A narcotics in the trunk of Eric Pierce's car last night."

"Did Evi1Geni-us set Pierce up or is Eric Pierce Evi1Geni-us and not limiting his criminality to online torture and murder?" Shane asked.

"Or did Pierce hire someone to attack Yael—or maybe a list of potential someones—in the event he was arrested?" Alex put in.

"What do the profilers think?" Sloan asked Lincoln Frazer pointedly.

Lincoln Frazer put his hands behind his head and leaned back in his chair. Anyone else might look relaxed. He looked thoughtful. "Our current profile suggests an organized offender who fits well into society. Age range is still wide twenty to forty-five. White—same race as his victims. He's a good talker and socially competent but he uses those skills to manipulate. He's probably a first-born son whose father's work was stable but whose childhood discipline was inconsistent. He has a quick temper and will be known to lash out, probably violently, when angered. People like to keep on his good side. He probably considers himself quite the ladies' man. He's methodical and cunning and amoral."

Frazer sat forward. "From all accounts, Eric Pierce fits many of these criteria and judging from the drugs definitely leads a compartmentalized lifestyle."

A female agent spoke up. "His co-workers and boss said they generally got on well with the guy, but he had a rep as a bit of a Lothario when it came to dating."

"Fits." Frazer continued, "EG chooses victims he can control. Even the men taken were not particularly strong or athletic. Presumably he incapacitates them either with drugs or a taser to subdue them. Taser marks have been found on several victims including Wayne Stockwell. Once he has them where he wants them, he makes them beg. He makes them submit with his use of pain and restraints. The fact we now know that, at least in the case of Anya Baker, the auctions are not live means that he's the one choosing to torture and to sometimes sexually assault his victims prior to their death. The fact he manipulates others into paying him to commit his dark fantasies suggests a high level of narcissism. We see no empathy, no remorse, no conscience. We're dealing with the worst kind of predator and unfortunately, he's smart in both the ways of computing and the dark web and also regarding forensics." Frazer dragged his thumb over his bottom lip. "He hasn't given us anything concrete to work with despite multiple crime scenes. I can't say for sure whether Eric Pierce is Evi1Geni-us. He fits some of the profile but not all. I'd like to send some of my colleagues down to interview him, if possible."

Sloan nodded. "Of course."

"I do believe the fact he doesn't broadcast the audio at the time of the murders to be significant," Frazer added. "I think he's stealing their voices. Perhaps he doesn't feel like his voice has been heard in real life."

"Did the agents find any sort of 'murder kit' in Pierce's vehicle?" Alex asked.

"No. Nothing," Ashley Chen spoke up. She looked tired. Yael could sympathize.

"Did he generally drive his vehicle to local jobs?" Alex questioned. "We can search for it on traffic cams at the time of some of the murders."

"I don't know. I'll find out." Ashley wrote the question down. "Traffic cam searches haven't revealed anything as yet which makes me think he frequently swaps plates."

"How does he find his victims?" Sloan asked. "Have we figured that out yet?"

No one answered and Yael looked around. She raised her hand. "I'd like to dig deeper into any potential apps he might have used. Check the victims' purchase history on bank statements. I'll need increased access to financial and cell records."

Sloan nodded. "If you feel up to it."

Yael pulled a face. "My feet are healing fine."

"She's not talking about your feet, Yael," Shane said wryly.

She shifted in her seat. "I want to help figure this out. Catch whoever attacked my house last night."

"Okay," Sloan conceded. "We need to revisit all the reasons we picked up Eric Pierce and see if we missed anything."

"Ashley and I are going to review that information shortly," Alex said with a look in Yael's direction that she was sure was meant to be reassuring.

She felt a shiver of unease race against her shoulders. Did she mess up in some way? She didn't believe so but EG liked to muddy the waters...

"Our ballistics expert suggested last night's attacker used a Colt M4 carbine."

Shane stiffened beside her. "Some HRT operators use them."

Sloan nodded. "Interestingly enough we got a hit on the weapon in the system. This gun has been used in other crimes."

"When?" Shane asked.

"A series of bank robberies in Springfield, New Jersey. Last April."

Frazer frowned. "It's a big shift in MO for it to be the same guy."

"But not out of the realm of possibility?" Sloan pushed.

"No..." But Frazer drew the word out enough for it to sound highly dubious. "But EG killed Randy Gomer April 18." He looked at Alex. "We missed that one as we were lazing around the French Riviera prior to your wedding."

Alex nodded, his expression impassive. "Gomer was in Phoenix. When exactly were the bank jobs?"

Ashley Chen checked the notes. "Twenty-first, twenty-second, and twenty-seventh. He hit three banks on the last day. Got away with over a hundred grand total."

"He's clearing easily five times that amount per murder," Alex noted.

"And it's a lot less risk killing some poor bastard restrained in front of a camera compared to robbing a bank." Shane slouched in his chair.

Yael dragged her eyes away from his rugged form.

"I can't see it being the same guy but do we have any footage of the bank robber?" Alex tapped his pen on the notepad.

"I'll get a photo." Ashley nodded and made another entry on her list. It never got any shorter, Yael realized.

"We've been chasing this guy for far too long." Alex echoed her thoughts and looked pissed.

Yael clenched her jaw. Why couldn't they catch this person?

She remembered something that, in the craziness of the last twenty-four hours, had slipped to the back of her mind. "What about the ex-con who stayed at the motel the night Wayne Stockwell was murdered?" The search to find and question him had fallen under the radar with everything else that had happened.

Ashley leaned forward and typed something into her laptop. She looked up with a gleam in her eyes. "There was a hit on the prints in his room confirming his presence there. Ronald Borisky." Ashley read his file. "The guy is a known fence and we have a warrant out for his arrest."

"You think EG set up a meet with this guy at the motel to buy the gun he used to kill Lloyd Zenko?" Shane sat forward.

Alex's gaze was sharp. "EG never used firearms that we know of before the Zenko murder. It's pretty much the only thing he hasn't used to kill victims in the past."

"But he planned to kill a former Marine with explosives experience and I'm guessing EG didn't want to risk arriving without a gun. You know what this means..." Shane said, excitement lacing his words.

Alex grinned. "Yeah, this Borisky character has presumably seen Evi1Geni-us's face."

"Why use a fence when you can go to any store or gun show and pick up a weapon?" Yael asked with a shudder.

Shane tapped his pen in a rapid beat on the table. "One, a lot of stores have surveillance cameras. Two, maybe our guy has a record."

"And felons can't buy firearms..." Yael finished.

Sloan's gaze turned sharp. "Nice work, Yael. You should have been an agent."

Yael smiled tiredly.

Shane nudged her with his shoulder. "Smarty pants."

She snorted softly. "Sure."

"We need to make finding Borisky a priority." Sloan stabbed her notepad with a pen. "Above all the other priorities on the list." There was a twist of humor in her tone. "Next on the agenda is the shooting last night at Yael's home. Because of the sheer volume of evidence, I requested another ten agents from HQ.

They arrive today."

"I analyzed the surveillance feed from the security cameras," Alex said. "The shooter is the same height as the guy in the Evil-Geni-us videos. Same basic build. So is Eric Pierce—but we know Pierce didn't attack Yael's home last night."

"How did he find out Yael's address? I thought you said it wasn't public record?"

"It isn't and he shouldn't have been able to. Not that fast." Alex stared at Yael with a pained grimace. "I'll keep looking into it."

Sloan looked at Shane. "What's the update from HRT?"

"Agents tracked the scent down to the creek and then to a field on the other side. K9 unit lost the scent near the road so we are assuming he left a vehicle there. Evidence Recovery Teams are checking the area looking for tire tracks."

"How deep was the water?" Alex asked.

"Less than six inches. It's been a dry year." Shane shifted and his seat creaked. "The agents isolated and photographed some shoe prints so we have an impression. Size tens. No brand yet."

"If he had any sense, he'd dump the rifle and the shoes in the nearest river," Alex stated.

"Or ocean," Frazer added.

"Any eye witnesses?"

The guy with dark hair introduced himself. "I'm SSA Sheridan with CNU. Special Agent Kanas and I were at the bar last night to raise a toast to Kurt Montana." His lips pressed into a thin line before he continued. "We made ourselves useful by questioning Ms. Brooks's neighbors. Thankfully no one else was injured although some bullets did penetrate the house directly opposite. The owner was visiting DC for the weekend so he wasn't hurt. No one saw anything before the attack but several of Ms. Brooks's neighbors reported seeing a man in dark clothing running into the woods after the shooting stopped. They called the cops at four minutes past ten. A patrol unit arrived in under ten minutes and the first FBI agents shortly thereafter." He closed his notebook and looked straight at Yael. "Sorry we didn't find out more."

She nodded gratefully. It had been nice of them to help out last night and now sacrifice their Saturday to the case. She understood though. This UNSUB threatened everyone's safety even though he seemed to have settled on her for now.

She thrust the thought aside. She had more protection than most.

"We need to find the shooter and contain him," Sloan said. "We need to figure out where the shooter obtained the weapon—highest priority is finding the ex-con, Borisky. Then continue to determine how Evi1Geni-us grabs his victims and how he found Ms. Brooks's home address. And, finally, we need to know whether or not we messed up in our identification of Pierce as Evi1Geni-us. Time to get to work, people."

"Sounds like a piece of cake," Shane muttered irritably.

Yael shivered.

"Seems like we're in luck with one of those items," Ashley spoke up quickly. "Traffic cop outside Fredericksburg pulled over our ex-con Ronald Borisky for having a broken taillight a couple of hours ago. Driver's license came back flagged with the warrants."

Sloan smiled. "Who wants to go get this guy?"

26

Shane walked into the county jailhouse to a lot of dubious looks from the local cops. He guessed he didn't much look like a G-man in his green tactical pants, black t-shirt and boots. The gold shield he wore was proof enough though.

"FBI Agent Shane Livingstone. Here to pick up a prisoner for transfer." He handed over a sheaf of paperwork to the desk sergeant along with a request that the evidence response team would be along shortly to remove Borisky's vehicle. To say the techs were working overtime was an understatement but everyone took an attack on the FBI very seriously—and as Yael was on the task force, they'd now had two.

Normally, they'd send along a local agent to question the prisoner, but Fredericksburg was so close to Quantico it made sense for HRT to come get the guy.

To Shane's surprise it took less than fifteen minutes before a big dude wearing dirty jeans and a filthy gray sweatshirt was brought out with his hands cuffed behind his back. He had a round face with a triple chin and dark scruff from too many days of not shaving. His eyes were beady, set deep in his face, the whites bloodshot.

He didn't look scared of the fact he was being detained by the FBI. He looked positively chipper.

Shane signed a form. Nodded to the officers. "Appreciate the good work on this one."

Borisky snorted. "I was on my way into the police station when they pulled me over. Hey, what are you going to do with my car?"

Shane gave the guy a hard stare. "We're going to examine it for evidence relating to a recent murder."

Borisky's eyes widened then he nodded. "I want it back in one piece. It's a good car."

Shane exchanged a look with the police officer and took Borisky by the arm and walked him to the Bucar he'd borrowed from ASAC Sloan.

Shane could have asked Novak or one of his other buddies on the team to accompany him, but he figured it would be better to ask his new partner. After all, Griffin technically had more time in the Bureau as a case agent than either him or Novak. Didn't mean they hadn't been good at their jobs but Griffin had an excellent record.

Will Griffin sat in the passenger seat scanning the traffic coming in and out of the jail. Given the lengths EG had gone to in order to kill anyone who'd seen his face, they weren't taking any chances. They also had an unmarked SUV following them with Cowboy and Meghan Donnelly acting as backup.

Shane fastened Borisky's seatbelt. With his hands cuffed it wasn't the most comfortable position but Shane wouldn't risk him attacking one of them from the backseat.

Griffin shifted slightly so he could watch their prisoner on the ride. Shane climbed in and turned over the engine. He gave Cowboy the signal over the comms that they were ready to leave.

He got a click of acknowledgment.

"So, Ron—"

"No one calls me that. Everyone calls me 'Boris.'" Borisky had a gruff Eastern European twist to his Bronx accent so that wasn't surprising.

"So, *Boris*"—Griffin's lips twitched at Shane's exaggerated pronunciation so at least his new partner had a similar sense of humor—"Can you tell me where you were on Tuesday night?"

"Sure I can, but I want a deal first before I tell you anything."

"A deal?"

"Yeah, I don't want to go back to prison. I tell you what you want to know and I go on probation."

"You're already on probation."

Boris shrugged and pulled a face. Shane watched him in the rearview. He caught sight of the other vehicle three cars back. His brows rose. Meghan was driving.

"How about you tell us what you know and we'll tell the judge to go easy on you."

Boris shook his head and wiped his nose on his shoulder. "Nah. I want a lawyer."

"What happens if someone else dies in the time it takes for you to cut a deal? Maybe shot with a gun you sold? How lenient do you think the judge is going to feel then?"

Boris's mouth downturned.

"Or maybe we discover you're the one who offed the kid at the motel."

Boris's eyes closed in what looked like genuine remorse. "I didn't touch that kid. But when I heard someone had turned up dead, I wasn't surprised."

Will Griffin gave a short laugh. "Then I guess the other attacks won't come as a shock either."

"Tell us what happened," Shane urged.

"I want a lawyer."

Shit.

They sat in silence and let the miles build.

When Boris looked as if he'd relaxed, Shane tried again. "What did the guy look like?"

Boris sniffed. "Like an ordinary guy. I mean it wasn't until after…" He cut himself off.

"How'd he contact you?"

Boris gave him an *are you kidding me* look.

"Boris, let me tell you something. We already know you were at the motel. We have you on surveillance camera and your fingerprints in the room."

The man's eyes shifted.

"The other guy though? He wiped his picture right off the system and we can't match prints or DNA because he used so much bleach in the room, I almost went blind walking in there. All we can prove right now is that a weapon you've had in your possession was used to shoot a nightwatchman at a motel the same night you were there."

Boris pulled a face.

The nightwatchman had been suffocated not shot, but Boris seemed to accept the latter. Nothing in the handbook said an FBI agent couldn't lie to someone's face if it would get a suspect to open up about a case.

"I want to know what other weapons, suppressors and scopes you sold him."

Boris blew a breath out of the side of his mouth. "No scopes." He pursed his lips. "Look, I said I'll tell you everything but I want a deal first. It's not my first time around the block." He was insistent and Shane knew they weren't going to get anywhere with the guy.

"Call Sloan." Shane handed Griffin his work cell with Sloan's number programmed in. "Tell her to have a DA waiting for us when we get to Quantico."

Shane held Boris's gaze in the rearview. "Anyone dies in the meantime from weapons you sold this sonofabitch and I'll make sure you do your time in a max security federal penitentiary. Understand?"

"I am not being difficult. I'm protecting myself." The guy's voice turned whiny and Shane wanted to punch him in the throat.

He gripped the steering wheel tighter and exchanged a glance with Griffin. He seemed to understand how angry Shane was. Because of this asshole in the backseat some psychopath had been able to get hold of an automatic weapon that last night had almost killed Yael. Shane wasn't here to make friends or shoot the breeze.

"Why'd he come to you and not buy them legally?"

Boris sweated. Shane *may* have turned up the heater.

Boris gave a shrug. "My guess is he has a record of some kind. He was paranoid about cameras and anonymity."

Was Evi1Geni-us in the system? Could he have a record? Have served time? It made sense. Psychopaths had terrible impulse control.

"You deal with a lot of tough guys," Shane said slowly. "This guy rattled you. Why?"

Boris flicked a glance at him via the rearview. Nodded. "Gave me the creeps. I've spent time with a lot of very bad people but no one ever looked at me like that before. He had dead eyes—like a shark, you know?" A bead of sweat slid down the side of his face. "He was short on payment by $100 which is a lot, you know? Told me he had it in his room." Boris swallowed noisily. "As soon as he left, I did something I have never done before in my adult life. I decided to forget the cash and get in my car and take off. I knew he was gonna come back and try to shoot or taser me."

"He carried a taser?"

Boris nodded. "Said he wanted an upgrade and laughed about it."

Shane exchanged a glance with Griffin. It looked like they finally had a witness. Borisky was the wrong size and shape to be Evi1Geni-us and didn't seem to have the IQ required to fox some of the best computer brains in the world. But then maybe looking and acting like Borisky was exactly what it would take to fox them. Assumptions were dangerous. He'd learned that in Special Forces.

They entered the USMC base and headed to Building 64 where Sloan had arranged to take custody of this man in order to question him. Shane signed him over to Sloan's temporary guardianship and then drove Will Griffin back to the HRT compound.

They pulled up in time to watch Meghan slam the door of the vehicle she was driving and stomp away.

Cowboy got out the SUV more slowly and ambled to meet them. "Borisky tell you anything?"

"Not yet, but he will." Shane raised a brow. "What did you do to Donnelly?"

"I don't think she likes me," the man admitted. "Said I was *hick* and *annoying* and *sexist*—I asked if she meant *sexiest* because I get that a lot."

"You need to go make peace with her."

"I wasn't even hitting on her."

Shane cocked a brow.

Cowboy heaved out a gusty sigh. "Fine. I'll go find her."

"And apologize."

"For what?"

"Everything. Tell her you're our burden to bear."

"Ha. I'll tell her. But I was treating her the way I treat all the guys."

"Well, that explains it then because you are hick, annoying, and sexist."

"I'm not sexist. I wouldn't even be here without one of the bravest women I know pulling strings and putting in a good word for me with a few of the higher ups. What I am, Agent Livingstone, is a gentleman."

Shane snorted. "Ryan, your idea of being a gentleman is letting the lady come first."

"That's the only rule that truly matters." Cowboy grinned and then sobered. "I was only seeing if she had a sense of humor." He dropped his voice to a stage whisper. "She doesn't, by the way. In case you were wondering."

"She does when you get to know her." Griffin stood up for her —as he should. They'd gone through Selection and NOTS together.

"Well, I'm glad she's with Charlie because I think, otherwise, a bullet might accidentally stray in my direction in the shooting house." Cowboy gave him a repentant smile. "I'll go see if she's cooled off, but if I don't turn up for work tomorrow you better bet your ass she's murdered me and disposed of the body."

Griffin flinched.

Shane blew out a quiet warning, "Ryan… For fuck's sake."

Cowboy's lips twisted. "Sorry, Griff."

Griffin nodded and straightened his shoulders. "It's okay. Mandy for sure would have busted your balls."

It was the first time the guy had mentioned his dead girlfriend by name which suggested he was dealing with her death better than Cowboy dealt with the loss of his wife. Ryan knew it too because he shot Shane a look from under his brows. Shane had worked with Ryan Sullivan for three years and the guy still clammed up if anyone asked about her.

And then Meghan was striding out of the building still wearing work clothes but carrying a backpack. She shot them all a look and Griffin raised his hand in greeting. She nodded in return.

"'Kay. Better go sort this before she leaves. Later, guys." Cowboy strode toward the female operator hopefully planning to beg for forgiveness.

"I actually think that's one mission he could fail," Shane mused, watching the pair's body language.

"Want to grab a beer?" Griffin asked.

Shane shook his head. "Can't. I have to get back to the task force. I want to know what Boris tells them. See if they came up with any useable leads in the meantime." He looked at his teammate whose mouth had sunk into an unhappy line and paused. "How about you join me? I'm sure Sloan wouldn't mind an extra pair of hands. But it's mainly grunt work."

Griffin's eyes lit up. "I excel at grunt work. Let's go."

———

Yael slugged back her fizzy water and ate a banana like a good girl. Mallory had arrived with a whole bunch of healthy snacks for the task force. It was amazing how quickly Yael had grown fed up of fast food when it was all she'd eaten for a few days.

It hadn't escaped Yael's notice that Jack Reilly was acting as Mallory's unofficial shadow today. The danger was real. Alex didn't take chances with his wife's or daughter's safety.

The fact Mallory was armed probably eased some of his anxiety.

What was that like? Loving someone whose job was inherently dangerous? The thought hovered unwanted in her mind, distracting her from her focus, but maybe she simply needed a quick break.

Baby Georgina sucked wetly on her fingers as Mallory chatted to Ashley Chen and SSA Sheridan's fiancée as if they were all old friends.

And there was that aching void again. The fierce burning desire to be part of a close-knit group. To have friends who didn't turn on you when they found out your brother was a cold-blooded murderer.

Yael bowed her head to hide her errant emotions. She sent Laura a quick text to check up on her again. Her colleague didn't reply but she was probably sleeping.

Ron Borisky was being questioned by an ADA in a secure room upstairs.

Yael had gone through each of the victim files, although she hadn't watched the actual footage of the murders. There was no obvious pattern. Victims ranged from a plumber, a schoolteacher, a stay-at-home mom, a mall cop, two students—one male and one female, a judge, and a factory manager. Nothing immediately linked them, although she wanted to dig deeper into their respective backgrounds by going through financials.

Alex slid into a chair beside her with his laptop open. "Hey. I decided to keep searching for where Lloyd Zenko might have crossed paths with EG and then decided to check if the cell they found on Eric Pierce intersected with Zenko's in the last year."

"What did you find?"

"Nothing."

Yael frowned. "He could have used a burner. They could both have used burners."

Alex nodded. "Yeah."

She knew Alex was starting to doubt that Eric Pierce was Evil-Geni-us. If she was honest, so was she. But the data had fit so perfectly…

"Did you run Pierce's cell against the murder locations?"

Alex nodded. "No hits. But there were hits for other locations at the time of the murders."

Yael's jaw tightened as she stared at Eric Pierce's HR file. "Someone from that firm was assigned to locations in the vicinity where the murders took place. Did EG swap cell phones with Eric Pierce, or…" She looked at Alex as details clicked into place. "Swap employee files."

Alex leaned forward and pointed to the screen. "All anyone would need to do is switch employee numbers and all the wrong info would populate regarding work schedule."

"We crosschecked work locations with murders and came up with someone EG set up as a patsy." Yael wanted to curse. "But EG must work at the same firm. He has to know we're onto him which is why he switched the employee numbers."

Yael checked the associated banking details with Eric Pierce's employee number but they lined up with Pierce's home address.

EG definitely knew they were onto him which was why he'd tried to kill her last night.

She needed to tell Alex that her attacker had taken her family's portrait. It was only a matter of time before EG figured out her real identity and revealed it to the world.

It didn't change anything. There was nothing she could do to change it. Worrying about it wouldn't help them catch this guy. It might get her taken off the task force and she couldn't afford for that to happen.

"Can we ask a manager if they remember who they sent to Houston over the New Year? Or see if they have another employee number on record for Pierce that someone else is now using?"

Ashley nodded and turned away to make the phone call.

"He probably already covered his tracks. I doubt he'd use the number originally assigned to Pierce. Too easy to trace," Yael said despondently. She pulled up the list of employees for the company. Over a thousand. She looked at Alex a little deflated. "He could have already deleted his real file or altered the photo and data in the HR database. That's what I'd do to confuse the issue. Mix up a few random files so we don't know which are true and which aren't."

Alex stared at her, the wheels of his brain clearly in motion. "Presumably he'd switch with someone on the same salary and paying the same amount of tax otherwise Eric Pierce might notice and raise questions with HR. Presuming EG is still on the payroll."

"He was as of two weeks ago and I doubt he'd work for free." Ashley put her hand over the phone mic, clearly on hold. "Narcissists don't like to give anything away."

"The guy has millions in crypto but draws a salary?" Another agent queried.

Yael frowned. "It's not that unusual. Even people with money get bored. And maybe he's using his access to the company's security equipment or data to further his crimes…"

Alex narrowed his gaze. "Let's compare all the salary payment transaction numbers from a year ago with the current HR files."

"Company is gonna get back to me ASAP. I think they are trying to limit the possible fallout from this so they are checking with lawyers every step of the way now." Ashley brought her laptop and sat down beside Alex. "I'll crosscheck the details on the DMV."

Excitement raced through Yael. This could work.

"Let's go through each record individually. I'll pull up the bank records for salary payments and you see who we pull up on the HR files. Ashley crosschecks photo on the DMV," said Alex.

Yael nodded. It was a lot slower doing this individually but less chance of them missing an anomaly.

Shane arrived and came to stand behind her and touched her shoulder. Yael noticed they were surrounded by a crowd of people. Mallory, Jack, and the baby had left.

After the first hour people wandered off to do other vital things. Shane took the seat beside her, watching all their screens intently.

Sloan came into the room. "We have a general description from Borisky of a white male about 5′ 11″, hundred-eighty pounds. Dark almost black hair. Blue eyes. We have a sketch artist working with him as we speak for a better picture."

"What did you have to give him in exchange?" Shane asked without looking up.

Yael glanced at Sloan. The woman gave her a slightly evil smile. "I promised the Department of Justice wouldn't charge him as an accessory to first-degree murder. He'll be charged with handling and selling weapons etc., which would normally mean straight back to prison, no passing go. But the ADA promised a suspended sentence *if* the picture Borisky helps create leads to an arrest."

Someone must have explained what Yael and Alex were doing as Sloan said, "If you can get me a photograph in the next couple of hours, I can show Borisky a line up and see if we can get a positive ID." She checked her watch. "I'm having him transferred to the nearest federal holding facility later tonight."

Yael clenched her jaw and rolled her shoulders. They were going as fast as they could but it still took about forty seconds per person which meant it might take them all day to work their way through the massive list.

They had a system going. Alex said a name. Yael and Ashley

pulled up the matching HR and driver's license files. It was monotonous and boring after the first hundred.

Shane handed her a Coke and she took a quick sip. She needed the sugar hit.

"Ethan Grice," Alex intoned and spelled the last name.

Yael's search came back blank. She sat forward. "Wait. There's nothing here. No HR file…"

Yael watched Ashley pull up DMV files for the name. The document loaded and horror gripped her insides.

"Shit." Shane stood and his chair clattered across the floor.

"You recognize him?" Alex asked.

"Yeah." Yael's mouth tasted like sawdust. "That's Laura's new boyfriend."

27

"Hey! I found a link between Ethan Grice and two of the victims…" Yael said from her position bent over a laptop in the corner of the small kitchen area.

"What is it?" Shane asked with half an ear tuned into the preparations HRT were making.

"Up until four years ago, victim number three, Derek Vincent, was a correctional guard at Dresden Detention Center where Ethan Grice served time. Vincent was fired for misconduct and fudged the details about that period on his resume. And guess who Grice's public defender was? One Phillipa Everard who went on to marry a guy called Douglas Laurent."

Phillipa Laurent was the judge who'd been murdered.

"Any idea what the misconduct Vincent was accused of was?" Shane asked with a sinking feeling in the pit of his stomach.

Yael's big brown eye met his. "He was accused of sexual assault but he was never charged. I assume the prison service wanted to sweep the allegations under the carpet."

Made sense for something that egregious to paint a target on Vincent's back. "Do you think he hid people he had a genuine grudge against amongst innocents or were all of the victims specific targets?" Shane asked.

"I suspect he hid those he saw as guilty amongst innocent victims. It's a good way of getting revenge without getting caught," Ashley Chen interrupted, coming over to where they stood. "I'll pass that onto BAU-4 and see what they say. Good work, Yael."

Yael nodded and went back to staring at her screen.

Shane watched his teammates get ready for the assault.

The task force had set up in an empty hotel suite at the far end of the corridor from Laura Bay's hotel room.

Ron Borisky had picked Laura's new boyfriend out from an array of five other dark-haired men, including Eric Pierce, as the person he'd sold two handguns, one with a suppressor, an assault rifle, and ammunition to. Pierce was looking more and more like someone *Ethan Grice* had set up, knowing that the former would lawyer up and look guilty because of the drugs he was apparently selling after hours.

Shane didn't feel sorry for the guy in the hospital. He'd drawn a weapon on an FBI agent rather than answer a few simple questions. He dealt drugs that destroyed lives even though he had a well-paying job.

The rest of the task force were assembling all the background data they could find on Ethan Grice while other agents and HRT assembled at Laura's hotel. Radar suggested the room was empty but no one wanted to take any chances.

They'd cleared the entire hotel, going door-to-door and asking people to wait outside on the opposite side of the building as a precaution against Laura's room being rigged with explosives. Not likely as EG had lost his bomb capability when he'd murdered Lloyd Zenko. But it didn't take an FBI profiler to tell them this psycho was escalating and fast.

The suspect was unpredictable and enjoyed hurting people. No one was taking any chances.

Shane ached to get out of this damn cast and join his teammates, but at the same time he enjoyed being part of the overarching investigation, especially as it gave him the opportunity to spend more time with Yael.

They were getting closer to capturing Scotty's killer and the person who'd gone after Yael with an assault rifle. They were assuming that Ethan Grice AKA Owen Froese—another fake identity he'd used to connect with Laura online—had left the bar with Laura last night having spotted Shane and realizing, possibly unwittingly thanks to Laura, that Yael was alone and unprotected. Presumably EG had finagled Yael's address out of the other woman—Shane didn't like to think about how.

It was conjecture but that's all they had right now. That and the fact Laura wasn't answering her phone or email and appeared to be missing.

And it fit. It all fit.

Alex Parker and Ashley Chen had ordered all company and task force passwords and encryption codes changed immediately *again* so that Laura couldn't reveal vital information. She hadn't had full access to the files but she knew what had been said in meetings and no one was taking any chances. Alex had put people on scouring the systems—at his firm and the DOJ—for any corruption or viruses that the EG may have inserted.

Theory was EG had somehow identified Laura as the person tracking the crypto payments and had presumably tracked her online habits and used a dating app to approach her in real life without arousing her suspicion.

Yael seemed stunned by developments.

It was unclear *exactly* when EG had taken Laura hostage. Someone had wiped the hotel's security camera footage completely for the last two weeks and had captured a twenty-four-hour loop that they'd set to play constantly. Hotel security hadn't caught on yet. Ironically the hotel used the hardware and software systems from the security firm Ethan Grice worked for—which must have seemed like a gift to the sadistic prick.

According to Laura's text messages to Yael, she'd come down

with food poisoning during the night, but it was more likely EG incapacitated her immediately upon leaving the bar. He could have drugged or tasered her. Left her tied up in the trunk of his vehicle before parking on the side of the road, crossing the creek and mowing Yael's townhouse down with automatic gunfire.

Shane looked at Yael whose dark eyes appeared haunted. She'd probably been texting with EG. She'd even planned to come here and see Laura tonight.

EG hadn't replied when Yael had told Laura she was on her way and asking her did she need anything. It would have been too perfect for the guy to be sitting waiting for her only to be met with fourteen heavily armed HRT assaulters and two overprotective canines.

But the guy was almost certainly long gone.

Anger hardened inside him. Ethan Grice had not only killed his best friend, stolen a woman's life partner and their children's father. He'd also terrorized numerous innocents both for fun and for money. He'd terrorized Yael whom Shane was starting to have real feelings for.

Alex had tried tracking Laura's cell but no luck. It had been turned off since just before the attack last night and only turned on again to periodically check and send texts. The location of the cell was cloaked.

The asshole had probably gotten off reading about how terrified Yael had been. Pity EG hadn't tried to trace Yael's cell last night. The welcoming committee would have been pleased to meet him.

Yael looked pale and taut, spine rigid, eyes downcast. She flinched when he touched her arm and he told himself not to take it personally.

"This is all my fault," she muttered for the twentieth time.

"This is one hundred percent not your fault." Alex Parker had the focused look of an operator right now. A man on a mission. "I should have prevented this from happening. I should have caught this guy a long time ago. I underestimated him and that's on me."

The scene was familiar to Shane. Everyone blaming themselves rather than the fucker responsible.

Shane watched from the doorway as Echo team stacked up at the door. They'd used radar, fiber optics, and a drone to surveil the inside of the room. Everything looked empty and undisturbed.

Ford Cadell held Hugo who looked focused and ready to work even though it was doubtful there was anyone to apprehend inside. Shane tensed as they let Griffin unlock the door with the hotel keycard. This was a good real-life training opportunity. The team moved in fast as soon as Griffin opened the door.

They were back outside the room again in under ten seconds. Shane strode down the corridor with Novak to meet Cowboy. He was aware of Yael following quietly behind them, clearly worried about her friend.

Ryan shook his head. "Room's empty."

Yael put her hand across her mouth. Alex Parker sucked in a deep breath.

Shane knew they'd mentally prepared themselves to find Laura's mutilated body inside the bathroom. "Did it look as if there'd been a struggle?" Shane wanted in to see for himself but knew it wasn't going to happen anytime soon. Evidence techs were going in first. Sloan's orders.

Cowboy shook his head. "Bed's made up. Room looks unoccupied."

Chances were the bastard had taken her with him from the bar and, if Shane was a betting man, he'd say Laura Bay was odds on favorite to be EG's next online victim, unless the FBI found her first.

"Laura definitely checked in." Shane impatiently scratched the skin under his cast. He was tempted to cut the plaster off but Novak would only send him back to the hospital for a new one which would cost him time.

Cowboy nodded. "No indication she ever made it to her room though."

They wandered back to the suite while Evidence Techs took over. Shane figured it was a waste of time considering the amount of DNA that must pass through there on a weekly basis. It was another avalanche of evidence to bury the details that might actually nail the suspect.

"Have they located her car?" Yael asked.

Ashley Chen looked up from where she was typing on a laptop. They'd put out a BOLO earlier. "Nothing. Yet."

Yael looked like she wanted to say something.

"What?" Shane urged. She had such good instincts. He wanted her to believe in herself more.

"You said her vehicle wasn't at the bar. I think she would definitely have left it here along with her luggage. She drove here last night after she dropped Tim off at his hotel down the road."

Tim Theriault was watching for any new crypto activity on a laptop near the window. The young man seemed traumatized.

"Owen or Ethan or whatever the hell his name is, picks her up and drives them to the bar. Laura likes a few drinks so she'd be happy to make someone else the designated driver. And she'd want her luggage easily accessible when she came back, but she'd want it safe."

Ashley frowned. "An agent checked the parking garage but I'll have someone check again for the make and model."

"Or EG took it," Novak suggested.

"I doubt he'd risk it. And Laura's car is top of the line. He'd be wary of anything we can track," Alex said. "As far as we know he's still driving the car he stole from Wayne Stockwell with false plates."

"What about her laptop?" Yael asked.

"Either he has it or it's in her vehicle."

Yael's expression collapsed. "I can't believe he's taken her. That even with us all looking for him he was right in front of us the whole time. The bastard chatted to me in a bar and I didn't even realize it was him. Everything he does is to maximize people's pain."

She looked away, wiping her eyes. Pretending she hadn't been about to cry.

Shane wanted to give her a hug but he needed to let her be professional in front of her boss. "Why'd he scrub so much video if Laura only checked in last night?" asked Shane.

Maybe they'd come here for a quickie last week. The idea was repulsive now but Laura had been into the guy and thought he was a normal date.

Yael frowned at him. "You think he could have booked a room here too?"

"Why not? Ethan Grice knew it was only a matter of time until we found his identity via his workplace. Eric Pierce was his version of Lloyd Zenko's tripwire and told him when it was time to execute his escape." Shane crossed his arms. "He had to be staying somewhere close by." He was officially on vacation from his place of work. Shane didn't figure the guy had planned to go back. FBI Charlotte were searching for his home but had come up with nothing. "I doubt he's been moving from place to place all this time. He'd want to have a base and he was already in the area a week ago when he went on that first date with Laura."

The FBI had discovered he'd wiped his dating app records from the system. Online, it was as if he'd never existed. All that remained was a payment to the company which was from another stolen credit card.

She sat up straighter. "That actually makes a lot of sense. That's why he wiped so much security footage. Perhaps he installed the security system here or saw it listed in company documents. But either way he knew he could manipulate the cameras and software here. Maybe we should send out a message to any hotel in the country with this security system to be on the lookout."

Ashley nodded and made a note on her tablet.

Yael tilted her head. Shane loved watching her brain kick into high gear. "He might even still be here, watching."

Alex stared at her thoughtfully. "He's probably long gone, especially with the FBI clearing out the hotel…"

Shane remembered Wayne Stockwell's bloated body in the bathtub. "And he probably wiped down the room with Clorox."

"But he might have missed something. We need to find out if he was here. And what he was driving when he left."

Alex typed something on his laptop then looked at them. "There is no booking for an Owen Froese or Ethan Grice."

"We need to check with the front desk and see if someone recognizes him. He can't have killed everyone he came into contact with and he can't have an unlimited supply of fake identities."

Shane hoped both things were true.

"Housekeeping might not have cleaned yet or they might have missed something. And my guess is he wouldn't expect us to figure this out. He'd assume we'd assume he wiped the video because of Laura being here." Yael looked determined now, which was a whole lot better than beaten.

Right now, they had no physical evidence linking EG to Yael's shooting or Ethan Grice to that or the other murders. They needed his DNA to connect the crimes on top of any circumstantial or electronic evidence they assembled.

Alex stood up.

"Where are you going?" Yael asked.

"To talk to the desk staff. See if someone remembers our guy."

Yael followed him out and after a brief hesitation and a look at his teammates so did Shane.

They were in a race against time. If EG stuck to his usual schedule they had three days before Laura Bay became his next online victim. Shane didn't want Laura or Yael to have to go through that. He didn't want Ethan Grice to run any more circles around them. He wanted the guy under arrest or bleeding out in the dirt. He wanted Laura Bay rescued alive and unharmed. He wanted Yael happy and his best friend back. One of those things was impossible, but the others…

He would fight to make them happen.

They were watching all the murders in the task force briefing room and there was definitely something more personal about the mutilation and murders of Derek Vincent and Phillipa Laurant.

Yael's mouth went dry watching the visceral fear in their eyes that said as loud as words that they knew they were about to die.

They both had a pair of nylons tied around their open mouths. The victims could scream and make noise but the words were not discernible to someone who knew how to read lips. The FBI were now paying extra special attention to the victims who were gagged this way but it could have been another method of obfuscating targets who could identify him.

Yael felt sick from watching the violence and cruelty Ethan Grice inflicted on people.

Grice had been incarcerated for two years for hacking into the Defense Intelligence Agency and then trying to sell secrets on the dark web. It was before Cramer, Parker & Gray, Security Consultants had been hired to conduct pen tests on government agencies and identify possible threats in order to figure out how to fix them. It was possible EG held a grudge against people with the same skills he had who were profiting from something that had sent him to prison.

"Dammit." Alex's expression was tense.

She'd never seen her boss rattled before and it worried her.

"EG just posted. The next online auction starts tomorrow at 9 a.m. EST."

"He's never had that small a gap between abductions and murders before," Yael protested. She put her hands on her head. That didn't give them enough time to track him down.

Alex met Yael's gaze and she had to blink away tears. This wasn't some unknown victim, which would have been bad enough. This was *Laura*. Their friend and colleague.

Evi1Geni-us had had twenty hours since shooting up her house to get wherever he was planning to go. It was also possible he hadn't left the area at all and that he'd follow his usual pattern of killing near the abduction site. The guy had money. He could hire a jet and be out of the country. He could be anywhere in the world by now.

All fifty-six FBI divisions had been put on high alert. Ethan Grice's image had been circulated to law enforcement and the media and he'd claimed an official spot on the FBI's Most Wanted list.

They'd found the hotel room where Ethan Grice had stayed but a search had turned up nothing more exciting than the brand of shampoo he preferred. Evidence techs were collecting DNA samples in the hopes of coming up with *something* tangible.

The task force office was relatively quiet. Most people had headed over to the Academy building to grab something to eat before the canteen closed for the night but Yael couldn't bear to leave her terminal. She couldn't stop searching for some clue as to where this guy or Laura might be.

Shane offered her a slice of pizza but her stomach lurched and she shook her head and turned away from him. She knew he was confused by her emotional withdrawal but no matter how often Alex tried to take the blame, this was her fault. She'd spoken to this man. He'd looked her in the eye and smiled.

She had a crick in her neck and her lower back ached from hours in the chair, but she couldn't leave. She needed to catch him. Needed to put him behind bars. Had to help find Laura before it was too late.

Alex was on the dark web signed in to one of his bad guy personas.

He was typing fast.

"Alex?" Ashley's voice rose in warning. "What are you doing?" The woman looked pale and tired.

Her boss's mouth was grim.

"Oh shit." Ashley closed her eyes and let out a big sigh.

Yael's mouth parched when she saw what he'd posted into a forum that regularly talked about these and other crimes.

Alex had accused EG of setting up a fake show. That there was no way EG could have escaped the cops last time if it really was live and that the voting system was rigged. EG was stealing his money and he wanted a refund.

Alex looked up and held Ashley's gaze. "Do you really think he will be any crueler to her simply because I call him out?"

The agent shook her head reluctantly. "Might have been useful to run it past the profilers first."

"I did."

Ashley grunted.

"Frazer agreed we have nothing to lose at this stage and, if we get lucky, EG might get angry or be arrogant enough that he makes a mistake."

"But it's not you he'll be angry with," Yael protested. "It's Laura."

"Look." Ashley put the screen onto a monitor they could all see. "He's online."

Yael started tracking where the information was coming from but the guy was using a much more sophisticated VPN this time. One that would take time to hack. But she was good too. She needed to prove it.

EvilGeni-us: *"Crippen" works for the FBI. His real name is Alex Parker and he has a cybersecurity firm if anyone wants to take a crack at his business. If you're wondering how I know that, it's because one of his employees will be my next special guest. And, yes, last time I recorded the fun so I could leave a surprise for the cops—which you all got to watch as a free bonus, so stop complaining motherfuckers. This time I'll prove it's live so come with your own ideas for making her scream. She's a pretty one. I'll take my time with her. The FBI won't find me. She'll die and they'll watch. You pay and I'll play.*

. . .

The responses varied from people immediately logging off, to support for EG, to users demanding a refund. But EG didn't stick around to listen to complaints and Yael hadn't begun to isolate his signal which was bouncing around like a ping-pong ball off three different proxy servers.

Then he was gone.

Alex bowed his head.

"You need to warn the others," Yael said woodenly. "Every hacker on the dark web will be trying to damage us or our clients tonight."

Alex sent off a text to whoever was on duty in DC to be on the watch for cyber-attacks. The most obvious one would be a denial-of-service attack. If the company took the website down for a few hours it would take the wind out of their sails and beat them to the punch. It wasn't as if that's how they pulled in most of their business anyway. It was just the public facing front.

"Laura knew all the IDs I used that received invites to the auctions. She had to in order to track the crypto. How do we get into the next auction?" Alex was pissed. They were effectively blind when they most needed to see.

"I can get us in," Ashley said quietly. "I have a dark web persona who's been invited before and LAPD have a cybercrime unit that's been posing undercover. I know the detective there. I'll reach out as a backup."

Alex nodded. He looked defeated though, which he never did and Yael felt the same way.

"You need to take a break," Shane said quietly in her ear.

"Don't tell me what I need to do," she said sharply.

"You need to eat."

"I ate earlier."

"That was hours ago." Shane dragged her chair out from her desk with her still sitting in it. "Come on."

Alex shot them a glance. "Might be a good idea to take a quick breather. It's going to be another long night."

"Fine." Yael closed her laptop and stomped out of the room into the dark frigid evening.

28

Outside the building Yael glared at Shane as he waited until he was close enough to open the door of his truck before popping the lock. She climbed inside, hoarding the anger and fury and pain that burned through her being.

"I don't appreciate being told what to do," she snapped.

"You think I hadn't figured that out yet?" Shane's expression tightened as he slammed the door shut.

Even though she was pushing him away the thought of him going anywhere hurt. How messed up was that? She was falling for him, she realized with a jolt. After all the years of never falling for anyone, of only dating people she didn't like, she was falling for this man who was everything a younger, more innocent version of herself had ever dreamed of.

They were driving now through the gloom.

"This was a mistake," she bit out.

He shot her a look.

"What was?" His voice was hard and angry.

"You and me getting involved."

Now she'd made him furious. She could tell from the way the muscle in his jaw ticked. He veered off the road along a short dirt track, pulling to a stop at the side of a lake.

He got out of the truck and stood outlined in the headlights, staring at the water.

She undid her seatbelt to go to him but hesitated. Looking at him made her mouth water with want. The broad shoulders and narrow waist. Strong legs planted in a wide stance. Had he done it deliberately? Stood there showing her everything she was going to lose?

She knew she couldn't keep him. Had known it from the moment they'd started this unlikely entanglement. He wouldn't stay.

After a full minute he turned and looked over the hood at her even though she must be hidden in darkness.

She tensed, her heart rate picking up like some hunted animal.

She killed the lights, not wanting to see what she was going to miss with every beat of her heart.

He came around to the passenger side of the truck and opened her door, pulling her until she stumbled onto him. Shane cupped the back of her head and lowered his lips to hers as he pressed her up against the rear door of the cab.

Immediately her pulse went into overdrive and she kissed him back.

His mouth was hungry and insistent and she wrapped her arms around his neck and strained to get closer. They were alone out here, the night so pitch black he was nothing but a shadow. No one was around. No one could see what they were doing. Thank goodness because she didn't want to stop.

He smelled like crushed pine needles and a hint of warm spice. His skin was hot and smooth, the muscles beneath bunching.

Lust ripped through her bloodstream like a rocket launch before blastoff.

She kissed him as if she was starved—starved of attention, starved of affection, starved of love. The possessive curl of his fingers against her face and angle of his mouth fed that hunger. Made her want to sink into him and never let go.

Why did he make her feel like this? Every time he touched her, she ignited and no matter how much she knew it was a mistake to let him get closer, she didn't want it to stop. Even though she knew he would break her heart in the end.

He tugged her t-shirt over her head. The metal of the door was shockingly cold against her back. She didn't care. All she cared about was the fact this man was devouring her and she was devouring him right back and right now it beat everything else going on in her life.

His hand closed over her breast and he lowered his mouth and kissed his way down her body, sucking her nipple until her hands clenched in his hair. His fingers were busy with the snap of her jeans and then he was peeling them down her legs along with her panties, careful of her bandaged feet.

"Hurry," she urged him as she kicked them off.

But he surprised her by dropping to his knees and draping her one leg over his shoulder and forcing her thighs wider with his shoulders before leaning forward to taste her hot center.

Her hands sank into his shoulders and she let her head drop back against the hardness of the cab while his mouth softly kissed along her folds until settling with determined pressure against her clit. His good arm reached up and tweaked her nipple and she felt the clench of reaction arrow from her breast to her core as a shudder worked through her. She shattered in a rush of sensation.

He climbed to his feet, pulled a condom from his back pocket and handed it to her. Her hands shook as she ripped it open. He undid his belt, shoving his jeans off as she slid the condom over his rigid flesh.

"Hang on to my neck," he growled.

She did as he told her. "What about your arm?"

"My arm is fine." He hoisted her legs around his hips and she clung to him as he positioned himself against her. Then he pushed inside and they were both shaking as he started driving in and out of her. He cushioned her head as best he could but she didn't care.

She wanted that unrestrained passion, that mindless lust that seemed to consume him as much as it consumed her.

He shifted her and she felt small and delicate even though she was anything but. She was writhing and thrusting against him and her hands absorbed the strength of him as he pistoned in and out, stimulating her clit over and over until she teetered on the brink of another climax.

"Let go, dammit." His voice was rough but the kisses he placed on her lips and throat were so gentle they fluttered over her skin like butterflies then turned into dragons as the avalanche of sensation crashed over her again and her nails dug into his back as she cried out. She felt him stiffen as he ground against her, pulsing between her legs before they both held themselves completely still as they gradually floated back down to earth.

He withdrew carefully and placed her feet gently on the ground, dealing with the condom while her world slowly stopped spinning.

He stared down at her for a long, silent moment, his expression only faintly visible in the moon and starlight. "You going to tell me that was another mistake?"

Her brain screamed that, yes, this was a mistake but her pounding heart would do it over and over a million times with this man. And that was the problem.

I seem to date women who want more from me than I am willing to give.

His words echoed through her mind. She grabbed her t-shirt off the ground and pulled it on, snatching her jeans off the dew-laden grass. She snorted out a laugh, knowing the sex solved nothing. It couldn't fix the thing that was most broken about her. And would only hold him until the next thing came along to challenge his adrenaline-junkie heart. Or until he found out the truth.

When she was dressed again, she said quietly, "Are you really going to tell me it wasn't?"

He took his time righting his clothes. She went to climb back in the truck when he grabbed her wrist and turned her gently around to face him.

"You know, Yael, one day you're going to have to stop running."

She froze, then jerked away. "This from a man who doesn't like commitment?"

He stood back even though she could tell he wanted to touch her. "I want you to trust me, to confide in me."

"And I want you to trust me enough not to have to." Her heart squeezed painfully and she lowered her head.

"I do trust you." He frowned. "I know at first I was a little suspicious—"

"What do you mean?" She crossed her arms over her chest.

He hesitated, dragging his hand through his thick hair in a way that made her want to melt. "Just, you know, I wanted to make sure you weren't somehow in league with, *erm*, you know."

Shock lanced through her. "What?"

"It was a possibility I couldn't ignore."

She stiffened. "Wait. You suspected I might be working with that monster?" The knowledge lashed at her, reminiscent of the pain of the worst days of her life. "You actually thought I might be involved in the torture and murder of all those people?"

He shook his head as if to deny his own words. "I was fucked up after Scotty died, and then losing Montana…"

"When did you figure out for sure that I wasn't part of EG's evil scheme?"

He didn't say anything.

"When?" Her voice carried across the lake.

She heard him swallow.

"I checked your phone when you were in the shower that day after we found Zenko."

She was stunned. She hadn't suspected anything and yet, after all these years of being disappointed by people, it shouldn't hurt quite so much. The moonlight skimmed his profile. The man was absolute perfection and he'd made her want him more than she'd ever imagined wanting anyone. And it was all a lie. "Was that the reason you insisted on staying close to me?"

"At first," he admitted. "A small part of it, anyway. The other was to make sure you were safe, and also because I don't have any computing skills and you obviously do." He raised his face to look at the sky.

"You used me." Pain seared across her chest. He'd stuck close to her so he'd be the first to know when and if they tracked down EG's real identity. He'd gotten to know her out of suspicion and utility. The sex was probably an unexpected bonus.

"I think you're amazing, Yael. I was a fucked-up idiot who fucked up." He dragged his hand over his hair. "I think what we have could be special. I want to see where this can go…"

Inside she felt ice cold. "I thought you didn't do relationships."

"I might. For you." His voice cracked.

Silence stretched between them until he finally broke it. "I'm not talking about getting married, but dammit, you could at least meet me halfway here."

"I did meet you halfway, Shane, but you lied to me and I don't know if I can forgive you for that." The truth rang out, shocking in its honesty. And maybe halfway wasn't enough for a real relationship, not one built on lies.

He swore before they both climbed into the truck and drove silently back to Building 64.

She opened the door to get out, knowing she needed to end this now while she had a hope of surviving with her heart even vaguely intact. "I'm not looking for anything complicated, Shane. I thought this was a bit of fun to ease a stressful situation. I thought you understood that."

She forced herself to look him in the eye when she lied. He was going to hate her soon enough anyway. "It's probably best if we keep everything between us strictly professional from now on."

Alex came to the main entrance with a tense look on his face. "I think I've found something."

Yael jumped out and went into the building without waiting for Shane. She couldn't bring herself to face him. It hurt too much.

29

Several hours later, Shane was still pissed as he and Alex Parker covertly approached Ethan Grice's home on the edge of Charlotte, North Carolina. They'd flown down here on Parker's company jet.

Yael was still onboard the aircraft, along with Ashley Chen. The rest of the task force was split between Quantico and staging at Andrews Air Force Base, ready to take off as soon as they had a potential location on Grice. SWAT teams around the country were on high alert as were HRT's Blue team who were currently training on the west coast.

The fact Yael had pushed him away seconds after she'd come apart in his arms was driving him nuts—as if the sexual connection they shared was nothing out of the ordinary. He was still furious, with himself mainly.

For the first time in years, he was the one trying to prolong a relationship. They seemed to share something amazing. The fact he hadn't been completely honest at the start made him feel like a jerk, but he'd had legitimate concerns and hadn't been thinking straight.

Now she'd shut him out and he didn't like it. Not at all.

Male ego? Maybe.

He understood that she was angry with him for the lack of trust and the invasion of privacy but, considering EG *had* infiltrated the task force via Parker's team, his initial suspicion wasn't so far-fetched. She was spooked but he didn't think it was his actions that scared her—more the thought of getting involved with someone and he totally got that. She was still in danger from this psycho motherfucker though. It wasn't like he could walk away and let her fend for herself, even if he wanted to.

He figured that they needed to catch this asshole and then he could work on things with Yael.

"Reminds me of Mallory's home when we first met," Alex said wryly, glancing at the houses on the edge of the trees.

Shane grunted again. He liked Alex well enough but he didn't want to talk about the guy's perfect life or ideal wife.

Alex shot him a look. "You and Yael have a falling out?"

"What gave it away?"

"Oh, I don't know. Maybe the icy silence or awkward atmosphere on the flight down here? Or maybe your current brooding demeanor. I take it there was an argument?"

Shane made another non-committal sound. He couldn't make out the guy's expression in the darkness. They were both dressed completely in black including balaclavas and thin gloves. No FBI markings or insignia. They both glowed a ghostly green through night vision goggles. This was an off-the-books op that Ashley Chen said it was better she knew nothing about.

"Hard to argue when the other person refuses to talk to you." Pretending she'd only been into him for the sex? It was laughable. He'd done plenty of only-for-the-sex relationships and this wasn't it. Yael was too complex for a relationship to be that uncomplicated or two dimensional. What really surprised him was the fact he wanted more.

"I fucked up," Shane admitted. "I was suspicious of her at first. Figured if anyone was a leak in the task force it would be someone like her, or you." He shot Alex a look in the darkness. They kept their voices barely above a whisper. "People who can manipulate the internet into saying whatever it is you want it to say. She wasn't too happy when I admitted that to her earlier."

"Ah. I'm used to people being suspicious of me and, frankly, I don't trust anyone I haven't checked out all the way back to kindergarten." Alex paused again and Shane did too. "But Yael has had some bad life experiences."

"Yeah? Join the club."

"You've always had someone to fall back on. Your family, your SF buddies, your teammates."

Alex Parker seemed to know a lot about him. Maybe it was Shane's questions at the motel the other day. Maybe it was the fact he was sleeping with his employee—or rather *had* been sleeping with his employee before he'd been unceremoniously dumped after the best sex of his life.

Alex continued, thankfully oblivious to Shane's wandering thoughts. "She hasn't had anyone in her life for a very long time."

And now her best friend had been kidnapped by a maniac. Shane's mood slumped deeper into the dumps.

"In fact, she's only recently realizing that there are people in the world she can trust."

Shane stared at Alex's shadow and the not-so-subtle reprimand. "What happened?"

"It's not my story to tell," Alex stated simply.

Shane ground his teeth with frustration.

"For the record, I don't think she's told *anyone* about her past. Not even Laura."

"But you know all about it?" Shane asked.

"I figured it out before I offered her a job."

"Did she know that?"

Alex shook his head. "No. Unlike some people, I know when not to push."

Fuck.

"I know what it's like not to know who you can trust. To never feel completely worthy of the people you care about..."

Shane did care for her and thought she might care about him

too. The feelings he had for her were stronger than he'd expected them to be and not something he'd planned for. What had started out as leveraging her knowledge about computers had turned into so much more.

But perhaps it was better to end things now, before either of them got hurt. He didn't have the sort of job that lent itself to relationships. Gone for weeks at a time and on call for the rest. Plus, she wasn't good for his focus, and lack of focus got people killed.

He thought about Scotty and Grace and acid crawled up his esophagus. They'd both lost everything. This wasn't the time to be thinking about his love life. This was the time to concentrate on catching Scotty's killer. Maybe then they could all move on with their lives.

They continued moving stealthily through the woods, still some distance from their target.

Alex wasn't done with him yet.

"Before I met Mallory, I didn't let anyone close. I told myself I did it to protect them but in reality, I was scared. Scared of rejection. Scared of not being deemed worthy if they knew the whole truth."

Shane shot the guy a glance. Was he talking about being an assassin for the CIA? "I doubt Yael has a history of covert ops."

Alex laughed reluctantly. "She does not, but she's a gentle soul and has reasons to guard her emotions."

That gentle soul had tossed him aside like he was a live grenade. Hadn't seemed to matter to her whether or not he had any feelings on the issue.

After a few more minutes they reached their destination.

"That's the place."

They watched for five long minutes but there was no sign of activity from inside. Alex started silently across the frost-damaged lawn. They reached the backdoor and, in under a minute, Alex had picked the very expensive lock.

"Wait." He held up his hand, pulled out some sort of device and turned it on. Then he sent a text and twenty seconds later the whole neighborhood went dark. Alex eased open the backdoor and headed straight to the alarm system that was starting to beep on auxiliary battery power. The beeps got closer together and Shane braced himself to move fast if the alarm went off.

A triple beep told Shane the system was disarmed and they were in.

"Won't EG know someone's in his house?" Shane whispered.

"Not with my little gadget. And I've turned on a signal blocker that prevents any listening devices or cameras from transmitting within a ten-meter radius in case he has some hidden inside the house. If EG notices the interference on any of the feeds hopefully he'll put it down to the power outage."

"How long until the power company turns it back on?"

"We should have about thirty minutes. If EG investigates the issue he'll see that there is an area outage. And Yael is all set up to follow anyone checking for outages who is not situated in the immediate area."

Shane's mouth tightened. "Smart."

"Yael's idea."

Like Shane hadn't already guessed that.

Alex flipped up the NVGs and they both turned on their red-beamed flashlights. The rest of the FBI didn't know about this place yet. Alex wanted to search for the crypto before Evidence Response Teams got in here because doing otherwise would slow them down. He wanted to barter Laura's life for EG's fortune.

"You really think he left the money here?"

"Yep. He doesn't trust banks and he doesn't think we'll find this place." The house was registered to a corporation and hidden under layers and layers of shell companies. "I doubt he'd risk carrying it all on his person in case he was mugged or apprehended. It probably isn't all of the money but I'd wager it's the bulk of it."

Shane knew that, ideally, they'd stake out the place and arrest the fucker when he came home to pick up the cash. But EG had Laura and no one wanted her to die.

"Where do we start?"

"Panic room."

"You saw the blueprints?" Shane asked in surprise.

Alex shook his head. "Simpler than that. As soon as I located the property, I found an old real estate listing. It mentioned a panic room."

"He never did any killing here, right?" Shane didn't want to contaminate evidence of a crime scene if he could help it.

"Not that we know of but anything is possible."

A shiver ran over Shane's back. Ethan Grice was a serial killer with no morals and zero empathy. Who knew when he first started his grisly trade.

Shane followed Alex to a large bookcase and they quickly figured out the opening mechanism and pulled the doors wide. Behind the cases was a steel door.

"Four-inch-thick steel with a 10-gauge carbon steel inner plate. Eleven bolts form the locking mechanism which also has electronic lock guards."

"Great. How do we get in?" Shane eyed it. "I could probably blow the hinges and bolts."

"The amount of explosives required might destroy everything inside which is fine except I want the hardware wallets intact."

The thought of giving Grice the money left a bad taste in Shane's mouth but he wasn't sure he could live with the alternative either. Hopefully they could catch the guy during the exchange—*if* he took the bait.

Alex leaned closer to examine the electronic lock which had shifted to some sort of auxiliary power system. He removed the faceplate and attached another small electronic gadget to some of the wires. Then they waited.

Every second ramped up the tension. The hairs on his nape rose. What if the sonofabitch had boobytrapped this space?

Fifty seconds felt like an eternity but finally the lock clicked and Alex pushed on the lever, spinning it in a circle until it unlocked and came ajar.

Shane halted the door with his foot and ran the flashlight around the crack of the opening. Satisfied, he moved his foot. "Looks clear."

They headed inside. There was a comfy couch set up in front of a TV and gaming console. A desk and a computer that was currently turned off.

A large refrigerator stood in one corner and there was also a small chemical toilet. The place was equipped with enough supplies to last for a month, easily.

A sweatshirt hung off the back of the chair but apart from that, the room didn't give anything away about the person who owned it. No photographs or artwork. No books or magazines. It wasn't much cozier than a prison cell which held a high degree of irony.

Alex went over to the desk and carefully opened the drawers. "Bingo."

Shane took some photographs on his phone. Alex slipped something that looked remarkably like a couple of data sticks and key fobs inside an evidence bag that Shane handed him.

Shane checked the rest of the room and found two more wallets beside a small surveillance unit placed near the door.

"Here."

Alex took photos and scooped them up into the bag also.

"Why does he have so many? I thought you could store billions on a single wallet?"

"Probably in case he loses one—doesn't want all his eggs in one basket. I expect he's carrying plenty with him in case he needs to run, but this is his retirement plan."

"Looks like he planned to hide out here if the cops ever tracked him down. Might have worked too."

"FBI will put a watch on this place in case he decides to come back here, but once he realizes we cleared him out, I doubt he'll be back unless he thinks we missed something."

They headed out of the panic room and closed the door. Alex reassembled the keypad before removing the gizmo off the alarm panel. Silently they headed out the door, into the trees, leaving no trace they'd ever been there. Alex sent a text to Yael and a few seconds later distant streetlights and houses once more started to glow.

Shane checked his watch. Time was ticking for Laura Bay. "Think he'll go for it?"

Alex remained silent.

It was pretty much the only hope they had right now.

"Where are they?" Bile burned the back of Yael's throat every time she thought about Laura being at that monster's mercy. She glanced at the time. 2:03 a.m. They only had a few hours until the auction went live and every psychopath in the world got to bid on the worst way to torture and humiliate her friend.

Ashley checked a text on her cell. "They're back."

She went over to the door of the jet and opened it. Shane and Alex came inside and Ashley quickly secured the door behind them.

Yael tried not to think about how good Shane looked dressed all in black. Why one man looked like the best thing in the world despite bristling with weapons, whilst another turned her stomach holding nothing more sinister than a screwdriver, she wasn't sure. "Did you find it?"

Shane nodded and a wave of relief filled her.

Alex pulled a bag of six different hardware wallets out of one of his pockets. He handed them to Ashley.

Yael sat at the computer and embedded a beacon into the metadata of one of the images Alex sent her. It would tell them where, when and on what device the image was opened.

The plan was for Ethan's boss to email Grice's work address telling him he had something he needed urgently from the guy. The email itself would be the photo along with a message from Alex asking EG to contact them on a cell number if he wanted his crypto back. If he hurt Laura, he'd never see any of it again.

Grice had turned his work email settings to render HTML without images but Yael had superseded his previous instructions. There was a good chance that he wouldn't realize until it was too late. Hopefully it would give them a glimpse of his location. At worst it would let the bastard know Alex had the guy's fortune in crypto.

In the meantime, they had to wait.

Shane stored his assault rifle in a room at the back of the plane and Yael tensed when he came and sat beside her. She met his stormy green eyes.

"Don't worry. I can act professional." Shane's lips pulled back in a half smile. "Even when I don't want to."

A lump formed in her throat and the unexpected threat of tears had her blinking and looking away. She nodded. Grateful and heartbroken all at the same time.

She watched Ashley and Alex work on the email and finally agree upon the text before they sent it off. It was possible EG wouldn't check any email accounts for fear of being tracked, but the alternative was announcing they had the crypto on the dark web which EG would probably view as both a humiliation and a challenge. This sort of coward was bound to take his anger out on the innocent.

Yael clenched her fists. "What do we do now?"

Ashley flicked a glance at her then at Shane. "We wait."

"We'll take off and head west for a while." HRT had planes on both coasts ready to go in minutes. "Why don't you get some sleep?" Alex suggested.

She could barely keep her eyes open. "I don't want to."

"I'll wake you if we hear anything."

She shot Shane a glance and the atmosphere seemed to thicken between them. She blew out a large breath. Nodded. Sleep made sense. She was exhausted and she didn't want to think. She closed her laptop and found a couch where she could lie down.

30

Ethan opened his phone to look for the nearest drive-thru along this deserted stretch of highway when he saw he had an email notification from his boss. Sneering, he clicked on the message, expecting either gossip about the arrogant prick Eric Pierce who had hopefully died of his wounds or a request to cut short his vacation and come in to work as they were now short-staffed.

Imagining the look on his boss's face when he discovered who Ethan really was, and how Ethan had used his job to help evade capture? Ha. He felt a surge of anticipation while the message downloaded. Then utter panic had him careening onto the shoulder and punching the brakes.

Fuck, fuck, fuck.

He hit the disconnect button and sat breathing hard as sweat dampened his brow. Blood roared through his ears until he couldn't hear anything except the frantic beat of his own heart.

Fuuuuuck.

His VPN should hold up but the Feds might be able to locate the cell tower his signal had jumped onto. He needed to move. He needed to get as far away from here as possible. Still, he didn't go anywhere. He examined the photograph again. And fury grew until it was lava punching through his veins. They'd stolen his money. Alex Parker and that bitch had broken into his home and stolen his crypto. It would take them time to hack into the wallets but he didn't kid himself they wouldn't be able to. Parker had the resources and brains to eventually figure it out. All that work and strife and those motherfuckers had ripped him off.

Ethan didn't believe they'd give it back. Any attempt to negotiate would be a trap designed for him to tumble into and then back to jail. Death row was not somewhere he intended to spend the rest of his life.

Maybe if he could get to Africa or some country that didn't have an extradition treaty with the US. Take this bitch with him. Negotiate from there. He had enough online connections that he could turn around and get on a boat and have a new identity arranged before they hit port on the other side of the ocean.

His hands wrung the steering wheel.

Red and blue lights flickered in his rearview and he realized a patrol car was behind him.

"Shit."

He watched the cop slowly get out of his vehicle, adjust his hat and start walking toward him.

Ethan rolled the window down an inch as he rested the pistol out of sight.

"Sorry, Officer. I pulled over to check my cell phone."

The man leaned closer. "You aware you have a broken taillight?"

Ethan blinked twice. "No, sir. I wasn't." The road was empty. No headlights in either direction.

"License and registration."

Muffled sounds from the cargo area had the cop's eyes going wide. Ethan fired twice through the door, straight into the man's torso.

"You had to fucking ruin my fucking day, didn't you, bitch!"

Ethan screamed. There was only one reason the taillight could be damaged.

A sob came from the back.

He pulled on his gloves before climbing out and stepping over the large man's body. Quickly, he opened the trunk to make sure she was still tied up. Laura stared up at him with reddened eyes.

She flinched away from the cop car's headlights. Her hands were tied together but somehow, she'd pushed the fitting out. He quickly put it back in place. Then he grabbed his taser and hit Laura with a five-second cycle. Her eyes rolled and she shook like she was having a fit.

"Do it again and I'll hurt you so bad you'll wish you were already dead."

He slammed the door shut and grabbed the cop by the feet and dragged him into the thick grass at the side of the road. He snatched the body cam off his jacket.

He rolled the guy down the embankment, sitting on the frozen ground and kicking him with both feet. Next, he jumped in the patrol car and pulled out the dash cam, as well as the computer. He turned off the lights and the engine, got out and pushed the car off the road, steering it down the embankment toward the dead officer. Then he opened the cargo door on the SUV again as Laura scooted away from him. He pulled out another set of fake plates and quickly put them on the vehicle. It was fucking cold and even with gloves his fingers were almost numb. Ten minutes later and a car was just starting to head his way, headlights visible in the darkness. He pulled carefully onto the highway and punched the gas. He was going to make sure Laura and Yael and Alex Parker all wished they hadn't pulled that stunt. Then, after Laura was taken care of and his coffers replenished a little, he'd leave the country and start a new life.

Ethan knew how to make money on the internet and how to avoid getting caught. He'd been doing it for years. It wouldn't take him long to re-amass his fortune.

Unfortunately, it wouldn't take long for Laura to die, either. For the millionth time he cursed Yael's good luck and his bad. But he'd make her suffer with his current plan and, one day, when she was least expecting it, he'd make her pay.

31

Shane had caught forty-winks but was now wide awake and trying not to stare at Yael as she worked on one of the couches toward the rear of the small plane. Dark circles shadowed her eyes. Her expression was drawn. Worry for her friend etched every line. At least she'd gotten a little rest.

"How are your feet?" he asked her.

She looked up, startled. "They're fine. A little sore but healing."

He nodded, wanting to say a million other things and unable to utter a single one.

Tension was ramping up as the start of the auction loomed.

"Storm approaching from the west. I'm going to have the pilot refuel in Wichita while we can still land," Alex said quietly.

Shane nodded. Wichita was as good a place as any and central if they ever figured out a location for Grice. They still had no firm idea where this guy was. Alex's crew in DC were working tirelessly to find some trace of him in the electronic universe but so far this guy was a ghost.

Everyone was on edge. They'd had a glimmer of excitement when EG had opened the email but he had a sophisticated VPN that Yael had only been able to narrow down to the Kansas, Nebraska, Colorado area.

EG hadn't responded to Alex's message yet and he was either considering his options or he'd decided recovering the money wasn't worth the risk of death or incarceration.

Ashley Chen was in the restroom freshening up. Everyone was going to need to be at the top of their game for the next few hours.

His work cell buzzed.

"Hey, text from Sloan." It had gone out to everyone on the task force but he read it out anyway. "Highway patrol cop was shot and killed on a rural road near Limon, Colorado around 3:20 a.m. last night." Anger curled in Shane's stomach. Another senseless death. "Cop stopped a green Subaru with a broken taillight. Suspect got away and stole the cop's body and dash cams before he fled the scene. Sloan and company believe this could be our UNSUB."

"That was around the time someone opened the email..." Yael's lips were pale as they pressed tightly together.

"I guess he didn't take it too well," said Shane.

Alex swore.

"Still no reply from the email?" Shane asked.

"Nothing. He knows the chances of getting that money back and getting away are close to nil," Alex stated numbly.

Alex opened up a program that showed cell towers near where the cop was killed and identified them and downloaded the cell-phone numbers that had connected to them between 2:45 and 3:45. Then he pulled up a program and ran the numbers through another database.

"One of the phones that connected to one tower in the area for a brief one-minute window was a burner cell and yep, it matches the model that opened the email," Alex said. "Phone was sold in Charlotte last year." He looked around Shane to Ashley. "See if you can find out any information on who might have bought the phone."

"Send me the details," Ashley said, grabbing a coffee on her way across the room. "Where exactly is Limon?"

He and Alex leaned over a map and Shane felt a tingle of anticipation that suggested they were onto something. They were close to that area.

"It looks like our guy but where's he going? And why drive out all this way in January?" Ashley mused.

"Oh god."

He turned. Yael was staring at the map and at Alex with huge eyes, a growing look of horror on her face.

"You don't think..."

"Think what?" Ashley prompted harshly. "This is not the time for guessing games."

Yael flinched at the sharpness of the other woman's tone and Shane had to batten down his protective urges. Professional, remember?

Professional sucked.

Yael tipped up her chin and leaned closer to the screen, zooming out on the map a little. "My family has a personal association with a town near Colorado Springs. A dark one." Her shoulders slumped and she seemed to shrink in front of him. "I mean, it could have nothing to do with his intentions."

"Or it could be everything," Alex said quietly.

"What association?" Shane asked.

"My brother was responsible for a school shooting there." She swallowed repeatedly. "He also murdered our parents."

Ah, shit.

Shane's heart broke for her. So this was her big secret. Her big shame. It was a hell of a burden for anyone to carry.

Ashley didn't look surprised. Looked as if the other agent had already figured it out. And Alex knew. Shane's feeling of frustration grew. Not because this was about him, but because he wanted Yael to know he was here for her. And maybe he just had to prove it to her by supporting her now that the truth was out.

"Aside from the fact he fixated on you in Quantico, why do you think he would risk traveling all this way?" Alex asked.

"I don't know." Yael sounded angry, which was good. "To twist the knife? To hurt me because hurting people is what gets him off?"

"Would he risk going to the school?" Shane asked. "Or your old home?"

"The house was torn down by a developer a few years ago." Yael shook her head. "I don't know about the school."

"It's Sunday so the school is a viable option." Alex pondered. "Maybe that's why he sped up the auction? I doubt he's expecting us to track him via aircraft and he didn't plan to get pulled over or kill a cop. But he might abort his original plan after opening that email. Conducting the auction anywhere in the area would be enough to drive home the point. Especially when he reveals Yael's real identity and connection afterward."

Shane jolted. *Real identity*?

He looked at her but she wouldn't meet his gaze.

"Do we call in the local PD for help checking the school or not, Shane?" Ashley asked for his opinion to his great surprise.

"If we have a lead on a possible location, I want us to be the first ones checking it out. I'm not sure I trust a small local police department to be up to the job when this guy has evaded law enforcement for years. Nor do I want to catch a bullet from an inexperienced officer when they see us arrive on scene heavily armed." Shane checked the map. "Let's get Sloan to call in HRT's Blue team from the west coast in case this turns into a hostage situation. Keep Gold team on the east in case we're wrong about EG's location. It's going to take Denver's FBI SWAT time to get down there and into position, probably longer if the storm is as bad as the weather service predicts and if we're wrong…" Laura could be dead by then. He checked his watch. Considered the various options. "Have our pilot head for the airfield closest to the school. Ask SWAT to stage nearby but out of sight as soon as they can get there. Explain we have a small team doing some initial recon. The three of us can check out the building while Yael stays in the jet and tries to pinpoint EG's location."

"The auction is about to start," Yael reminded them all. "Communications might be dicey with the bad weather. I don't want to be cut off if you need my help."

"You can work in the car," Alex said, heading to the cockpit to tell the pilot to change course.

"What car?" Shane asked pointedly.

"On it." Ashley followed Alex to also talk to the pilot, while Shane updated Sloan.

When Alex came back a few moments later, Yael still hadn't moved from where she stood with her hand gripping the back of the cream leather seat.

She cleared her throat. "There's something I didn't tell anyone. I didn't imagine it could be in any way relevant at the time."

"What is it?" asked Alex with a lot more patience than Shane was feeling.

"The night of the attack. EG took a photograph of my family off the sideboard."

"I never saw any photographs," Shane stated.

Yael crossed her arms over her chest. "I only put it out that night."

And it being stolen had probably reinforced all her beliefs that keeping her past hidden was the right thing to do.

"If he hadn't figured out who you were before that night all he had to do was run facial recognition on that image and he'd get about a million hits," said Alex.

She nodded.

Ashley looked annoyed. Alex shrugged. Shane wished to hell Yael had trusted him enough to share this with him.

"Let's gear up," Shane told them, making sure to keep his tone neutral. They started gathering the equipment they were going to need when they hit the ground.

"Was this the real reason you decided we were over?" asked Shane under his breath as he leaned down beside her.

Her fingers trembled as she stuffed various power bricks and a second laptop into a bag. "That and the fact the good people of this town put me on trial as an accessory to mass murder. I guess they didn't trust me either."

He flinched. *Jesus.* His suspicion was the worst possible thing he could have done to her.

"Do a Google search. The internet is full of bullshit conspiracy theories where I somehow instigated the whole thing and got away with it." Her eyes filled with tears but she blinked them away. She always did.

"You lost your parents…" He was struggling to understand.

She zipped her laptop bag and grabbed her coat, swinging it over her shoulders. "Apparently that was part of my wicked plan." She sent him a defiant look. "I inherited a lot of cash and was the beneficiary of two large life insurance policies when my parents died. The companies tried their best to make sure they never had to pay out."

"Time to strap in," warned Alex.

"You could have told me," Shane said quietly, sitting in the nearest seat.

"It doesn't change anything."

"Like fuck it doesn't. You could have trusted me," he reiterated.

"The same way you trusted me?" She refused to meet his gaze and he burned to make her understand that things were different now. "It doesn't matter. I'll be moving on when this is over. Some people will make sure of it."

He blinked in surprise. "You're going to run away from it your whole life?"

"What do you care? The sex was great but right from the start you told me you weren't interested in relationships."

"I told you at the lake—"

"We'd just had the best sex of our lives at the lake and you felt guilty as hell for lying to me," she whispered fiercely.

Shane's tongue welded to the top of his mouth. Everything

had changed, but how did he convince Yael of the fact? He had to catch this killer and fulfil the vow he'd made to his best friend. Even thinking about a future with Yael felt like a betrayal of Scotty's memory, a betrayal of his widow and fatherless kids.

Yael gave him a baleful stare and turned away to carry on working, desperately searching for a fixed location on EG.

He didn't have time to deal with their personal issues. Neither of them did. It was costing them focus on the mission and that was the damn problem with relationships.

The jet touched down with barely a bump and Shane glanced out the window with an annoyed sigh.

"Fucking snow."

Yael looked up warily.

He unclipped his seatbelt before they came to a stop and pulled on an extra layer before he gathered his weapons and ammo. Everyone wore a flak jacket under their top layer. None of the others were fully prepared for a snowstorm and he didn't have all the cold weather equipment he'd usually favor for warfare in this kind of environment. He and Alex had night vision goggles.

"Can you turn off the power for the school if we give you a signal?" he asked Yael. "Maybe we can catch him off guard in the dark."

Yael nodded. "I should be able to."

"Do not leave the vehicle. No matter what." He tossed Ashley a pair of thin but warm gloves. He couldn't do much about her leather boots but maybe they'd get lucky and they wouldn't be outside much and the snow wouldn't be too deep.

Perhaps that was all wishful thinking in a case that had never gone their way.

He had a basic comms system with him and he handed everyone an earpiece. "Clip the other end to your collar," he explained to Yael. "Press the button if you want to speak. It'll only work within a short distance of about a hundred yards." What he wouldn't give for Gold team's comms system.

He tossed Ashley his black knit cap and she pulled it on without a word of complaint. He handed Yael the red bulldog hat she'd worn a few days earlier on the hike to Zenko's cabin. A lot had happened since then.

"Oh, no." There was a shake in her voice even as she held her head high, focused on the job. "The auction just went live."

Feelings for her stormed through him but now wasn't the time. He needed to catch this killer and then maybe figure out his life. This was for Scotty and for all the other victims of the psychopath. Capturing Evi1Geni-us was the only way to keep Yael safe. He just hoped she gave him a chance to prove himself to her again. To prove he wasn't like all the other assholes who'd doubted her in the past.

32

Ashley had arranged for a four-wheel-drive SUV to be delivered to the tarmac where their jet landed. Alex insisted on driving. They were still five miles from the school and it seemed to be taking forever to get through the snow-covered highways.

They were driving through a blizzard in the dark because they needed the odds to be stacked against them even more than they already were. Why couldn't something be easy for once? Why couldn't that poor traffic cop have arrested EG rather than becoming another tragic victim?

Yael wanted to tell Alex to hurry but the back wheels were already fishtailing dangerously. Crashing would destroy their chances of getting to Laura in time.

The auction had started ten minutes ago and Yael's stomach revolted every time she thought about her friend suffering.

Ethan Grice had again muted his mic on the live video but was presumably recording the sound on another device. Laura's blood already stained the white sheet beneath her. Her screams had been silenced, replaced by the dulcet tones of Grieg's *Peer Gynt Suite*. Yael would never be able to listen to that music again. The comments box was cheerful and lively and the suggestions there made Yael gag. Viewers were paying thousands of dollars to watch EG inflict pain on a woman who'd never hurt anyone.

EG had put Yael's stolen family portrait on a table in view of the main camera and there was no way the world wouldn't figure out who she was and what her link to both the school and Laura was in the next few hours. No doubt the crazies would be blaming her for all Evi1Geni-us's crimes in the next news cycle.

She ground her teeth. As long as they could save Laura it didn't matter. She'd lived through vilification before.

What didn't kill you made you stronger...

Yeah, if that old adage was true her bones would be tungsten steel by now.

When would this end?

From the looks on her companions' faces it ended today, but what if they were in the wrong place? Or what if one of them was hurt in the process? She didn't think she could bear it if that happened.

Did EG truly expect to get away with this?

Alex had taken EG's money, but he was about to make a whole lot more if they didn't stop him in the next hour. And maybe he carried more crypto on him. Probably. Enough to escape and start a life with a new identity. Maybe they hadn't found the motherlode they'd presumed or he had so much it didn't bother him to lose a few million.

Shane sat beside her giving Alex directions to her old high school, a place she hadn't visited since the day of the shooting. A day when her own brother had pointed a gun at her and then laughed, instead shooting the boy she'd been sweet on who was standing beside her.

A boy who, minutes earlier, she'd invited to the school's Sadie Hawkins dance, and he'd said yes.

She shook her head to clear the image. The boy's parents had been some of the most vocal in their condemnation of her and she didn't even blame them.

Shane had removed his arm from his sling which he'd tucked inside his ballistics vest.

The three of them were ready to take this bastard down. Yael's own contribution felt weak at best. She'd isolated which transformer to turn off to kill power to the school.

Ashley had her laptop open in the front passenger seat and was mirroring Yael's screen. "I'm afraid this isn't looking good for Laura," she said grimly.

Ashley's evil online alter-ego had received an invitation as she'd anticipated. Yael recognized the moniker and had honestly never imagined the seemingly depraved individual was actually a beautiful, uptight, badass federal agent, which was probably the point. You didn't send a kitten into a lions' den and expect it to come out alive.

Speculation in the comments proved it was only a matter of minutes until viewers identified Yael and her family. And maybe Ethan Grice had overplayed his hand because it wouldn't take long for the location of the crime to be discovered and presumably someone in the law enforcement community watching would call in the cops.

"What can you see now?" Alex asked.

"EG is in the frame wearing his usual get up. He's draped large white sheets around the place as backdrops," Yael stated. "Laura is duct-taped to a table on top of another white sheet. He has the second camera situated above her following his usual MO."

"The way his pants sag to the right suggests he's carrying a gun in his pocket and we can assume he still has his assault rifle nearby. Look at that flooring." Shane pointed out. "That worn paint line on the edge of the field of view looks like the sort you'd find in a gym."

"I agree," Ashley said. "Does it look familiar at all, Yael?"

Yael bit her lip. "It's been a long time, sorry. I don't remember the floor of my old school gym." Even as she said the words, flashes of running screaming through the bloodstained cavernous space bombarded her.

Her mouth flooded with saliva and she swallowed repeatedly.

"You all right?" Shane's warm hand splayed over her back.

Her heart pounded and she took in a deep breath and held it until her lungs felt as if they'd burst, then she released it slowly and gave him a quick nod.

She was barely hanging on, but the scent of Shane supplanted those older memories with images of the two of them together. Bittersweet, as she'd already lost him.

The warmth of him engulfed her as he peered closer at her screen. It made her want to sink into him and beg him for another chance but she knew it would only prolong the agony.

She held herself stiffly, not responding or allowing herself to be coaxed. The temptation of Shane Livingstone was addictive and seemingly never-ending.

Her mouth went dry as the enormity of the truth hit her. She was more than halfway in love with this man already. The pain of losing him would not be worth the short pleasure of a fling. Pushing him away was an act of self-preservation, not self-pity.

She shoved thoughts of the two of them out of her mind. Saving Laura and catching this bastard were all that mattered. Afterward she'd find a way to avoid Shane for the duration of this case.

She homed in on the signal data. "I think he's there. I'm seeing a lot of internet activity coming out of the school."

"Could be kids doing extracurricular activities or the janitor streaming porn so let's not get ahead of ourselves." Shane glanced out the window. "Weather conditions mean we have zero drone or satellite availability and zero backup until SWAT arrives."

"What do we know about the gym?" Alex asked, concentrating on the road and driving so fast Yael wanted to close her eyes.

"Assuming it hasn't changed, old media reports suggest there are two inside exits plus two exits via the locker room," said Ashley, "and a double door that opens to the outside."

"He's not going to get far if he makes a run for it on foot in this storm." Shane checked his handgun and Yael flinched. He caught her gaze and suddenly seemed to understand her hatred of firearms. "I'm leaving you with a weapon."

Or maybe not.

She shook her head. He ignored her and placed a lethal-looking black handgun down the back of the seat pocket in front of her.

"I don't want it."

"It's there anyway. No safety but the first shot requires a lot more force on the trigger than the rest. Point and shoot. That's all you need to do. It's for self-defense."

She held his green eyes. The idea of touching the weapon was an anathema to her.

"You shouldn't need it, but it will make me feel better to know you have some way of protecting yourself should this guy slip past us, okay?"

Reluctantly, she nodded. She didn't want Shane to be worried about her when he was facing an armed and dangerous suspect. She knew her apprehension was founded on old fears and neurosis. She wanted Ethan Grice stopped so he never hurt anyone else ever again.

From the determined light in Shane's eyes, he clearly wanted the same.

But the idea of shooting anyone, here…

"I'll give you a signal when we want the power to go off. Three clicks in your ear if I'm unable to speak," Shane said. "We don't want it to go off too early and warn him we're coming."

"If he's here we don't want him to suspect we've found him," agreed Alex.

Yael went back to the screen. Armed with the knowledge of where EG was, she should be able to track his signal faster and maybe hijack the Wi-Fi or figure out his IP address and maybe hack his machine directly while he was busy with his torture fest. She could cut off the feed to the spectators.

They were almost at the school now. Yael recognized the neighborhood and the play structure she'd used as a kid.

The others pulled their weapons and prepared to exit as Alex drove to the back of the building. They all spotted a green SUV partially covered in snow.

Alex reversed until their SUV was out sight of the other vehicle.

"Even if this isn't Ethan Grice it is most likely our cop killer," Shane stated.

And no one believed in that level of coincidence.

"Make him an offer of two million to keep the woman alive," Ashley ordered. "See if that will distract him long enough to prevent him killing her in the next few minutes. We should be inside by then. Let's go."

Alex got out but, thankfully, left the engine running. He tossed Yael the evidence bag with EG's fortune. "Look after this."

Her throat swelled. That he trusted her so much was humbling.

Shane gave her a stern look. "Lock the doors. Use the gun if he tries to get in here. Point and shoot."

"Be careful," she whispered.

He leaned over and kissed her quickly on the lips, as if he was done pretending they meant nothing to one another. He pulled back, his eyes smoldering with the heat of wanting something so badly you burned for it.

The side of his mouth kicked up. "Always am." And like that he was gone.

Her mouth went dry with fear. Fear and self-loathing, and the agony of what she was terrified might be love. That she didn't have the nerve to tell him exactly how she felt made her clench her fists in frustration. Did they have a chance of rescuing what was between them after all?

She watched her colleagues run toward the school in the

snowy darkness, hating the worry that now started to bloom—for Shane, Alex, and Ashley. On top of the all-consuming fear for Laura. All because of one man's twisted actions.

If any of them died she would be devastated. She shook herself out of her inertia. Stared at the code in a side panel on her laptop screen.

If she could tap into Ethan Grice's system or even slow him down by trying to penetrate or disrupt the live feed…

Her machine suddenly got a hit on his IP address. Shit. She started typing furiously and opened a program to probe his machine for possible vulnerabilities in the background.

She typed in the offer Ashley Chen had outlined. *"Two million for the woman alive. I want her for myself. I'll give you three others in exchange."*

It took a moment for EG to see the comment and respond. When he did, he tilted his head to one side, then gave an exaggerated shrug and shake of his head in rejection. He moved on to creating the next torture poll instead.

Dammit.

Yael shivered. Laura wasn't leaving that place alive unless the others saved her.

And suddenly she was inside his machine. Oh my god.

She desperately wanted to shut him down, but if she did that he might panic and run. He might escape when he was so damn close, she could almost smell him.

Instead, she inserted a trojan into his operating system. If he got away this time, she'd track him down and paralyze his machine at will.

She smiled grimly. Not so clever now, EG. They were closing in on him from every direction.

"Hold on, Laura. We're here. We love you."

33

The first thing Shane did was run over and punch his KA-BAR knife through the front tire of the Subaru. This motherfucker wasn't going anywhere and if it was a case of mistaken identity, he'd go buy the owner a new tire and fit it himself.

He scanned the area before he dashed back to the others. There were no obvious footprints but the wind was fierce, driving the snow horizontally into his face and blinding him. Visibility was twenty feet and closing. The storm was forecast to become a whole lot worse in the next couple of hours.

Shane, Ashley, and Alex entered the building around the corner from where their SUV was parked, away from the entrance closest to the Subaru. Alex made short work of the lock and Shane was impressed. He planned to expand his current skillset from explosives and breachers to include lock picks and add a little subtlety for those occasions when stealth was paramount.

Presumably Ethan Grice had similar locksmith skills. The alarm inside the school was also disarmed. Shane eased open the door a crack before checking for explosives using a small, red-beamed flashlight.

"Clear," he murmured quietly. "You two head that way and cover the south and east exits. I'll take the west." Which Shane figured was closest to EG's vehicle. They took off at a quiet jog through the darkened corridors while Shane headed in the opposite direction. A fire exit sign gave off enough of a glow that he could easily make his way without the NVGs. The gym was in the middle of the building with the north wall abutting the playing field.

Shane moved silently along the corridors and forced himself not to think of Yael walking these same halls the day her brother had sacrificed his humanity and condemned his sister to a lifetime of pain. He loved his family but if any one of them pulled a stunt like that, he'd put a bullet in them himself.

A scream rang down the hallway and ice sped along his veins. He had no doubt they were in the right place this time. He forced the need to hurry out of his mind. He couldn't afford to rush. He worked his way through the maze of school passageways until he found the gym.

Another soul-chilling scream of pain pierced the air.

At the doorway to the gymnasium, he paused and texted Sloan an update. Presumably she'd roust the troops now they had a confirmed location.

Laura screamed again and the sound stabbed into his spine like nine-inch nails.

Fuck that asshole.

EG had covered the glass of the doorway with sheets, but lights were visible inside. The smell of gasoline made Shane pause.

He pressed his comms and said in barely a whisper, "You guys smell gas?"

"Yep," Ashley answered.

"Any visual on EG?" he murmured.

"Negative. He's nailed sheets to the doors," said Ashley.

"Negative." Alex.

"Fuck."

"I'll check the locker rooms entrances," Alex said. "There's no way this guy doesn't have an escape route mapped out."

Shane texted Sloan again, this time to have cops secure the perimeter and have fire trucks on standby and to have everyone approach without sirens.

"EG looks like he heard something," Yael's voice warned through his earpiece. "He's stopped doing what he was doing and walked to near the camera. Want me to cut the power now?"

"Yes. Let's get inside as fast as possible," Shane said in an undertone. And hope the fucker hadn't wired the place the way he had last time.

"On three." Shane counted down and as soon as the lights went off he shot the lock off the door. The gunshots echoed through the space, but Shane was used to it and didn't even flinch. He kicked open the door but a sudden *whoosh* of flames forced him back.

"Christ, he lit up the place." He held up his cast to shield his face. He certainly didn't need his NVGs now. "I can't see anything through the flames."

"Same here. He spread gasoline on gym mats all around the room," said Ashley.

"EG has disappeared. Oh my god, Laura!" Yael exclaimed. "The sheets behind her just went up. Quickly, she's going to burn to death."

Motherfucker. Shane kept his rifle up and ready as he rushed through the flames toward a small piece of the gym floor that hadn't yet ignited. The smoke was thick and the dry wood was starting to catch. The gym mats were releasing thick noxious clouds of gases. He smothered flames that had caught on his pants and singed his leg. He kept moving, searching for Ethan Grice, searching for a safe space amongst the heat and fire, trying to figure out how to get across the wide expanse to Laura.

The heat was intense and made him want to retreat but he kept pushing forward.

The sound of gunfire ripped through the air. "Alex, Ashley, report."

Then he spotted Laura near the edge of the gym as the sheets burned to nothing.

But there was no clear path through the flames. An ember singed his cheek. *Fuck*. He was going to burn to death. Great. This fucker was going to escape and he was going to roast.

Yael's face flashed before him and he knew he wanted more than a few nights of stolen passion.

No way was he going to die. No fucking way.

He caught a glimpse of a red fire extinguisher on the wall out of the corner of his eye and lunged for it. Turning it on, he sprayed the floor in front of him and started walking toward the bound woman.

"I found Laura. Alex? Ashley?" he yelled because the asshole already knew they were here and the fire was so loud he couldn't hear a thing.

Shane drew his knife and cut the tape securing the naked woman to the table. Her eyes were massive with fear and horror. Wounds bloody. She was screaming incoherently but he couldn't make out the words over the roar of the fire.

He couldn't worry about any potential damage as he hoisted her over his right shoulder. The risk was less than the almost certainty of burning to death. The smoke was choking him, his throat raw as he coughed incessantly. He twirled around to look for a way out through the flames. EG wasn't here so how had he escaped?

Shane's injured arm ached but he kept the rifle strap on his shoulder and finger on the trigger as he made his way through a snaking path of heat and flames. He found a door to one of the locker rooms. It was locked from the other side. Shit. The fire was building behind him and his skin sizzled.

He stood back. "If anyone is in the male locker room unlock the door or get the hell away from it."

"Negative. We're heading that way though," Ashley's strained voice came through his earpiece.

"Wait." He blasted the lock and kicked open the door. He half stumbled inside coughing, the relief from the flames instant but wouldn't last long as the fire spread. He kept his weapon raised as he moved past the rows of benches into the corridor.

His earpiece screeched suddenly as if someone had scrambled the signal. He pulled it from his ear before it burst his drum.

He glanced into the corridor and saw Alex and Ashley stumbling toward him, Alex bleeding from a bullet wound in his upper arm.

"She okay?" Ashley nodded to Laura who'd gone limp against him.

"I don't know but she was alert when I found her." They kept jogging, retracing the way they'd come, alert for EG, Ashley watching their six. He hated the fact assault rifles were once again in this school and that Yael's name would inevitably be associated with the headlines. The coverage would hurt her and he didn't want that. He didn't want her to run. He wanted her to stay. With him.

Why would she when she thought he wasn't serious about her?

He needed time to persuade her. Prove to her he was worth the price she'd inevitably have to pay with long periods spent alone when he was away with work.

"You okay?" he asked Alex.

"Flesh wound."

"He jumped in front of me when Grice shot at us," Ashley said with annoyance.

"Didn't want Lucas chewing out my ass if you were hurt."

Ashley gave a soft huff of laughter. "*I* will kick your ass later. As will Mallory."

"Where is he?" Shane wanted this guy so badly he could taste it.

"He ran towards his vehicle."

That was way too close to Yael.

"Shit." With a glance at Alex, he took off at a run. He had to make sure Yael was safe.

34

Yael had watched in horror as flames formed a wall behind Laura. Then the video feed died, no doubt killed by the fire, which melted the wires and fried the computer circuits.

Her earpiece let out a loud screech and she yanked it out of her ear. *Damn*. Either the fire had melted something important or EG had enabled some sort of device designed to block law enforcement communication.

"Dammit."

What had happened? Shane had found Laura, but was she all right? Was Shane?

The thought of something happening to him made her want to scream. She'd seen EG in action before. She'd watched a member of HRT's elite team die the last time they'd tried to apprehend the guy because they'd underestimated his hateful cunning.

The idea of losing Shane hit her with the force of a sledgehammer. She'd been so busy trying to protect herself from the danger of falling for him that she hadn't realized it was already too late. She cared about him more than she'd cared about anyone in a very long time.

She should have told him. Who cared if he ran screaming in

the other direction? At least that would be an honest reaction. At least she'd have been brave for once in her life.

Her computer was useless right now. The feed dead. There was nothing left for her to track. But Ethan Grice, the self-styled Evi1Geni-us, was nearby and he was probably pissed, and he was definitely dangerous. She remembered him firing the assault rifle at her a couple of nights ago. Unlike Alex's SUV, this vehicle wasn't bulletproof.

She glanced at the school, the scene of all her worst nightmares.

She didn't want to ever feel as helpless as she had on that day fifteen years ago. She didn't want to be a sitting duck, too scared to defend herself.

Her hand shook as she slipped it into the seat pocket and retrieved Shane's parting gift. The weapon was heavy and lethal-looking. Gore rose up in her throat until she eased the sensation with another firm swallow and deep calming breath.

It was a tool. Nothing more.

She slipped the handgun into the waistband at the back of her jeans, feeling unnerved from the touch of the cool resin. She leaned forward and scooped the electronic key fob from the console so, even with the engine running, if anyone attempted to steal the car they wouldn't get far. She opened the door and got a fierce face full of winter as she struggled against the blustery wind.

She locked the door behind her and stuffed the fob into her jeans pocket.

If EG escaped because of her inaction, she would never forgive herself. If he hurt any of her friends, especially the man she'd stupidly gone and fallen for, well, she couldn't bear to think about it.

She ran to the corner of the building just in time to see the black-clad figure stumble out of the school doors. She plastered herself to the rough brick surface so he didn't see her. He climbed into his SUV and drove about five feet before the Subaru wedged solidly in the snow.

She peeked and saw one of the tires was flat.

Yes!

She heard him curse as her heart pounded. She pressed herself against the building as he got out of the car. She grabbed the handgun and clutched it tightly. She couldn't let him get away but the thought of pointing a gun at another human being, even one as depraved as this man…

She stepped out from the side of the building, gripping the heavy gun with both hands.

"Hold it right there!"

Ethan Grice looked up in surprise. "Well, well. Yael, or should I say, Yasmine? How does it feel to be back on the old stomping grounds? And with a gun? *Tut tut*."

He held up his cell with one hand, obviously filming her. The assault rifle strap was hooked over his head and he had his finger on the trigger.

"Why are you still hiding behind a mask? The cops know who you are, Ethan Grice."

He gave a sharp laugh. "You're one to talk about masks. You've been hiding behind one for years."

He took a step toward her.

She pointed the nose of the pistol right at him. "Don't come any closer."

"You won't shoot me. Laura told me all about how much you hate guns before I came by to deliver my little housewarming gift."

Yael's hands shook.

He fired off a burst of bullets and Yael yelped and darted back behind the wall. She was about to run when the sound of raised voices had her freezing.

She peeked around the corner and Ethan had started to swing in the direction of three teenagers. What the hell they were doing here in a blizzard she had no clue. She yelled out, "Run away! Run away!"

She aimed at Grice's legs and pulled on the trigger. It took an unbelievable amount of force as she frantically squeezed until finally the gun bucked in her hands.

"You fucking bitch!" he screamed.

Had she hit him?

The kids turned and ran around the side of the building. Hopefully they'd keep running all the way home like she had fifteen years ago. Fingers crossed they didn't find what she'd found that day.

Ethan swung back to face her and started firing wildly. A piece of shattered brick sliced her cheek, narrowly missing her eye. She didn't stop to worry about it.

She sprinted back toward the SUV, then realized that would make her an easy target.

She lunged for the doors where the others had entered the school earlier and dashed inside. Her footing was slippery from the snow and ice. She almost went down and, in the process, wrenched her knee.

Dammit. She staggered to her feet and turned right, hopping and running. "Shane! Alex! Ashley!"

She could hear Grice opening the door behind her and racing after her along the corridor. She couldn't believe she was back here. She couldn't believe she was once again fleeing a madman with a gun. At least this one didn't share her DNA.

A sharp, hot pain lanced her side.

She fell and rolled onto her back, gripping the gun at her side. "You are such a loser, Ethan. We took your money and shut down your sick enterprise. Laura's alive and we'll track down everyone who ever donated to your auction and put them in jail right alongside you."

His lip curled. "And you call me sick. You have no idea what they do to people in jail." He dragged off his mask and tossed it aside. "You think I started off like this? I'm a product of the precious justice system so I'm thinking that maybe it doesn't work quite the way it is supposed to."

She watched his fingers start to tighten on the trigger of the rifle.

"I'm sorry for what happened to you," Yael said quickly. "I'm assuming that's why you killed Derek Vincent and Phillipa Laurant?"

He hesitated. She wanted him to put down his weapon. She wanted to live. She wanted Shane, she realized. Wanted him desperately.

"They both got what they deserved. She persuaded me a plea deal would be the best thing I could hope for. He—" Ethan Grice looked haunted as he swallowed loudly. "He got exactly what he deserved."

"And the others? The innocents you murdered?" she asked.

His expression turned calculating then. "*Everyone* got exactly what they deserved. Just like you're about to."

"Grice!" Shane yelled down the corridor.

Ethan glanced over his shoulder and swung the rifle towards Shane who carried a naked and bleeding Laura over one shoulder.

No way could Yael let Ethan hurt either of them. The momentary distraction gave her time to aim the gun and pull the trigger, over and over again, five times. Tears filled her eyes and she didn't know whether or not she'd hit him or if she was about to die. She closed her eyes against the reality of what was happening.

The noise and the stink of gunpowder brought everything roaring back into focus.

"Yael. It's okay, honey." Shane's voice came from beside her which was good because that meant he wasn't dead. He wasn't dead.

Thank god.

She felt him gently removing the weapon from her rigid fingers. She let go with a massive feeling of relief.

She hated guns. She would always hate guns.

"You got him. He won't hurt anyone else ever again."

"Did I kill him?"

"Yeah. You got him."

Emotions pummeled her like a tsunami, the most surprising of which was an immense feeling of sadness. Not necessarily that Ethan Grice was dead. He was evil and cared nothing for others. But for the fact she'd been forced to take his life, to commit violence in a place that had already seen so much suffering.

Shane started coughing. Smoke was filling the corridors.

The fire. She'd forgotten about the fire.

She could hear a siren in the distance now and she found herself trying hard to stay in the present.

"Laura? Is she alive?" Her mouth was so dry she could barely speak.

"She's unconscious but alive. I don't know if she'll make it. She lost a lot of blood."

That made her want to weep. Her dear, wonderful, vibrant friend. Shane took her hands in his and tried to tug her to her feet but the pain was so intense she cried out.

"Are you hit? Fuck." Shane's voice went from deep to high-pitched so fast she would have laughed if her entire side didn't feel as if she was being stabbed over and over again with a very sharp blade.

She groaned in answer and found herself roughly rolled onto her front. The cold floor cooled her burning skin.

Shane started muttering more curses than Yael had heard in her lifetime. "Alex, Ashley. Yael's been hit."

"We need to get out of here. The whole place is going up," Alex shouted.

"Let's get to the SUV and try to keep them warm there," Ashley suggested.

"Keys in my back pocket," Yael croaked.

She felt him reach in and grab the keys, then move her clothes and press something warm firmly against her bare skin. She flinched. Her vision was getting spotty. She could feel the blood draining from her body and remembered how Lloyd Zenko had looked in the moments before he died.

The bullet was still inside her. She raised her one hand and edged Shane's hair off his forehead.

"Sorry I dumped you. I was scared of falling for you. I didn't want the heartbreak of being left behind. I should have trusted you. I'm not very brave."

Shane hoisted her into his arms. Alex had Laura over his shoulder. "Not brave? What the fuck are you talking about? You're brave as hell. I'm the one who's scared of commitment."

She wanted to laugh but her world was going dark. She felt herself moving through the air, passing through these old familiar hallways that still haunted her dreams. Wondering if this had always been her fate.

35

"Don't you dare close your eyes," Shane yelled at Yael.

She blinked. Once, twice. A smile tugged at the corner of her mouth followed by a gasp as they hit the wall of snow and ice outside. Ashley opened the rear compartment and Alex laid Laura gently in the back and covered her with his coat. "She's unconscious."

Ashley dove into the front seat as Shane slipped in the rear with Yael, pushing her laptop onto the floor.

Alex clambered awkwardly into the cargo area and pulled the door closed. Ashley drove smoothly away searching for the nearest medics.

"Where's Yael been hit?" asked Alex.

Shane laid her flat on the backseat as he knelt in the footwell. "Right side near her hip bone."

He had no idea if the bullet had shattered inside her or not but there was no exit wound that he could see. He didn't know whether to risk undoing her pants or if the tight jeans could be acting like a bandage. His first aid training could get him through a lot of things but it couldn't fix a bullet wound while in the back of a moving vehicle without medical supplies.

"Yael. Hey. Open your eyes, sweetheart."

She blinked them open again, those gorgeous dark velvet eyes of hers recognizing him through the pain.

He needed to keep her awake.

"You got him, Yael. You stopped that son of a bitch even though you had to conquer your own demons to do it. That is the bravest thing I've ever seen."

Her eyes narrowed in a mix of pain and disbelief but he was telling the truth.

"I am so amazed by you, by your strength."

Her skin was clammy and pale and he was terrified because the last person he'd seen who'd looked like that had been Scotty, moments before he'd passed.

"Do you think I'll have to stand trial again?" Her voice was reed thin.

"What? No."

"He was starting to turn away from me to shoot at you." She swallowed noisily. "Before that he was pointing the gun right at me."

He couldn't believe she'd been concerned about that and yet it wasn't surprising considering what she'd been through in the past. "You killed him in self-defense. The guy wasn't about to let anyone walk out of there alive. Not me, not you, not Laura. You nailed a serial killer and deserve a goddamned medal."

Relief washed over her features and her eyes started to drift closed.

"Hey, stay with me, Yael." He pressed his coat against her wound and she cried out making him die a little inside. "There are things I need to know."

"Like what?" Yael blinked.

"Like what it feels like to ride pillion on Myrtle."

"Sublime." A small smile touched her lips.

Shane laughed even as his heart was being torn in two. He needed to keep Yael focused. He couldn't let her slip away from him. "I know you're still mad at me for being suspicious of you and snooping on your phone."

"If it helps, I'm also mad at him," Alex said, leaning over the back seat. His gaze told Shane he knew what he was trying to do. Keep her awake. Keep her alive. Alex glanced at Laura but there was little they could do. The only way they could save these two women was by getting them professional medical attention ASAP.

"Somewhere along the way I discovered I enjoy spending time with you. Watching your mind work, watching you type away at a thousand words a second…total turn on."

Yael's brows crinkled and he could tell she was being hit by a wave of pain. "You get aroused by touch typing?"

"Kill me now," Ashley grouched from the driver's seat but it was obvious she was trying to inject a little humor into a dire moment.

"And you're wicked smart. Without you, the task force would still be sitting around in Virginia waiting for the next crime scene." He cleared his throat. "I love your brain and badass computer skills and those sexy tattoos of yours."

"Not the tattoos." Ashley slapped her own forehead.

Shane spotted an ambulance coming their way and felt a collective sigh of relief go through the three of them.

"What I'm trying to say if the spectators would quiet down." He sent them a mock quelling glance but didn't miss the way Yael's lips quirked at the corners. "I'm sorry for being less than honest at the outset, but I'd really like a chance to prove myself to you even though we all know I will never be truly worthy."

Yael's teeth started to chatter as Ashley lowered the window and flagged down the approaching ambulance. Shane hoped to hell Laura lived. But if anything happened to Yael he wasn't sure he'd survive.

Her eyes started to drift again.

"So, what do you think, honey?" he said loudly, desperate to keep her attention here in the moment. "About giving me that second chance?"

Her beautiful eyes opened again, briefly, and she smiled. "I think I'd like that. I think I'd like that a lot."

36

TWO DAYS LATER

Laura groaned in the bed beside hers. They were in a private room of a private hospital in Colorado Springs.

"Hey, you're awake." Yael tried to sit up and winced. "How are you feeling?"

The bullet that hit Yael had shattered when it struck her hip bone but luckily only into three pieces. The largest had lodged into her pelvis. One had damaged her glute muscles which made it painful to sit, the other had nicked the external iliac vein. A centimeter to the side and she'd have bled out before Shane could have carried her to the car.

"Like I might live," Laura grumbled.

Yael pressed the call button for the nurse because they'd wanted to know when Laura woke up so they could run a few more tests.

Laura was recovering from an array of injuries and lacerations and she'd probably have scars over pretty much her entire body, although not on her face. Alex had offered to pay for plastic surgery but Laura was too weak for any procedures right now. They'd arrived in time to prevent Ethan Grice from using any of the power tools he'd had lined up, apparently having raided the school's workshop.

All things considered, Laura had had a lucky escape. She was traumatized though. She'd cried all day yesterday and had to be sedated.

"I was so worried about you," Yael admitted. "I'm sorry we didn't get there faster."

"I'm grateful you arrived at all. When the room went up in flames, I thought I was going to burn alive and that was the single most terrifying moment of my life." Laura sniffed. "Anyway, it was my own damn fault."

"How were you to know?"

"You always warned me of the dangers of online dating. I should have been more careful."

"It wasn't your fault. I mean, hopefully the next guy you meet is not a serial killer but I love how brave you are going after relationships. Pursuing your own happiness…"

Laura held herself carefully as she laughed a little. "It's more the pursuit of orgasms and I think I might give it up. I have a vibrator that's a lot less trouble and a whole lot *more* than most of the men I meet, if you know what I mean." She wiggled her brows.

Yael laughed, the way she was supposed to.

"I'm thankful I didn't sleep with Owen or Ethan or whatever the hell his name was, but only because he 'didn't want to rush things.'" Laura reached for a glass of water on the bedside table. "Ouch."

"His sexual abuse in prison obviously deeply affected him."

Laura blinked rapidly. "That's no excuse."

Yael leaned over as far as she dared and held out her hand. Laura took it and squeezed. "I know, but I didn't want you to worry that you'd lost your touch."

Laura chuckled reluctantly, then sobered. "I keep thinking of that police officer who died on the side of the road after I poked out the rear light."

"It was the smart thing to do. You weren't to know it wouldn't get noticed until you were on a deserted road."

"It was piss poor luck. That poor man." Laura held back a sob.

After a moment of silence, Yael said, "You can talk to me, you know. If you need to."

"Thank you. That reminds me." Laura licked water off her lips.

Yael tensed.

"I overheard the nurses gossiping when I went up for the CT scan. I was half out of it at the time, but I woke up in the night when you were asleep and checked out the news headlines."

Yael's mouth parched and she looked away.

"Apparently, my best friend is notorious in Colorado under a different name. Who would have thought?" Laura shifted up the bed a little, obviously struggling to get comfortable. "I wish I'd known. I'd have been less pushy about trying to hook you up."

"You're not mad?" Yael looked at Laura anxiously.

"Oh, honey, I am furious. That authorities traumatized a fourteen-year-old girl in punishment for her brother's actions. If that isn't a patriarchal society at work, I don't know what is."

Yael played with the fold of the sheet. "Everyone who's found out in the past has always believed what was written in the press."

"I once witnessed you rescuing a *skunk* on the side of the road. I might not be good at picking men, but I'm *fantastic* at picking girlfriends."

The knot in Yael's throat tightened. She hadn't anticipated such easy acceptance, not from Alex, not from Laura, especially not from Shane. She knew perhaps that was partly on her. She guarded her past so assiduously it probably made her look guilty. Now her secret was in the open again and this time it didn't feel quite so terrible.

Unfortunately, the press was still after an inside scoop and kept attempting to sneak in to get photographs or an interview. Alex had posted bodyguards on the doors to keep them out. Didn't stop the nursing staff asking probing questions—about her past and Ethan Grice's death. Yael had only told them what was already in the media. The story would come out eventually but she wasn't about to feed the frenzy. Even the thought made her nauseous.

The school had been badly damaged by the fire. She felt terrible that the community was once again suffering but she'd finally made peace with the fact that it wasn't her fault.

She'd atoned for everything she could. More than she'd needed to in the end.

The door opened and in walked a nurse who was smiling broadly at her favorite operator.

Shane was part of the investigation into what had happened and had been spending most of his time on scene at the school, seeing what evidence they could uncover from the burnt ruins of the gym. He'd also had to explain exactly what had gone down to ASAC Sloan and the other higher ups. The task force commander had come to see Yael late last night and had held her hand for a little while and thanked her for what she'd done.

"Hey there." Yael couldn't quite quell the quiver in her voice as she tried to play it cool.

Shane leaned down to kiss her, his hand cupping the back of her head as he took it deeper, kissing her until she trembled with emotion.

"How are you feeling?" he asked, pulling away but keeping hold of her hand.

"Good. Better than yesterday. Did I thank you for saving me again yet today?"

Shane shook his head. "I didn't save you."

"Well, you saved me," Laura said with what sounded close to a laugh.

"How are you feeling, Laura?" Shane asked the other woman.

"A little less fragile than yesterday."

"Good to hear," said Shane.

"Time for a CT scan," the nurse announced.

They both watched as the nurse made Laura climb, complaining, into a wheelchair to go upstairs.

"We won't be long," Laura joked. "Better make it snappy. I'll warn the bodyguards not to interrupt."

"You're incorrigible." Yael laughed and ignored the heat she could feel spreading up her neck.

Shane smirked. "You look cute when you're embarrassed."

"She always looks cute," Laura exclaimed as the doors closed.

Yael rolled her eyes.

"Laura seems a little better."

"She does."

"Did she say anything about her ordeal?"

"That she was grateful you turned up when you did, and that they didn't have sex and I think that also means he didn't rape her, which is something."

Shane nodded. "It's a lot."

Yael shifted and winced.

Shane frowned. "Are you sure you're okay?"

She nodded. "Just healing from a bullet wound. I'll be fine."

One side of his mouth curled up in a focused grin. "Badass." He picked up her hand and kissed the tattoo on the inside of her wrist.

A shiver ran over her shoulders and down her spine.

"I am planning to give you a few shooting lessons though. So next time you can maybe pull the trigger with your eyes open."

She blew out a deep breath. "I'm sorry."

"Stop apologizing."

"It's difficult after so many years of insurmountable guilt," she admitted, needing to be completely honest with him. "I have spent a lifetime alternating between apologizing to people or pushing them away so I didn't get hurt by their reaction when they finally discovered the truth." She turned her head toward the window. "It's why it hurt so much when you told me you'd doubted me."

"Yael," he whispered in anguish, slowly exhaling, before touching her cheek. She looked back at him.

"There will never be a time that I am not sorry for what I did. I was destroyed by Scotty's death. The belief that it was my fault, that I should have been the one to die in his place—" His voice caught. "And then Montana going down in that air crash." He shook his head. "Give me the chance to make it up to you. Give me the chance to love you."

Shane's green eyes were vivid against the drabness of the hospital room.

She loved those eyes. She loved everything about him but she wasn't quite ready to tell him that. Not yet.

She swallowed. "I'm not sure if you appreciate what life with me might be like. Even now some jerk will be online saying that I'm somehow to blame for both what happened fifteen years ago, and for what happened two days ago. Some conspiracy theorist will have some bullshit story how it's all connected to some Deep State nonsense or how EG was some kind of invention by the FBI to garner support."

He smiled at her and kissed her fingers. "And you'll help shine a light on the truth and track down the bad guys."

Tears swam in her eyes and she blinked rapidly.

"You really are the bravest person I know." Shane stared at their clasped hands. "I can't imagine how difficult life must have been for the teenager you were, especially having lost your immediate family all on the same day. I'm willing to be half as brave as you are if you give me the chance to stand by your side." His fingers tightened on hers and he stared deep into her eyes. "I will not let you down, ever again."

"Promise?" she asked with a watery smile.

He kissed her deeply, pulled away slowly. "Promise."

Yael's pulse raced. When it slowed back down again, she exhaled heavily. "I guess I'd better take those shooting lessons from you then, huh?"

Those green eyes of his positively glowed. "Does this mean we're going on a date?"

She shook her head. "Our first date is not going to be on a firing range."

"Where then?"

Yael hadn't thought about it. Their entire relationship had evolved when she'd been avoiding the attentions of a serial killer. The thought of being free to do exactly what she wanted was liberating and at the same time terrifying.

"How about sailing?"

He tilted his head. "You like boats?"

"I don't have a lot of experience but I've always liked the thought of learning to sail… That, or scuba diving."

He grinned. "A friend of mine in the BAU has a sailboat. I'm sure he'll let us borrow it."

"You know how to sail?" Yael asked in surprise.

"One of my many skills." He leaned in closer, intent on her mouth, but only giving her a brief peck. "I'm also a certified scuba instructor." He quirked a brow and somehow made the suggestion of teaching her to dive sound dirty.

"Hey, where's your cast?" she asked, noticing his left arm was no longer encased in plaster.

He rolled up his sleeve and rotated the arm. His muscles corded and Yael felt a stab of lust.

"I spoke to a doc here and managed to get an x-ray which showed both bones were healed. I had the guy speak to Novak and then my boss gave permission to leave the cast off, although I have a plastic one for if it gets sore. I have orders to rest it for another two weeks and then I'm good to start training again with the team."

Her heart fluttered suddenly as she held his dark green eyes. What did that mean for them?

Shane kissed her again. The fact he was so open about them being involved now, that he displayed his affection so lavishly despite everyone knowing the truth about her brother and what he'd done, made her want to well up with emotion. She forced it away. She wouldn't cry. Ethan Grice was dead. Everyone else had survived. She wouldn't let her brother's evil destroy her happiness. Not again.

It was amazing how clarifying her most recent brush with death had been. How liberating.

"So, does this mean we're actually giving this relationship thing a try?" he asked.

She gripped a handful of sheet tight. "I'm game if you are."

He slowly uncurled her death grip from the cool cotton and cradled her hand gently between his palms. "Funny, but I don't want to play games this time."

"Neither do I. Shane." She swallowed hard and forced out the words she needed to say. "I think I'm falling in love with you. So, please, if you aren't serious about a relationship tell me now."

His expression grew serious again and he tucked her hair behind her ear. "Honey, my job is not great for relationships. I sometimes spend months away from home and often I can't even call to say why I can't call. But if you think that's something we might be able to handle, together…then I'm all in with giving this thing between us a real chance."

She smiled, her heart feeling lighter than it had in years.

They leaned toward one another, both grinning like loons, but a loud knock on the door interrupted, and then the door burst open with Laura being pushed along by the matronly nurse.

"That was quick," Yael said on a laugh.

"I warned you."

The nurse helped Laura into bed and Yael couldn't help worrying about her pallor. Some of it was the lack of her usual makeup. Some of it was pain.

The nurse left and Shane took a phone call. He went to the door and suddenly some of his team members were striding toward them pushing two wheelchairs. They were in civilian clothes and yet they looked every inch the operators they were.

"You remember Ryan Sullivan?" asked Shane.

Yael nodded.

"This is Aaron Nash, Will Griffin, and Hunt Kincaid," Shane introduced the others.

"We've come to rescue you." Griffin smiled.

"Goody," came a raspy croak from the next bed. "Rescue me too, would you?"

Ryan asked soberly, "How are you feeling, Miss Laura?"

"Like I was kidnapped and tortured by a psychopath but the psychopath's dead and I'm not, so that's okay?"

"You were lucky to survive," Will Griffin said solemnly. "You don't have to bounce back straight away. Take some time to recover."

The fact Laura was joking about the incident with people she didn't know was a great sign.

"What do you mean, rescue me?" Yael asked.

"Alex Parker sent his jet for you two," Nash said. "We squeezed two hospital beds onboard and he even hired a nurse for the trip."

"A very attractive nurse," Ryan Sullivan added.

"Who you are not going to distract," Shane admonished.

"I already distracted her on the way down here." Ryan looked unabashed as Kincaid and Griffin stared at the ceiling.

"But what I don't understand is why are *you* guys here?" Yael asked, looking at the three HRT operators. "You don't work for Alex."

"We're your official FBI escort." Will Griffin sent her a smile that suggested this should be obvious.

"What about our bodyguards?" Yael asked in confusion.

"We're better looking," Ryan told her with a straight face.

"They're coming too," Kincaid told her with a twinkle in his eye. "They're the muscle. We're the brains."

Yael clasped the bedsheets in her fists. "I don't understand."

"You're family," Ryan said simply. "We're bringing you home. Or at least to a hospital closer to home."

She fought the tears she knew she shouldn't shed because if she started to cry she wouldn't stop. The knot in her throat was getting bigger and bigger and she couldn't speak.

Shane squeezed her fingers. "Hey, I forgot to tell you. I heard a funny thing on the radio earlier."

Yael sniffed and blinked, crisis over. He always did that. Pulled her back from the brink of tears. Although he had held her when she'd woken up after surgery yesterday and let her weep all over him.

"What did you hear?" She finally choked out the words.

He turned her hand palm up and stroked his fingers over the snake coiled over her wrist. "I heard there was a mysterious donation of several million dollars toward rebuilding of the school."

"Really?"

He leaned back and didn't let go of her gaze. "It was you. I know it was you."

"You have millions of dollars in the bank?" Ryan asked with an exaggerated stroke of his chin.

Yael snorted. "Not anymore." She squeezed Shane's hand before telling them everything. She didn't want any more secrets. "It was from the life insurance policies I received when my parents were murdered. I never wanted that money but after what the insurance companies put me through, I took it. I put it in the bank but didn't touch it. Until now."

Shane leaned down and kissed her on the lips. "I think you're amazing."

"I think you're pretty amazing yourself." She side-eyed the audience, noting the happy smiles they all wore.

"Your house is all fixed up," Shane said, pulling away reluctantly. "Or we can stay at my apartment when you are released."

"Already?" She didn't miss the implication that they were going to be staying together for the time being.

"Alex said one of his partners took over the logistics. Haley Cramer?"

"Haley fixed my house?"

"I bet it looks even better now than it did before." Laura smiled tiredly. "Haley has exquisite taste."

The guys helped them both transfer into the wheelchairs. Shane began pulling her personal items out of the bedside locker and putting them in her lap and then covered her up with an extra blanket. Will Griffin did the same for Laura.

"Are you ready to be wheeled out of here?" Shane asked.

"Are you sure I can't walk?" Yael grumbled.

"That would be a negative," said Shane.

"Nyeht." Ryan.

"Non." Kincaid.

"Nein." Griffin.

"Nee." Laura.

"That's a 'no' then." She laughed even as she mentally prepared for the onslaught of attention going through the hospital. Her incision still hurt but the painkillers were hardcore. She was going home and for the first time since her brother's murderous spree fifteen years ago, she didn't feel alone.

Shane pulled a ball cap over her hair and Ryan handed her a pair of aviators that almost didn't stay on her nose. Then with a nod to the bodyguards they wheeled her out of the room, so fast her head spun.

Shane pushed the chair.

"You're going too fast." Yael laughed as they almost ran down the hallway.

"And here I was thinking we weren't going fast enough."

She caught his gaze and all the emotions she'd been feeling for the last week hit her.

"You going to put on the brakes again?" he asked, obviously not talking about the journey out of a side entrance of the hospital.

She shook her head. "No."

"Good."

And she laughed again, even though it hurt and even though these guys were completely ridiculous. Shane was hers now. She wasn't giving him back.

EPILOGUE

ONE DAY EARLIER

Alex eased silently through his front door, then locked it behind him and rearmed the security system. The soft beep was the only noise to break the silence in the minute after midnight.

Rex came toward him with a wagging tail and a quiet woof. Next month would mark a year since Mallory rescued the Golden Retriever after the poor guy's owner had been murdered up in Boston and the dog had been shot.

"Hey, buddy." He crouched down to stroke the dog's soft fur as Rex whined optimistically, ever-hopeful it was snack time. His undiminished trust in humans never ceased to amaze Alex. This dog was a better person than he'd ever be.

A voice came out of the darkness. "You're hurt."

He looked up and saw his wife standing on the stairs in plaid pj bottoms and one of his old t-shirts. "It's a flesh wound. I would have told you if it was anything serious."

He and Mallory had made a promise to one another not that long ago—no more lies. And Alex stuck to that because his wife and Georgie were precious to him. He would never jeopardize their love for anything, so he did everything he was allowed to do to keep them safe and happy. And for Mallory "happy" meant informed.

She came toward him as he rose to his feet. Put her hands lightly on his shoulders and rose on tiptoe to kiss his lips. Alex dragged her to him with his good arm and made it a proper hello.

He rested his forehead against hers as she sank against him. "Ashley called you."

"No," she said softly. "Lucas."

He led her through to the kitchen because he was thirsty. The moonlight lit up the space with a cold blue light. He grabbed a glass of water and drank it down. Tossed Rex a dog biscuit.

"Take off your shirt."

Alex paused, then did as she asked knowing that this, unfortunately, wasn't a *take off your shirt because you are about to get lucky here right now* moment.

Slowly, deliberately, because he didn't want to tear the stitches, he eased out of his t-shirt and tossed it on the island.

Mallory winced as she took in the wound that had sliced through the outer edge of his upper arm leaving behind an ugly four-inch gash. The intern had done their best to repair the muscle beneath before pumping him full of antibiotics.

She bit her lip with a worried frown and raised her gaze. "Lucas said you were protecting Ashley."

Alex grimaced. "She's not very happy with me."

"I don't blame her," Mallory said evenly.

Alex grimaced again because both women were highly trained professionals and perhaps Ashley had been lining up the perfect shot that would have taken EG out of the game and he'd pushed her aside to "safety."

"Lucas said to say 'thank you.'" Mallory reached up and stroked his face. "I'm grateful you are both okay."

Alex nodded, relieved.

"How are Yael and Laura?"

Alex sagged. Two of his employees had almost died, both of

whom he'd failed to adequately protect. He swallowed tightly. "Alive."

Mallory stepped into his embrace and he held her to him. "It wasn't your fault."

Maybe not directly, but the fact Alex had been chasing that particular serial killer for so long meant it felt like it was. Ethan Grice had targeted Laura because of Alex's hunt, and then latched onto Yael for the same reason. But Grice was dead now and couldn't hurt anyone else ever again.

Alex would have stayed with Yael and Laura in Colorado, but he'd had to get home. They were in good hands. Shane Livingstone seemed like an excellent agent and an even better man.

"Yael's secret is out," he said.

"She okay about that?"

Alex snorted. "I think she'd rather no one ever knew, but at least this way she can finally move on. Not all secrets are quite so...*forgivable*."

She kissed him and his hold on her tightened. The thought of his secrets being revealed, of losing his wife and his child... He had protections in place but he never took a single moment for granted.

"How's Georgie?" he asked.

Mallory grinned. "Fussy. Noisy. Hungry." She yawned tiredly. "I'd just fed her when I heard you come in. I think she has another tooth coming through."

He took her hand. "Come on, you need some sleep before work."

She let him drag her to the stairs and they climbed them together, side-by-side.

She slipped under the covers as he stripped off the rest of his clothes. Her phone started to buzz and she pulled a face before picking it up.

Alex recognized the ringtone. Frazer.

"Hello." Mallory's eyes shot to his as he stood in front of her.

Alex didn't want her having to go out into the darkness in the middle of the night but he'd long ago stopped trying to control his wife's actions, especially in relation to her job.

"You want me to come in?" she asked.

Alex braced himself for disappointment because, after nearly dying today, he'd wanted to hold Mal while they both slept.

"Okay. I'll be there at eight." She hung up.

Relieved, Alex climbed in beside her, snuggling close when she lay down. He put his injured arm outside the covers and around her waist.

"What happened?" he murmured.

"Looks like a Mexican drug cartel tried to abduct the US Vice President's daughter last night."

Alex's grip on his wife tightened. The last thing he wanted her involved with was the cartels. "Frazer wants you on the case?"

She drew his fingers to her lips and kissed them. "No, he put me in charge of the office while he's in DC helping to coordinate a response."

Alex released a sigh of relief then they both tensed at the telltale whimper from the nursery across the hall. He kissed his wife. "I've got her. Get some sleep."

"What about your arm?" Mallory asked with concern.

"Not a problem." He eased out of bed as the volume of Georgie's protests started to intensify.

"Hey, Alex," Mallory murmured softly. "Did I tell you how much I love you today?"

He glanced at the clock. Ten after midnight. "Not yet."

She yawned widely. "Well, I do."

He leaned down and kissed her brow. "I love you too, Mrs. Parker." More than she could ever know. Rex hadn't been Mallory's first rescue. That privilege belonged to Alex, and it was something he felt profound gratitude for, every minute of every day.

"Sweet dreams," he whispered, and turned away to address the increasingly demanding cries of the other miracle in his life.

Thank you for reading *Cold Silence.* I hope you enjoyed Shane and Yael's story. For my next novel featuring the FBI's Hostage Rescue Team order *Cold Deceit* today!

> When forensic anthropologist Zoe Miller stumbles across a murder victim in the blisteringly hostile Sonoran Desert, she sets off a chain of events that puts her in the crosshairs of a ruthless killer. And it's FBI HRT operator Seth Hopper's job to keep her safe.

Don't miss my next *Cold Justice - Most Wanted* novel, featuring agents from the FBI's Hostage Rescue Team. Order "*Cold Deceit*" today!

Sign up for Toni Anderson's newsletter to receive new release alerts, bonus scenes, and a free digital copy of The Killing Game: www.toniandersonauthor.com/newsletter-signup

USEFUL ACRONYM DEFINITIONS FOR TONI'S BOOKS

ADA: Assistant District Attorney
AG: Attorney General
ASAC: Assistant Special-Agent-in-Charge
ASC: Assistant Section Chief
ATF: Alcohol, Tobacco, and Firearms
BAU: Behavioral Analysis Unit
BOLO: Be on the Lookout
BUCAR: Bureau Car.
CBT: Cognitive Behavioral Therapy
CIRG: Critical Incident Response Group
CMU: Crisis Management Unit
CN: Crisis Negotiator
CNU: Crisis Negotiation Unit
CO: Commanding Officer
CODIS: Combined DNA Index System
CP: Command Post
CQB: Close-Quarters Battle
DA: District Attorney
DEA: Drug Enforcement Administration

DOB: Date of Birth
DOD: Department of Defense
DOJ: Department of Justice
DS: Diplomatic Security
DSS: US Diplomatic Security Service
EMDR: Eye Movement Desensitization & Reprocessing
EMT: Emergency Medical Technician
ERT: Evidence Response Team
FOA: First-Office Assignment
FBI: Federal Bureau of Investigation
FNG: Fucking New Guy
FO: Field Office
FWO: Federal Wildlife Officer
IC: Incident Commander
IC: Intelligence Community
HRT: Hostage Rescue Team
HT: Hostage-Taker
JEH: J. Edgar Hoover Building (FBI Headquarters)
K&R: Kidnap and Ransom
LAPD: Los Angeles Police Department
LEO: Law Enforcement Officer
ME: Medical Examiner
MO: Modus Operandi
NAT: New Agent Trainee
NCAVC: National Center for Analysis of Violent Crime
NCIC: National Crime Information Center
NFT: Non-Fungible Token
NOTS: New Operator Training School
NYFO: New York Field Office
OC: Organized Crime
OCU: Organized Crime Unit
OPR: Office of Professional Responsibility
POTUS: President of the United States
PTSD: Post-Traumatic Stress Disorder
RA: Resident Agency

RCMP: Royal Canadian Mounted Police
RSO: Senior Regional Security Officer from the US Diplomatic Service
SA: Special Agent
SAC: Special Agent-in-Charge
SANE: Sexual Assault Nurse Examiners
SAS: Special Air Squadron (British Special Forces unit)
SD: Secure Digital
SIOC: Strategic Information & Operations
SF: Special Forces
SSA: Supervisory Special Agent
SWAT: Special Weapons and Tactics
TC: Tactical Commander
TDY: Temporary Duty Yonder
TEDAC: Terrorist Explosive Device Analytical Center
TOD: Time of Death
UAF: University of Alaska, Fairbanks
UNSUB: Unknown Subject
ViCAP: Violent Criminal Apprehension Program
VIN: Vehicle Identification Number
WFO: Washington Field Office

COLD JUSTICE WORLD OVERVIEW

ALL BOOKS CAN BE READ AS STANDALONES

COLD JUSTICE SERIES

A Cold Dark Place (Book #1)

Cold Pursuit (Book #2)

Cold Light of Day (Book #3)

Cold Fear (Book #4)

Cold in The Shadows (Book #5)

Cold Hearted (Book #6)

Cold Secrets (Book #7)

Cold Malice (Book #8)

A Cold Dark Promise (Book #9~A Wedding Novella)

Cold Blooded (Book #10)

COLD JUSTICE – THE NEGOTIATORS

Cold & Deadly (Book #1)

Colder Than Sin (Book #2)

Cold Wicked Lies (Book #3)

Cold Cruel Kiss (Book #4)

Cold as Ice (Book #5)

COLD JUSTICE – MOST WANTED

Cold Silence (Book #1)

Cold Deceit (Book #2)

The *Cold Justice* series books are also available as audiobooks narrated by Eric Dove, and in various box set compilations.

Check out all Toni's books on her website (www.toniandersonauthor.com/books-2)

ACKNOWLEDGMENTS

I've been wanting to write about the FBI's Hostage Rescue Team since I started the *Cold Justice* series wayback when. Then certain factors conspired against me and I spent a few years exploring other units within the FBI that I was also burning to write about. As a consequence, I feel as if I've been building this particular world in my head forever. Now it's here and I hope you enjoy reading it as much as I enjoyed writing it.

My thanks, as always, go to my critique partner, Kathy Altman, who has the dubious honor of seeing the messy first draft. Many thanks to Rachel Grant for the great *beta* read and excellent advice. And also to Jodie Griffin for the feedback and general cheerleading of my books in real life and on Twitter.

Credit to my editors, Deb Nemeth, Joan Turner at JRT Editing, and proofreader, Alicia Dean. Your input is much appreciated. Thanks to my assistant, Jill Glass, who is such a great help when my brain explodes. Thanks also to my amazing cover designer, Regina Wamba, for her gorgeous artwork. Eric G. Dove is (still) on his sailboat recording the audiobook version, living the dream! Thanks for being the voice of the *Cold Justice* books and for being such an easy person to work with.

Huge amounts of love and gratitude to my husband and kids for their constant support. This one is, again, for Gary. Book #25 published during our twenty-fifth year of marriage. Seems appropriate.

ABOUT THE AUTHOR

Toni Anderson writes gritty, sexy, FBI Romantic Thrillers, and is a *New York Times* and a *USA Today* bestselling author. Her books have won the Daphne du Maurier Award for Excellence in Mystery and Suspense, Readers' Choice, Aspen Gold, Book Buyers' Best, Golden Quill, National Excellence in Story Telling (NEST) Contest, and National Excellence in Romance Fiction awards. She's been a finalist in both the Vivian Contest and the RITA Award from the Romance Writers of America. Three million copies of her books have been downloaded.

Best known for her "COLD" books perhaps it's not surprising to discover Toni lives in one of the most extreme climates on earth—Manitoba, Canada. Formerly a Marine Biologist, Toni still misses the ocean, but is lucky enough to travel for research purposes. In January 2016, she visited FBI Headquarters in Washington DC, including a tour of the Strategic Information and Operations Center. She hopes not to get arrested for her Google searches.

Sign up for Toni Anderson's newsletter:
www.toniandersonauthor.com/newsletter-signup
See Toni Anderson's current book list:
www.toniandersonauthor.com/books-2

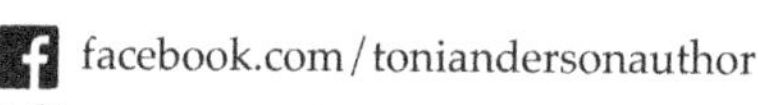
facebook.com/toniandersonauthor
twitter.com/toniannanderson
instagram.com/toni_anderson_author

Made in the USA
Monee, IL
31 July 2024

62990886R00215